# Where She Belongs

### By
### LIZ DORAN

Copyright 2016© Liz Doran
All rights reserved. No part of this document may be reproduced or transmitted in any form or by any means, electronic, mechanical, photocopying, recording, or otherwise, without prior written permission of Liz Doran. Nv4

# Dedication

This book is dedicated to my ever-supportive husband,
Friedhelm Rogel.
Thanks for all the adventures.
Love to Sebastian and Christian for being such kind
and special sons.

Special thanks to JD Smith Design for creating a wonderful cover.

Thanks too to the lovely Jennifer Kremmer of Book Anvil for help with developmental editing.

# Table of Contents

| | |
|---|---|
| CHAPTER 1 | Pg 9 |
| CHAPTER 2 | Pg 15 |
| CHAPTER 3 | Pg 19 |
| CHAPTER 4 | Pg 29 |
| CHAPTER 5 | Pg 35 |
| CHAPTER 6 | Pg 49 |
| CHAPTER 7 | Pg 61 |
| CHAPTER 8 | Pg 75 |
| CHAPTER 9 | Pg 95 |
| CHAPTER 10 | Pg 107 |
| CHAPTER 11 | Pg 115 |
| CHAPTER 12 | Pg 125 |
| CHAPTER 13 | Pg 129 |
| CHAPTER 14 | Pg 141 |
| CHAPTER 15 | Pg 149 |
| CHAPTER 16 | Pg 161 |

| | |
|---|---|
| CHAPTER 17 | Pg 171 |
| CHAPTER 18 | Pg 179 |
| CHAPTER 19 | Pg 187 |
| CHAPTER 20 | Pg 199 |
| CHAPTER 21 | Pg 209 |
| CHAPTER 22 | Pg 221 |
| CHAPTER 23 | Pg 239 |
| CHAPTER 24 | Pg 265 |
| CHAPTER 25 | Pg 273 |
| CHAPTER 26 | Pg 283 |
| CHAPTER 27 | Pg 289 |
| CHAPTER 28 | Pg 297 |
| CHAPTER 29 | Pg 309 |
| CHAPTER 30 | Pg 315 |
| CHAPTER 31 | Pg 325 |
| CHAPTER 32 | Pg 335 |
| CHAPTER 33 | Pg 347 |

| | |
|---|---|
| CHAPTER 34 | Pg 355 |
| CHAPTER 35 | Pg 361 |
| CHAPTER 36 | Pg 375 |
| CHAPTER 37 | Pg 385 |
| CHAPTER 38 | Pg 395 |
| CHAPTER 39 | Pg 405 |
| CHAPTER 40 | Pg 419 |
| CHAPTER 41 | Pg 431 |
| CHAPTER 42 | Pg 439 |
| CHAPTER 43 | Pg 447 |
| CHAPTER 44 | Pg 457 |
| CHAPTER 45 | Pg 467 |
| CHAPTER 46 | Pg 477 |
| ACKNOWLEDGEMENTS | Pg 486 |
| ABOUT THE AUTHOR | Pg 487 |

# WHERE SHE BELONGS

## CHAPTER 1

Roisin Delaney looked out of the window onto the arid dusty piece of land with gnarled trees and unrelenting sunshine from her Spanish home. She could see her husband Javier dozing in his favourite wooden chair on the old porch. A scraggy chicken pecked in the dust, an optimist considering the fact that all it was likely to find was a few windswept seeds. A few strands of Javier's thick black hair fell onto his face, giving him a roguish but endearing appearance. The slight bulge of his belly rose and sank in rhythm to his breathing. She could almost hear the sound of a thin whistle with every exhaled breath. He shifted his position and turned to look at her. Uncanny how people seemed to know they were being watched.

"What's for dinner, love?" He called.

She sighed and shouted back at him. "Rice or eggs, dear. Nearly ready."

He looked at her as if to protest but seemed to think better of it and mumbled something under his breath.

She moved away from the window and sat

down at the table, flicking through the holiday guide that came with the paper. There were times when she felt so restricted and in need of a change of scene she thought she would burst. This was one of them. They were in deep trouble, and if she didn't make some sort of a move they'd go even deeper into the downward spiral of the past few years.

Up until five years previously, Javier had always been a highly motivated person, the type who'd roll up his sleeves and tackle any job. It seemed as if there was nothing he could not do. But then he had taken one risk too many by putting all their money into the construction industry. Nobody could have foreseen its rapid collapse, least of all him. The consequences and speed with which this financial tsunami had struck left them with shattered faith and depleted spirits. Some recovered faster than others from such a shock, but Javier was not one of those people. He reminded her of a deflated balloon slowly losing air. The holiday house they had built in the next village was close to being repossessed by the bank and their funds were dwindling rapidly, hence the almost empty cupboard. Roisin felt as if she was in a bad nursery rhyme. She couldn't change the words, never mind the storyline.

She turned on the radio, switching channels until she found a cheerful song to lift her mood. When she heard Javier's footsteps, she tidied the papers and put them into a neat pile.

Javier came in and sat down at the table, grabbing the paper and shaking it out. After a few moments, he let out an exasperated groan. "Bastard banks."

She pierced a hole in one of the eggs and balanced it on a spoon ready to drop it into the boiling water. "What's wrong love?"

"Did you see this?" He jabbed at the front-page article listing the bonuses of all the top bank managers over the past few months.

"What good does it do, Javier? You're going to give yourself a heart attack if you carry on like that."

"It's not right. What am I supposed to do? Ignore it, like you? Stick my head in the sand!"

"Oh, I'm not ignoring it, believe me. I'm just as annoyed as you are. But we must make the best of things." She went over to stand behind him and began massaging his shoulders. "Go on up and have a shave and a shower, love. You'll feel better, and when you come back dinner will be ready."

He folded the paper and flung it down on the chair before walking with heavy steps toward the stairs. If only she could get through to him.

As she heard him moving around upstairs, she contemplated her situation and her choices. Perhaps all was not lost. She believed situations could turn around and that there was always a solution.

A familiar shadow flashed by the window, taking her out of her reverie. She looked at the clock. It must have been the postman, not a welcome visitor these days. The only letters they seemed to receive lately were bills and bank statements. She waved to him, but decided to wait until later to check the box.

Little things made her happy these days. Creative cooking, adding small touches of cheeriness to her house, a ribbon, a piece of cloth, fresh herbs, wild flowers. She removed the eggs and rinsed them under the cold running water before checking the cupboard for inspiration. Two tins of sweet corn, three tins of tomatoes, a few potatoes turning green, pasta and a half bag of rice. She found a tin of sardines and put it on the counter. Humming along to a catchy pop song, she went outside to the patio and snipped off some fresh herbs. Despite the gravity of their current situation, she smiled, making up fancy-sounding names for the dishes she created.

Starter: Roasted sardines on a bed of croutons marinated in sage walnut oil. Oil was good, good for the brain, good for the heart and a lubricant for the joints.

Main meal: Curried eggs served with zesty tomato rice. Hey, not bad, she commended herself.

Dessert: Apple snow with rhombus of rhubarb. Less is more. It's all in the name. If all the best gourmet restaurants charged an arm and a leg for fancy names and Lilliput portions spread out over several courses, then why couldn't she?

She set the table with her best linen napkins; the ones she had bought at the local flea market, taking them home and boiling them before ironing them so they looked good as new. The jug of flowers finished off the rustic touch. It was still bright, but she lit a candle to enhance the mood. Let it be peaceful, she thought. She heard his steps coming down the stairs, not quite so heavy of foot this time.

He popped one of the croutons into his mouth. "Who are you expecting?" he said.

She put the warm plates on the table. "Just for us, love. Come on, before it gets cold."

He patted her on the bottom and sat down to eat. They ate in relative silence. When she served dessert, he even complimented her. "I have to say, Roisin, you can work magic with slim pickings."

Roisin thought it might be a good time to broach the subject of their future. "Have you decided to take Miguel up on his offer?"

A shadow fell across his face and he pushed aside his dessert bowl. "Don't get me started, okay! I'm too old to work as a waiter."

She bit her lower lip. "I'm sure it'll only be a temporary solution, love. Things are constantly changing." She placed her hand over his. "Why don't you give it a try? It might do you good."

He stormed over to the cabinet and took out the whisky bottle.

"Don't patronise me," he said between clenched teeth.

"Please, don't start drinking," she said. "You're not yourself when you drink."

He ignored her and poured a shot, downing it in one go. Then he poured another. She went over and screwed the top on the bottle before putting it back in the cupboard.

The slap resounded through the room and made her ears buzz.

She struggled to keep her balance and held onto the edge of the table. When she dared lift her defiant but teary eyes to him, she saw the look of surprise in his eyes. He tried to put his arms around her. "Roisin, I'm sorry. I didn't mean to hit you." Over and over again, he repeated those words, telling her that it would never happen again. She shrugged him off and turned to leave. Before closing the door behind her, she saw him slumped on the chair with his head between his hands, sobbing.

She held her hand over her reddening cheek and turned to him. "That's the last time you'll ever hit me," she said, almost surprised at how numb she felt. She turned and walked out the door.

Upstairs, she tossed and turned in her bed wondering what to do. He had gone too far this time. She heard him slamming around downstairs. No tears came, but a ball of anger and helplessness stuck in her stomach and her throat. She felt like vomiting. Her thoughts ran to and fro like erratic fish in a bowl that was becoming too small, gathering momentum at every turn. She commanded herself to stop and breathe, and while she lay there contemplating, she suddenly knew what she had to do. She got out of bed, wet a cloth with cold water and held it against her flushed and sore cheek. Then she grabbed a light cardigan, ran a comb through her hair and drove off to her friend Anastasia.

Her new resolve had given her a sense of power. Even the chickens scampered out of her way. Drama queen, she thought. The scene reminded her of one out of a cartoon. Poor chickens, she wouldn't damage a feather on their puny backs. This time Javier wouldn't change her mind, no matter what. If she gave in now, nothing would change. Maybe leaving would help both of them.

*When the pot boils over, it's time to remove it from the heat.*

# Chapter 2

She drove away at high speed and could barely remember how she made it to Anastasia's house. At least the roads were familiar. She could probably drive with her eyes closed.

Although she had vague memories of maneuvering the hilly roads and passing by the olive groves, her mind had been all over the place. The more she thought about it, the more she knew she would have to make a move. She had no choice in the matter. And now she was angry enough to finally do what she had been contemplating for months. It was about survival, for both of them.

Anastasia was standing on a ladder, cleaning windows, when she drove up. She stopped what she was doing and turned to Roisin, who stepped out of the car. "What a surprise." Her words caught in her throat when she saw Roisin's expression. "Roisin," she said, as she stepped down from the ladder. "What's up, love?" I thought we were going to meet on Saturday?" Anastasia came toward her friend and put her arm around her. "What on earth happened to you?" Roisin began to sob and hated herself for it. Sympathy always had that effect on her. Anastasia guided her inside.

"It's nothing," she said between sobs. "It

looks worse than it is."

Roisin slumped down in her favourite armchair.

Anastasia was busy pressing ice cubes from the plastic freezer container. Two flew out and slid across the floor. Anastasia retrieved them and wrapped them with a few others inside a thick dishtowel. She handed it to her friend "What on earth happened? That looks nasty."

Roisin took the ice pack and held it to her face. "Thanks," she said. "Any chance of a glass of wine?"

Anastasia couldn't help but smile at the image of her friend holding a bag of ice to her face and a glass of wine in the other as she recounted the gourmet meal she had created for Javier. She was laughing and crying at the same time.

When she finished recounting what happened, Roisin slid back into the chair. "All jokes aside. It is not very funny. I'm utterly exhausted from all this drama and heaviness." She went to put the wine glass back on the table, but her friend took it off her. "I've made up my mind, Anastasia. I'm leaving here as soon as possible."

Anastasia, who had been tidying up the kitchen, stopped to challenge her. She paused for a few moments as she let it sink it. "You're serious about this, aren't you?" She stood there with her right hip jutted forward and waved the tea towel at Roisin as if practicing fencing. "It will all blow over in a few days. Do you want to throw everything you have worked for away, just like that?"

Roisin glared at her, wide eyed. She raised her

voice. "Are you kidding me? How can you say that?" She pointed to her face. "Don't you see what he did?" She shook her head with vehemence. "No, Stasia. He crossed the line today."

Anastasia, who had had her own fair share of relationship problems fell silent again. After her third failed marriage, she had had enough of men. She refilled their glasses. "So nothing I say will change your mind?"

"Nope." Roisin took a sip of the wine but pushed it away again. "Sorry dear, but this stuff gives me headaches. I should know better than to drink it." She thought for a moment and felt it necessary to defend herself to Anastasia. "You don't know how hard it has been these past couple of years. I tried everything in my power. He's a changed man. You know I try to have a balanced, fair view of things…"

"Yes, you always do, but I don't think your head is clear at the moment," her friend said.

Roisin continued as if she hadn't heard what her friend said. "What worries me most is the fact that we are beginning to lose mutual respect for each other. I still love him, but I can't live with him like this. There were too many things, too many hurdles to jump over."

Anastasia placed her warm hand on Roisin's and squeezed it. Her look of empathy required no words.

Roisin wiped her eyes and sat up straight in the chair. "You know me too well, but believe me when I say, I do not make this decision lightly. I'll do what has to be done. What's lost is lost, what's won is won. Simple as that. That's how life is. You love it, leave it or change it."

"Did you tell him yet?" her friend said.

"Tell him. Are you kidding me? I couldn't even think straight. Besides, it wouldn't have been wise. But I will, tomorrow." *She hoped.*

Anastasia's forehead creased in a line of wrinkles. "But where will you go? I hate to say this, Roisin, but it's not as if you're on the good side of thirty anymore."

"Don't worry. I'll find something. At least I want to prove it to myself. This passiveness has to go." Nothing her friend could have said would have made any difference anyway. She had never felt so sure about anything in her life before and hoped she would not falter when the mood passed.

Anastasia told her about the time she chopped her boyfriend's hair off when he was in a drunken stupor one night. She had caught him cheating the week beforehand but hadn't said a word. "You should have seen his face the next morning," she said. "It took all my strength to keep up the innocent façade. It never once entered his mind that I could have been the culprit. I told him it must have happened on the way home, or that someone must had played a practical joke in the pub." She continued with other escapades and soon they were laughing so hard that Roisin had almost forgotten about her problems.

# Chapter 3

When she awoke the next morning, her aching face brought memories of the previous day crashing back. Her first thought was of Javier. She knew he would be ashamed of his behavior and she almost felt sorry for him. She turned on her back and reenacted the scene in her mind. Now she felt angry and her anger made her feel nauseous. She dreaded having to confront him and would have preferred to take the next direct flight to Dublin without seeing him at all. But that was unrealistic; she had classes to teach and things to sort out. Besides, it was not her style to just run away. On the other hand, she knew the longer she waited the less likely she would be to follow through on her plans. Even now, her anger began to dissipate. She dreaded telling him of her decision. It would be the same old story. Either he'd go into a rant, or he would plead with her to stay, telling her she'd never make it on her own.

Maybe he was right.

When she was back home she applied some make-up to cover the bruise that was developing into a nasty-looking blotch on her cheek. That afternoon, she had two young adult students who were working on improving their English. At least dinner was assured for a few more days. It was surprising how far she could make money stretch when she had to. The irony of the situation was that because of the rise in Spanish people going abroad to look for jobs, she and her colleagues were doing well. Languages were badly needed, especially English and German. Germany, particularly, had a shortage of certain workers, especially in the Health Care business. Now young people who were forced to look farther afield for work were flocking up to learn English and German, and it seemed as if the whole of Europe was undergoing a major change. Despite this rise in need, she was still earning nowhere near enough to pay for insurances, mortgages and sustain herself and Javier. In fact, the more she earned, the more taxes she had to pay and soon she would also lose her car which would mean she could no longer travel to work. It was a nightmare.

On her way out the door, she mustered the courage to check the letter box. There were a couple of letters that looked like bills, but she immediately recognized her sister Helen's handwriting on one of the envelopes and that cheered her up. She decided to deal with the unpleasant one first and ripped it open. It was another threatening letter from the bank, nothing new. She shoved it back into the envelope, went back inside and left it on the kitchen table. Later she would read her sister's letter.

*

When her students had left, she packed her books away and decided to treat herself to a coffee at the café down the road. At least she could read the letter in peace there. She still wondered why Helen was writing to her at this time since her birthday was a couple of months away.

The café was almost empty, and she chose a seat by the window, overlooking the main street. After placing her order, she took out the letter and opened it, savouring the moment. Not too many people wrote real letters any more. There was a card inside with a watercolour scene on the front. She opened it and a wad of money fell out. Surprised, she began reading.

*Dear Roisin,*

*I know how you get homesick when spring comes in. This is an early birthday present. Don't feel bad. I can well afford it at the moment. It's up to you what you want to do with it, but it should cover the cost of a ticket.*

Roisin paused for a moment and stared out the window. She believed in signs, and this was one! The timing was perfect. Of course, she would have to come up with a few hundred more, but it was a good start. She continued reading. Helen went on to tell her about the family and her work but steered clear of uncomfortable questions. Roisin smiled as she read her sister's comments about some of the locals. *Remember old Padge the Badge? Can you believe it? He's driving all the way to the south of France in his tractor to raise money for the local dog's home. Isn't he great? Mary, his wife has him all set up with a smart phone and a camera. You can follow him on YouTube. He doesn't speak a word of French and says it's far from French he was reared and if the locals don't understand him, it's their loss. Isn't he a howl? He's bringing a little mascot with him, a knitted leprechaun he bought in Dunnes, and he'll*

*also be taking his little terrier along for the ride.
Mary told Jackie Leeson that he's taking French
lessons on the sly. They always say it's the quiet ones
you need to watch.*

*Let me know when you're coming. We'll be
looking forward to seeing you. Just give a ring.*

*Love to Javier.*

*p.s. Maybe you should pack a bigger suitcase
this time!! You know you can stay with us for as long
as you want.*

Roisin slipped the card and the money back into the envelope as she sipped her coffee and thought about all the times she and Helen seemed to have been telepathically connected. It was always at times of extreme stress that her sister either dreamt about her or called her just when she needed it. She, too, had often felt a sudden urge to pick up the phone just when Helen was going through a difficult phase. Once she had even woken up exactly at the moment when Helen had delivered her last child. And that was without even knowing she was in hospital, since little Simon had arrived early. As it turned out, it had been a particularly difficult birth. She found that all out after the fact, when Helen called her the next day.

So in a way it was no great surprise that the letter arrived when she needed it most. This was her ticket to freedom, and if ever there was a sign of providence, this was it. She had been racking her brain about how to get the money for the ticket. The rest she could figure out later. The hardest thing would be to make the break. She hoped she could live with herself. Her grandmother's emerald ring would have been her last resort, and she had prayed she wouldn't have to sell it.

She checked her watch. The travel agency would be open for another hour. Without further ado, she jaunted down there. Both desks were occupied so she had no choice but to take a seat in the waiting area. While she sat there thinking about Javier, doubt began to set in again. She wore a string of wooden beads that dipped to her cleavage and she kept twisting them until they snapped. Heads turned as the beads rolled onto the floor and she scrambled, red-faced, to pick them up. She could barely believe she was really doing this. But when the time is ripe, everything falls into place. Or so she believed.

Back in her seat, she heard the travel agent explaining the connection details from New York to Chicago to a young fellow in his twenties. She hoped, if he was planning on a better future, he wouldn't be disappointed. Young people were hit particularly hard with this new crisis. In fact, it seemed as if no land was left untouched.

Finally it was her turn. She smiled at the young man as he passed her on his way out. His brief smile faded quickly, but he broke eye-contact and turned his gaze to the door. She wondered what he was going to do in the U.S. It was a long way from home.

Thirty minutes later she had the ticket in her hand. In two weeks she would be flying out of there. Decision made. The sting of the slap held remorse at bay. No pity party, she thought. Now all she had to do was break the news to Javier.

Before heading for the car, she strode to the

end of the wide main street, turned off to the left along the narrow alleyway which was a shortcut to the Church of Madonna de Seville. The church was cool and quiet and the scent of Frankincense hung heavy in this silent womb away from the glaring sunlight. Shafts of light came in through the circular stained glass windows, giving it a sense of magic. There were a couple of older women sitting at the front pews, praying silently. An orb of red light hovered over their heads. It was a reflection from the stained glass, but magical nonetheless. She blessed herself with holy water and went over to light a candle for safe passage and assistance on the next leg of her journey. She also lit one for Javier and asked for forgiveness for what she was about to do. So many emotions had swept over her in the course of two days, from anger to sorrow, from regret to sadness and even a frisson of excitement at her new adventure. It had done her good to remove herself from the house for a few hours. Coming into town always cheered her up and gave her a new perspective on things. It helped, too, that she was forced to pull herself together for her students. No matter what, she had to act professionally in her job and she always enjoyed those lessons. It was with some regret that she had to tell her students she was leaving, but she had given them the name and number of Julie, a woman from Manchester, who was happy to take them on as she was new to the area and building her clientele.

*

Days passed and she couldn't muster the courage to discuss her plans with Javier. But she did call her sister. No telling how long they'd have a telephone. She and Helen had been very close when they were younger, but ever since they both got married, and Roisin had moved away, they had drifted apart. It was inevitable in a way. She had witnessed it so often. Some friends lose touch after they marry and are often too busy with child rearing and juggling jobs, leaving no time for keeping up friendships. Moving away changes everything too. She had realised, too, that Helen could not cope with difficult subjects, and so she had steered clear of mentioning what was truly going on between her and Javier. But Helen had a kind heart, and in her own way she always tried to put things right.

Her sister's voice was a bit groggy, as if she had been sleeping. Roisin had the impression Helen was making a special effort to be diplomatic when she thanked her for the letter and for the money. "Don't worry, Helen," she said. "I'm not going to impose upon you." But her sister told her not to be silly and repeated what she has written in the letter. "You can stay as long as you like."

Roisin told her she would love to take her up on her offer for a few days but that she wanted to go somewhere completely fresh, probably somewhere on the west coast, near the sea.

"But how are you going to survive. There aren't many jobs available these days. Maybe you'll change your mind when you get here."

"You're probably right," Roisin said. She thought it better not to pursue the subject. It was a waste of time trying to discuss anything with Helen, as lovely as she was, she was more stubborn than she cared to admit. Besides, Roisin would have to test the waters when she arrived and see if she was still brave enough to head out on her own.

"But how did you know?" Roisin said. She had never told her sister the full extent of their domestic situation or the private problems they had been having for the past couple of years, although she had probably hinted at it on occasion.

"I don't know," Helen said. "It was just a feeling. What did Javier say?"

Roisin hesitated for a moment. "I haven't told him yet." She tried to hold back the emotion that threatened to overcome her, but her voice gave her away as it always did.

"But you'll have to tell him before you leave. Are you packing that big suitcase like I told you?"

Roisin took a deep breath. "I'll get it sorted. Don't worry Helen…" She had to cut the call short because she could hear Javier coming in.

There never was a right moment to tell him. She was afraid of his reaction and afraid he might dissuade her too. Instead, she wrote him a letter. Letters were always easier. There was no one to answer back, no one to shout you down. She inserted some of the money she had earned from her teaching job into the letter and left it in the middle of the table.

Her suitcases were packed and ready. As she heard Anastasia's car pulling up outside, she took one last look around her cosy stone kitchen. Her eyes rested on the old Aga, the walnut table, and her pride and joy, the lamp she had made out of wire and painted flags with inspirational quotes or funny one-liners. She used to like to pick one at random, like reading a fortune cookie, and so she chose one and turned it over to read. *If you keep looking back, you'll never go forward.* Good on paper, but not always easy to live by. Why did it have to be like this? If she could, she would have erased all the negativity of the past. She would have loved to be the type of woman who could get through to a man like Javier, to make him see sense, but it was a futile wish. She sighed and checked her handbag one last time to make sure she had everything and went outside to meet her friend.

# Chapter 4

At the airport, panic began to well up inside her. She did what she always did in such situations and forced herself to concentrate on something else. This too will pass, she thought. No turning back. Providence aided her now as her eyes were drawn to a small child, like a clockwork toy, who ran past her toward the escalator, red shoes clacking on the marble floor. She ran after the child and grabbed her just in time. The toddler wriggled and tried to escape. Roisin looked frantically through the crowd. Where were the child's guardians?

A harried young bearded man wearing a checkered shirt came running toward her. He carried a small baby and pulled a luggage trolley behind him. Pearls of sweat like small blisters covered his forehead. He reached out for the child. "Sorry about that. The little mite is faster than Jack Flash." She smiled, letting him know it was okay, and soon he was off into the throng of other travelers.

The flight attendant's voice sounded from the speaker, requesting the passengers for her flight to prepare for boarding. As she went back to her seat, she thought that perhaps if she had had a child it would have changed everything. But that was not their fate. At least now she was only responsible for herself.

Later, when they were up in the sky, a new wave of doubt began to threaten her. She blinked a few times, forcing herself to change the inner chatter and the snapshots flashing through her mind. It was useless. *Had she made the right decision?* Anastasia's words jumped back and forth in her mind like a Ping-Pong ball. "What will you do in Ireland? There's nothing there for you."

The worst thing was that her friend's words echoed her own fears. What would it be like going back? She hadn't lived in Ireland for nearly two decades, but her yearly visits had kept the place alive in her mind. Sure, there were things she'd miss about Spain. The sunshine, for instance. But then, a soothing image of rich green fields, stone walls and overgrown hedges arranged haphazardly along the road made her feel optimistic. She imagined she could almost smell the air. Javier always said he associated Ireland with the smell of turf fires. There he was popping into her thoughts again. Lately he kept saying that not only were jobs drying up in Spain, back home things were drying up too. So, what was better? Drowning in debts in Ireland, surrounded by angry and shocked faces who didn't know what had hit them, or staying where she was? She thought about how some parts of Spain had been suffering from drought these past years. Rationing water was becoming the norm rather than the exception. At least that was unlikely to happen in Ireland. She wondered, too, what was going on in the world. It seemed as if no land was left untouched by the financial and climate changes.

The hostess came clattering down the gangway with her trolley. Roisin was glad to have a distraction, and she turned her attention to the in-flight menu. A little snack would take her mind off her useless worrying. When a ray of brilliant sunshine threw a golden sheen on the cabin, she saw it as a good omen, as if the universe was giving her a nod of approval.

*

After she had collected her luggage and gone through the green lane to the waiting area, she scanned the sea of faces waiting to greet their overseas visitors. Dublin airport had changed so much these past years. A low buzz spread through the waiting area. She watched people hugging and chatting, carrying suitcases, stopping for coffee. A young black man wearing a colourful t-shirt and a string of beads around his neck cut across her, nearly tripping her up. She turned to watch as he threw his arms around an elderly black couple. The man, presumably his father had tears in his eyes as he hugged the younger man. The unmistakable sound of Eastern European languages added to the din. This was definitely not the same country she had left all those years ago. Such a variety of skin tones contrasting with the Irish faces. She was home, but home wasn't quite as she had left it.

She spotted her eight-year-old niece, Deirdre,

running towards her with outstretched arms. Deirdre's creamy complexion was slightly flushed. "Auntie Roisin's home," she said as she threw her arms around her aunt. Roisin hugged her back. Her brother joined them, smiling. "Roisin," he said. "Good to see you. How was your trip?" He grabbed her suitcase. "What have you got in here, a dead body or what?" He pulled out the handle and dragged the suitcase behind him.

"Thanks a million for coming, Brian."

"Sure isn't it the least we can do." He gave her a warm hug. "Good to see ya," he said.

Mark, who had just turned four, was trying to hide behind Brian, but his curiosity threatened to win out over his shyness. He didn't want to miss anything. While Roisin hugged her niece and gave her the long-legged fluffy rabbit she had bought in the duty free, she winked at Brian. In the meantime, Mark had come out of his hiding place. She bent down to his level and gave him the bag with his box of Lego. "Don't open it till you get home, Mark, or you'll lose all the pieces." He smiled and took it from her.

"Say thank you to Aunty Roisin," Brian said.

Mark had taken the box out and was showing it to his daddy. He looked up with a shy smile and said, "Thank you Aunty Roisin."

"Let's get your bags in the car first," Brian said to Roisin. "We can stop for coffee on the way home, if you want."

She put her passport back in her bag and flung it over her shoulder. "No need to stop for me, Brian. I had something on the plane." All this emotion had made her weary, but when she saw the flicker of disappointment in his face, she changed her mind. "On second thoughts, a nice hot cup of coffee sounds great."

"Yea, well whatever you want yourself," he said. "The kids were looking forward to seeing the planes land. I wanted to get here earlier but you know me, working on a job till the last minute." His twinkling eyes followed his daughter who was running towards the viewer's window.

"I'm in no hurry, Brian." And she wasn't.

The car journey from Dublin to Knockadreen saw her soaking up impressions as if for the first time as she scanned the scenes passing by her eyes--the rich green fields and pretty houses scattered sporadically across the landscape. Everything seemed so close and comforting. She sniffed the air through the open back window. Did it really smell like turf fires?

Puffed-out clouds sailed across the moody skies, and the watery sun blinked from a distance, creating shadows. An artist couldn't have done a better job. She soaked in the mystical layers of knotty old trees, the organic tidy grey rock boundaries separating the blocks of green and the soft sloping hills. She couldn't wait to go walking.

"Can we go for a picnic later, Aunty Roisin?" Deirdre said, as she continued humming a little tune to herself.

She turned her head to smile at her niece who was rubbing her nose into the fluffy rabbit she had given her. Mark still held his Lego box in his clasped hands as he nodded off to sleep. "Of course we can," Roisin said.

# Chapter 5

She awoke the next morning to the sound of rain splattering on the windowpane. In the half-light she adjusted her eyes. A shelf full of dolls stared back at her, and she remembered where she was. Poor Javier, what had she done?

The inviting smell of freshly-brewed coffee and bacon wafted down the hallway and she lay there, contemplating her situation. What was he doing now? He must surely have tried to contact her. The first person he would have tried to contact would have been Anastasia. The next on his list would definitely be Helen, but he was probably too proud to call, or too ashamed.

She dreaded the questions that were sure to arise at breakfast. How could she explain why she had made such a drastic move? They wouldn't understand it. She shifted, stretching her long legs. Funny how distance put everything into perspective. Now, she was flooded with memories of him and all the nice little things he had done for her. Making her coffee in the morning, or whistling as he downloaded music on her MP3 player. Was he still angry with her?

A gentle rapping diverted her attention. "Aunty Roisin, are you awake?" It was Deirdre.

"Come on in," she said. The door opened and she swung her legs out of bed and reached for her kimono.

"You're looking very lovely this morning, missy. Let me look at you." Deirdre giggled and twirled around. She was already a beauty with her long, black wavy hair and now she was slimming down and shooting up.

"Come on, Aunty Roisin," she said, tugging at her arm. "We're all waiting for you, and I'm hungry."

"You go ahead. I'll be there in a jiffy."

Mark came running toward her as she entered the kitchen. He was a gorgeous child, with dark wavy hair and the wide-eyed exuberance and innocence of youth.

"Pity I have to go to school. Mammy, can't I stay at home today?"

Pauline tussled his hair. "Nice try, Mark. You'll see her when you come back. Besides, you have sport today, your favourite. Have you got your sports things packed?" He skipped to his room to retrieve them.

Roisin pulled her kimono tighter around her waist as she took a seat at the table. *At this rate I'll never get back into those jeans.* "You're such an angel, Pauline, for going to all this trouble".

Pauline flushed and smiled. "Well, we love having you." While she poured Roisin a cup of coffee, she inquired about her plans. "Brian said something about you looking for a job on the west coast."

"Yes, that was my plan."

"But wouldn't it make more sense to stay here? At least you'll have family around you. The kids were so excited about you coming home."

"Well, it's not as if I'm moving behind the moon." She laughed and poured herself another cup of coffee. "And I'll still be able to see you all regularly."

An awkward silence ensued. Roisin didn't want to go into the details of why she felt it necessary to go to a new town, somewhere where nobody knew her. Here, everybody knew one's business. Brian had had his head buried in the paper, but she noticed him and Pauline exchange a quick glance. Obviously trying to distract from that embarrassing moment, he shook his head in exasperation. "Those bloody politicians. They won't be happy till they have us on our knees." He drained the dregs of his coffee and folded the paper. "Are you right lads? Time to go."

Pauline began stacking the dishwasher.

"Come on, Pauline. You do whatever you have to do. I'm doing this," Roisin said.

Pauline smiled and rushed to get ready while the kids gave their aunt a goodbye kiss. "Can we go for a walk after school, Aunty Roisin?"

She wiped her hands on the towel. "Of course we can. Sure, didn't I promise you?"

Brian honked the horn as Pauline checked her reflection in the hallway mirror. She turned to Roisin. "See you later. When is Helen coming to collect you?"

"Around ten, but I'll make sure to be back to take the kids for a walk."

\*

With the house to herself, Roisin stood at the kitchen sink washing some glasses. It was a cheerful spring day. Maybe Helen would drive her over to Donovan's later on. She could enquire about their car rental prices and, if it wasn't too expensive, she'd rent a small car and drive over to the west coast in a couple of days.

After she had rinsed the last sudsy glass, she couldn't resist but go outside and inhale the air. The back door was locked so she opened it and stepped outside. Tall hedges created a private spacious garden. She walked down through the archway where she had a good view of the low-lying fields. Lifting her face to catch some sun's rays, she almost tripped over Mark's football. It was great to be back and to have some time alone to let it all sink in.

When she went to go back inside, the door was locked. What a stupid thing to do. Now what? Helen would be arriving in less than an hour and she still had to shower and get dressed. What a start!

The next few minutes saw her rushing from back to front trying all the windows. No luck. She tried to think of where she would put a spare key as she lifted flower pots, stones and anywhere else that came to mind. Maybe they had installed special anti-burglary locks. She remembered her brother telling her there had been a spate of burglaries in that area the previous year. What would she do next? She could either wait outside until her sister came, or she could walk down to one of the neighbor's houses and call her brother. That would definitely be her last resort. Besides, she didn't have his number, or anyone else's for that matter.

Laughing at her silliness, she wandered down the driveway and stood on the road, looking left and right to see if there was any sign of life. From the gateway she had a clear view of an uneven stone wall opposite her. Behind that there were more fields and a line of trees off in the distance. Smoke billowed from a nearby farmhouse. She was about to go back to the house and wait out the back when a car sped around the corner toward her.

It was too late to turn back towards the house as the driver slowly pulled to a stop alongside her. Since she couldn't make a retreat, she tried to look as normal as possible. The driver, a dark-haired man with a healthy-looking complexion, who looked to be in his mid-forties, had a smirk on his face, not unkind but clearly amused. He lowered the passenger window. "Are you all right?"

"Fine, thanks." She tried to pull her robe even tighter.

He raised his left eyebrow while the hint of a smile played on his lips. She pushed some stray stands of hair from her face and, trying to make light of an absurd situation, she said. "I just locked myself out." A flush rose up her neck. She swallowed and smiled at the same time.

"Can I do anything for you? Maybe you want to call someone?" He handed her his mobile phone.

"No, no, thanks. It's okay. My sister will be here any minute." She couldn't remember the last time she had felt so embarrassed. In order to hide her shyness, she forced herself to stand tall and try to act as if her predicament was the most natural thing in the world.

"Well, if you're sure," he said.

She insisted she was fine. "Honestly. It's very nice of you, but not necessary."

He smirked and drove off at a slow pace. She could see him looking back through the car mirror before she turned toward the house again. There was nothing for it but to hang around until Helen showed up.

She hurried her pace toward the shed. At least that should be open. It was. She scanned the interior to see if there was anything with which she could occupy herself until her sister came. Perhaps a dart board or a skipping rope? If she remembered correctly, there was a gas heater Brian used when he was working on winter evenings. She would be half frozen to death if she had to wait much longer. Apart from some summer furniture and a few garden tools, there wasn't much of note. No sign of the heater either. Just as she was about to slam the door with frustration, she spotted a bunch of keys over on a hook by the back window. Maybe she'd be lucky. She was!

\*

She laughed out loud when she thought about what had just happened. Stop it, she said to herself, as she rinsed her hair under the gushing water. His face though! Maybe she should have turned her hand to acting. This was so typical of the kind of thing that happened to her. She stepped out of the shower and rubbed herself dry. By the time she was dressed and applying her make-up, she had convinced herself these things happen all the time. Still, she hoped she wouldn't be bumping into him again. If she had at least been dressed... She was running late and had barely managed to dry her hair when the doorbell rang.

Helen's face lit up when Roisin opened the door. 'It's about time,' she laughed. 'I thought you'd never come down. You're looking well,' Helen said. 'Come on before it gets too late. I have to take the dogs out.'

'Nice to see you too,' Roisin said. They always did this. No great emotional farewells or greetings. They carried on as if they had seen each other the previous week. In the car again, Roisin had a laughing fit.

"What on earth got into you?" Helen said.

"It's too embarrassing to talk about," Roisin said, but she continued to tell her anyway.

Her sister saw the funny side of it. "You never changed, Roisin. It could only happen to you."

They drove back to Helen's house to get the dogs. "Afterwards we can go for lunch somewhere. What do you think?" Helen said.

"Sounds great." A smile began to play on Roisin's lips as she thought of seeing all her old haunts again, the lake, the hotel and all the familiar places. It seemed as if every time she came home there were new roads or houses on that particular route. The lake was not too far from town, making it a popular place to live. And yet it had not been too built up, thanks mainly to the local Planning Commission. They carefully monitored every new building proposal. The committee tried to ensure that small factories and workshops were kept in the Industrial area and that a certain uniformity of architectural style, one that fit in with the existing style, was adhered to. They had learned valuable lessons after the big housing crash and the ensuing scandals as people became aware of builders throwing up shabby, insufficiently insulated identical housing estates and shooting prices skywards. Some of these eyesores were still sitting empty, particularly near Dublin, and although the city needed affordable housing, that was not the way to go. Many pockets had been lined with shady deals and little regard for quality and aesthetics.

The weather was picking up, and it promised to be a fine sunny day

"How about heading out to the lake?" Roisin said. "If we have time I'd like to drive out to Donovan's afterwards and check the car rental prices. I was thinking of heading off to the west coast tomorrow to check out for jobs."

Helen cleared her throat. "I'm not sure that's such a good idea. You don't know anybody out there. Wouldn't it be much easier to look for something here?" She had been folding some laundry and stopped for a moment to direct her attention to Roisin. "I hate to say this, but it's a bad time to move over here. Jobs are rare enough as it is."

Roisin almost gasped, opened her mouth to say something and closed it again. "I'll be fine, don't worry about me."

Helen continued folding clothes, almost throwing them down on the pile.

"This will work out, Helen. You know it's always been a dream of mine to live near the coast. If not now, then when?"

Helen put the last item on the top of the folded pile, crossed her arms in front of her chest and turned to Roisin. "Have you heard from Javier yet?"

"No, not yet. I'll call him as soon as I'm settled."

Helen grabbed her jacket from the back of a chair. "It's not as if you didn't warn him often enough. I really don't think you have any reason to berate yourself, Roisin. You haven't been happy there for years."

"I know, but he was such a big part of my life for so long. She sighed. "The only way I can survive now is to keep on going. No looking back."

"I suppose you're right, but I still think you should have talked to him before you left. He's a proud man." She shrugged her shoulders. "It's none of my business, I suppose."

*Damn right*, Roisin thought. *First she encourages me to come and now that I'm here she's laying a guilt trip on me.*

"We'd better get going," Helen said. She put on her jacket and Roisin followed her out to the hallway. She knew if she said anything there'd be hell to pay for it and so she kept her mouth closed but hardened her resolve to get her own place as soon as possible and pay her sister back.

As soon as they opened the door, the two dogs rushed over to them with tails wagging. They were two beauties. One of them, a red setter, had boundless energy. She began licking them, rushing from one woman to the other and creating a lot of excitement. The other dog, a black and white mongrel had such a shy temperament. He was stocky and already going grey around the snout, but had a most sensitive nature. "No, don't jump," shrieked Roisin, to the setter. She hunkered down on the ground and took turns ruffling their coats.

Helen sat in the car, tapping her fingers on the dashboard. The dogs jumped into the boot. "The morning is almost gone," Helen reprimanded her, when Roisin joined her. Helen turned the key in the ignition and checked the rearview mirror. "We'd better get a move on," she said.

Roisin didn't like her sister's tone but decided to ignore it. If she stayed here, she'd feel obligated to her and that was the last thing she wanted. Another reason why she wanted a place of her own.

They took the new road out to the lake. A lot of changes had taken place over the past few years. The once narrow roads were hardly recognisable with all the wider bypasses. It was as if the road surgeon had become carried away with his scalpel, creating roundabouts and bypasses till the once-characteristic roads were hardly recognisable, but at least the traffic flowed better. It had been a necessary operation, but sad nevertheless. Roisin found it difficult to find her orientation as they cut across town on a totally unfamiliar road. Spin me round twice and I'm lost, she thought. Convenient and faster yes, but somehow she missed the curvy country roads and low brick walls. This route blocked the green vistas, and although the landscapes and grassy areas were immaculate and decorated with an abundance of spring flowers and saplings, she needed to make the mental adjustment. Soon they took the exit to the lake, and the landscape began to look more familiar, more organic. "Oh, look!" Roisin said. "McCarthy's is still there. Remember getting pop ices on our day trips to the lake?"

"The son took it over," Helen said. "It hasn't changed much on the inside either."

Memories came flooding back. Roisin tried to see her home with fresh eyes, as if she was a tourist, but scenes of yesteryear continuously flashed onto her inner screen.

*

The parking lot at the lake was almost empty. Her sister opened the hatch door and the dogs leapt out, tails wagging furiously. "Let's take a dog each," she said, as she handed her the lead. I'll take Rex; he's used to me and he'll yank you all over the place if you don't keep him under control." Poor Rex. He needed a lot of exercise and was bursting to go and explore.

"Let's go over to the little bridge, you know where the cafe is?" Helen said.

"Of course I do. Remember I worked there one summer? Have you forgotten?"

"Oh yes, you did. It's hard to remember with all the jobs you've had,"

They walked at a fast pace, mainly dictated by the dogs. The slate-grey water stretched out for miles. A few lonely fishing boats bobbed along on the calm waters, and she remembered catching pinkeens, the baby fish that used to zigzag their way through the clear, shallow water so many years ago. She could almost smell the sun cream and hear the happy families playing by the waterside.

"Roisin, are you even listening to me? You haven't heard a word I've said, have you?"

"Sorry. I was taking a stroll down memory lane."

They released the dogs from their leads and let

45

them run. "So, tell me about your plans," Helen said.

"What plans? I'm going to head out west, get myself a job and a house by the sea and hope for the best." Helen's silence told her that her sister was skeptical of her decision, but Roisin didn't care. To break the silence, Roisin told her sister about the fellow who'd pulled up as she'd walked out onto the road earlier.

"Do I detect an interest?" Helen said.

Roisin shrugged her shoulders. "I just wondered if you might know him. He said he lives up the road from Brian."

"And how am I supposed to recognize him from the scant details you gave me?"

"Ah, forget about it," Roisin said.

She could feel her sister's eyes on her and they both laughed.

"I think you're having a mid-life crisis, Roisin Delaney."

"I don't believe in mid-life crises."

"What is it then, whatever you're looking for?"

"Excitement, perhaps. If this is a crisis, it feels exciting. Don't you ever wish you could take a different road?"

Her sister thought for a moment. "We all do. I'm sure of that, but most of us stay on the safe road. Besides, I really am happy with my life. Todd is very good to me. We are healthy. Yes, life is grand."

"So, you think I'm selfish?"

"Where did you get that idea?"

"Just wondering. Maybe I feel guilty for leaving him."

"What choice did you have? It will shake him up. I just don't think it's over yet."

Roisin picked up a flat stone and rubbed it between her fingers. A soft, refreshing breeze sent a shiver through the young leaves, and tiny ripples spread across the water. "Why don't we go to The Lilacs after this and have an Irish coffee? I'd really like that, even though it's not a respectable hour to be drinking alcohol."

"Who cares about decorum? We have something to celebrate. You finally did it, Roisin."

# Chapter 6

First they drove up to the car rental. Roisin was surprised at how reasonable it was to rent an economy car for a few days. They had a special deal – ten days for the price of seven - undoubtedly an advantage of the recession. She arranged to pick up her car in a couple of days, postponing her trip by a day. Perhaps it was too early to leave immediately.

Later, they sat in the luxurious surroundings of The Lilacs with a view onto the vibrant greens of the golf course.

"Why are you looking at me like that, Helen? Come on, spit it out? You think I'm mad, don't you?"

"Well, yes. The thought has often crossed my mind. You're really serious about doing this, aren't you? I mean, leaving Javier is one thing, but heading off into strange territory is another. What kind of a job can you expect to get, especially in this economy? And what are you going to live off while you're waiting."

Roisin stared out onto the green, watching a man in a bright red cap preparing to take a swing at the ball. "How staid you've become. Don't you remember all the times we took off on a whim, the adventures we used to have?"

"They were different times, and we were

younger."

"I'll manage. Wait and see. In fact, I was never more serious in my life. I just know I need to give it a try." She sipped the coffee through the frothy cream. "If it doesn't work out, or if I change my mind, it won't be the end of the world. We've got to live our dreams, Helen. You should know that."

Her sister looked thoughtful.

Roisin continued. "If I don't do it now, it'll be too late. Life is an adventure. I don't want to read about it, I want to live it. I'm going to rent a little cottage on the west coast. You know—a nice little house near the sea." Her eyes turned again to the golfer as he moved on to the next spot. "I see myself living on the edge of the Atlantic, surrounded by nature, with easy access to all the wonders of civilisation. It must have high-speed internet access, a great coffee house, a jazz bar, a fantastic farmer's market and a good health spa."

Her sister laughed. "I just don't want to see you making a mistake, that's all. Reality can be pretty harsh."

Roisin's laughter was a bit too high pitched. "Where do you think I've been living? Would you stop trying to put the fear of God into me? I'll be fine." She looked at her watch. "How about doing a bit of retail therapy? I might buy myself a new dress; I'll need one for my interviews anyway."

\*

The kids were giggling in the next room as they watched a group of animated, noisy creatures on television. Roisin had packed a little backpack with some drinks and snacks and a warm blanket. She called them and they came running.

Deirdre led the way. "We always go as far as the graveyard," she said. Roisin thought it a strange place to have a picnic but if that's what they wanted it was fine with her. There was no pedestrian path, and occasionally a car came driving past, much too fast for her liking. She was amazed there were so few accidents. The roads had not been made for so many cars. It would cost a small fortune, not to mention months of disruption, to widen them. They kept within the boundaries of the imaginary footpath. Mark told her about his football team and how he had scored a goal the previous week. Deirdre interjected with her latest horse-riding stories, stopping to pick daisies. She began making a daisy chain. "Daddy said Uncle Javier called last night," she said.

"Oh, really."

"Yes, I heard him tell Mammy Uncle Javier was in a state." Nothing like children to rub the conscience.

"Don't be worrying about that, Deirdre. He'll be fine." Roisin felt sick to her stomach at this news. What did Pauline mean by 'in a state?' Now she was beginning to get seriously worried about her husband.

Her niece looked thoughtful as she pushed the final daisy through the loop before putting it round her neck. "My best friend's Mammy and Daddy are getting a divorce. She's very sad about it."

"Just think about it, your friend will have two houses to visit in future. Isn't that great? I would have liked that when I was a child."

That seemed to do the trick. Roisin steered the conversation to safer areas. "I have a little surprise for you both," she said.

"A surprise! Tell us," they cried in unison. "What is it?"

"You'll have to wait and see."

When they arrived at the graveyard, which was almost hidden by overgrown hedges and ivy, Mark fiddled with the latch of the iron gate. It was like a neglected, hidden place, with lime-scaled headstones adding to the old-world atmosphere. Mark bounded ahead, making a beeline for the stone bench at the far end of the graveyard.

They loved the special snacks she had bought. The old-fashioned gobstoppers were a big hit. She had found them in a new specialty shop that sold sweets she remembered from her own school days. Still sucking on the giant gobstopper, Mark pleaded with her to tell them a ghost story.

"Forget it," she said. 'I'm not going to be responsible for you having nightmares."

They swore they wouldn't tell.

"I never have nightmares," Deirdre said.

Mark nearly spat out his gobstopper and began to tease his sister. "You're too scared to even sleep without the light on."

"Now, now children. We'd better be getting back. Don't you still have to do your homework?"

"But we just got here," Mark said. He crossed his arms in defiance and refused to budge until she told them something scary. She sighed and settled for a story her old neighbour, Mrs. Corcoran, used to tell her when she was a young girl. If she could handle it, they probably could too, especially in light of the fact that they were exposed to a lot more than she had ever been at their age.

Roisin used to visit the old lady who lived next door to them when she was a young girl. The old lady always made her a cup of tea and they'd sit there looking into the flames of the fire as Mrs. Corcoran puffed on her cigarette and toll her ghost stories. That memory had never left her and was particularly precious since she had never had a chance to get to know her own grandmothers. She began to tell the first story that came to mind.

*Once there was a woman who was lying in bed with her newborn baby. She was still weak from giving birth, and she kept dozing off in a half-awake, half-asleep state. The door creaked and she opened her eyes in fright. Her first thought was that it might be her husband so she turned to look at the clock which sat on the little table beside her bed.*

*It was far too early for him to be returning home from work. The woman felt so tired and could barely keep her eyes open, but the creaking noise continued. A strange coldness crept into the room it was filled with a hazy mist, making it hard for her to see clearly. She tried to move, but was frozen with fear. Who was there? She clutched her baby tight in her arms and hummed a soft lullaby. Seoithín, seo hó, mo stór é mo leanbh..*

Roisin sang in a haunting voice, little more than a whisper. She was beginning to give herself goose bumps. It was time to start heading home soon. The children were like statues, hanging on to her every word. Had she overdone it?

*The woman kissed the baby's forehead. She lifted her weary head to look toward the door again, but she couldn't see anyone. There was nobody else in the house and nobody who could come to her rescue. As she continued watching, terrified of what she might see, a small alabaster figure began to move toward her, slowly, ever so slowly as if it was sliding along the floor. With every forward movement, the figure grew bigger and bigger.*

Once again, Roisin took a sideways glance to see the effect her story was having on the children. Both children moved closer to her. Deirdre had a far-away look in her eyes, whereas Mark's eyes were wide open. She remembered how thrilling she had found Mrs. Corcoran's stories, back in the day.

"What happened next?" Deirdre whispered.

Roisin continued. *Her first instinct was to hold the baby even tighter, to protect her.*

Roisin was still for a moment. She was suddenly overcome with sadness. She had never held her own child in her arms. She swallowed. It was time to take the story into a lighter tone.

*The baby began to cry and then the woman realized that the alabaster figure had been merely a shadow caused by the weak afternoon light shining in through the window, or perhaps it was an angel coming to alert her to stay awake for her baby.*

*When the baby's daddy came home later that day, he found his wife clutching the little one to her breast. She had a high fever and so did the baby. He could never understand what prompted him to return home earlier than usual that day, but he knew something was not right.*

Roisin clapped her hands to break the spell.

*He was able to take them to the hospital and both mother and baby were in the best of hands and soon on the way to recovery.*

The sun was beginning to fall low in the sky which set the graveyard in a gloomy light.

Mark has a wistful look in his eyes. "Do you think it was really an angel?"

"I think it might have been, but I also think we'd better be making our way back before it gets dark," Roisin said as she began putting things away. She hoped she would be able to change the mood on the way home by telling them a silly story. And that's exactly what she did.

*

Later on that evening when the kids were in bed, Pauline thanked her again for taking them on the picnic "I wouldn't have had a moment's rest listening to them if you had forgotten."

"Well, I enjoyed it too. I'm making up for lost time."

Brian had one eye on the news as he spread butter on his scone. "You heard Javier called yesterday?"

Roisin answered a little too quickly. "Yes, I heard. How was he?"

Brian turned his full attention to her and sighed. "What do you think? He didn't sound in great form."

Roisin didn't say anything.

"I don't know, Roisin…" Brian looked over to Pauline as if hoping she would take over and finish his sentence. Seeing as no help was coming from that direction, he said. "I think you should sort things out between you. It's kind of hard on us. What are we supposed to say to him? " He bit into his toast and sat back in his chair as if indicating that he had said all there was to be said.

Roisin's face reddened. She didn't want to have to answer to anyone. This was precisely the reason why she wanted to move on and live her own life. They had not been there with her when she'd had to put up with Javier's depression and constant negative moods. She couldn't bear to feel criticized and judged, but at the same time she understood how they felt. After all, they had never had any issues with her husband.

"No, you're right," she said. "If he calls again, just tell him I'll be in contact soon."

Brian mumbled something about going to watch the match next door. When he was out of earshot, Pauline said, "Just ignore him. He'll get over it. He always does."

Roisin's eyes welled up with tears and she fumbled in her bag for a tissue. "What choice do I have? Of course he sees everything from the man's perspective."

Her sister-in-law went to the cupboard and took out a bottle of red wine. "I know just the thing. How about watching a film? There's a whole stack of DVD's up in our room."

Roisin nodded and pulled herself together.

She didn't want any scenes.

She came back later with three DVD's and placed them on the table. "Thriller, romantic comedy or sci-fi?"

After some deliberation, they chose *It's Complicated* starring Alec Baldwin and Meryl Streep, although both of them had watched it before but forgotten most of the details. This type of film made you see the hilarity of life and gave you a sense of detachment from your own problems. By the end of the film they had finished the bottle and lightened their spirits. Roisin even considered forgiving all and calling Javier. She said as much to Pauline.

"I'd wait until tomorrow at least," her sister-in-law said. "You're still coloured by the film. And you're tipsy. Not a good combination."

"Yeh, you're probably right.' She tried to stifle a yawn. 'I think I'll head up to bed. It's been a long day. Thanks again, Pauline, for everything."

"Sure, it's great having you. I told you that."

She went into the living room to say goodnight to her brother but he was fast asleep with the remote control in his hand, snoring loudly.

The next morning she awoke with a headache and a dry throat. She should have known better. Red wine rarely agreed with her. She went up to the kitchen and drank a huge glass of cold water and made herself a coffee. The others weren't awake yet but it was only 7.30. Since it was a Saturday, it was unlikely anyone else would be up for another couple of hours. She grabbed a book from her bag and went back to bed, but after reading a couple of pages, the words began to swim on the page. When she awoke, she heard muffled, urgent voices coming from Brian and Pauline's room across the hall. She hoped she wasn't the cause of the argument.

Later at breakfast, there was no sign of any ill will. She joined them afterwards in town and, while they went to do their weekly food shopping, she did some window shopping. As she walked down the street, someone tapped her on the shoulder. She turned around to see the fellow who had offered to give her refuge from the cold the previous day.

"I thought I recognised you," he said, extending his hand to her. "The name's Tom Cullen, by the way." Before she could answer he said, "Did you get in all right?"

She smirked. The question was superfluous, but she held her tongue and nodded.

"If you're not doing anything else tomorrow night a friend of mine is playing out at The Well."

She smiled. "I'm afraid I have other plans." *Did she really say that?*

He brushed it off. "Well, if you change your mind, just let me know. They're excellent musicians and it'll all be very casual."

She hesitated a moment.

"It's the least I can do after leaving you out in the cold yesterday."

She tried to halt a blush that was creeping up from her throat. He seemed so kind and thoughtful and if she refused him he might feel rebuffed.

He took her silence for a possible yes. "Great, then. I'll pick you up tomorrow at 9."

*Say something, you idiot.* "Well, I suppose..." She smiled. "I'm Roisin, by the way." Not wanting to embarrass herself any further, she turned to go.

As she walked away, she thought, Did this really just happen? Immediately she thought of Javier. She could hear him scolding her. What was the harm in going out to hear some music with a man she hardly knew? It wasn't as if she would even be around for long. There was no fear of becoming embroiled in a new relationship, and besides, she was sure it was just a friendly gesture on his part. At least it would get her out of the house for a while.

# Chapter 7

The next evening after dinner, she told the others she was going out. Of course they wanted to know where, and with whom. No reason to hide anything, she thought. She told them about how she'd met her new friend as she was standing on the road. "I bumped into him again yesterday in town," she said.

"What's his name?" Brian asked.

"Tom Cullen. I think he lives up the road, not too far from here."

"Enough said. Tall fellow with dark hair, well dressed?"

"That sounds like him, why?"

"I hear he's a bit of a boyo. You might do well to keep far away from him."

Roisin's look said enough, and Brian raised his hands in defeat. "Don't say I didn't warn you!"

"I like to make my own decisions about people." She immediately regretted her sharp tone. "Sorry Brian. It's just a date, no commitment. I think he was being kind, nothing more."

"Yes, and what'll I say if Javier calls again?"

"Just tell him I'm not here, and I'll contact him later on in the week." She stood up. "Anyway, I'd better be getting ready, he'll be here soon."

In truth, she was relieved to be able to leave the room. She placed her new dresses on the bed.

Which one would she wear? After much deliberation, she chose the low-cut burgundy one, not only because the A-line complimented her figure, but the wool and silk fabric fell beautifully and didn't crease.

The doorbell rang just as she was applying a touch of lipstick. She grabbed her jacket and bag, hoping to reach the door first, thus avoiding awkward introductions. Mark got there first, and Brian was already halfway down the hallway when she arrived. She caught a glimpse of Tom's handsome visage as he stood chatting to her young nephew.

"Hi, Tom." She made a bee-line for the door.

"Come on in for a minute." Brian held out his hand in welcome.

Tom shook his hand before brushing her cheek with his lips. They went into the kitchen.

"Take a seat," Brian said. "I heard about my sister's little mishap yesterday. Good thing you showed up when you did."

"Well, I'm sure you would have done the same," he smiled. He ran his fingers through his thick wavy hair. It seemed more like embarrassment than anything else. She had time to observe him as he chatted to her brother. He was handsome with a strong, square jaw, more rugged than smooth, good teeth and clear intelligent eyes that held a touch of mirth. If she was any judge of character he was no pushover, someone who knew what he wanted, but he had heart. Was he really a womaniser? Brian must have had a good reason for his comments. He was not the type of man to criticise others without good reason; in fact he had great empathy for human weakness.

She decided there and then to cut the interrogation. "Didn't you say it started at nine, Tom? We'd better get going."

Tom stood up, the relief on his face evident. Brian accompanied them to the door. "Well, enjoy yourselves. I'll leave the back door open. By the way, Roisin, your husband rang a while ago. I forgot to tell you earlier."

She laughed, more out of nervousness than amusement. In fact, she could have kicked him. She blew him a kiss. "You're getting old, Brian. Don't you remember you already told me?" She would have told Tom herself, but the way Brian blurted it out made her out to be a woman of loose morals.

"Yeh, yeh. Sorry."

When they were inside the car, she said. "I feel like I'm seventeen again."

"Ah, don't worry about it. He was just making small talk."

"Yes, he's the best in the world, but I'm too old for this."

"You look lovely, by the way," he said.

"Thank you. Anything would be an improvement on yesterday."

She repeated to herself that this was not a date and that he was just being kind. What an unusual thing for her brother to say. He had made a point in saying your husband, rather than Javier. He had surprised her, but then she knew he was a traditionalist at heart. Who knows what he was thinking. She wasn't going to ruin her evening worrying about it. Besides, Tom didn't seem to even notice.

The old manor house, which now served as a pub and restaurant, was set in a large enclosed garden with wrought iron gates and lovely old trees, stone pillars and terraced pathways. The last time she'd been home, her brother had told her the new owner planned on renovating it and turning it into a wellness spa. Now of course, all such plans were abandoned. The recession had changed all that. Pity, she thought. The location would be perfect for a retreat. It was idyllically situated in a small valley nestled amongst unspoiled fields and hedgerows, a true sanctuary. It was one of those nights when you imagined you could reach up to the sky and cradle the moon in your arms, it hung that low. The indigo sky was pregnant with stars, and the moon cast a pearly light upon the landscape, making it look magical.

The sound of lively music floated through the open door. Tom stepped aside to let her enter first. He held his hand in the small of her back. She could smell the faint scent of his after-shave which held a note of something woodsy and a hint of bergamot.

The bar area had smaller nooks and the large, stone fireplace to the left added extra warmth. Flickering flames danced a hypnotic pirouette, casting shadows on the candle-lit room. A friendly buzz of chatter filled the space. As they debated where to sit, a tall gangly fellow in a tweed jacket came up to them. He gave Tom a friendly punch on the back.

"How're doing, Tom? Good man. What are ya havin?

Tom turned to her. "Roisin, this is Gorman, an old school friend. Gorman, this is Roisin."

"Nice to meet ya, Roisin. What are ya drinkin?" Gorman asked over the din of the music. "Come on over and join us. He pointed to a table by the window."

Tom looked at her for confirmation. She smiled.

While Gorman ordered their drinks, Tom led the way over to the group of people at the table. The singer's rich voice filled the room as they nestled in amongst the small group. Tom introduced her to Claire, a vibrant red head with an open face and friendly smile. Then there was Mary, a petite fair-haired woman who gave her a cheeky grin, and Sinead, a dark-haired handsome woman with a lion's mane of hair who eyed her with suspicion. She was briefly taken aback by this woman's scrutinising demeanour. She's thinks I'm trying to steal him, she thought.

Another fellow, Richard, a short bear of a fellow with twinkling eyes and dark curly hair, gave her a warm handshake. Soon, Gorman came back with the drinks and she sipped her first glass of Guinness. It had been years since she'd had a glass of the dark stuff but it always looked nourishing and didn't taste too bad with the addition of blackcurrant juice.

"So, where are you from?" Sinead's smile didn't extend to her eyes. Tom never mentioned you before. Did you Tom?"

"I'm from around here originally."

"Did you know each other before?" Sinead's eyes flicked from her to Tom.

"No, we only met yesterday." She nudged

him, silently hoping he wouldn't tell about how they met.

"Sshh. Sinead. Listen to these lyrics," Tom said, friendly but firm.

The band played their unique cover version of Tears and Laughter, one of Roisin's favourites. Tom leaned over and whispered, "Everything okay? Pay no attention to Sinead's Inquisition. Her bark is worse than her bite."

She shrugged her shoulders and raised her glass to him, grinning. She felt Sinead staring at her and returned her glance without flinching.

"So, what brings you to these parts?" Sinead said.

"I'm just visiting family." She detected a smug look in Sinead's eyes.

Still not satisfied, Sinead leaned in closer. "How exactly did you meet him?"

Roisin cupped her hands over her ears, indicating that it was useless trying to talk over the din. She hoped Tom wasn't planning on hanging around for too long with the crowd afterwards.

The band announced they were taking a short break. Bad timing.

"Another drink, Roisin? What about the rest of ye?" Tom took his empty glass and reached for hers.

"Let me get this one," she said, getting up from her seat.

"Absolutely not. You're my guest." He went up to the bar. Sinead didn't miss a chance and zoomed in on her as soon as he was out of earshot.

"Bit loud back there. I asked how you met

Mr. Charming." Sinead flicked a glance in Tom's direction. He had one foot crocked up on a ledge at the base of the bar as he gave his order to the barman.

Roisin considered her answer for a moment. "You wouldn't believe me even if I told you. Let's just say I bumped into him on the road yesterday?" Was it yesterday? She had lost count of time.

"So, are you married?" The woman glanced at her hand where the mark of her wedding ring could clearly be seen.

Roisin feigned partial deafness again and made a flippant comment about the noise level.

Tom came back carrying a couple of drinks.

"Roisin here tells me you bumped into her on the road yesterday," Sinead said. "You're a fast worker, Tom Cullen."

"Now, now, Sinead. Drop it, will you?"

Sinead looked dejected, and Roisin couldn't help feeling secretly pleased he had helped her out of an awkward situation. She leaned closer to him. The alcohol was beginning to go to her head. It always made her more amorous so she knew she'd better not drink too much. "The band is very good. Thanks for inviting me, Tom. I'm so glad I came."

"Yes, they're great, aren't they?" Finn, the lead singer, is an old school friend of mine. They could've gone far if they'd wanted to—not cut-throat enough though. Now they mostly do cover songs, but that fellow has poetry in his soul."

It was Diarmuid's turn to zoom in on her, but there was no malice in his voice. "So, do you work in town, Roisin?"

She swallowed. "No. I'm just visiting." She

told him she'd lived in Spain for the past few years. He, in turn, told her he'd once been to that part of the world several years ago. "Those Spanish are a wild bunch. We're tame in comparison." Talk about the pot calling the kettle black. "*Slainte*," he said, "*To your health, Salut, Cheers* or whatever you say in those Spanish plains." With mirth in his eyes, he sucked a gulp of Guinness through the white creamy froth. Sporting a frothy moustache, he continued with his banter. "What do you do to earn a crust?" She had been away too long and was no longer used to people showing such an interest in her personal life.

"A bit of everything really. You could say I'm having a gap year. Just hope I don't fall through." She knew Sinead was hanging on to every word. She even laughed at her lame joke which was said more in nerves than anything else. Sinead's expression had softened considerably which she put down to the fact that she now knew Roisin wouldn't be staying around for long.

When the band broke up for the night, she felt pleasantly tired. It had been a long day. She said her goodbyes and secretly hoped she wouldn't bump into Sinead again.

\*

"Like to come in for a nightcap?" Tom said as he approached his house.

She froze for a moment. "Well. It's getting late and I've a lot to do tomorrow." *Fool, why did I say that!* Although it was true that she had a busy day ahead, she didn't want things to end there. They'd hardly even had a chance to get to know each other.

"Oh, come on. "Just one drink?"

Like Oscar Wilde, she could resist anything except temptation. Not that she had any intention of having more than a night cap and getting to know Tom better.

She finally gave in. What was the harm in it? "Oh, why not," she said.

He set about igniting the sticks and paper which were already prepared in the grate. Was he always so organised or had he prepared this for her, she wondered. With a deft hand, he set the room aglow with candlelight and flicked a switch on the CD player. "Make yourself comfortable. I'll be back in a few minutes."

She went over to the bookshelf and leaned her head slightly to see what kind of books he liked to read. There were some popular contemporary thrillers and several Steven King books. Funny, she wouldn't have associated him with the great master of horror. There were books on song writing, some on architecture and a wild mix on subjects ranging from astronomy to bird watching. Bird watching of all things. She grinned.

"So what's the verdict?"

She spun around as he handed her an Irish coffee. "You'll definitely sleep well after this."

"Oh, I never have trouble sleeping." Why couldn't she think of something witty to say?

She took a sip, a chance to hide her smile. "I notice you're fond of bird watching." She looked up and challenged him with her eyes.

"I have many interests. Bird watching is just one of them." His voice, deep and hoarse, added to his attractiveness. He walked over to the couch and sat back, patting the space beside him. "Aren't you going to make yourself comfortable?"

"Just a minute. I'm not finished yet." She opened a book on architecture, more as a distraction than anything else.

"Come on. Put the book down."

No longer able to delay, she put the book back onto the shelf and went over to the couch. She sat down, leaving a decent space between them. This was silly. She'd been with Javier for so many years that she no longer knew how to do this anymore. Distant memories of her dating years came rushing back. How easier it had all seemed back then. He broke the silence. "Do you really have to leave so soon?"

"Yes." She kicked off her shoes and made herself comfortable. "I've set my mind to it and when I set my mind to something I always pull it through. I've already reserved a rental car." He played with a tendril of her hair and she snuggled closer to him.

"You've no idea how much effort it took for me to make this move. I want to live by the sea." She took another sip of her creamy beverage and looked at him sideways, from under her eyelashes.

He looked thoughtful. "I couldn't imagine uprooting myself and starting all over again. Maybe I'm a safe player. I've been here all my life, except for a trip out of my comfort zone when I was in my twenties—went to New York. That opened my eyes—never been so lonely in my entire life. Here, people know me, for better or for worse."

Her toes were beginning to get cold. There was a folded blanket on the couch. "Mind if I borrow this," she asked.

"Take away", he said. "Better yet. Let me warm them up. I'm an excellent warmer-upper." He took her cold feet into his hands and began massaging them briskly.

She sat back, facing him, with her legs outstretched. "You really are good at this," she said. Normally she couldn't bear anyone touching her feet because she was so ticklish, but he knew exactly how much pressure to apply. "Don't you have any dreams, any bucket list?" she asked him.

His hearty laugh filled the room. "Yes. I suppose I do. Impossible dreams. I'd like to fly into deep space. That's not likely to happen, not in my lifetime. We're tiny specks in a vast universe—mere ants in the grand scheme of things." Roisin pulled her feet away, giggling.

"Warm enough now?" he asked as he wrapped the blanket around her feet.

She closed her eyes, enjoying the sound of his voice and looked up lazily to watch him as he went over to the fireplace. He put a few more lumps of coal onto the dying embers. When he came back, he knelt beside her and kissed her gently on the mouth. He had taken her by surprise, and she felt like Sleeping Beauty being given the kiss of life. Familiar sensations which had been dormant for far too long stirred in her. She disentangled herself gently. He grinned at her, rubbing his chin.

"Sorry, I couldn't resist," he said. She leaned into his shoulder. If only she could switch off her brain and banish the guilty feelings. This was all out-of-character; she was normally a loyal soul. Gently, she sat upright and began fixing her hair. "I think I'd really better call it a night Tom." This time her voice was hoarse.

"So, what about your husband?"

"What about him?"

"Why isn't he with you?"

"It's complicated, Tom."

"I won't press you. But are you sure you're doing the right thing?"

"What, this…being here?"

"Everything. Going out west on your own. I cannot imagine why he let you go."

"He didn't."

"So you left? You must have had your reasons."

"I had no other choice." She sighed. "Let's not talk about this now."

"As you wish," he said, and reached for his jacket."

He drove her home in relative silence. She was furious with Brian, but more furious with herself. What would she tell Javier when he rang? This could all have been avoided if he hadn't been so stubborn. How many times had she tried to tell him what was wrong? It was as if he couldn't help himself. Now it was too late. No going back.

Tom pulled in to the curb beside Brian's driveway. He turned off the engine. "What are you doing tomorrow?"

"Going out to the lake with the family." She mustn't let this chance pass her by. "But I'll be in town late afternoon." Did she really say that? *Roisin Delaney, there's no hope for you now.*

His eyes lit up. "Great. Maybe we can meet in

the afternoon. There's a new café called the Grasshopper on Chapel Street. I'll be there at four." He leaned over and placed his warm hands over her cheeks, pulling her toward him. This time his kiss was more demanding. She gently pushed him away. "I'm sorry, Tom...it's just that...."

"Come on, Roisin. The night is still young. We can drive out to the lake now, watch the moon teasing the water."

She laughed. "What, and watch some owls?" She gave him a friendly punch. "No, really. I don't want to do anything I'll regret. It's too early for that right now."

"Ah, Roisin. You can't leave me like this?"

"Don't tempt me. I just can't right now." She kissed him on the cheek and squeezed his hand. He was still sitting there when she reached the front door. She blew him a kiss and went inside. With the door firmly closed behind her, she leaned against it, her heart fluttering as she chided herself. Why did she feel so guilty; it wasn't as if she had planned any of this. At least the house was silent. She had no desire to be asked awkward questions.

# Chapter 8

The next morning, she awoke to the sound of tapping at her bedroom door. She slowly opened her eyes and propped herself up. One glimpse of her tousled hair in the mirror was enough to make her flop back down again.

"Morning, Roisin," Pauline called through the door. "Are you going to join us for breakfast? I have the table set, and we're all waiting for you. Better to start out while the sun's still shining?"

"Come on in." Roisin reached for her robe and tidied her hair a bit. Her sister-in-law poked her head around the door and laughed.

"Looks like you had a late night last night. Did you enjoy yourself?"

She nodded, rubbing her eyes. The clock on the wall said 8.30. "I'll be right with you, Pauline."

She slid her feet into her slippers, freshened herself up and joined the others in the kitchen. The crackling fire spat out welcoming sparks, and the kettle buzzed away on the warm stove. Optimistic music rang out from the radio. The kids giggled as Brian tapped his fingers on the wooden table in time to the music and pulled funny faces while mimicking the lyrics.

He looked up, smiling, when she came in. "Well, the dead arose and appeared to many."

"Auntie Roisin. I thought you'd never get up," Deirdre said.

Both of the children started chatting to her, like little chirping birds. "Are you coming out to the lake with us?" Mark pleaded.

"Absolutely, but first I'm going to enjoy this delicious breakfast."

"How did your evening go?" Brian asked.

"Great. Good music. I met some of Tom's friends too. He's a really nice man, you know."

"Did you kiss him?" her niece asked, giggling and covering her mouth at the same time.

"Deirdre! What a thing to say." Her mother apologised to Roisin.

"Of course I didn't kiss him, Deirdre. That would be disgusting, wouldn't it?" Roisin leaned over to her niece and planted a big kiss on her cheek.

Their good-humoured banter continued as the two women cleaned up the breakfast things. Brian had to do a quick job out in the shed.

\*

She hadn't been to Lough Brandon for many years and it brought back memories of summers spent swimming and picnicking. A slight drizzle fell slowly from the slate-grey sky, but they were dressed appropriately for these early spring days. Brian and Mark skimmed stones on the water and the females gave it a go too although they weren't very successful.

"Let's climb the hill over there?" Deirdre splashed through puddles in her flowery wellies as she went toward the hill.

"Hold on a moment, let's just tell the others.

Maybe they want to join us." Pauline called out to Brian and Mark who were still skimming stones on the water.

"Ah, Mum. This is brilliant fun, I don't want to climb any hills," Mark said.

"First one up gets a hot chocolate when we're back in town," Brian said, and he began to walk toward the hill.

Soon they were climbing. Running was out of the question. It was a slow and steep incline and Brian was struggling, much to the amusement of Mark whose little legs were much faster. The children were trying to outdo each other. They didn't seem to find it in the least bit strenuous. Roisin enjoyed listening to their happy teasing. From its summit they could see the misty hills and low valleys of the surrounding countryside in various shades of green and earth tones. The sun attempted to shine through, turning the grey to shades of lilac-grey. Roisin wished she'd taken her camera with her, but she'd have plenty of opportunity to take all the photos she wanted. Snippets of her conversation with Tom kept intruding on her inner landscape. Her body tingled as she remembered their embrace, his kiss and his warm, deep voice. Their meeting had been so fortuitous and she hadn't yet had a chance to digest all that had happened so far. She felt a little thrill about seeing him later.

She looked at her watch. "By the way, I have to be in town at four o'clock. Maybe you could drop me off on the way back."

"Sure," Brian said. Are you meeting Helen?"

"No, I'm meeting a friend." She steered the

conversation away from further uncomfortable questions. Deirdre, the little minx, gave her a knowing look. She was a smart little girl, wiser than her nine years.

*

Back in town, she had some time to spare so she went into the book shop where an old school friend worked. Their friendship was one that didn't need constancy. Although she didn't keep in regular contact, she knew they could always take up where they had left off. If luck was on her side, Carmel would be working. She looked around but didn't see any sign of her friend, so she started browsing through the prominently displayed novels. Shop lights always made her eyes smart, and there were so many books on the market, making it hard to choose. She reached for one with an attractive cover and began reading the blurb. A hand on her shoulder brought her back to the present and she spun round to see who it was.

"Roisin Delaney. Is that you? You have the life! Home again on holidays, I see, and you haven't aged a bit. I'd recognize that mane anywhere."

"Hi, Carmel. I was hoping you'd be working today. Where were you hiding?"

Carmel put the pile of books she was carrying on the table. "I was out the back. Why don't we go for a drink later on during the week? We can catch up properly."

"I won't be in town too long this time. How about later on this evening? I'm meeting someone in a few minutes but we could catch up afterwards?"

Her friend checked her watch. "Sure, why

not? Would seven be too early? No, make it ten past. We can meet at that new hotel near the market place."

Roisin gave her a huge smile. "Great. I'll see you then."

The town was busy with people rushing to and fro. It hadn't changed too much. Despite the fact that new tapas bistros, coffee shops and eateries were popping up everywhere, some of the old family-run shops and pubs which had been there since she was a girl still stood proud. Baskets of spring flowers added a touch of colour and gaiety to the place. But there was also an uglier side with boarded windows and pound-shops in the less-prominent streets.

The Grasshopper, a relatively new trendy café, was tucked into a side street. True to its name, the façade was painted in bright greens and yellows. She braced herself before going in and hoped she didn't look too wind-swept after her day at the lake. As soon as she entered, she spotted Tom sitting off to the side and chatting to a young, blond waitress.

She ambled over to him. "Hope you haven't been waiting long," she said.

He held out a chair for her and took her jacket. "No. I just arrived. What about you, how did your outing go?"

She settled in and picked up the menu. "It was lovely. I'm enjoying being with the family again. Just bumped into an old school friend too. We're meeting up later this evening."

His face dropped. "I was hoping we could spend a bit more time together, seeing as you're leaving tomorrow."

She was surprised at his candour but she liked

it. Strategic games didn't appeal to her, and honesty ranked high in her list of virtues. She felt a flush of pleasure as she remembered their last meeting. "Well, I wasn't sure how much time you had and I didn't want to make presumptions." That was partly true, but she also didn't want to appear to be too eager. The waitress arrived back to take their order.

Roisin watched him as he browsed through the menu. She wondered if he had ever been married or if he had any children. She also wondered if she'd even see him again after this. Her brother's words of warning echoed again in her mind.

"I'll just have a plain, black coffee," he said. The waitress left with a cheeky grin and a small curtsy.

Tom turned his attention to Roisin, taking her hand in his. She snatched it away.

"Sorry, Tom. I don't think I'm very good at this."

He took her hand again and raised it to his lips. "You seem uneasy today," he said. "I hope you're not regretting your decision to go out west, are you?"

"Not really. It's just that it's all so new. I have no idea if I've made a mistake coming here at all."

"Just follow your heart and you can't go wrong." His eyes showed genuine concern, and something told her he'd had his own share of sadness.

She gently pulled her hand back and smoothed her hair. The last thing she wanted was to be seen holding hands with a strange man by someone she knew. "You never did tell me what you do for a living, Tom."

He fiddled with the plastic menu holder, rubbing his fingers along its edge. "I used to be an architect but there's no money in it now. I suppose I could call myself a writer. I've written a few plays. They had reasonable success here in Dublin and I'm also working on a novel. It's hard going though. But I'm not complaining. At least I made a few wise investments in the past. How about you?"

She sighed as a flush of colour rose up her neck and into her cheeks. "I'm a Jill-of-all-trades. Started out as a children's nurse, but I couldn't deal with the really sad cases. Besides, there would be too much to catch up with now. In Spain, I turned my hand to many things, even selling olives, cheese and oils at a market stand." She told him about her freelance teaching classes and all the interesting people she had met. "Anyway, I suppose if all else fails, I can work in a call center. My French isn't too bad, but I speak fluent Spanish and understand a bit of Italian." She sighed. "One thing I do know, I'll have to get a job soon."

"If you're not too fussy, something will turn up."

She smiled. Finally someone was optimistic about her plans. That was encouraging.

"So, what time are you heading out tomorrow?"

"Around lunchtime. That'll give me time to explore the countryside near Lissadore before it gets dark. I'm really excited, a little scared too though. I'm not used to being alone."

"I hope you don't think I'm prying, Roisin, but do you have children?"

She hadn't expected that, but for some reason she didn't mind telling him. "I met my husband when I was twenty and have been with him ever since, until very recently, that is. Sadly, we never did have children."

He sat back and stretched his long legs. "Tell me about your husband."

She took a sip of her cappuccino and stared into the frothy cream before lifting her face toward him. "He's a good man, but somewhere along the way life became too heavy. We didn't have much in common any more. I knew I could either accept my lot or make a move. He wasn't willing to take a risk. But I suspect that was more out of pride and stubbornness than anything else. It was the hardest decision I've ever made."

"No time for regrets, eh? I never married; I was too busy playing around. I'm sure a psychologist would say I didn't want to end up stuck like my own parents." He leaned forward and a look of sadness filled his eyes. "I saw my father slowly losing his sense of fun as responsibility took over. And my mother always seemed to be worn out by it all. I swore I would not let it happen to me. Sometimes I wonder if I made a big mistake."

"Are your parents alive still?" Roisin asked him.

"No, both of them died within a year of each other. Seems they couldn't live without each other after all."

She squeezed his hand gently. "Tell me about your novel?"

A frown formed on his brow. "Are you sure

you want to know?"

She nodded.

He rubbed his chin, as if wondering where to start. "Ok, wait for it. It's about the effects of global warming. The main character is an Irishman,"— He grinned when he said this—"One of the few who survived the great floods that swept through most of Europe at the beginning of the twenty-first century. It's set around 2050, not too far in the future because my imagination doesn't stretch that far." He laughed.

"Science fiction, Fantasy? An Irish Waterworld?"

He shifted in his seat. "Not really, it's more pseudo-science and a lot of imagination. It's basically about the human struggle, the cycles of nature and our helplessness against its force." A small frown formed between his eyebrows. "Everybody knows the ice caps are melting. We've had abnormal flooding in most European countries, not to mention the U.S., India and Bangladesh, Kuwait etc. alone in the past year. Look at what's happening now in Pakistan? Devastating forest fires in Australia and the U.S., drought in Africa and Mediterranean countries. The evidence is overwhelming that we're in the middle of a massive change. Maybe my book will help to wake people up…although I doubt it." He sighed. "People are more interested in the latest celebrity gossip than environmental factors."

"Maybe they feel helpless, and that's why they bury their heads in the sand. It's far too depressing otherwise. Besides," she added, "There are so many things to worry about. We can all do our little bit silently."

"Maybe you're right. But I can't help letting it get to me." He stretched out again in the chair, looking more relaxed. "Sorry about the rant, but this is something close to my heart." He waved to someone passing by. "Now tell me more about yourself."

"Where should I start? You already know about my work, that I was married to the same man for most of my adult life; I have no children, and I want to live by the sea on the west coast of Ireland."

"How come you ended up in Spain?"

"My husband is Spanish." She shifted in her seat and grinned at him. "This is like twenty questions, Tom."

His eyes sparkled with humour. "Well, you can't blame me for showing interest, can you? What does he do? Does he share your creative spirit?"

She thought about this for a few moments while she took a sip of her drink. When she looked up, she almost lost her concentration at the way he was watching her; his look was so intense, but kind too. "He's creative in his own way. At least he used to be. We used to design and make our own kites. He designed them and I painted them. He's also a very talented photographer." She sighed. "I don't know…for the last few years he stopped doing all that and became obsessed with news. Bad news, of course, about the state of the world, the failing economy, injustice. It became unbearable listening to his rants. He used to be a computer consultant, but jumped on the building and investment bandwagon. Big mistake. You know the score."

"Sorry. It must be a man thing."

"We all need to let out our frustration every now and again. It's just that when it becomes the sole topic of conversation…you know what I mean?"

An awkward silence set in. The setting was different, but she felt as if she was reliving an old moment with her husband. Everything Tom said was true, of course, but she'd felt that way with Javier too. He'd always managed to sway her as she'd listened to his arguments, but she didn't want to be constantly confronted with the harsh realities of life, not now anyway. She sighed and did what she'd always done in such moments: she switched subjects and chatted about the town and all the changes that had been made. Unlike Javier, Tom seemed to have no problem letting go of an issue.

"You should definitely take the scenic route and stop off in The Bard's Den, a great little cosy pub in Dune. It's off the main Galway road so it should be on your route if you're heading west."

She scribbled it down in the notebook she always kept in her bag. Then she checked her mobile. "Oh, look at the time. I'm supposed to meet Carmel in ten minutes."

He looked disappointed. "Where are you meeting her? I can take you there."

He gestured for the waitress.

"No, don't be silly. It's only up the road." She reached for her purse. "This is definitely on me. It's only coffee, for goodness sake." She paid and they both got up to leave. What if she never met him again? As if reading her mind, he handed her his card.

"Please call me as soon as you've found a place. Maybe I can come and visit you—it's only a few hours' drive and I'm often out that way. Promise me, and if you need anything, I'll be more than happy to help if I can."

"Thanks, Tom. I don't know what I did to deserve your kindness." She was beginning to think her brother must have been mistaken. Either that or she was not a good judge of human nature.

They walked in silence toward the market square together and her mood began to dip as she thought of Javier again. She remembered when they had first met and how in love they had been and the hopes they had had for a long future together. They used to make plans, imagining the kind of house they'd build, how many children they'd have and it used to be so easy to imagine it all with him. Never did she contemplate them drifting apart as they had done these past years.

Soon they were standing in front of the smart hotel. It was lit up behind a sprinkling fountain. She hesitated, unsure of how to make this break. Tom leaned in towards her and kissed her again; it was as warm and sensual as that of the previous night. He held her in his arms, and she didn't pull away this time. "I'll be waiting for your call. Doesn't matter if it's tomorrow, next week or next year," he said.

She whispered, "Thank you, Tom…for everything. I'll call you once I've settled in."

Before she entered, she turned once more to wave him goodbye. His silhouette was illuminated by the fountain lights, casting a shimmer over his wavy hair. An emptiness overcame her as she realised how alone she was. Was Tom playing with her feelings? He seemed so sincere, but she couldn't believe that he, a man with his charm and personality, was not involved with somebody else. Was he just interested in her because she was new in town? She pulled herself together. *Don't be silly, Roisin Delaney. This was not in the plan. So much for plans!* She pushed back her shoulders and entered the warm hotel lobby.

A few comfortable armchairs were placed invitingly near the lit fireplace. The soft lighting cocooned the space into a cosy oasis. In the restaurant, which was off to the right, she saw a few couples dining in candlelight in the elegant surrounds. The natural tones were continued in contemporary style with dark wooden tables and indirect lighting. An entertainer crooned out soft music on the piano and it wafted out through the lobby. She recognised an old classic by Nat King Cole as she sank into an armchair. Her friend bustled in a few minutes later.

Carmel's cheeks were flushed from the cool evening air and her jaunt up the street. "You beat me to it. Sorry about that but I was held up at the shop. I can't wait for a drink. What are you having?"

"I'm trying to decide. What about you?"

"Gin and Tonic, that's my drink. Go on, I'll order you one too." Carmel got up. "Why don't we go into the bar?" It was almost empty at this time of the evening and they chose a little table overlooking the fountain on the market square.

They gave the barman their orders.

"So, what's new with you Roisin? You sounded so mysterious back in the shop."

"Well, I suppose I'd better tell you. This time, I'm here for more than a holiday. I'm driving out west and looking for a job and a place to live."

Carmel's mouth fell open. She held her hand to her chest in a dramatic gesture and exhaled a puff of air.

"It's fine, really," Roisin said, as she tried to halt the tears forming in her eyes. "Well, it's not fine." She wiped her eyes and attempted to smile. "It's strange to feel so alone after all these years, but I had no choice really."

Carmel reached over to console her friend. "You never said anything. Why didn't you call me?"

"I suppose I never thought I'd do it. I've been playing with the idea for a while now but I wasn't sure of my own feelings, for Javier…for Spain…for anything anymore." She sighed. "It never seemed appropriate to go into details of my life." She took a sip of her drink. The cool liquid felt good as it reached her throat. "I've made this decision and I'm going to follow through with it, for better or for worse." Even to herself, her words rang hollow.

"But why not stay around here where you know people? Look, I'm sure I could get you a job in the bookshop, at least part time. If not, I could ask some of the golf crowd. It's all about connections, Roisin, especially around here."

"Yes, and that's exactly why I want to move away. You know I've never been one for gossip and I know how people are. There'll be all sorts of speculation and prying. Maybe, God forbid, some of the old crowd might feel sorry for me, as if I've failed."

"You know you'll be a one-week wonder, Roisin, and then people will forget. They have their own problems to worry about. That's the way of the world. Think about it, will you?"

"Alright, I'll tell you what. If, for some reason, I end up destitute out there in the west, I'll send you an S.O.S. I just want to prove something to myself this time." She shifted in her chair. "Anyway, enough about me. What have you been up to?"

"Same old, same old. Nothing much ever happens around here. Work and family, the usual domestic routine. Did you hear poor ole Davy Johnson had a heart attack? They buried him last month."

"What? You can't be serious. He was only a few years older than us. I'm truly shocked. I haven't seen him for over two decades."

"Well, he was a heavy drinker and smoker. He played hard and, in a way he backed out gracefully. Sad for his wife and young children though. Davy is probably up floating in the clouds with a pint in his hand."

Roisin smiled at the image. "I didn't even know he got married." Davy used to hang around with her brother. It seemed like a lifetime ago. She remembered him as a fun-loving fellow who never seemed to take life too seriously, but she had never had a serious conversation with him. Still, she felt sad to hear he was no longer with them.

"Yes, he married a girl from Corley. She had her work cut out with him. Rumour has it that he drank most of his earnings. The kids are gorgeous though. They have his dark curls and green eyes. I saw them at the funeral."

They continued catching up on old news and Carmel filled her in on all the goings-on in town.

Something warned her not to mention Tom. Although she would have loved to share her feelings with someone, the last thing she wanted was Tom to hear it back. Their new-found friendship was far too fragile for that.

Later on in the evening her friend suggested they order something to eat. While Carmel went to freshen up, Roisin sat contemplating her upcoming trip. She felt as if part of her was missing; it had been Javier and her for so long. They were like a matching pair of socks or well-worn shoes. Had she made a big mistake? She had never done something like this before and now she wasn't sure if it was even a good idea. She wondered what Javier was doing, and she touched her face where he had hit her and remembered how desperate she had felt. No matter what, she had had no other choice. No point in looking back now. Part of her looked forward to the adventure, at least she had made a move.

They relished the meal as they continued recalling old school stories.

"Old Mr. Byrne is still alive and kicking, driving everyone mad." Carmel dipped her fork into a baked potato. "Do you remember the day he caught us playing hooky? Nobody before or after has ever been able to make me feel so small."

Roisin laughed heartily. "Seriously, he wasn't right in the head." She swallowed the wrong way and began coughing. Carmel handed her a glass of water. Roisin took a few sips and patted her chest. "That'll teach me," she said, "but imagine letting him loose on poor innocent kids? Do you know I used to have dreams—nay, nightmares about him for years after I left school?"

Carmel placed her cutlery neatly on the plate and dabbed her mouth with a serviette. "Well, he still hangs around town and acts like he's a martyr to his cause, whatever that might be. Whoever said schooldays are the best days of your life should be strapped up by their toenails.

"Speaking of toenails..." Roisin said. "I believe Martina opened a new nail store and is raking in a fortune. I never could understand the craze about false nails, but then again..." She examined her own nails. "Maybe I should try it out, at least once. My nails leave a lot to be desired."

Desire! Roisin's thoughts turned again to Tom and immediately felt bad again about Javier.

As if reading her mind, Carmel said: "You never did say much about your husband but I sometimes wondered why you almost always came over here on your own. Did he have some sort of terrible habit?"

Roisin laughed. "No, not at all. The opposite, in fact." She moved her plate away and looked at her friend. "He was always reliable but far too busy working. And then when he lost his job, it was devastating for him...for both of us, in fact. It was as if he gave up bothering. It's hard to explain. I have far too much spirit left in me. Do you know what I mean?"

Carmel nodded enthusiastically. "So, you decided to do a Thelma and Louise."

Roisin laughed. "No, nothing like that. Haven't done anything criminal." She sighed. "I feel so bad for Javier. He's probably still in shock. You see, he never thought I'd leave him. In fact, he sometimes provoked me, dared me to try, especially when he felt cornered. It got so that even I didn't believe I could make it on my own. I must admit I'm proud of myself. He accused me of being full of empty threats." She looked up at her friend who was sitting back in the chair with legs crossed as if she was head psychologist. Something about the image made her laugh. "So now you have it, Carmel. I'm merely a statistic. Something finally snapped and all that pent up tension dissipated, just like that."

"Don't you think that's normal? Most couples go through those phases. I hope you haven't over-reacted."

"Who's to know? I just know I had to take charge of my own life. For better or for worse. When you're married you're so inextricably linked to your partner, emotionally, financially, spiritually." She shifted in her seat. "Well, maybe not spiritually. The truth is that there was no more impetus in our relationship. It was dragging me down, and I could barely keep myself buoyant, let alone him. Talk about an anchor pulling me down."

Carmel shifted slightly in the chair and drained the dregs of her coffee. "I always thought yours was the true love story, full of romance and adventure. Maybe you just need to get this out of your system?"

"Yes, maybe I do. We'll see." She tried to stifle a yawn. "Sorry, I'm wrecked. I have an early start in the morning."

"Me too. You have my number, right? Give me a buzz and let me know how you're doing. I can't wait to find out. Oh, and listen. If all else fails, remember what I said about the bookshop. You'll never be stuck, you know that?"

Roisin placed her hand over her friends and gave it a gentle squeeze. "I know. I really do appreciate your offer, but I hope I won't have to take you up on it."

She hugged her friend and walked over to the taxi stand.

## Chapter 9

The receptionist at the car rental asked to see Roisin's international driver's license. Roisin handed it to her and the receptionist keyed in some details before reaching for one of the glossy brochures on the shelf. She flicked it open with her index finger and glided her purple lacquered fingernail over the price list, listing options as if she was auditioning for a role.

Roisin smiled at the woman, interrupting her. "Before you go any further... I've already made enquiries. Ten days for the price of seven, economy class car. That should make it €270, right?" She continued. "Is there a drop off point on the west coast in case I decide to stay there?"

"Yes, that should be no problem," the woman said, as she handed Roisin a business card. "We have drop-off points in Galway and Westport. Both of the addresses are listed here." She typed in the details and within a few minutes the contract slid out of the printer. "Just sign on the line here and you're ready to go."

Roisin perused the contract. Satisfied that all was in order, she signed it and handed over her card.

"Well, I think we've covered everything. Your car is out the back. One of our employees will go through the mechanics with you. Should you have any problems, call this number." The woman with the purple lacquered nails looked over her reading glasses like a school teacher and said. "That's it then. Good luck on your journey."

Roisin thanked her and went out the back to retrieve her rental car. It was a green, compact, economy car, a symbol for her new road to freedom.

She put her luggage into the boot, sat inside, turned on the ignition and took off smoothly out toward the dual carriageway. She had already said her goodbyes earlier that morning and now she truly felt free for the first time in years.

The sky looked promising, casting its warm, pinkish hue onto the surrounding countryside. Optimistic thoughts coupled with anticipation filled her mind. Would she find a job, a house? Would she regret her decision to leave Javier? A small shudder ran through her as she thought of those last days and how suddenly she had made her decision to leave her old life behind her. She could barely believe it herself. The car and the glimpse of sunshine seemed to be good luck omens. Within an hour she was whizzing along the road, singing along to Brian Ferry's quirky voice on an Oldie radio station as she passed by patchwork fields in different hues of green, edged by unruly hedges and rickety stone walls. Occasional splashes of buttercup yellow broke up the tidy quilt effect as bushes of gorse appeared at intervals. The shimmering light did a quick step through the fields, and peaceful clouds sailed across the landscape as if they had all the time in the world.

The roads weren't too busy at this time of the morning. Roisin twiddled with the radio looking for something to hold her attention and make the trip more enjoyable. She paused when she heard the voice of a famous Irish actor who had made a name for himself in Hollywood. He talked about the tragic death of his wife. His voice became hoarse as he tried to suppress his emotion. Roisin's eyes filled with tears. Nobody is spared, she thought. What if something happened to Javier? She would never forgive herself, although she knew it was stupid to think like that? *Stop those maudlin thought now!* She saluted her inner voice, the critical one, and switched back to listen to some contemporary pop songs.

Ahead, a sign pointed her to Galway. It was only 57 km away. She remembered Tom's recommendation to stop off at that pub and pulled over at the next possible stop and checked the map. She had no idea where this place Dune was. In fact, she'd never heard of it. According to the map, she should take a turn to the left in about ten miles. Sure enough, soon she saw a sign and turned off. She'd have her lunch in the Bard's Den and still have enough time to explore Lissadore before it got dark.

Dune was a small town tucked amongst hilly, unspoiled landscape. On the way, she'd passed a pilgrim's hill and a few small lakes which looked like dark shiny eyes peering out at her. Fishermen cast their rods on the water's edge and a few little boats bobbed on the calm waters.

The farther she drove, the less building development she encountered. It was easy to imagine life as it would have been before the dawn of electricity. Not that she'd wish to live in those times. Progress might have its downside but she was happy to be living in the era of modern conveniences and easy mobility.

The town probably housed no more a few thousand people. She drove right through the main street, following the signs for parking. It was almost lunchtime so most of the office workers would be filling the local pubs and cafes soon. The daytime pub culture was kept alive by shoppers popping in for a coffee and office workers eating out at lunchtime. Now there seemed to be a lull as the streets were almost empty. Colourful shop fronts and eating places lined the narrow streets. She stopped a young woman and asked her for directions to The Bard's Den.

"It's just up the road on the opposite side, beside The Bank of Ireland. You can't miss it."

The Bard's Den was as cosy as its name suggested. A golden Celtic sign adorned the glossy dark green door. Outside, a blackboard presented the daily specials. Lobster soup with home-made brown bread, colcannon and lamb chops, vegetarian lasagna and braised pork roast with green beans. The prices were reasonable too. She entered the snug and slightly dark interior and chose a window seat with a clear view onto the bar area and the street. The unmistakable smell of beer and the delicious smells of cooking permeated the place. Shiny brass beer taps and the framed excerpts and sketches of Beckett, Shaw, Joyce, Heaney and Yeats were lined along the richly embossed wall-papered interior. Her eyes fell on a quote by Oscar Wilde. *There are only two tragedies in life: one is not getting what one wants, the other is getting it. So true.* That fellow Wilde was a wise one—a man who had remarkable insight into human nature.

She decided on the lobster soup and home-made bread. If she ate it slowly, savouring every mouthful, it should be more than enough to keep her going for the day. Today was the first day of her new dietary regime and she was determined this time to follow it through. More exercise, less food. Maybe she'd take up jogging. Who was she kidding? She envisaged herself running through the Irish countryside, hair flying in the breeze—nay, make that breeze a strong wind and add rain and fog to the scene?

The waitress, a sullen-looking, plain girl whose hair was tied severely back in a ponytail, sauntered over to her table and took her order. The door opened behind her and she felt a blast of cool air hit her back. A young woman dressed in a business suit and carrying a smart, red briefcase bustled by her, sighing. Roisin watched her as she stood checking out the room. There was something dramatic about her movements. She wasn't a large woman but she took up a lot of space. She spun around and made a beeline for Roisin. "Would you mind if I sit at your table? I have to keep my eye on the main road and this is definitely the best spot."

"What could she say?" She smiled and nodded.

"Thanks so much. I'm Maggie Cassidy. Sorry to barge in on your space —All these free tables and where do I want to sit?" She placed her briefcase on the inside chair, almost knocking over the condiments in her flurry of activity.

Roisin extended her hand. "Nice to meet you. I'm Roisin." Even though she enjoyed meeting new people, especially interesting ones, she found the woman's behaviour a tad odd.

"What are you having?" The woman sported an almost jet-black bob. She definitely had a look of Cleopatra about her with her cream-coloured skin, dramatic eyes and scarlet lipstick.

Roisin smiled at her. "I'm having the lobster soup and brown bread."

"Okay, I'll have the same." The woman gestured to the barmaid who stared over at them as if they were from another planet.

"Another lobster soup, please," Roisin called out. The barmaid nodded and moved her ungainly body towards the kitchen.

"Someone should give her a dose of enthusiasm." Roisin's new companion snorted, and although it was rude, her laughter was contagious. She turned her attention to Roisin. "So, what brings you to these parts? You're not from around here, right?"

This woman had no idea about diplomacy or boundaries, for that matter, but Roisin liked her. "I'm just passing through—on my way out toward Lissadore."

"Lissadore. Are you kidding? That's where I'm from." She stood up in one brash movement, moved closer to the window and peered through the glass. Then she spun around and turned her attention on Roisin. "…Yeah. Where was I? Lissadore—it's great in summer but gets a bit dreary in the winter months. Then again, I'm not overly fond of winter." She bit on her nails as her eyes darted back and forth from Roisin to the street. "So, what are you going to do there?"

Roisin considered whether to evade the question. Should she tell this inquisitive woman to mind her own business? But Roisin could tell by the woman's expression that she didn't mean any harm. She seemed to be the type of person who had no filter between the things she thought and the words she uttered.

"I'm going to look for a job and rent a little house by the sea." Roisin rolled her eyes skyward as she realised how naïve she sounded.

The woman guffawed again. "Sorry. I don't mean to be rude, but have you any idea how much a little house by the sea costs? As for jobs, forget it. Haven't you heard—the country is in a recession? Look around here. We're the only two in the pub. Point proven." The woman took a sleek camera out of her bag and moved closer to the window again. She attempted to hide behind the heavy velvet curtain as she began to snap photos at a rapid rate. Roisin looked out to see what all the fuss was about. A nondescript bald fellow in a suit, who looked to be in his mid-fifties, strolled along the opposite pavement. He made an abrupt stop and stared directly over at them, or so it seemed.

"Stupid me," Maggie said. Forgot to turn off the flash. Oh drat! I think he's spotted me." She ducked under the table and whispered: "Don't look at him."

"It's too late for that, I'm afraid." Roisin broke eye contact with the man. *What kind of a weird film had she stepped into*? She took another peek out of the window but there was no sign of the man any more. "You can come out now. He's gone."

Maggie Cassidy gave her head a whack as she emerged from under the table. She rubbed her head and frowned. "Did you get a good look at him?"

"Yes, but would you mind telling me what's going on? Are you stalking that fellow, or is he stalking you?"

Maggie yanked her head around like a cuckoo on the alert for predators. "Where did he go? I've got to keep tabs on him."

"Well, you're not doing it very subtly." Roisin laughed, delighted now to be part of this strange woman's antics.

"It's no laughing matter, believe me."

The waitress arrived with their steaming soup, and plonked it in front of them, almost spilling some. There was a hint of a smile on her otherwise stony face. Either she had got some good news when she was in the kitchen or the message came through to lighten up.

Roisin had no idea what to make of Maggie Cassidy. Should she just play along? What if she was being filmed by one of those candid camera programs?

Maggie took a spoonful of soup as if nothing had happened. Her face held no trace of intrigue or drama.

"Seriously, what was that all about?" Roisin said as she sprinkled some pepper on her soup.

"Oh, forget it. Let's just say the less you know the better." The woman buttered a slice of thick brown bread and took a bite.

"How can I forget it? Who was that man?

Now that you've involved me in your little theatre piece, you can't just leave me hanging."

Maggie ignored her questions, leaving Roisin with no option but to drop it.

"What do you do for a living?" Maggie asked her. "Let me guess." She placed the tip of her index finger on her lips and locked her eyes onto Roisin's face. "You're a nurse? No, wait, you could be a singer in a band, or a book-keeper." She didn't even give Roisin time to react as she listed off myriad professions. "Am I getting hot?"

Roisin couldn't help but laugh again. "You're definitely warm. Mind you, you didn't leave anything out. What gave me away?"

"Just a feeling. So, are you going to tell me or what? Hold on a sec. I'm going to try it again. You like making things, right?"

Maggie pointed to Roisin's shoulder bag that was hanging on the side of the chair. "Perceptive," Roisin said. She had made the bag out of rich woven fabric depicting a series of Indian scenes. It was one of her favourites because she had made it to her individual specifications."

"And the necklace? Make it yourself too?"

Roisin fingered the beads. "Yes, I did. Every so often I have a figary and go on a creative binge."

"It's not that hard to read people if you know what to look for." Her tone changed to a more serious one. "I suppose I do owe you an explanation of sorts. I am certainly no Miss Marple. Let's just say I'm doing my civil duty. That's all I'm saying for now."

Both of them had finished their soup, but Roisin was intrigued enough to want to know more about this strange woman. She ordered a cup of tea and her companion followed suit.

"So why did you choose Lissadore?" Maggie touched up her lipstick and ran her fingers through her hair which had become tousled during her escapades under the table.

"Coming full circle, I suppose. I was ready for something new. New beginnings, you could say." Roisin locked her hands together and smiled at the woman. "I spent a few days in Lissadore many years ago. It was a glorious summer. I swam and camped and listened to live music in the local pub. And I've always wanted to recapture that time. "

Maggie seemed lost in thought. "Do you think that's possible? We're never the same people, are we?" She didn't wait for an answer. "Everything becomes stale after a while…if you're a certain type of person. Lissadore is no different." She perked up then. "Although summer is always full of surprises. The tourists definitely add a bit of spice to the soup. There's more night life and all sorts of activities, and when the sun shines, it is the best place on earth. What more would you want. Oh yeah, did I mention it's great for business? I do most of my business in the summer months."

"I'll be so busy in the beginning setting up my place and looking for a job that I won't have time to be bored. Besides, it's up to me to make the best of it."

"But you'll need Lady Luck on your side too." She pulled out a business card from her bag. "Call in and let me know how things work out. I'd love to know."

Roisin looked at the card and thanked her.

"I have a small design boutique where I make and sell accessories: jewellery, hats, scarves and bags. I mainly sell to tourists but I also sell a few items to the Kilkenny Design Studios, Avoca and one or two others. A couple of students from the Design College in Rathcooley help out in the shop, so I do alright..." She stopped in mid-sentence, but obviously thought better about saying whatever it was she had meant to say.

Roisin nodded and made the appropriate sounds of interest. She was tempted to ask if the woman happened to be looking for extra staff, especially now at the busiest time of the year, but she didn't want to be pushy.

Maggie continued. "I'm working a lot with felt at the moment, but I have to follow trends too, to a certain extent. I get my wool from a local sheep farmer and a local woman colours it. She uses vegetable dyes. I like experimenting with different materials, so I use silk and felt a lot. She reached in her bag and took out a red felt ring with a little silk orange rose in the centre. "This sort of thing."

Roisin smiled. "My only attempt at working with felt cured me forever." She remembered the time she and her friend sat for hours preparing felt for a friend's birthday present. It was messy and time-consuming. The scarf she had made could have been used as a door mat, it was that stiff.

"Give me a call when you get settled in. At least it's worth a try. By the way, try McElroy's Estate Agents. They're a good bunch. Tell them I sent you."

"Thank you so much. I'll definitely check in on you within the next couple of days."

She scribbled the Estate Agent's name on the back of the business card and put it in her purse. The pub was beginning to fill up. She was glad she'd missed the lunch-time crowd. When she passed by the window she saw Maggie chatting animatedly to a group of young women.

The woman, for all she knew, could be a total basket case, but she was a nice basket case. Roisin walked back to the car with a spring in her step.

# Chapter 10

Soon she was on the road again. The closer she got to her destination, the more excited she became. Having met Maggie, she felt even more positive about her new adventure. All traces of her old life were temporarily wiped away, as in one of those children's plastic drawing screens. You draw and delete, draw and delete – a new blank screen every time. Of course she knew nothing was truly deleted or forgotten, but this was her survival mode and she'd sworn to herself not to wallow in the sticky mud of past memories. The new page was, as yet, unwritten, but the few glyphs she'd scratched so far appeared so be forming a cohesive shape.

The diluted sun seemed to dance in the distance, like a beacon of hope. She could feel the sea pulling her closer, reverberating with a deep place within herself; a place that existed long before she was born in this land. That old familiar and much-loved smell of seaweed, cockles and salty air came in through the vents. She lowered the car window and took a deep breath. Part of her wanted to call Javier and show him, through her eyes, what he was missing. She wiped the slate clean again. She wanted to share her little thrill with someone. Maybe she'd underestimated what it meant to be secure in the comfort of one's clan. She'd have to learn to deal with this feeling of solitude, at least for the time being. Her thoughts darted to the future. She saw herself at her kitchen table in an unknown house, the window opened to catch the sunlight, and the sound of maritime birds squawking in the distance.

She spotted a scenic parking place up ahead and pulled up, turned off the ignition and stepped outside. She had to stand on her tippy toes and crane her neck to look over the protective sea wall that wrapped around part of the beach. It had taken a lot of battering, especially with the mighty storms that had hit both coast and inland these past years. She'd been keeping tabs on that sort of thing, reading the Times online too. Beyond the barrier, there was a magnificent view onto the Atlantic. At least the waters were calm and cheerful. Diamonds of light danced on the surface, disturbed only by gentle, undulating ripples. The scene mirrored the sense of peace she felt. She lifted her face up to the sky, allowing the sunlight to kiss her skin. All her life she'd been searching for something. Maybe she'd finally found it. It had taken her years to realise that happiness is made up of these rare moments and that it wasn't a constant thing but came at intervals, so you wouldn't lose hope.

She took out a notebook and pencil from her bag and captured the scene in quick strokes, shading in parts to add more depth—that hill over there, the curve of the shoreline and the jet-black rocks still wet with sea spray. She added the swooping gulls, the rippling waves and the dancing sun. Memory, she knew, could be a master deceiver, which is why she captured such scenes in writing or in sketches.

Tonight, she'd fill in the details of her past couple of days. Finally she'd be alone, with time to let it all seep in.

How many more miles? It couldn't be far. She continued driving, soaking up the country scenes, the pretty houses nestled in amongst hills or almost hidden by tall hedges. The sun played hide and seek behind the clouds, sometimes casting a shadow and throwing a dismal light onto the canvas, only to come out again within seconds, illuminating the entire scene. It was a moody land, a mystic place.

A sign directed her to Lissadore. She turned off onto the smaller road, which led to the town, and continued on until she found a parking spot at the end of the main street. Her memories of the town had indeed played tricks on her. It looked much smaller now, with the main street housing most of the pubs, shops and restaurants. The main road took a sharp turn and she knew if she kept on going, she'd be driving right into the ocean. She followed the sign for parking and drove up a narrow alleyway, barely wide enough for one car, let alone two. She drove around a couple of times. Somebody pulled out—another good omen. After having turned off the ignition, she pulled a ticket and strolled back out onto the street, taking in impressions as she went. She could hardly wait to take a walk along the beach, although the wind was picking up. It could get pretty wild along the west coast; a fact she had conveniently suppressed. She held onto her hat as a strong gust of wind blew up from the coast. No matter. She'd finally arrived and she wanted to celebrate the fact somehow. First things first though. She had to look for a place to stay. It was unusual, after all these years, to be at nobody's beck and call, no boss and no husband to answer to.

    She took out the card Maggie had given her. In tasteful cursive print, she read *Eye Catchers – the little things you can't do without.* 7 Barley Cove. The street was full of signs. Shop signs, parking signs, no parking signs, dinner specials, live pub music with an arrow pointing to the left, up another alleyway. She walked the length of the street, looking left and right until she saw the sign for Barley Cove, down near the pier. At least she could peek in the window. There was a buzz in the air and people seemed to be in a holiday mood. A happy-looking couple eating ice cream passed her. In an instant, a wave of sadness and loneliness overcame her as she thought of Javier. It could have been so different between them. She wished she could have turned back the clock. They were that couple once, laughing and sharing the same jokes. If only she could summon back those times. She sighed. Gazing into the past was a futile exercise. No fire can survive if it is not given fuel. Her chin began to tremble at the memories. She hadn't expected to miss him that much and wondered how he was getting along. Now, all those things she had found so annoying about him didn't seem to matter that much. The thought even entered her head that she might have provoked him into hitting her? No! That was silly talk. She missed him, but she knew if she had stayed where she was, everything would have become worse. The fact that he had lashed out was out of character. He had been desperate, but she had done everything in her power to help him and all to no avail.

The town buzzed with shoppers and local business people. She noticed several shops selling surfing gear—not surprising, because Lissadore was becoming a popular place for surfers. Many of them were younger folk, so they didn't frequent the local restaurants much. They tended to hang out at the youth hostel and ate most of their meals there. They were also oblivious to the latest fashion and designer labels. There were no major industries here either. Most of the local folk worked in hotels, guest houses or shops. Some of them commuted to the bigger cities. The town lived on tourists, so she expected it would soon begin to fill up when the weather improved.

As soon as she saw the shop, her mood picked up. It would be wonderful, she thought, but too good to be true, if she could work there. The shop front stood out from the others she had seen. Floating green-blue bubbles on a white background gave it a contemporary feel. It wasn't exactly what she had expected when she remembered how Maggie had described her wares. Roisin had expected something more traditional, but just looking at the contemporary shop front made her feel cheerful. She looked in the attractively-displayed window. Exquisite beaded bags, wrist-warmers, hats, scarves, jewellery, and a selection of knick-knacks were displayed—not too many, but enough to attract any woman with an eye for design. The items were pricey but definitely quality—individual works of art. She peered closer and saw hats and bags, scarves and jewellery on shelves and hanging from hooks on the wall.

She'd seen as much as she wanted to see and

decided not to go in just yet. That pleasure could wait for another day. She watched as a lanky young man, with an unusual haircut and skin-tight jeans, dusted the shelves with a long fluffy wand.

As she continued walking, she tried to imagine herself solidly planted in this town, close to the coast and as near to her dreams as she'd ever be. She observed the passers-by, all the while looking for signs of familiarity, wondering how real such signs would be, if she could ever feel a sense of belonging. She had no sense of self here yet; she was merely a spectator. And yet, she had thought this out; she'd taken the steps she needed to take, but she felt scattered and dissected like pieces of a shattered hologram, refusing to come together to form the whole. Parts were overseas; parts of her were somewhere in the past, or in the future. She could see vague reflections of these pieces from the corners of her eyes, as if they were teasing her.

Her inner and outer reserve slowly drifted away, as if someone had opened a valve, and she felt the familiar sense of detachment come over her once again.

*Banish your demons*, she chided herself. She was getting closer to the end of the street as it tapered off; joining with the old stone wall which formed a protection from the sea. The sound of the gentle flow of water from below drew her eyes to the wide expanse of beach which stretched for over a mile in the distance. Large grey rocks, like fat, immobile sea lions added structure to the scene. She put on her sunglasses and walked down toward the beach. At least the wind had died down.

A few lone walkers dressed in bright jackets strolled along the strand. Otherwise it was remarkably empty. There was no sign of surfers here, but she assumed they were a bit farther up. Maybe it was too early in the season. She took off at a brisk pace and breathed in the air, enjoying the novelty of finally being here. The sea air cleared her head and cooled her cheeks. She wrapped the wooly scarf closer to warm her neck.

On her way back, she sat atop one of the large boulders and thought of the time she had been there with Javier. They had spent a few days there camping before moving over to Spain. It had been such a romantic time; he had his new camera, the one he had saved so hard for from his student's job, and they had walked up and down this very beach every day, hand in hand, stopping for an ice cream or fish and chips on the way back to the campground. She closed her eyes and listened to the sound of the waves and the squawking of seagulls as she revisited those memories. She opened her eyes again to see the sun dipping into the low-lying hills.

# CHAPTER 11

Back in town, it was time to look for a place to stay. She wandered up and down the street, looking for a Bed and Breakfast to catch her attention. It shouldn't be a problem so early in the season, but she didn't want to take any risks. Nestled in between two family homes, she spotted a B&B sign with a floral motif on a tall, narrow house that was painted lilac. It looked so pretty and fresh. She walked inside the open door. The colour scheme had been repeated on the inside. She found herself humming *Purple Rain* silently as she waited to see how friendly the staff were. If they were nice she'd stay, if not she'd move on. A faint citrus scent floated through the air. To the left, pictures of wild flowers common to The Burren added to the room's calming atmosphere.

She heard footsteps coming down the stairs. A woman, carrying a jug of water, came bustling in. Her reddish blond hair framed her soft round face. She looked as if life had been kind to her, and when she smiled, her dark blue eyes lit up.

"Oh, hello. I didn't hear you come in. Can I help you?" Without taking her eyes off Roisin, the woman poured a little water into the ceramic dish of the aroma lamp causing a sizzling sound.

"Yes, I was wondering if you had a spare room for tonight, or possibly even two or three nights."

The woman flashed another smile at her. "Well, it's early in the season so we do happen to have a couple of spare rooms. Is it a single you're looking for?"

"Yes, that's right. Just for myself."

"Right. That's grand." The woman flipped open her laptop, which was on the reception desk, and checked through her bookings. She turned her attention to Roisin once again "I just want to make sure these rooms are free until Friday before I get your hopes up."

After a few minutes, the woman said. "I have two rooms I can show you now. If you'll follow me." She smiled and passed the friendly test. "Is it your first time in Lissadore?"

"No, but it's been a long time since I was here. It looks different from how I remembered hit. But that was a very hot summer and a long time ago."

"Everything looks nicer on a sunny day. At least we have rain," the woman said, "More than California or Australia. It's shocking isn't it? I just wish we could give some of ours to them."

Roisin followed her up the narrow stairway, careful not to miss a step. The wallpaper repeated the lilac and wild-flower theme. It was different from any other guest house she'd seen in Ireland, but then again, she'd been gone for a long time and many things had changed.

When they reached the landing, the woman turned around and extended her hand. "By the way, I'm Fidelma Purcel. Everybody calls me Fidi."

"Roisin Delaney, lovely to meet you."

The woman swung open the room to the right. Roisin knew immediately she was going to stay here, at least for one night. The room was clean and cosy. Small personal touches added to its attractiveness. The bed was decorated with fluffy pillows, and a cotton throw, in hues of stone and lavender. A bunch of daffodils filled a large glass vase on the low sideboard. An elegant side table with pen and note pad finished off the scene. She nodded in appreciation. "It's beautiful," she said.

Fidi opened the door to the small bathroom revealing an immaculate and modern bathtub, shower and hand basin. Roisin looked forward to a long soak in the tub.

"The nightly rate is fifty euro off-season. If you decide to stay for three nights, I'll give you a special offer of one-hundred and thirty. How does that sound?"

Roisin watched as a wispy cloud float by over the church steeple. She had a great view from the window onto the street. She turned her attention to Fidelma and smiled. "That's generous. Thank you."

The woman continued. "Breakfast is served between eight and ten a.m. We have a Scrabble evening tonight down in the communal lounge. Otherwise, you've got your own television and internet access in the room. If you feel like going out, there are a couple of good pubs on the main street."

Roisin leaned over to smell the daffodils. "Things have really changed a lot since the last time I stayed in a B&B"

"Not really. You'll find most places still pretty much the same. I have a little passion for interior design and always try to give people a warm welcome and offer them the type of place I'd like to stay in myself. Thanks for the compliment. I enjoy meeting new people from home and abroad, and I want them to have a memorable holiday. Happy people spread the word. I hope to see you tonight at Scrabble."

Roisin smiled. The idea was ludicrous. Somehow she couldn't see herself sitting down playing Scrabble with a bunch of strangers. "You can park your car out the back," the woman said. More good news. At least Roisin wouldn't have to leave the car unattended.

After parking her car and taking her bags up to the room, she flicked through the channels. Too wound up to concentrate, she decided to go downstairs after all and check out the Scrabble game.

Downstairs, she followed the sound of voices and found the group in a room off reception. Fidelma Purcel was sitting amongst the small group who were busying themselves choosing their letters. All heads looked up when Roisin entered. "I'm glad you decided to join us, Roisin," Fidelma said. "We're just about to start."

Roisin took her place at the table. Fidelma introduced her to the others. There was an American couple, an older man and woman he assumed were local, and a younger fellow who was introduced as Jimmy Tyrell. "This is my father, Paddy, and his partner Esther," Fidelma said, pointing to the older couple. "My father never misses a game of Scrabble and poor ole' Esther has no choice but to join him."

The older man smiled at Roisin and mumbled something. His partner, Esther, flushed, and pursed her lips. Fidelma continued, smiling over at the younger couple. "Joe and Rachel Liddy from Chicago. They checked in a few days ago."

Roisin smiled and gave a little wave.

"Jimmy here is always on the lookout for his dream partner. Isn't that right, Jimmy?" Jimmy winked at Roisin and quipped back, good naturedly.

"What'd you say, Fidelma? You're looking for a partner. Won't find one here." He lifted up a blank tile to Roisin, smiled, and buried his head once again in concentration. This could be an interesting evening, Roisin thought.

It didn't take her long to immerse herself in the game. The American couple proved to be fun company and not shy of expressing their opinions, in contrast to Fidi's father who had a habit of swallowing his words before they had a chance to escape the confines of his mouth. She hardly understood a word he said, but he managed to cause his partner to blush several times. Fidi's eyes betrayed her calm exterior. She was like a child on alert to her alcoholic father's antics, ever watchful and ready to react. Yet she managed to pull off an air of hospitality and relaxation. The older man was definitely no fool. He managed to surprise them all by using all his letters and winning the seven-letter bonus points, which put him clearly in the lead. Jimmy Tyrell was too busy trying to be witty to put much effort into the game. Roisin played a decent game, and Fidi looked delighted that everybody appeared to be having fun. Half way through, she said, "Okay, break time. I'm sure you're all thirsty." She turned to Roisin. "We don't touch alcohol during our Scrabble evenings. It ruins the concentration. I'll just pop out and make the beverages."

Jimmy Tyrell loved to talk, especially about himself. He had moved there from Dublin about a year ago and had opened an organic shop on the main street. She gathered, from some of the teasing which had been going on earlier, that he was passionate about his mission to convert the locals to organic fare. Not only that, but she found out he was an up-and-coming figure in the local Green Party chapter. It was all well and good, but she had the distinct feeling that these people were not interested in hearing about his overpriced soya milk products or his super anti-oxidants. At one point, Fidelma's father made a quip about people selling seaweed products. "Money is all that talks these days," he said. Esther nudged him, but he continued. "Live by the seasons. Eat eggs, butter, the odd bit of meat, fresh vegetables. Have a laugh, a smoke and the odd drink. Didn't do me any harm."

"We're on the same page there, Paddy, with a few exceptions," Jimmy said.

Roisin was a great believer in doing good deeds but not going on and on about it. She was a great believer in going back to natural farming and buying home-made, pesticide-free products, but she knew that most families on average incomes couldn't afford to buy in a shop like Jimmy's.

Fidi, ever watchful, called her over. She left Jimmy extolling the virtues of one of the local cheeses to the two Americans who listened with open, enthusiastic eyes as they promised to pop into his shop before they left.

"Is Jimmy talking your ears off," Fidi asked? Roisin laughed. "Well, he's certainly a man on a mission." She poured herself a cup of tea. "Still, he's quite convincing. I might try one of those nutty baguettes he was talking about. I'm thinking of driving around tomorrow to look for a place to live."

"Ah, so you're planning on moving here? I didn't want to be indiscreet but I did wonder if you were on holidays. You mentioned earlier that you've lived abroad for years. So, what's it like to be back in good old Ireland?"

"Strange in a way. I'm acclimatising, but I love the banter, the friendliness and the countryside. I know the real test will come when I settle into a routine. So far everything is working out better than I'd expected. I just need to find a job and then a place to live."

Fidelma nodded. "What kind of a job are you looking for?"

"I'm open really. Anything that pays the rent, but I'll need a job before I can commit to renting. Catch 22." Roisin flashed her a smile. "If you hear of anything, do let me know. I speak Spanish and enough French to get by."

"Maybe you could try the hotels or even some of the shops. Check out the notice board down at O'Reilly's supermarket. They often have jobs advertised, and on Wednesday you can try the local paper." The woman smiled apologetically. "I wish I could help, but I have Esther. She's a great asset, I can tell you." She laughed. "I don't know how she puts up with me da. He's grand really, but old school, if you know what I mean, and likes to keep women in their place."

"I'm sure I'll find something," Roisin said. "If I can't find anything here, I'll just have to look in Galway and commute, I suppose." Yesterday I met a lovely woman called Maggie who has a little boutique here. I'm going to pop in and see her later.

Fidelma raided her eyebrows. "I just had an idea. If you don't mind putting the cart before the horse, I might have a house for rent. A friend of mine has a little house about a mile out of town overlooking the ocean. It's been empty since last autumn. Would you like me to arrange a viewing? It's not fancy, mind you, but it certainly has charm."

Roisin's eyes lit up. "That sounds just like what I'm looking for. I really don't want to live in an estate, or a bedsit."

"I think she's more interested in finding the right kind of tenant, someone who will take care of her beloved house."

"Why is she renting is out if she loves it that much?"

Fidelma grinned. "She met a Canadian and moved to Vancouver. She doesn't want to sell it yet, better to leave one's options open."

"Wise woman," Roisin said.

"What about that woman you met yesterday, the one with the shop? What's her name again? I must know her if she has a shop here. This place isn't exactly huge."

"Maggie Cassidy is her name. Her shop is called *Eye catcher*."

"Ah, Maggie Cassidy. Yes, I know her—not very well, mind you. Maggie moves in different circles." Roisin noticed a subtle change in Fidelma's expression, so subtle that she almost missed it. Discretion and a sense of loyalty to Maggie prevented her from probing further.

Although it was obvious that Fidelma had something to say about Maggie, she was too much of a lady to spread idle gossip. Roisin admired that. She cleared away the cups and saucers. "Suppose we'd better be getting back to our game or we'll be up all night," Fidelma said.

# CHAPTER 12

The gentle morning sun shone in through the slats in the blinds, tempting her from her deep slumber. She pulled the duvet up over her shoulders, enjoying the last remnants of sleep and listening to the birds chirping their enthusiastic nesting songs. Encouraged by their song, she lay there planning the day ahead. Perhaps she could view that house Fidi told her about. Her thoughts wandered to the people she'd met the night before. Fidelma's words about Maggie moving in different circles echoed in her mind. There was something strange about the way she had emphasised it. Apart from that, she was curious to know why Maggie had acted so strangely in The Bard's Den—all that business about snapping photos and hiding was most peculiar.

The dining room was empty when she entered, but she could still smell the remnants of bacon, eggs and coffee and hear the comforting sound of dishes being clattered around in the next room. No sign of Fidelma though, but Esther came in with some toast.

The previous evening she'd thought of Esther as the kind of woman you would have passed on the street without noticing. There was nothing remarkable or catching about her, no shine in her eyes, and no spring in her step. It was as if she wanted to be invisible. Her figure was prim and tight, or at least what one could see of it. She was a permed, twin-set type of woman, the type who wore fitted tweed skirts and had her hair done once a week. Her mousy grey hair was fine, the thin strands held together by hairspray. Watery, delicate grey eyes which avoided direct contact made one feel as if she'd withdrawn into herself and was just biding time.

She was like a different woman this morning, full of smiles and chatter. "Help yourself to the breakfast buffet, Roisin. If you need anything else, just give me a shout." Again, her face coloured bright red, from her throat all the way to her hairline, and she waved her hand like a fan. "These hot flushes. I'm sure it escaped nobody last night." She took a miniature plastic fan out of her cardigan pocket and flicked a switch. "That's better," she said as a cool breeze circulated in the space between them.

"Have you tried sage?" It's supposed to be good for that sort of thing," Roisin said.

Esther turned off her little fan. "Sage? The only time I use sage is at Christmas to stuff the turkey. If you say it helps, I'll certainly give it a try." She leaned in toward Roisin.

"I've been feeling so irritable and down in the dumps lately. These hot flashes are embarrassing enough but the mood swings make me want to stay in bed all day. I'll do anything at this stage. How do I prepare it?"

"Break off a few leaves, a tablespoon per cup, pour boiling water over them and leave steeping for about five minutes until the essential oils are released. Then strain, you can add honey as a sweetener."

"That sounds easy enough. How often do I

need to drink it?"

"I wouldn't drink more than about two cups a day. It has valuable minerals so you'll feel like a new woman soon enough. Don't expect miracles immediately, though. Give it time."

"I'll definitely let you know if it works. Are you an herbalist or something?"

Roisin laughed. "Lord no. I wish I had pursued one thing in my life. It might have made things easier. Do let me know if it helps." Somehow she doubted whether the woman would bother preparing the tea though. She'd probably forget about it as soon as she left.

"Well, I'm going to make my tea as soon as I've finished here, but I'd better be getting on with it before the others come down." The woman continued with chores, humming to herself.

Roisin hastily ate her breakfast, anxious to set off exploring the surroundings. Although she could hear the rain splattering against the windowpane, she hoped it would clear up later on. *All seasons in one day.* Luckily, she had brought some sturdy boots and a waterproof coat so she put them in a small bag and stuffed in her camera and sketch pad. The only thing that began to weigh heavy on her heart was her financial situation. She had to find a job and a place to live as soon as possible. Were her skills even up-to-date? Nowadays everyone wanted people with computer knowledge. She imagined hotels had their own computer programs, and she had hardly any experience in the service industry, or anything for that matter. Most of her remaining money would be eaten up by the deposit, and the rest she'd need to survive for the first couple of months. She checked her mobile and saw that she'd missed some messages. One was from her sister, enquiring about her progress. She would call her later on. The other was from Tom. He texted: *Everything okay? Call when you have a minute*. She smiled to herself as she sent her reply: *Was in the Bard's Den. It was definitely worth the visit. Love being by the sea. Things going smoothly. Off to look for a house now.*

When she passed the reception, Esther gave her a note. "By the way, Fidelma just called and asked me to give you this address." She took the note and read: *Cowslip Cottage, Lissadore Road, Co. Clare*. "She said you can pick up the key at Delia Walsh's house. It's the next house down the road at the end of the boreen. Good luck to you. I hope the weather clears up."

"Me too. I'm going to drive around and take a few photos."

"Maybe it's not a bad thing for you to see it in the rain. It will give you a taste of what it's like in winter."

*Here we go again*. "I know. You're not the first one to remind me. Anyway, I'd better get going and make the most of the day."

She decided to check the shop first but wondered if Maggie Cassidy would be there. For some reason she felt uneasy about coming face to face with the woman who had behaved so strangely the previous day.

# Chapter 13

When she entered the shop, Maggie was propped up on a high stool behind the counter, stringing pearls under a magnifying glass. She looked up and brushed the hair from her face. "Ah, look who's here. I was thinking about you. Where did you stay last night?"

Roisin wiped her feet on the mat. "In The Burren House. Do you know it? I actually played Scrabble with the owner and some guests. Never thought I'd see the day. It's a beautiful house. I decided I'd start on the right foot. A room with a view and all that."

"I've never been there myself, but of course everybody knows everybody in this small place. I don't know Fidelma well but we bump into each other every now and then. I don't think I'm one of her favourite people though. If you stay here, take my advice." She pulled a string of beads through the wire and looked up, no trace of a smile this time. "Form your own opinions about people and guard your thoughts. People are not always what they seem. Gossip spreads like wildfire in provincial towns and villages." Her serious face changed again and she laughed.

"Believe me, Maggie. If there's one thing I've

learned it's exactly that. I was never one for hanging out with a clique. Besides, I've spent the past decade living in a small village. Basically, people are the same all over the world, I suppose."

"Let me show you around the shop— my baby, my pride and joy."

"I couldn't resist taking a peek yesterday," Roisin said. "When I arrived, I went looking for your shop. It's really lovely, but I didn't go in." She looked around and nodded. "I'm very impressed, did you make everything yourself?"

"No, are you kidding? I have one or two people who help me every now and then, but one has to keep coming up with new ideas in a shop like this. You wouldn't believe how quick people are to snatch an idea and copy it." She placed the beads in a little tray and walked over to the shelf. "See these scarves; they're made of the finest felt mixed with raw silk. I embroider the Celtic designs myself. All handmade and very popular with locals and tourists alike." She took Roisin around the shop, taking her time to describe the various accessories and clothing items.

"When do you get time to make them?"

"I make time. It's all about priorities, I suppose. And then I have one or two students come in to sell two days a week. That gives me time to create. Being self-employed is totally different than a nine-to-five. Sometimes I work nights or at the weekends. Come, I'll show you."

They went out back to the workspace. It was crammed with fabrics, sewing machines and all sorts of sewing accessories. A long wooden table took up most of the centre space. Shelves with plastic boxes lined the walls. They were labelled. Some of them were transparent, and she could see wires and all sorts of beading materials, sewing silks and other accessories. Paper patterns and cardboard templates were attached to magnetic boards with scribbled instructions beside them. There was a small window in the room looking out onto a garden space. Tall grasses drooped, heavy with pearls of water, and an old Cherry Blossom held onto its buds as long as it could, waiting for the right moment to show her pretty dress, once again. A rickety old wooden fence separated the garden from the neighbouring backyard. The view out onto the garden would certainly inspire creativity.

"I love the garden," Roisin said.

"A woman after my own heart. It was one of the decisive points in my renting here." She sighed. "The rents are very expensive though. I'd never make enough to live on if I relied purely on the sales in this shop. They fluctuate far too much. I present my creations at the annual trade fair." She was talking very fast, barely stopping to breathe.

"Do you enjoy doing the trade fair?"

"Oh yes, I love it, despite all the work. It's always been lucrative for me, and an invaluable networking opportunity. At the moment I have a large order for the Kilkenny Design Studios, and I sell a few items to other shops around the country." She sat down on one of the swivel stools and began turning it lightly with her feet. "Sorry for talking your head off."

"No, not at all."

Maggie stopped swivelling. "I know it's early,

but any luck yet with a job?"

Roisin swallowed and creased her forehead. "It doesn't look great, but it's early days yet. If all else fails I'll have to work in a call centre. They'll snatch me up with my language skills. Otherwise it'll be a shop or hotel. Something will turn up. It always does." She got up to leave. "I'd better get going if I want to make the most of the day and do a bit of exploring."

Maggie chewed on her lower lip. "I know—it's not the easiest of times, is it? Keep me in touch. You're welcome to come in for a visit any time."

*

The Deli was almost empty when she entered, but it was still early in the day. She expected lunchtime to be the busiest time. A bouquet of scents filled the interior, a mingling of fresh bread, herbs and other indefinable culinary delights. Jimmy was busy transferring olives into glass containers. "Morning, Jimmy." He swung around and grinned. "Ah, the Scrabble Queen. The game was great last night, wasn't it? Here, try these olives." He pricked a toothpick into a shiny, black fruit and handed it to her. She savoured the nutty flavor. He handed her a cracker with cream cheese. "Easy Jimmy, I've just had breakfast." She popped the cracker into her mouth and let it slowly crumble, releasing the flavours of the cheese.

"Hmm…delicious."

In the meantime, he prepared a wholegrain roll with sun-dried tomatoes, mozzarella, black olive slices and basil for her to take on her trip. If only he'd drop the sales pitch he'd be a lot easier to take. He was like a walking, talking advertisement—for goat's cheese, tofu, for a better world, a world without cars or food additives. There was something endearing about his optimism though. She liked his open, round face, his narrow, twinkling eyes and his exuberance.

The rain had indeed cleared up a bit but she could tell by the sky, the heaviness in the air and the fat low-lying grey clouds that there was more to come. Her enthusiasm to see the house overrode her reluctance to get drenched. She threw on her raincoat and rushed to the car. Within a few minutes she was there. It probably wouldn't take more than fifteen minutes to cycle from town and that was good news, seeing as that would most probably be her mode of transport in future.

She drove up the long, winding driveway and got out of the car. As soon as she saw the house, a feeling of disappointment overcame her. It looked forlorn with overgrown trees crowding in an unkempt garden and a garden gate hanging on its hinges. Part of her wanted to turn around and go back, but she wouldn't write it off yet. What could she expect with her limited means? So far everything had worked out better than she could have ever imagined. So what if the house wasn't perfect.

The paint was flaking off the old cottage door and the wooden window frames weren't much better. She peered through one of the windows, brushing away the cobwebs with the elbow of her jacket, but couldn't see much. No wonder the place had been on the market for so long. She turned around and stopped for a few minutes to take in the spectacular view.

There were misty hills off to the right, a lane enclosed by hedgerows at the bottom of the garden, and she could smell the sea and hear the gulls in the distance. A protective leafy chestnut and a large oak tree stood sentinel on either side of the house. Should she decide to take it, she would have the best of both worlds, privacy in this gorgeous landscape and closeness to town. At least there was still plenty of light entering the house, but it would get cold in winter. Even now there was a stiff breeze coming in from the Atlantic. The view onto the rolling fields to the sides and the back added a sense of space. On either side of the wooden door, plastic plant hangers held dried out scraggy weeds. She was surprised no one had tried to make it more attractive for potential tenants.

    She jaunted down to the road, turned left and along the boreen to the neighbour's cottage to get the keys. The neighbour's house was of a similar style, but in much better shape than the one she had looked at. It was a traditional cottage dwelling typical to this area and in stark contrast to some of the newer sprawling houses she had driven past on the way here. They were all glass and double garages, generous balconies and meticulous landscaped gardens, probably built during the economic boom of the nineties. She didn't envy the owners' huge mortgages though.

    She rang the bell and waited. The slightest movement of the lace curtain drew her attention to one of the front windows, and she saw a little bespectacled face looking back at her. The curtain fell back and soon she heard footsteps approaching the door and the noisy release of the safety latch and a couple of turns of a key. The door opened a slit. A tiny woman, who looked as if she was about eighty, peered out at Roisin. She had hair the colour of Connemara stone. It was pulled back tightly and tied into a bun. Her limpid blue eyes shone from a finely-structured face with delicate skin, like paper. Light thread veins shone through the skin on her cheeks, giving her a slightly flushed appearance. She wore a long-sleeved blue floral dress buttoned to the neck. "Hello, dear. You must be Roisin. Come on in. Mrs. Purcel told me you were coming."

The old woman's hand felt cool to the touch. Her voice shook slightly, as did her hand. Roisin noticed Mrs. Walsh looking past her out onto the driveway as if on alert for somebody. She barely had enough space to squeeze through to the hallway before Mrs. Walsh closed the door behind her.

The old woman led the way for her to follow through to the narrow hallway. The smell of baking hung in the air. She noticed the floral theme continued onto the walls which were covered in a faded pink and cream wallpaper. A framed picture of The Sacred Heart with its eternal lamp burning underneath brought memories flooding back, of everything oppressive about her own childhood, school, nuns, processions and weekly mass. Roisin's grandmother used to have one of those lamps too, as did many Irish households. The woman beckoned for her to follow through into the living room.

"Would you like a cup of tea, dear? I'm sure you're parched?" It struck Roisin as funny. She had forgotten about some of the quaint sayings. With all that rain, it certainly wasn't the Sahara, but she thanked Mrs. Walsh and waited in the living room while the woman went to make the tea. More floral wallpaper. She suspected she'd be served tea in floral china cups too. The hypnotic sound of a brass ticking clock on the old dresser lulled her into a dreamy state. It was like stepping back in time, and although everything was fresh and clean, it probably hadn't been redecorated for many years. A blazing fire crackled in the hearth, adding to the cosy atmosphere. Roisin's gaze moved onto the mantelpiece where a set of family photos in silver frames were lined up like trophies, displaying what she assumed were various family members. A basket with wool and knitting needles sat beside an armchair, and a television set was tucked over in the corner.

Roisin went over to the side window to look out onto more fields divided by rows of neatly stacked, low stone walls. She wondered if she would be able to see *her* house from there, and she craned her neck. Yes, there it was, not obvious but with a bit of effort she could see it. It was comforting to know there was at least one house nearby. Not that it was likely the old woman could be much help if there was a burglary, but better than feeling completely alone.

Mrs. Walsh came in rattling a tray with tea and fruit cake, and Roisin got up to help her. A small smile formed on Roisin's lips when she saw the delicate porcelain floral cups. "You really didn't have to do that. I seem to spend my time drinking or eating since I arrived."

"It's no trouble at all, dear," Mrs. Walsh said, as she settled herself into the armchair and took a sip of tea. "Sure, isn't it part of being in Ireland? Mrs.

Purcel said you lived abroad for several years."

"Yes, but it's great to be back. A lovely time of year, too."

"I'm sure you'll love it. Betty was very happy living here. I do miss her a lot. She was like a daughter to me. Do you enjoy gardening? Betty's garden used to be her pride and joy." The old woman sighed. "Don't be put off by the state of it now. It looks worse than it is."

Roisin wondered if Mrs. Walsh would be keeping tabs on her, making sure she cleaned her windows, watching her comings and goings, that sort of thing.

"If it works out with the house, I'll definitely do my best," Roisin said. "I enjoy pottering in the garden, but I'm no expert. Have you always lived here, Mrs. Walsh?"

"Yes, all me life. Can you believe I've never been outside the country? The farthest I've been is Cork, but that's going way back." She began pouring out the tea. "Mind you, I do like to do a bit of armchair travelling." She pointed to the television in the corner. "I was too busy really, and there was never enough extra money for travelling. Of course, nowadays things are much easier than they were back when I was a young mother." She handed Roisin a plate. "Help yourself to the cake, dear. When Mrs. Purcell told me you were coming, I wanted to have something to offer you. I like a bit of fruit cake myself." She placed her cup of tea on a side table and sat back in her chair as nimbly as a much younger woman. "Sure, there were no modern conveniences like they have nowadays." She giggled like a schoolgirl. "Never mind me, I'm sure you don't want to hear me rambling on about the past."

Roisin rested her teaspoon on the saucer. "No, please. I love hearing about what life used to be like. Do your children live around here?"

Mrs. Walsh told her that the only relative now living nearby was her grandson. She evaded the issue of the other family members so Roisin left it alone.

The phone rang several times, and she noticed the old woman's eyes darting back and forth as she shifted in her chair. Each time, it rang off before she had a chance to answer. The old woman's eyes had taken on that hunted look again but she quickly pulled herself together. Roisin wondered what on earth could be the matter. She found it hard to imagine why the old woman should be afraid. As if in answer to her unspoken question, Mrs. Walsh said, "I don't bother answering it most of the time. Someone keeps ringing the wrong number, or else it's those telemarketers. I saw a program on the television the other day warning us about them. There's so many cheats out there and it pays to be on your guard."

They continued making small talk for a while, but Roisin was anxious to look inside the house and explore the area as long as it was still dry. Mrs. Walsh, alert to Roisin's body language, smoothed out her dress. "Well, I'm sure you'll want to be taking a look at the house." She stood up and went out to the hall. Roisin heard the dangling of keys. When Mrs. Walsh returned, she thanked her for the delicious cake and tea and assured her she's be back in no time.

"Take all the time in the world," the old woman said. "It'll be nice to have someone nearby again."

# Chapter 14

Finally, she had the treasured keys in her hand. She stood in front of the panelled wooden door. There was a little garden gate off to the right of the house, almost hidden from sight. She peered over the gate. The garden was a mess, but she could see that a week or two of weeding and pruning should get it back into reasonable shape. A variety of laurel, hawthorn, box and forsythia hedged in the space. She opened the gate, lifting it slightly to stop it scraping off the ground and walked in through. Slabs of concrete formed a curved path through the garden. The path was lined with overgrown lavender, thyme, sage and rosemary. Some smaller trees provided shade without crowding the garden. A stone-sculpture added an interesting focal point to the lawn, and over to the back there was a wooden bench underneath an apple tree. She imagined herself pottering there, snipping herbs, or reading under the apple tree on a fine day.

She left the garden and walked around the house where an extension had been added on. The structure looked solid, and the view from the back window would be peaceful. She walked back towards the front and turned the key in the lock as she held her breath in excitement.

The first thing she noticed was the chilly air. That was probably normal since the house had been empty for several months. The hallway was spacious, nice and bright with light biscuit-coloured walls. The wooden floorboards appeared, at first glance, to be in good condition. At the other end of the hallway there was an open door leading onto the kitchen. She walked on down and stepped into the roomy kitchen. The first thing she saw was the old enameled Aga stove which took centre stage. A smile played on her lips. Couldn't beat an Aga. The old floor tiles, chipped in part, added to the atmosphere of the room. Mentally, she saw herself taking down those ugly net curtains and giving the place a good coat of paint to get rid of the awful oppressive orange. There was a stack of wood neatly packed in a basket beside the fireplace, waiting to be ignited. She wondered who had put it there. Hardly Mrs. Walsh.

Built-in kitchen units complemented the country-cottage look. They had seen better days though. She opened doors and drawers to make sure everything was in good condition. Some of the doors barely hung on their hinges, but that could easily be fixed. Otherwise, they looked okay. A large solid pine dining table and chairs stood off to one side of the room. She sat down at the table, facing the back garden, and imagined herself having breakfast there. The view from the patio windows onto the back garden was stunning, just as she had imagined. Beyond the back garden in the distance, she could see the hazy lilac sky offering a promise of sunshine later. The monochrome tones added to the sense of space and silence. She felt her shoulders relax and closed her eyes, tipping her head back and releasing a sigh of contentment. Her decision was made.

If her sense of orientation was intact, she'd be able to walk out to the shore from the back garden. It shouldn't take longer than twenty minutes. Finally, her dream was coming true. She'd be within walking distance to the sea.

The living room was a bit dim, but it had potential. If she could rip out that old red carpet and give the room a splash of fresh paint, clean the windows and add some personal touches, it would be great. Apart from a worn out armchair and couch, there was no other furniture in the room. That would be a blessing, because she wanted to keep it as uncluttered as possible. For the time being, she could buy a couple of pretty throws and drape them over the furniture.

She opened the door out onto the hallway again and found a small lavatory and a utility room. The toilet and washbasin were fine, apart from a hairline crack in the sink. She turned on the tap and let the water run for a few seconds and flushed the toilet. Everything worked. No dripping sink, no rusty water. Again, the window needed cleaning. In fact the whole place could do with a good cleaning, but it wouldn't take long to have it sparkling.

There was a small window at the top of the landing, a bit too small for her taste but at least it shed some light on the space. Two good-sized bedrooms, one ensuite, on one side of the hallway and a smaller guest room on the opposite side. When the saw the bathroom, any reservations she might have had were definitely quashed. Not only was it bright and spacious, a nostalgic bathtub with brass fittings and clawed feet stood in the centre of the room. There was a skylight built in so she could lie there and look at the stars, or if she wished she could look out onto the landscape through the well-positioned large window. The former owner must have shared Roisin's love of a long soak in the bathtub. Perhaps she had been working her way through the house with the intention of doing a complete renovation. Roisin chuckled as she realised what song she was humming. It was *Love Came to Town*. She had been thinking of what Fidelma had told her about the owner being swept off her feet by a Canadian.

In the end bedroom, to the left of the house, she pulled aside the curtains and ripped open the window, letting in some fresh air. A lone seagull soared through the air. Its shrill cry split the silence. A quick movement caught her eye, and she craned her neck to see what it was. An irate-looking man stood in front of Mrs. Walsh's door. She heard him calling out and banging on the old woman's door. From what she could see, he was of medium height and balding, with a crown of fair or greying hair. Something told her he was the reason for the old lady's anxiety. Roisin's protective sense took over, and she rushed down the stairs, half walking and half running back to the old woman's house. By the time she reached the driveway, a black van swerved out past her, splashing her as he passed. The driver was hunched over the steering wheel, but she could still make out a black bomber-style jacket and his round, balding head. He drove the van at a terrific speed and barely missed her, but didn't appear to have seen her.

Mrs. Walsh took her time answering the door, but those few minutes gave Roisin the chance to catch her breath. The old woman finally opened the door a crack. This time she couldn't hide the fright in her eyes.

"Are you alright?" Roisin asked. "What did that man want? I saw him from the window of the house. Was he threatening you?"

"It's alright, dear. I'm able to take care of myself." Mrs. Walsh's tone was weak but dismissive. Her face instantly transformed and she acted as if nothing had happened. "Tell me, what do you think of the house?"

Roisin decided not to pursue the matter. It was, after all, none of her business, and it was obvious that the old lady wasn't going to confide in her.

Roisin smiled. "It needs a good clean and coat of paint, but otherwise I think it'll be perfect. Just what I was looking for."

"That's great, dear." She opened the door fully and invited Roisin to step inside for a few minutes. The old lady did a quick scan of the driveway and the road before she closed it again and attached a chain on the lock. "I don't think there should be a problem." Mrs. Walsh's eyes avoided Roisin's and she seemed to hesitate before saying. "I'll have to check with Betty of course, and she needs to have some verification of your finances. If you could get that to me within the next couple of days, that'd be great."

"Sure, that should be no problem," Roisin said. Inside, she was panicking. "Do you think it would be sufficient if I had verification from my new employer?" Roisin asked.

"I'm not sure, to be honest. I think she might need a bank statement or something like that. If it's any help, I'll put in a good word for you. I'm sure Betty is more interested in knowing her house is in good hands. Are you planning on staying here for a while?"

"Oh, yes. Definitely. My plan is to settle here."

"So, you'll be working in Lissadore, I presume. You did mention an employer."

The woman would probably report all this back to Betty, but she had nothing to hide. "Yes, I have an interview next week. Formalities really. It's with a call centre." She remembered Mrs. Walsh's earlier words about being bothered by people calling her on the phone. "It's not that kind of a call centre; it's one of the good ones." Roisin crossed her fingers, a silly, superstitious thing to do. She was amazed at how fast she was making up this stuff, but it was all about survival and she needed that house.

"Oh, that's great, dear! I hope you will be very happy here, no matter what decision Betty makes. And if she agrees and you move in here, I'll invite you over and we can get to know each other a bit better." Mrs. Walsh cupped her hand over her mouth like a little girl. "Silly me— I've already got you settled in, but I'd feel safer having someone nearby. Ireland is not what it used to be, you know." She sighed. "There are a lot of strange characters around these days and dangers lurking, even in lonely places like this." She had that worried look in her eyes again. Roisin wished there was something she could do to help her. She took her leave, promising to come by with some documentation as soon as possible.

Roisin's heart sank when she considered how she was going to get a bank statement. She hadn't even set up a bank account yet.

# Chapter 15

Right, she thought. That's it. Bite the bullet, swallow your pride. You have to do this. She had seen a sign for a job agency in town. There was an immediacy now about her search. No more dillydallying. She'd go to the bank and enquire about setting up an account. She drove back to the B&B, put on one of her new dresses, her good woolen coat and her leather boots. She brushed her hair and applied some fresh lipstick.

Back in town, she went into the first bank she saw. Banks made her nervous. Maybe Javier had left more of an indelible mark on her than she would have liked. She walked in with an air of authority. The teller, a woman about her own age, mid-thirties, looked up with a friendly smile. She wanted to see her passport, of course, for identification, and made small talk while Roisin searched in her bag. Roisin handed it to her. The woman opened it. "Spain!" she said. "What on earth are you doing here?" Roisin shrugged, said it was a long story. The teller smiled again, and Roisin explained that she was waiting for confirmation for a job but needed to produce a bank statement for a prospective house she wanted to rent. Roisin laughed nervously. "I'm going for a job interview next week," she said, as way of explanation. The woman nodded sympathetically and gave Roisin a form to fill in. "You can take a seat over there," she said, pointing to a little table over in the corner. Roisin thanked her and went over to the table. She hated having to fill in all her personal details. It seemed as if nothing was simple any more. She looked at the form, began filling in her name. At least she had kept her own name, which made things easier. Married/Single? Her eyes swam over the list of questions. She stood up, no time or nerve for this now. She'd find a different way. She looked over to try to catch the teller's attention, but she was busy with another customer.

Outside, she breathed a sigh of relief and jaunted up the street to the agency. Banks made her feel claustrophobic. An enthusiastic young blond, who looked as if she'd just finished school, asked her to take a seat. Roisin looked around the room. There wasn't much going on. The woman offered her a beverage and told her she'd be with her in a moment. The moment turned into ten minutes, and Roisin watched as she shuffled a few papers, clicked on a few keys and examined the screen, filling in a few details. Finally, she looked over in Roisin's direction, gave her a toothy smile and asked her how she could help.

Roisin told her she was looking for a job. What else would she be doing there? She tried to curb her cynicism as the woman handed her an application form. She spoke to Roisin as if she was a child or a hopeless case. "Take your time and fill in as much as you can," she said.

Roisin did as she was told, smiled weakly at the woman and handed the form back. "I'll send you my Curriculum Vitae via e-mail, if that's all right?"

The woman perused the form, looking up to every so often. "So, what kind of a job are you looking for?"

Roisin took a deep breath. "I'm pretty flexible really. Office work, hotel work, reception, that sort of thing."

"Right," the woman said. "I see you've recently returned from Spain. Are you looking for something permanent?"

"Yes, I am."

The woman turned to her computer and began tapping keys.

"How about customer service?" We have a company in Galway looking for someone in customer support for a major software company. They need a Spanish speaker." She looked again at the form. "I see your Spanish is excellent."

Roisin swallowed. Galway, an hour's drive away. Was her Spanish good enough? "I don't have a car at the moment," she said. "Don't you have anything nearer?"

The woman shook her head. "That's about all we have at the moment, I'm afraid."

Roisin's heart sank. Could you tell me a little more about the job? What's the pay like?

The woman rattled off some information about training, software license, business customers, a little under €10 per hour. They were looking for someone young, dynamic and a team player. Roisin smirked and nodded, taking it all in. She had no great interest in or knowledge about computer software, but there would be adequate training, the woman said.

The young and dynamic part was so cliché, and she doubted she could explain all the intricacies of computer software to a Spanish customer, especially if she didn't even understand it herself,

"I'll tell you what," the woman said. "I can send them your application and we can play it by ear from there. They usually respond quickly." Sure they do, Roisin thought, mentally slapping herself for being so cynical. These companies were always looking for suckers and desperate people.

"That would be great," Roisin lied, putting a big fat smile on her face. It was a lie of preservation. If she showed any reluctance, she'd lose her chance. She needed a job and if this was the first thing available, so be it. She thanked the woman, who told her to expect a call within the next few days, and left.

Next thing she'd have to do would be to find out how to get to Galway and how much that would cost. She called into the local newsagents and asked the young man behind the counter where the nearest train station was. "Ah, sure there's no train station here at all," he said. Roisin was determined not to be defeated. "Do you know how I'd get to Galway then, or even Ennis?"

"Your best bet," he said, "is to go up to the bus station. They'll let you know times and everything." She bought a magazine to show her appreciation, thanked him and went off looking for the bus station.

The town wasn't big, one main road with shops, hotels and restaurant/café's leading off to side streets. That was the core of it. There were a couple of new residential areas on the outskirts, the surfing school, a few hotels and a large golf course which attracted many natives and tourists alike. Most people used their own transport, and so it was no great surprise to discover that there were only a few buses going to Galway, via Ennis. There was no way she could live in Lissadore and commute to Galway. She needed a Plan B. The problem was that she didn't have a Plan B, and she didn't want to compromise her wish to live in Lissadore.

    What now? She'd explore the area a bit, hang out in a coffee shop and try to come up with a plan. She was glad Javier wasn't there to witness her first major obstacle. His parting words echoed in her mind. "You'll never survive on your own, Roisin. Don't come running back here when things don't work out." Well, she'd show him. She knew he had been acting out his anger and fear. It was his way of trying to get her to stay, but he should have known better than to taunt her like that. It merely reinforced her pledge to prove that she could not only support herself but thrive in the process.

    She decided to head toward the Burren and explore the area as long as she still had the car. That would take her mind off things. She should be able to reach it within less than an hour.

    The narrow curvy roads took some getting used to, and she had to be on the alert at all times. Several cars came whizzing past her when she least expected it. She was amazed there weren't more accidents on these roads. The sun, which had the power to make or break a day, decided to grace the sky with its presence, albeit a weak one. She still had to accustom herself to the proximity of towns in Ireland. On quieter stretches, she looked out onto hilly fields and vibrant spring grass dampened by the recent rain. Clumps of gorse and rock formation were sprinkled here and there with wild flowers, and sheep grazing in the meadows. On an impulse, she pulled over to a small lay-by to call her sister, who promptly answered.

"Roisin," she said. "What are you up to? I wondered when you'd call." Static ruined the clarity of the call, and Roisin took a few steps, hoping that would restore the connection. It did, although Roisin had no idea how that worked. If she thought about it for too long it seemed amazing she even had a connection. "So, how's it going?" her sister asked. "Have you had enough yet?" Helen laughed at her own little joke.

"Well, I'm here in the heart of The Burren, surrounded by sheep, cows and wildflowers. Can you hear the sounds?" Roisin held the mobile out to catch the sounds of nature. Sheep bleating, birds chattering away, accelerating the speed of growth. Roisin remembered reading once that the sounds of birds chattering helps nature to awaken. Although it sounded far-fetched, she liked to think it was so. But of course it was the light that was responsible, the clock of time, the repetitive cycle of death, rebirth and growth. She remembered Helen on the other end of the line and brought the phone back to her ear. "Isn't it glorious?"

The connection broke up again for a second. She heard Helen's voice loud and clear. "Those birds are making an awful racket."

"Did you get my message yesterday?" Roisin

said. "I haven't had a moment so far, but I'm sure I'll be seeing you soon enough and I'll tell you all in detail."

"I did," Helen said. "I still don't know what you're doing out there in the Wild West. Sure, wouldn't you be better off here?"

"What did you say?" Roisin said. "I'll have to call you back later. The connection is really bad. Love to everyone." She flipped the flap of her mobile. A little grin played on her lips.

The countryside became tighter or more compact as she drove past the craggy fields and mottled grey-stoned terrain which made this place so unique. Her thoughts strayed to the people she'd met so far. She couldn't help worrying about Mrs. Walsh. What about the fellow who had appeared to be causing the old woman stress? Her mind conjured all sorts of scenarios as she thought back to the old lady's frightened demeanour.

Javier, who was never far from her mind, came into her thoughts again. She remembered the way his face use to light up when he smiled, the glint in his brown eyes, his broad shoulders and the natural wave of his hair. But most of all she remembered his strong, warm hands. She missed him, after all. Even though she had certainly had her reasons for leaving, she hoped by now he had forgiven her for leaving the way she did. To stop herself from becoming too sentimental, she recalled scenes of the past few years when he had hurt and disappointed her. Sometimes he was rough in his manners. A particular scene came to mind. They had been at the local market, laughing one minute and, although she couldn't remember what had sparked the argument, he had stopped in the middle of the street, wagging his finger at her and shouting. She had been mortified and tried to walk away, but he had kept shouting after her. He didn't care where he was or who was around when he lost his temper. With time, she hoped they could learn to forgive each other and remember all the good times they'd had. He was a loner at heart—she knew that. Maybe now, he'd begin to pick up the lost pieces of himself, just as she was trying to do.

    She pulled into a little hamlet in the parking area of a charming thatched pub in Sinleach. She must have missed the signs, if there were any. The main road was barely wide enough to allow more than two passing cars, let alone a crowd of campers. Hard to believe that this small place held the largest traditional folk music festival in Ireland. It attracted thousands of international and Irish visitors every summer. Now, it looked forlorn. A church steeple peeked from behind a cluster of trees in the distance, and she'd spotted a few scattered houses along the way. She wondered if the little pub was even open. The door was closed and she couldn't see any lights. With a shrug of disappointment, she read an almost faded sign on one of the windows. *Closed from November to May*. Just a couple of weeks now and it would start buzzing again. She was looking forward to going to the festival.

    Not a soul had crossed her path on the way to the church. She walked around to the back looking for an open door. Like most churches, it was closed for casual visitors—another sign of the times. So much for the sanctuary of the church! So much, too, for respect for others' property. Some people didn't hesitate in stealing, breaking stained-glass windows, destroying things that didn't belong to them. Once they would have been in awe of an all-seeing God. Now, most of the previous believers scorned their former naiveté. Where was the all-seeing God when the innocents were being abused? Where was the justice? The church had lost a lot of respect. It would have to work hard to gain a modicum of trust from those who had strayed. Maybe it would even need a miracle. She shook off a sudden shiver and looked over her shoulder. *What was that?* A feeling as if someone had walked over her grave. Wasn't that how the saying went? An old iron gate hung half open, inviting her to enter the graveyard.

She pulled aside the creaking gate and walked along the narrow grassy path, stopping to read some of the inscriptions of the forlorn graves. Most of them were illegible, worn away by wind, harsh conditions and years of neglect. Crumbling headstones lay scattered throughout the mossy graveyard. A chill crept up her spine again as her eyes tried to focus on the writing. She traced the shape of the Celtic symbols with her finger. The leaves on the trees rustled. She couldn't shake off the feeling that she was being watched. She spun around to see if someone had crept up behind her. There was nobody there, but she could still sense the presence of something or someone in this space. The banshee sounds of sea gulls squawking in the distance added to her sense of unease. Without knowing why, she pulled out her notebook and scribbled down some of the legible names. Brid MacCauley, 1788-1843. The next grave belonged to a young man called Michael Brody 1810-1842. Beside this, a lone grave, no larger than a shoe box, caught her eye. A robin perched upon the grassy tufts watched her with beady eyes and head slightly tipped to the side, as if waiting to see what she'd do next. He didn't stir when she came closer to read the inscription. *Our beloved son, Paddy. 1876-1878.*

This area was badly hit by the Great Famine in the 1840's. Three million Irish inhabitants perished of hunger and another three million emigrated, some of them scraping the basic fare together to travel like herded animals on the lowest deck of passengers ships on the way to the far corners of the world. She tried to imagine how desolate life must have been in those times.

Time changes everything, but the imprint of past events often lingers in a place. She stood in the middle of the secluded space and felt the history of ages sweep over her. Apart from some families that had lived in these parts for generations, the rugged west coast of Ireland was not somewhere that attracted a new influx of settlers. Ironic really, when one considered how many tourists flocked there every year. Occasionally, a few freelance artists, musicians, botanists and writers came there on holidays, fell in love with the place and ended up staying.

There was something peaceful about graveyards. They made you reflect on the value of life and death. The robin fluttered its wings and took off into the unknown. Slowly, she made her way back to the car.

Time to continue exploring. She got in the car

and drove along the coastal road with no particular destination in mind. Maybe the chill she'd felt back at the graveyard was a mere trick of the imagination. Did the appearance of the robin hold any significance, or was it merely a coincidence? Would she, too, whittle away her remaining years in this place, or would she throw herself into some sort of activity to make her life meaningful, if only to her. No longer prepared to wait for things to happen to her, she would make the most of this second phase of her life. It was time to shed her passive cloak which, although it had served her well in the past, had become a bit too threadbare.

A brilliant ray of sunshine broke the sky, illuminating the road ahead. It bathed everything in a benevolent light and shed warmth upon the wild dramatic hills. She caught occasional glimpses of the frothy waves from behind low hedgerows and those endless stone walls.

When she turned off the main road, she was forced to wait as an old, stooped farmer wearing a cap and tweed jacket herded his cows across the road. Every so often, he half-heartedly tipped one of them with a spindly branch to encourage them on their way. She rolled down the window and said hello. In response, he gave her a toothless smile. "Great day now!" This was a typical greeting from stranger to stranger. It was either *great day, terrible weather, nasty morning,* or something to that effect. Weather was always a safe topic of conversation, a filler of gaps—just enough to show a stranger a willingness to communicate.

The man carried on humming a tune and

mumbling to himself. She watched him fade into the distance. He'd probably lived here all his life, just like generations before him. Sometimes she thought these were the lucky ones, the ones who needed no more in life than the same old routine, day in, day out.

Her thoughts turned to Javier again. Tears welled up in her eyes and she tried to manoeuvre the car through the narrow road flanked by grassy knolls, puddles and granite mounds. Overcome with emotion, the tears came tumbling down her face. She held her chest with one hand as if that would stop the pain. What she had done? Was it worth it? She was a woman straddling two countries, neither here nor there. She turned off the ignition, stepped out of the car and sat down on a large boulder, trying to calm herself by sucking in large mouthfuls of cool air until she began to feel better. It was good to finally release some emotions. She knew she had made the right decision but it didn't stop it from hurting. She wiped her eyes and returned to the car.

# Chapter 16

She parked the car and walked over to Jimmy's Deli. She could grab something to eat and a cup of his delicious coffee. It was already beginning to get dark and the Deli would be closing in about an hour. While she was standing waiting for her coffee, Maggie came in. "Do you want to take it into the shop and keep me company," Maggie said. "I was going to take a break anyway."

She nodded enthusiastically, although now that she was back in town the gravity of her situation came down upon her like a heavy cloud. She tried to hide it, but Maggie was perceptive. "Any luck with the house?" Maggie asked her when they were sipping their coffee in the back room of the shop. Roisin curled her hands around the cup and gave her a weak smile. "I love the house. It's just the kind of thing I was looking for. Privacy, great views and not too far from town."

"So what's the problem?"

Roisin pulled herself up, sighed and told Maggie about her dilemma. Maggie went over to the window and looked outside. She seemed to be lost in thought for a few minutes. Roisin hoped she hadn't made a mistake by confiding in her, but she was worried. How could she rent a house if she didn't have a job? Maggie spun around to face her. "I think I have an idea."

Roisin wondered what was coming.

"I've been thinking about this ever since you came into the shop yesterday, but I didn't want to say anything until I was sure. So here's the deal. I could hire you part-time. What do you think of that?"

Roisin's mouth went slack as she released her shoulders. Her forehead creased as she contemplated Maggie's offer. This was almost too good to be true. "Are you kidding me? I'd hate if you were just offering me the job because you feel sorry for me…Don't get me wrong, it's just that I don't really have experience with this kind of thing."

"Get away out of that," Maggie said. "We'll both benefit from this. I have big plans, Roisin." Maggie hesitated. "The only thing is, I can't guarantee anything. It could all collapse in a few months, not that I believe it will. At least it'll be something to get you started. You might even enjoy it."

Roisin's face relaxed in a smile when it truly dawned on her that she wouldn't have to work in some horrible job. She trusted Maggie.

"Does that smile mean you'll do it?" Maggie raised her coffee cup. "We'll be great! So, when can you start?"

"Eh…next week? The week after. As soon as I have a place, and if I'm lucky, I'll get this house," she said. Roisin looked around the workspace, taking it all in.

"It would be great if you could start next week? We'll give each other a trial period. You come up with some of your own designs and we'll play it by ear. I have a good feeling about this," Maggie said.

Roisin swallowed. "I don't see why not." She still couldn't believe her luck. And yet, a niggling voice warned her that life might throw a stumbling stone on her path. She didn't want to sound too enthusiastic. "Sorry for getting so emotional just now. I was beginning to despair. Thanks a million, Maggie." Now it was Roisin's turn to hesitate. "Em...there's one little thing," she said. "We didn't mention the money issue. I hate to bring it up, but I need to have some idea."

"How much were you expecting?" Maggie asked, in a matter-of-fact tone.

Roisin hesitated. She didn't want to ask for too much, but she knew she'd have to earn at least the minimum wage to be able to afford basic living costs. Maggie cut in. "How about if we start off with fourteen Euro an hour. Twenty percent commission on your designs if they're a hit. That's a fair rate, what do you think? Keep it to yourself though. I don't want any bad feelings between yourself and my other two employees. Although they're just selling. You'll be my creative right-hand woman."

Roisin did a quick mental calculation. It should be enough to pay her rent and basic living costs. If she lived frugally she could get by. With the knowledge that she now had a job, it would be so much easier to rent the house. She nodded enthusiastically. "I'm very happy with that. There's one other little thing," she added. "I'll need some sort of confirmation for the landlady. She wants a bank statement, but she might be happy with a job contract.

Would that be a problem?"

"Sure. I'll get that to you as soon as possible." They heard someone come into the shop. "I'll see you on Monday then," Maggie said, with a smile.

As Roisin left the shop, her thoughts raced with calculations. A car was out of the question, especially with the cost of insurance and tax. She'd have to get a bike. Yes, that's what she'd do.

*

A few days later, Roisin was in her new house. She turned on the radio at full blast and sang along to a Rolling Stones number as she armed herself with buckets of hot water, dusting and cleaning cloths and other paraphernalia. Everything had worked out after all. She had confided her situation to Fidelma, who had in turn made a call to the owner. The owner was understanding of Roisin's situation and was happy to have one month's rent in advance and rent the house out on a monthly basis for the time being.

Roisin opened all the windows, washed surfaces, vacuumed floors and began adding personal touches. She decided to wait a few months before painting the place. By then she should have a better idea of her future plans. In a couple of days she'd be starting her new job, and she wanted to get the house ready beforehand. Later on she'd tackle the garden, rip out the weeds and plant the new flowers and herbs. Helen and Todd were coming the next day with her bicycle and she wanted to make the house look inviting. The bicycle belonged to her sister, but had been sitting in the garage for months.

Todd was going to drive her car back and drop it off at the car rental. The more she thought about it, the less she liked the idea of being without a car, but she would have to get used to it, at least for the time being. She'd been busy setting up house, sending text messages and organizing a telephone. Most of all, she was delighted with the laptop which had arrived earlier on in the week. Javier had sent it with a note: "Not that you deserve it. Keep in touch. Javier." No kisses, no soft words of regret. A battle between pride and desire took place. Desire won. What good would it do if she rejected his peace offering? Would it serve anyone? Betty already had internet access in the house so she rang the telephone company and was surprised at how fast they had sent out one of their men to set things up.

A few hours later, she looked around the living room with a sense of satisfaction and pleasure. The fire was set to light; the tasteful art posters and candles brightened it up and added a personal touch. She'd also bought some scatter cushions which complemented the earth tones in the posters, and a woven blanket in russet and burnt orange tones. Before going out to the garden, she rewarded herself with a cup of tea. She plonked down on an armchair while she waited for the water to boil and opened her laptop. There were ten new emails, most of which she immediately dumped. Those annoying spammers didn't waste any time. Her mood plummeted when she saw a new message from Javier. She held her breath, afraid of what she would read, but she opened it anyway.

*"Dear Roisin,*

*How could you do this to me? Running away like a thief in the night. Is that all I mean to you after all these years? But…at least you got the ball rolling. Maybe I'll even thank you one day. So, what have you proven? We can live without each other. Don't you miss me just one little bit?*

*For what it's worth, I feel like a free man. Not because you left, but because it looks as if we've finally found a buyer for the house. If you had just waited…we were so close…. Roisin, you were always hot headed. We could have avoided this fiasco.*

*Anyway, hence the laptop. Pablo let me have it for a good price, and I thought you might need it.*

*I wanted to wait before contacting you in the hope that you would call me for help.*

*I was foolish enough to believe you wouldn't last long on your own. It's early days yet! Brian gave me your new address and has filled me in on your news.*

She released her breath, relieved for him. He had even partly admitted that she might have helped him. That was a major breakthrough. In all their years together, Javier had never expressed his vulnerability or taken her advice on board. But hot-headed. The pot calling the kettle black…. She continued reading.

*This isn't easy to write. You know I've never been good at this kind of thing. How can I convince you to give me another chance? We took each other for granted. I realise that now – too late as you always said. I foolishly thought if I got tough with you, you'd see sense. You can't just throw everything away, everything we've achieved together. You know I've never been the romantic type – you knew that when you met me. But I've always provided well for us…until recently. You can't accuse me of cheating on you either. I've always been loyal.*

*I'm even willing to come over there to be with you. For God's sake, Roisin. I'll give up everything and move over there. Isn't it possible that we can make another go of it? I know I've wasted too much time. You don't need to tell me what a fool I've been. Yes, yes. I can hear you sighing from here. You tried to tell me so many times but I never listened.*

*I'm not going to beg, Roisin. Just think about it? Give me a chance. I can come and visit you soon. You'll see these are not just empty words. If you don't want me to stay with you, I can book a nearby hotel. Remember the great times we had there?*

*With you gone, there's nothing here for me anymore.*

*I'll be checking my e-mails daily, looking for an answer. To hell with it anyway. I've already booked my ticket..."*

She gasped as her fingers reached to touch her throat.

She didn't know what to think about that. He sounded desperate but conciliatory. She bit her lip, trying to stop the tears. It was no use. She cried for him, for her, for missed opportunities, and for the spanners life throws in the way of happiness. The fact that he was miserable made her feel even worse.

This was so typical of the merry-go-round of their relationship. Why couldn't she just close the door and keep it closed? She had had good reason to leave, and now he'd realised he couldn't live without her. Too little, too late. But another part of her said that the past was the past. It was easy in theory but not easy to achieve. She wiped her eyes. At least he wasn't angry with her any more. That meant that he was beginning to thaw. Perhaps they could become friends once more, maybe even lovers, but one thing was for sure, she wouldn't live with him again. People do not change that much, not that she thought it was impossible, but basic nature remains the same.

Even if she felt sorry for Javier, she reminded herself that she was not responsible for him. He would suffer in silence and let it eat him up inside. She could picture him becoming more withdrawn as the days went by. Some people drink to drown their woes, others allow their woes to eat them up from the inside. He had developed reclusive tendencies these past years. It was unlikely that he'd suddenly take an interest in cooking. So he probably wasn't eating properly either.

A gamut of emotions, from resentment to sadness, ran through her. They were tinged with a ray of hope though as she thought back to the past few years. Living in Spain had presented her with many challenges, but she had overcome them all. It had taught her so much too. She'd done her most serious growing up there, having had to face obstacles she could never have imagined. She'd also lost some of her impulsiveness and light-heartedness, but maybe that was part of life no matter where one lived.

She remembered her tea and went to the kitchen. No moping, she reprimanded herself. If she gave in to these negative thoughts, they would pull her down. She poured boiling water over the black leaves, and watched the colour transform as her thoughts turned to Tom Cullen. He was different to Javier, but what did she really know about him?

She opened her phone and clicked through her last exchange with Tom. Her to him: *Hi Tom. It's me, I promised I'd keep you informed. How about coming to my house-warming party on Saturday week. It'd be lovely to see you again.* She had deliberated for ages, wondering how to sign off, but had left it at *Roisin xxx*. His answer had come that same evening. **Love to come. Have to rearrange a few things, but I'll be there.** He had signed off with his initial, **T**. That was all. The next morning, he had sent another message. **Don't forget to send me exact directions. I've taken a long weekend off and can combine business with pleasure. Yours, Tom.**

A few stray butterflies flapped their wings in her stomach when she re-read his words. She had replied with a smiley, afraid she might write the wrong thing. Perhaps she shouldn't have invited him, but she wanted to see him again. She wondered what kind of business he had to attend to, but dismissed the thought. She didn't need to know. Everyone she'd invited so far had accepted, and she felt nervous and excited at the prospects of seeing her friends and family again. A smile played on her lips as she found herself daydreaming about Tom. It was fun having her own house to decorate and nobody to cheer up except herself. She could do whatever she chose, when she chose. Not that Javier had ever really interfered in that sense, but the freedom she felt now was totally different to how she'd felt in the marriage.

# Chapter 17

Helen and Todd arrived around noon. She had been waiting with anticipation and nervously flitting around the house, making sure everything was in order. To her eyes, it was a charming haven. When she heard the car pull up she rushed out to meet them. She had tied her hair in a ponytail, wore minimal make up and casual clothes. She felt happy and knew it showed. She stood there, grinning as they came to greet her.

Both of them spoke at once. "Well look at you," her sister said. "You look as if you belong here."

Roisin smiled and showed them inside. "Did you have a good trip?"

She could tell that Todd wasn't in the best of form. "Go on, Helen," he said. "Tell her about our major blow up outside Dune. It felt more like Doom back there for a while."

Helen glared at him. "I thought we agreed not to mention that." She turned to Roisin. "Show us around, will you. I can't believe you've already found a place, and a job."

"I told you I would," Roisin said. Well, she hadn't really, but she did have to put up with a lot of naysayers, including Helen. Of course it could have gone the other way too.

The range made pleasant crackling sounds. "It reminds me of our kitchen back in Knockadreen," Helen said, as she yanked open cupboards and drawers. She strolled around the room, finally settling to gaze out the window. "Todd, how about if we moved here, near the sea? We could sell our house and buy an acre or two, become self-sufficient."

Todd raised his eyes to heaven, grinning. "For the love of God, woman. You're changing your tune. Weren't you the one who was against your sister moving out here?"

Helen glared at him again; she wasn't used to him contradicting her. He chuckled to himself. Every couple of years Helen had a new plan up her sleeve and it always involved selling up and moving somewhere. One year it was Mexico, then Goa of all places. Roisin understood this longing for change and often thought they must have had nomadic blood somewhere in their ancestral line.

"Let's go down to the beach after our tea," Helen said. We can take some photos."

"Good plan," Roisin said. "But I'd like to try out my bike first. Just to make sure it works properly, especially the lights and the brakes. I'll have to get used to all these hills. Why don't you both take a look around and I'll take it for a spin?"

She changed into sturdier shoes and threw on her denim jacket. It felt strange to be riding a bike again after so many years, but she soon got used to it.

She returned, flushed and slightly out-of-breath and joined Todd and Helen in the garden. Helen, who was sitting on the garden chair while

Todd inspected the soil asked her if she'd had any problems.

"It was grand, just have to get used to battling the wind and the hills."

Helen grinned. "Don't rave too much about it or I might want it back."

"Look at it as a loan, Helen. Whenever you decide you want it back, just say the word."

"Not at all. I think my biking days are over." She turned to Todd. "We like it here, don't we Todd?"

Todd nodded. "You've got yourself a nice place here. Great view. Are you going to plant a few vegetables?"

Roisin sat down beside her sister. "Hardly likely. I think I'm far too lazy for all that bother. I can get good stuff in the local shops, pesticide free even at Jimmy's. Did I tell you about Jimmy?"

Helen punched her playfully. "Don't you remember? You gave me a rundown of all your new acquaintances shortly after you arrived."

Roisin raised her eyes to heaven.

Helen carried on obliviously. "Whenever you decide to have a garden party, I'll be there—a working garden party, I mean. There's a whole rake of weeds that need urgent attention." Her eyes grew big. "We could make it into a real refuge." She got up and brushed the dust off the back of her jeans. "Todd, do we still have that garden set in the garage?"

Todd, who was scraping dirt off his shoes, mumbled. "No, sure didn't you tell me to get rid of it, 'cause it was taking up too much space."

Helen frowned. "Pity." She held out her hand

to Roisin. "Maybe we can get you one as a house-warming gift?"

"No," Roisin said. "I really appreciate it, but I don't want to burden myself with too much baggage…I'm delighted with the bike, though."

"Ha!" Helen said. "That means you're not willing to commit. You'll need a place to sit on sunny days—for visitors, too. This little bench is cute, but the paint is flaking and it's not exactly comfortable."

Roisin shrugged. Perhaps her sister was right about the commitment part.

"Well, how about going into town then," Helen said. "I'm falling asleep here. Maybe we can see the shop and meet the famous Maggie." She cocked her head to the side. "Did you ever figure out what she was doing in the pub that day? Sounds as if she's a bit eccentric."

"Eccentric—she's as batty as a whirligig. You'll love her, I'm sure. How about if we have lunch in Flynn's pub. The food is good there and they have music sometimes."

The two sisters chatted all the way down to the beach while Todd wandered off, taking photos. Although the sun was nowhere to be seen, the sky was full of contrasts that day, so it didn't bother them. The brisk walk did them good, adding colour to their cheeks. The ever-present wind played havoc with Helen's red hair, giving her a wild look. Roisin, who had more of a milky complexion, would have loved to have Helen's more olive tint of skin that browned so easily. They tramped on now, in silence, followed by Todd, snapping shots of them, of the patterns in the sands where the waves had left their creative markings, of the monochrome ashy tones of sky and sea, and the peace of it all.

*

Soon, rejuvenated after their meal, they lingered for a while over their drinks.

"That was so good," Helen said, as she tried to tame her hair. She turned her attention to Roisin, who was staring intently at two men who had just come in. Helen's eyes followed hers. "Hey, Roisin. Penny for your thoughts?"

Roisin leaned in closer to them. "Don't look yet, but I'm sure that's the fellow I saw at my neighbour's house the other day, the one who was harassing Mrs. Walsh. If I'm not mistaken, the other fellow is the one that upset Maggie that day in the pub, the day I met her. The plot thickens. Don't you think that's too much of a coincidence?"

"Wouldn't be the kind of company I'd choose. If I were you, I'd keep out of it. Just ignore them," Todd said.

"Yes, you're probably right, but I was worried about that old woman. What do you think they're up to? Drugs maybe?"

"Yeh, right Watson. And what would an old woman be doing mixed up with drugs? Don't you think you're letting your imagination run away with you?" Todd was showing Helen the photos he had taken. She took the camera off him and accidentally pushed the wrong button. The flash illuminated the dim interior.

Before she had time to react, the big fellow turned his bald head in their direction. They watched, horrified, as he glared over at them and began walking towards their table.

"Lay off with the photo taking, okay." He cracked his knuckles and jerked his chin up to indicate he meant business. Roisin giggled and shifted on her chair.

Todd stood up. "Hey, take it easy, man. She just pressed the flash by accident. What's wrong with you?"

The man, as if he suddenly saw sense, put his hand over his eyes in an overly-dramatic gesture. "Put the fucking thing out. The light hurts my eyes." He lowered his voice. "Careful where you flash around here, okay."

"No problem." Todd sat back down again, his brow furrowed. His hands shook as he took a gulp of beer. "I don't know what his problem is. Since when is it illegal to take photos in a pub?"

Helen pretended to be checking out the menu. "That fellow no more has a problem with his eyes than I do."

Roisin mumbled. "He has something to hide, if ever someone does. By the way, I'd like a copy of that photo."

Helen sat with her mouth agape. "I think we'd better pay up and go."

On their way back to the house, Roisin stopped at Maggie's shop. There were a couple of customers in there, one of whom was over at the mirror trying on hats.

The young man she'd seen earlier on in the week was busy arranging a scarf on a mannequin. He turned to her and smiled. "Can I help you?"

Roisin went over to him and introduced

herself. "Hi, I'm Roisin. I'm not sure if Maggie told you about me yet, but I'm due to start here on Monday."

His face transformed into a sunny smile. "I'm Darius." He pulled a funny face and rolled his eyes up to heaven. "It's my *nom de plume*. I'm studying Art and Design in Galway. Sure, Maggie mentioned you. She's a ticket, isn't she? She's up to her eyes getting ready for the show. I've never seen her in such a tizzy. All extra hands are more than welcome, so we'll be happy to have you on board."

"Thanks, Darius. I can't wait to get creative again. I'm just showing my sister and brother-in-law around and don't want to keep you." She indicated to the hat woman who was on the way to the counter. "Looks like you have a purchase."

"Ching, ching," he whispered with a cheeky grin. "Enjoy yourselves. I'll probably see you around next week sometime."

Helen was trying on a blue hat. "What do you think?" She admired herself in the mirror.

Roisin gave her the thumbs up. "Go for it."

"It's not exactly cheap," Helen said. She turned to her husband and blinked at him coquettishly. "What do you think, Todd?"

"I'm the last one you should be asking" he said. "You know me and fashion."

"Yes, but would you walk down the street with me if I was wearing it?"

"Since when did that ever stop you? If you really want it, I'll buy it for you."

"You're too good to me," she said as she stood on her tipped toes and planted a smooch on his cheek. A hint of a smile revealed a dimple on his stubby chin.

As they left the shop, Helen was full of chatter. The event in the pub seemed to be forgotten for the time being. "I think you're going to enjoy working there. It's right up your alley, really."

"I hope so. She might think I'm useless and fire me after a week."

"I'd say the biggest problem will be resisting temptation," Helen said. "I'd probably spend most of my earnings in the shop."

"No chance of that happening. Most of my earnings will cover basic living costs." And that was something that still niggled Roisin, but she was an optimistic person. Perhaps she'd even make a name for herself as a designer. She would certainly not share these hopes and dreams, even with Helen. Some things were better left unsaid because speaking them out loud and sharing them could awake expectations.

# CHAPTER 18

When they had left, she closed the door to the outside world, poured herself a glass of wine, and settled in to read a few pages of a novel, a luxury she hadn't had time to enjoy for days. Her mind was too preoccupied to concentrate on the novel, and she kept reading over the same lines. She forced herself to concentrate and was soon lost in the thriller. She thought she heard a cry and disengaged herself from the book. Silence. It was getting dark outside. She closed the curtains and debated whether or not she should light the fire but decided against it. It had been a long day; in fact it had been a long week. She intended going to bed early; it wouldn't be worth lighting a fire. She lit a candle instead and settled in on the armchair, covering herself with a blanket, as she re-entered the world of mystery and suspense.

    Once again, she thought she heard a commotion outside. It sounded like screeching. It's probably just a horny cat, she thought. She returned to her book. This time she was sure she heard shouting. It must be coming from the direction of Mrs. Walsh's house, she thought, as her front window was slightly ajar. She threw off the blanket, went over to the window and pulled the curtain aside. Of course she couldn't see anything. Still the noise persisted. Maybe the book she'd been reading was playing on her imagination. With a mixture of fear and curiosity, she went to the hall and opened the front door. This time she made sure to take the key with her.

The voices appeared to be coming from the direction of Mrs. Walsh's house. Roisin's heart beat rapidly as she contemplated for a moment what she should do. She abhorred nasty scenes. What if she became embroiled in a violent situation? There were enough cases of innocent bystanders being beaten up, or worse, while trying to protect a mugging or rape victim. Despite her trepidation, she grabbed her jacket and mobile and headed out. She couldn't stand by and do nothing. First, she called the police. She told the Garda about her previous observations and said she thought Mrs. Walsh was in imminent danger.

"I'll send someone out right away, Mam," he said. Roisin shivered, and it was not because of the cool night air. She was afraid, torn between going over to help the old woman and keeping herself safe. The sound of raised voices again brought her back to the present. She braced herself, put on her jacket and half ran, half walked down the driveway and over towards the old woman's house. That black van was parked down at the end of the driveway. Another dark Toyota was parked up front. She flipped open her mobile and took a photo of the registration number of both vehicles.

The downstairs lights were on. She could hear loud male voices coming from the living room and saw that the front windows were slightly ajar. That explained why the noise had carried all the way to her house. Either that or they had been outside. She hoped she wasn't about to walk into a hornet's nest.

Fired up by adrenalin, she masked herself with false bravado and pressed the buzzer. No answer. She looked around her, debating whether she should go back before it was too late. No, she was not a coward. Despite her racing heart, she pressed the doorbell again. She hoped the police would arrive soon. It was about ten minutes since she'd called them. The voices had died down. Somebody jerked the door open, and she waited with bated breath to see who it was. A young man stood in front of her. She registered his lank hair, his pale face and the fear in his eyes, which he unsuccessfully tried to hide

"Yes. What do you want?"

"Hello. I'm Roisin and have just moved in next door. Is everything all right? I heard shouting and was worried about Mrs. Walsh." She checked her mobile again. "It's a bit lonely out here, and I heard there were several robberies in the vicinity so I called the police. They should be here any minute." She congratulated herself on getting that in, for extra measure.

The big fellow she'd seen earlier in the pub appeared behind him and shoved the slighter man aside. His close-set eyes bored menacingly into hers, and she tried not to let him see her fear.

"What's the trouble here, Sean?" His voice sounded like it had been ground on rough sandpaper.

She took a deep breath and spoke with a steady voice. "I'd like to see Mrs. Walsh.

"She's not here right now. Who are you?" He came closer to the threshold and slanted his head slightly to one side. "Hey, don't I know ya from somewhere?"

Roisin cleared her throat. "No, I don't think I've had the pleasure, but I was just telling this fellow here that I was worried about Mrs. Walsh when I heard the commotion and so I called the police."

He squinted at her. "You did wha?" He wagged his finger at her. "Yeh, I'm sure I've seen you somewhere before."

"Look, I just want to have a few words with Mrs. Walsh. Where is she?"

"She's busy right now. Tell her, Sean."

Sean's voice shook. "Granny's not here right now." His eyes pleaded with her. She got the message. "If you come back tomorrow. I'm sure she'll be back by then."

At that moment, a squad car pulled up the driveway. She exhaled a sigh of relief.

"Watch what you say, Sean." The big fellow hissed at Sean. He turned to Roisin. "And you—keep your nose out of other people's business. I'll deal with you later."

She glared at him in defiance. "Your bully tactics don't work with me."

He disappeared back inside.

Two young-looking police officers stepped out of the car. The threshold light cast a reflection on the chubbier policeman's youthful face. His eyes were guarded by his cap. Roisin didn't even know if policemen were permitted to bear arms in Ireland. She seemed to remember reading that they were reserved for Special Forces.

The chubby policeman moved closer. "What's going on here, folks?"

Sean, the grandson, looked even more terrified than before. Despite the cool temperatures, his forehead was blistered with pearls of sweat.

"Nothin," he stammered. "This crazy woman started ringing on the doorbell, askin' for me granny…"

The garda raised his hand. "Hold on a minute. What's your name, sir? We have reason to believe that the woman who lives here might be in trouble. I'd like to talk to her."

Sean's eyes darted from the policeman's to Roisin's. "She's not here. I already told her."

"I'm going to have to search the premises. Step aside please."

Sean shifted his position, pulling back his shoulders and jutting his chin "You can't do that without a search warrant. I know me rights."

"Getting a search warrant is no problem. You would be wise to cooperate."

The young man looked confused. He finally let the officer in. The second officer turned to Roisin. "You'd better go back home now, Miss, but before you go I'd like to take down your details."

Roisin hesitated. "I didn't really want to get involved in any trouble. All I wanted was to protect the old lady. There's another fellow inside, a big fellow. He's the one I saw a few days ago, harassing her."

As she turned around, she saw, from the corner of her eye, a dark shadow running by the hedge, heading toward the road. "Look, he's getting away," she shouted

"Well, he can't get far," the policeman said.

"We'll find him." He went back inside the car, probably calling for backup. He called Roisin over. "Can you give me a description of that fellow you saw?"

Roisin described the man. "I think that's his van. It's the same one I saw the other day." She heard him pass on the information to the person at the other end. She couldn't imagine there were many officers in such a small place and they'd have to act quickly.

The Garda went inside. There was nothing left for her to do but to head back to the house. As she hurried up the driveway, aware of the loud crunch of her shoes on the gravel, she heard the sound of a car's engine starting up. Although she had a good view of the road, she was shielded by the thick hedge. The van took off at a fast pace, whizzing around the corner. She snatched a glimpse of the bulky fellow with the cropped hair who was talking into a mobile. As she debated whether or not to go back inside and tell the young garda, the police car swerved out of the driveway at an equally terrific speed. Its siren blared out into the silence of the countryside. She felt a certain glee to be part of all this action; it was the kind of excitement that both bewildered and terrified her, like waiting for an approaching storm.

Let the police do the rest, she thought. She'd done her part. She just hoped Mrs. Walsh was safe and that they would be able to capture that bully. His threatening words lingered in her mind. She was terrified of any kind of violence. Why is it in life, she thought, that every perfect thing is marred by some irritation? Now that she'd found her idyllic place, it would be such a shame to have to move, but move she would if things started to get rough. Why do some people run rogue, ruining the status quo for the rest of us, she thought. Her thoughts turned to Javier and how he had lost control. That slap, in retrospect, was a sign of his own impotence in the light of a difficult situation. But he was not a violent man and part of her wished the old Javier, the one she had fallen in love with, was there with her. One cannot turn back the clock, she thought. Too much had happened for that.

# Chapter 19

She awoke to the sounds of mad chattering birds and peeked through her half-closed lids to see the glaring red alarm clock digits. A thumping headache made every movement painful, and she pulled the cover over her head. With a sudden jerk, she realised this was her first day of work, so she dragged her body out of the warm covers and headed straight for the shower. The warm water helped to clear her head, but she knew if she didn't zap the headache, it would dig its nasty claws in for hours, if not days. No time to contemplate what she would wear; she pulled on a pair of jeans and a teal boat-necked jumper. With a few deft strokes, she applied makeup to her pale cheeks, adding a glow of blusher and eye makeup. It wasn't a day for bright colours. Inexplicably, her good mood of the past few days had abandoned her. For the first time in ages, she felt a sense of alarm at what she'd done, giving up her comfortable life just to satisfy an urge for something new. She spoke to herself in the mirror. *So what. He lost his temper. Was it the end of the world?* She threw her mascara into her make-up bag. *You're such a fool, Roisin Delaney, and now you'd better make the best of it.*

She arrived at the shop at 8.50 a.m. Although it wasn't open yet for business, Maggie came out looking as if she'd just spent a day at a fashion shoot, making Roisin feel decidedly plain and unadventurous.

"Come on in. I couldn't wait for you to get here."

Maggie's welcoming words already made her feel better.

"Let's get us both a cup of coffee before we start in. I'm so glad you're starting, especially now." She stopped for a moment and exhaled a whiff of air. "I'm up to my eyes, don't know if I'm coming or going." Maggie marched off to the back room. Roisin followed. The headache tablet she had taken was beginning to work, but she still felt a mild thumping in her temples with every step. The workspace, in contrast to the first time she'd seen it, looked as if not one, but several bombs had hit it.

"I'm going to clear this table over here for you," Maggie said, pointing to a table with a view out onto the garden. She prepared the coffee machine. It soon began to make cheerful, spluttering sounds. Maggie continued showing Roisin where everything was. "Here are some templates for bags and hats."

Roisin tried to look as interested as possible. Despite the apparent chaos, everything was clearly catalogued.

"Over here I've got all the material we're working with right now. You can help yourself. Mix and match to your heart's desire."

"You mean you want me to design something myself ...now?"

"Yes, of course. You're now my number two designer!" She grinned. "No need to look so shocked; I have full faith in you. Three bags and one hat by the end of the week—do you think you can cut it? Sorry, that was a pathetic pun, wasn't it?" Her laughter was like bell chimes on a clear day. No sign of the frantic woman Darius had described. "I'm going out to the front for a bit to tidy up. Don't panic, just pretend you're sitting at home sewing. No pressure."

*What on earth did I get myself into here?* Roisin took a sheet of paper and sat looking at it, feeling like an imposter. She couldn't draw a straight line, never mind a bag. The headache threatened to come back full force, and the pressure behind her eyes was building up and making it harder to concentrate. She massaged her temples and began doing a rough sketch, but quickly crumpled up the paper and threw it in the bin. It took at least three attempts before she was half-way pleased with her efforts. She contemplated admitting it was a mistake and leaving, but that would have made no sense. *Pull yourself together. It's not such a big deal.* She closed her eyes and imagined the type of bag she herself would find useful. Her first bag would be a casual, over-the-shoulder college bag design. It would be robust with contrasting lining, not too light either. Beside the first sketch, she scribbled: *insert for mobile, make-up, purse, pens.* That shouldn't be too difficult. The secret was in choosing the right fabric. She'd seen some floral tapestry-type fabric in one of the boxes, robust but feminine. The lining would be plain, but she could repeat the floral material on the inserts.

Maggie returned and poured two cups of steaming coffee. "This should get us going for the day. Help yourself to coffee whenever you feel like it." She peered over Roisin's shoulder. "It's looking good. Come, I'll show you what I've been up to."

Roisin followed Maggie out to the store room. Maggie opened a cabinet and took down a neatly folded pile of hats from the top shelf. "Try a couple of these on."

Roisin posed in front of the mirror, trying one, then the other. "Did Darius tell you I was here yesterday with my sister and brother-in-law?"

"Yes, he did. I don't know where my head is at the moment." She adjusted Roisin's beret. "I believe you helped keep us afloat yesterday. You two will get along fine."

"Yes, I think we hit it off." Roisin tilted her head slightly to the side. "I like this one. Although it's hard to tell about the colour in this light. Do you think this shade of red suits me?" Without waiting for an answer, she continued. "Helen's husband had to practically drag her out. My sister is afraid I'll spend all my earnings here. I'm afraid she knows me too well."

Maggie rummaged through another drawer. She handed Roisin a hat in a lighter shade. "You don't need to worry about spending your earnings in the shop. If there's something you really like, I'm sure we'll come up with an arrangement that won't break the bank. That hat, for instance—why don't you keep it? It's good advertisement for us. The only thing I ask is that you wear it whenever possible."

Roisin stood in front of the mirror and nodded. It was a better choice. "It's very generous of you, Maggie, but I can't just take it." She wanted to make sure the balance didn't tip too much in one direction and that it was a fair give and take. But Maggie wouldn't take no for an answer. Roisin raised her hands in defeat. "Only if you promise to let me buy you lunch." Maggie reluctantly agreed.

Roisin immersed herself into the creative process. It didn't feel like work as they chatted with ease. While Maggie buzzed up a scarf on her high-speed, fancy sewing machine, Roisin told her about her concerns for Mrs. Walsh. She told her about her escapades of the previous night. Maggie stopped sewing, her hand up to her mouth in shock. When she described the fellow she'd seen, Maggie's face took on a solemn expression. She shoved her chair away from the sewing table and sat back with her arms folded.

"Tell me exactly what he looked like?"

"Mean, deep-set eyes hidden under almost invisible eyebrows, a soft ruddy face. Lips too fleshy and too red. Clear blue eyes and cropped sandy hair. Big around the shoulders, about six foot two. Oh yes, and he drives a black van. I'd say he was about mid-thirties."

Maggie nodded. "Forget the police. They won't or can't do anything about it. Remember the other day when I met you at the Bard's Den?"

Roisin nodded.

"I was on my own assignment that day. Following a fellow in the dealer ring. They're merely foot soldiers, I know, making money and benefiting from an international smuggling troupe who traffic drugs in from the Caribbean—heavy stuff. I'm not talking about weed which is a whole other scene. My ex had a big problem with drugs, cocaine and the like.

They nearly threw him over the edge." She paused for a moment and turned her attention to Roisin again. "I've been on a personal vendetta to do my part to stop them, and I think if I have some sort of evidence I might be able to have some impact. She sighed. "It's not right. They're preying on the weak and lining their own pockets, with no regard for all the lives they are ruining. Believe me when I say it's a waste of time trying to get the cops to do anything."

Roisin pinned the template to the fabric. "We live in a corrupt world. There's a huge elephant in the room and hardly anybody notices it. It's the same with the tax evaders. We miss one little thing on our tax forms, they're down on us like a group of heavies. Did you know that Al Capone was only imprisoned for tax evasion? All the killings, all the robberies. But no, it was tax evasion that got him in the end." She looked up, balancing a pin between her lips. "So what's with that? How can they get away with it? It doesn't make any sense. And I've never been able to accept that these people..." She almost spat the words out. "...They run free while an old man is charged a heavy fine for not paying his television license." She grimaced as she attempted to stick a pin through the strong fabric.

Maggie let out a slow whistle. "Wow, Roisin. What happened to you?"

"I detest injustice, that's all. Mind you, the police certainly seemed to take it seriously when they came to the house last night. I was impressed."

"Oh, they go through the motions all right. Personally I think they're scared, although there is some hope now. I heard there's a new international task force working on stamping out smuggling activities. Supposedly the dealers are using this island to gain access to the continent. It's hard to catch them. They know the loopholes and have the lawyers. Can you believe it," she said, as she snipped the thread with her scissors. "We only have two navy ships to guard the entire Irish coastline…and all those tiny islands. How easy it is for them to sneak in under the blanket of darkness. How could our police force ever hope to deal with that kind of operation on their own?"

Roisin couldn't believe what she was hearing. It was not something she'd ever given a thought to, but it made sense. Everything was changing, and this was a new problem Ireland had to cope with. If the police didn't have the appropriate back-up, they'd be fighting a much larger force than they could ever hope to deal with. She switched on the iron and sewed the interfacing onto one of the fabric pieces. "I know nothing about all of this," she said. But did you manage to get any evidence so far, photos or even witnesses?"

Maggie slid the garment from beneath the needle and held it up in front of her. "I did get a few photos, but can't get anyone to talk. The people involved know the names of the dealers but their hands seem to be tied. I'm pretty certain I know the fellow you described. Heed my warning. Keep out of his way. He is not a man to mess with. These people have completely sold out. They'd literally sell their grannies to get what they want."

A shiver snaked up Roisin's spine. She'd been thinking it was just a harmless incident, and had no idea of its magnitude. Despite the gravity of the situation, she couldn't help but see the irony of it too. Here she'd returned to the green isle, the mystical land of her birth, only to find she was involved, albeit not directly, in an international drug scam.

"So what happened last night anyway?" Maggie asked.

Roisin stopped what she was doing. "I was settling in for the evening when I heard a commotion going on outside. It must have been the wind that carried the voices over. I have no idea. Anyway, I suppose I'd been worried about the old woman next door, so my senses were heightened. Maybe it was a bit of the old telepathy, who knows. When I visited her a few days earlier, it was obvious she was afraid of something. I'd seen that fellow banging on her door that day. Maybe I should have stayed where I was. Believe me, the last thing I want is to get involved in any shady business. That's not what I came here for."

The door chimes tinkled. Maggie pulled a face. "Will you be alright? I have to go out front?"

Roisin nodded. So far, she'd cut out the puzzle pieces of the bag and reinforced the bottom part with interfacing. Now came the fun part. She pinned them together but wasn't happy with the overall effect. There was something missing. She went over to the pile of fabric, flipping through the layers until she found what she was looking for.

By lunchtime, she had made the basic bones of her first bag. All she had to do was attach the lining to the main body, turn it the right way round and tuck in and sew on the handles. Her shoulders were tense after all the concentration. She decided to grab a bottle of water and a deli sandwich at Jimmy Tyrell's and take a rejuvenating walk along the beach. Thankfully, her headache was almost gone.

There was a navy blue car with blackened windows on the opposite side of the street. She could make out a man's shape in the front and remembered seeing that car when she'd arrived in the morning. The thought struck her that she was beginning to get paranoid, but still her instincts told her something wasn't right and she made a note to herself to keep an eye out.

When she returned from the walk, her head was clear. Maggie gave her a rundown of prices and showed her how to use the cash register and do credit card payments.

"Are you sure you'll be able to manage things on your own?" Maggie asked her. "I have to run a few little jobs. You have my mobile number in case you have any problems."

The rest of the afternoon passed in a mad frenzy of sketching, cutting, pinning and sewing. A few customers sauntered in providing a welcome break from her creative work. She realised how easy it was to sell something you believed in. Wasn't that the secret in life, she thought. To be able to adapt to situations as they arise. If only Javier had been willing to take on another job, even if he had considered it to be beneath him, it could have saved their marriage. But of course life if never so cut and dry and it doesn't pay to be too smug about anything. For no sooner had she been applauding the ease with which she had slipped into her new role than a difficult customer made her regret having been so harsh to judge Javier.

A tall, well-dressed woman, with small eyes like flints and thin lips, entered the shop.

"Hello," Roisin said. "Can I help you?"

The woman didn't answer but strode over to Roisin and demanded to see her boss.

"I'm afraid she won't be back for a couple of hours. Perhaps I can help you?"

The woman rummaged in her bag and took out a paper bag. She made a great show of taking out a scarf and almost throwing it on the countertop. "This is just not on," she said. "Look at this." She took the scarf and shoved it under Roisin's nose. "See here," she said, pointing to a part where the stitching had come undone and the silk had frayed. I didn't pay sixty-five Euros for something that was supposed to be hand-made with extra care. If I'd wanted shoddy workmanship, I could've bought a ten-euro cheap import item."

The woman's anger did not, in Roisin's opinion, fit the so-called crime. She was also not in a position to give the woman the money back, if that's what she expected.

"I'm terribly sorry. Have you got the receipt?" Roisin said.

The woman rolled her eyes in exasperation. "I don't go around keeping every flippin' receipt."

Maggie had told her she would get the odd irate customer. She'd told her that some people impulse buy and regret it, that they come back, sometimes months later, and try to get their money back. "You wouldn't believe what people are capable of," Maggie had said. "Don't let them bully you."

Roisin was not good at dealing with this sort of situation. She felt her face redden at the anger directed her way. It was hard to be diplomatic, but she tried to keep her voice even. "Why don't you come back tomorrow morning and …"

The woman cut her short. "I will not come back tomorrow morning. Do you think I have nothing better to do?"

"I'm afraid I am not in a position to resolve this situation right now," Roisin said. "And without the receipt, it will be up to Ms. Cassidy to make a decision. I could offer to repair it, at no extra cost, of course. It won't take long at all."

The woman huffed and snatched the scarf from Roisin's trembling hands. "This is ridiculous." She stuffed the scarf inside her bag and almost spat out the words. "You'll be hearing from me," she said. "I'm sure Ms. Cassidy will not be pleased to…"

The door opened. It was Maggie, back early, much to Roisin's relief.

Maggie came inside and nodded to the woman. "Hello Carla. How are you today?"

The woman began to take out the scarf and bitterly repeated her complaints to Maggie, who without raising her voice, examined the item and said. "I don't understand what the problem is. This is not one of our items. There must be a mistake, surely."

Roisin watched with amazement as Maggie managed to take charge of the situation without losing her calm. Finally, the woman stuffed the scarf back into the bag, mumbled something and went away in a huff. When the woman had left, Maggie turned to

Roisin and said. "She's not right in the head, that one. Don't let her get to you."

"That was horrible. I don't think I'll ever be tough enough to deal with somebody like her." She pretended to fan herself. "I feel a swoon coming on." Although she tried to make light of the situation, she allowed herself the short luxury of imagining returning to her relatively simple life back in Spain. Suddenly it didn't seem so bad after all.

# Chapter 20

The next couple of weeks passed in a satisfying routine. She greatly enjoyed being creative again but found it necessary to break the tedium of concentrated indoor work with lots of outdoor activity. Maggie proved to be a great companion. She was funny, at times eccentric, but easy to work with. Roisin was kept so busy that she didn't have much time to dwell on Javier or Tom or to think about whether or not she had made the right decision, and that brief thought of returning to Spain was soon banished from her mind. The shop was accumulating an interesting set of accessories. Their styles, although completely different, complemented each other too.

Living alone was even better than she thought. She particularly enjoyed not having to cook or clean for anybody besides herself. Most evenings, she went for a long walk along the beach or across the fields near her house. A couple of times she noticed a dark blue car parked up on the road behind the stone wall. It made her uneasy but she brushed it off as paranoia, although once the car had taken off slowly, keeping pace with her steps, only to speed away when she had picked up the courage to turn back and look at it. It was impossible to see who the driver was from that distance. Besides, she told herself, there were many dark blue cars about.

The police had come by and taken her statement, but she hadn't heard anything more about the incident next door. She was surprised to see Mrs. Walsh waiting at her doorstep when she cycled up the driveway one day after work. She got off the bike and parked it against the front wall.

"Hello, Mrs. Walsh. I've been meaning to go out and see you this week."

The old woman smiled and handed her a package wrapped in a tea towel. It was still warm, and the unmistakable aroma of fresh bread reached her nostrils. She thanked her and invited her in for a cup of tea.

Mrs. Walsh's cheeks flushed slightly as she came inside. Roisin showed her into the living room and left her sitting on a comfortable armchair while she made the tea. When she returned, the old lady was still sitting as she had left her, with her hands held together on her lap. Her face was still slightly flushed, but she no longer wore such an anxious expression.

"I just wanted to apologise for what happened the other night," Mrs. Walsh said, in short breaths. "You see ... it's my grandson ... he was always a wild one, always in some sort of trouble. The funny thing is ... he's my favourite. I could never be annoyed with him." She kept brushing back a lock of hair and pushing it behind her ear. She continued. "Sometimes I blame myself for spoiling him."

Roisin handed her a cup of tea and sat down in the armchair opposite her. She didn't want to break the flow of conversation.

"He was never able to settle down, never good at school—not that he's stupid by any means. Then he started hanging out with the wrong crowd. He ended up in prison for a few years. After he was released he had even less chance of settling down to a proper job. Nobody would give him a chance." The old lady took a handkerchief from her skirt pocket and dabbed the corners of her pale blue eyes. "I'm sorry," she said. "It's just that I feel so bad about all this and I don't know what to do."

Roisin came over and put her arm around the old woman's shoulder, but Mrs. Walsh brushed her off, obviously embarrassed. Roisin sat back down again.

"He got involved with drugs." The woman's eyes welled up with tears again. "What's going on in the world?" She sighed. "Ireland is not the same place it used to be. I know we had problems…but it was never like this." She straightened her shoulders and continued. "It wasn't long before he was out of his depth." She put her hand on Roisin's arm. "Sean has a heart of gold. He wouldn't hurt a fly. Deep down he's afraid of life…I don't know why." She took another sip of tea. "Then he met a local girl and fell in love with her. He wanted to change his life and get off drugs. I pleaded with him to go somewhere else where nobody knew him, to move abroad if need be. It was his only chance…his girlfriend was even willing to go with him, but even that road was blocked…because he had a record."

Roisin nodded, encouraging the old lady to carry on.

"Those drug fellows found out about it. He knew too much, and they weren't prepared to let him go. He went into hiding—even I didn't know where he was. That's when they began harassing me. I've been so frightened. Before he disappeared for a while, Johnny pleaded with me not to go to the police. He said it would make things even worse for him. Then you came and walked into a hornet's nest. I didn't know what to do. That night when you called the police, Sean had come out of hiding—he wanted to see me. Don't ask me how they knew...someone must have informed them. So, when they came to the house, Sean insisted I hide out the back. He told me they were dangerous men and there was no saying what they would do. If you hadn't called the police that night, I have no idea what would have happened." She sighed, finally unlocking her fingers from their tight grip. For the moment, at least, they're leaving us in peace, but I fear it's not the end of it."

"So what happened to Sean? Did he manage to get away?"

"He wouldn't talk that night. The police had nothing to go on. They know all right—they're no fools—but without evidence they can do nothing." She giggled like a young girl. "I like to watch those crime shows on T.V. Do you know how hard it is to convict these people? Well anyway, that's neither here nor there. The thing is Sean badly wants to start a new life. I know he didn't always do the right thing but he's all I've got and he's very good to me. I don't want him to leave, but I want him to make something of himself. It's not too late." She took a sip of her tea. "All this talking is making my mouth dry. So where was I? I'm not going to be here forever but I want to know Sean is sorted out before I go. I'm sorry, but it breaks my heart." The old woman hid her face in her cupped hands and began to sob again. Roisin went over to her and put a hand on her shoulder.

"Come now. Nothing is ever as bad as it seems." She patted the old woman's arm, trying desperately to find the right words. "Let's try some of Jimmy Tyrell's berry gin. It's delicious and will take your mind off things."

The old lady wiped her tears. "I'm so sorry. I didn't mean to involve you in this mess."

"I know, I know. Hold on a sec. I'll be right back."

She returned with two liquor glasses of dark syrupy liquid. "This'll do the trick." The old lady gave her a weak smile.

"Several people have mentioned the drug problem here already," Roisin said. "Surely there's something that can be done about it. If I were you, I'd put it all behind me. They probably wouldn't dare to harass you again. I'll tell you what. I'll give you my number. If you ever want to talk, or if they bother you again, just call me, no matter what time it is." She went to her desk and scribbled down her mobile number. "I felt kind of bad for interfering, but it was obvious you were worried about something when I last went to visit you. That's why I called the police immediately. I'd seen that fellow hammering on your door that day. Do you know what his name is?"

The old lady, relaxed by the warming drink, sat back on the couch. "His name is Bill Butler. I think he's from Cork or thereabouts."

"Do the police know his name?"

"I'm not sure. They don't tell you anything. But, they were very kind when they came that night.

After you left, Sean had to prove to the police that he was protecting me so he showed them where I was hiding. The hardest part was not being able to tell them anything. I wouldn't have been afraid for myself, but I didn't want things to get worse for my boy."

"Well, you don't worry about a thing. Everything will work out—you'll see. Maybe Sean won't have to go away after all."

\*

The next morning, Roisin told Maggie of the newest development. "There must be something we can do, Maggie, to break this cycle of crime. I'm going to pop into the police station and talk to that Garda, Sergeant Houlihan, the one that came out to the house. Now that I have a name, they might be able to hold him for something."

"I don't know—believe me, I'd give anything to put a stop to their racket, but I think it's far too big for us. Sure, we haven't got a clue where to start. Besides, the police need evidence. Without that, we haven't got a leg to stand on."

"Maybe they can put Sean under police protection."

"I doubt it, Maggie said. "Anyway, enough trying to save the world. We'd better get these scarves made. That exhibition is looming and still lots to do."

Maggie sorted through a pile of colourful brocades, velvets and silks. She chose a midnight blue velvet fabric and tried out various combinations with the silk, trying to get the right look. "What do you think?" she said. "How about if I create a lattice effect on one of the edges and reverse the effect on the back side?"

They sat together, sketching, planning and cutting.

"Why don't you come with me to the show in Dublin next month?"

Roisin dropped what she was doing. "I would absolutely love it." Thanks Maggie. "It'll be great to be there and see all of our efforts culminate in the exhibition. I think we've got a great collection so far. Why don't we take some photos and create a brochure which we can hand out on the day?"

"We'll have to do it ourselves though," Maggie said. "Getting a professional photographer isn't in the budget right now."

\*

The next few weeks passed by in a mad flurry as they continued working on their collection for the show. Roisin was so tired at night she didn't even have the energy to go for her long walks on the beach. She had seen Mrs. Walsh a couple of times. The woman seemed much more relaxed but didn't mention her nephew. Nor had Roisin seen any sign of the rougher elements of Lissadore. Perhaps, with any luck they had moved elsewhere, or they were keeping a low profile.

\*

The day before the house-warming party, both women, relieved to have met their deadlines, sipped sparkling wine. "I'm getting nervous about the party tomorrow. There's so much to do, and I'll be seeing *him* again," Roisin said.

"Who's *him*?"

*"Him* is a fellow I met the day after I arrived

in Knockadreen."

"What! And you never even mentioned him before. You're the secretive one."

"When did I even have time to think of anything else?" Roisin took in the cluttered studio in one sweeping gesture, almost spilling her drink. "My life has been upside down ever since I've arrived here. Besides, I'm still married, remember. I don't want to complicate things even more. Maybe I deliberately put him out of my mind. To make things even more complicated, Javier informed me that he's coming soon. So everything is happening at once."

Maggie raised her hands. "Okay, okay. I won't pry any more. You tell me when you're ready. I must admit though—I'm looking forward to seeing the mystery man at the party."

"Yes. Talking about party, I hate to be a burden but do you think you could give me a hand to get the food and drinks? I'll have a hard time getting it all with the bike."

"Of course. I was going to offer anyway but it slipped my mind."

As she tidied up her workplace, Roisin's mind wandered again to Tom. She had two of the guest rooms set up to accommodate her family and wondered what arrangements he had made for his extended stay. It wouldn't be appropriate for him to stay in her house.

\*

Later, the two women packed the groceries into the boot of the car. They were still flushed and silly from the effects of the sparkling wine and the thrill of being so close to reaching their deadline.

When she got home, Roisin kicked off her shoes and began putting everything in its place. She sat at the kitchen table and began writing her plan of action, along with a list of the foods she wanted to prepare. Three salmon and egg pastries—they could be eaten cold—sausage rolls and mini quiches. She had a great recipe for guacamole and salsa which could be used as dips for the tortillas. She'd also make about four different salads and two chocolate cakes for afterwards, in addition to her special fruit salad for dessert. She changed into comfortable clothes and prepared the cakes and the sausage rolls. While waiting for the sausage rolls to bake, she began totting up her expenditures since she'd arrived. She'd be getting paid soon, but she began to panic when she realised how quickly her funds were dwindling. She opened the window to let in the cool evening air. There was no immediate threat, but she'd have to be extremely careful from now on. No time to think about all of that now. She looked around the kitchen. What a mess!

By the time she had finished cleaning, it was ten o'clock. She yawned and made her way up to bed. But she couldn't sleep. She tossed and turned, folded her pillow, flattened it out again. What was she doing inviting Tom to her housewarming party? She turned on her back. Her heart began galloping at the thoughts of seeing him. She willed herself to slow it down. He's just a friend, she convinced herself. She wasn't doing anything wrong. Her thoughts turned to her new job. Things had worked out pretty well after all. Finally, adopting the mode of chief psychologist, she convinced herself that all was well. She remembered her purpose, her reasons for leaving, and it was natural to go through periods of doubt. She drifted off to sleep thinking that even though she probably shouldn't have left the way she had, she had done the right thing.

# Chapter 21

Helen and Todd were first to arrive the next day. Helen had said she would help with last-minute jobs but there wasn't much left to do.

"Well, you don't look any worse for wear," Helen said. "Come on, have a drink and relax before the mob shows up." She sipped her gin and tonic. Todd, with a Guinness in his hand, was busy munching on a sausage roll when the doorbell rang.

"Showtime, Roisin said and placed her drink on the table. "Here, watch this for me, will you."

It was the imposing figure of Blessing. Roisin had met Blessing in the supermarket when she'd first arrived. Blessing had been searching for a special type of sauce in the foreign foods section. She'd begun speaking to Roisin, who had been looking for Rebujito, a red wine mixed with lemonade and flavoured with mint. The conversation flowed as they both spoke of things they missed. They had agreed to meet for a coffee sometime, but had never got around to it, and so Roisin had invited Blessing to her party. Roisin was delighted to see Blessing arrive in her African traditional dress. Blessing's cropped curls were concealed in a vivid blue and white head wrap. Her voluminous body was wrapped in a long matching tunic dress, and her finely chiseled face looked like a mahogany carving. Broad cheeks supported heavily-made up eyes, giving her an overall dramatic effect. She carried a wicker basket covered with shimmery fabric and it perfected the exotic look. With a gleaming smile, which showed her perfectly strong and even teeth, she grabbed Roisin by the shoulders and gave her a warm hug. 'Here, this is for you, dear,' she said as she handed her an ebony figurine from the basket.

Roisin moved in toward the light of the hallway and held the figure in front of her. It was a beautiful, curvaceous African beauty holding a golden disk up to the sky. "I love it! Thank you very much." Roisin ushered her into the kitchen first. She kissed the figurine. "I'm going to put this in a special place," she said.

"Her name is Muhbati. She's one of the seven daughters of the sun. To receive one of these is considered good luck." Blessing handed over a ceramic bowl with an aromatic rice dish. Roisin barely had time to thank her again before the doorbell rang.

"Don't worry about me, dear," Blessing said. "I'll mingle."

Roisin's heart did a funny little galloping movement as she recognized Tom's car. She felt like a grinning idiot waiting for him to step out.

Before she had time to figure out what to do or how to react, he was standing in front of her. He handed her a little package and with one swift movement planted a kiss on her cheek. She could feel the warmth of his strong hands as they walked back toward the house. She was thankful he couldn't see her blushing in the semi-darkness. *Oh, get a grip. Help, I don't know how to do this anymore. I feel as if I'm losing my silly mind in the power of his presence.* Her hand fit so perfectly into his. She pulled herself together, something she was good at doing.

"I'm so glad you could come, Tom. Come on in. You're one of the first to arrive. Maybe that's not a bad thing. You don't want to be overwhelmed by too many inquisitive minds, if you know what I mean?"

"Don't worry. I can handle it," he murmured as they entered the house.

She needn't have worried after all. Helen and Todd were the height of discretion. Apart from the odd wink in his direction when he wasn't looking, Helen was friendly without being in any way obtrusive. The lively music was perfect for the mood and, with everyone settled in with drinks, she left them chatting as she went to answer the next doorbell's call.

Later, when everyone had settled in and busy getting to know each other, mostly in little groups, she went outside for a breath of fresh air. She heard the buzz of conversation and Blessing's deep rolling laughter echoing from within. All she could think about was Tom. She went around to the side of the house and stared up at the evening sky which looked like an indigo net holding a treasure of stars. He came up behind her. "How have you been, Roisin?"

She swung around to face him. "Oh…finding my feet, I suppose. It's even better than I thought. People are so kind."

"It's so nice to see you again," he said. He

moved closer and kissed her. This time she surrendered to his soft but determined lips.

Perfect timing, she thought as she heard someone rummaging behind her.

"Hmmn. Oops. I'm sorry…is that you, Roisin? I'm looking for some more tonic water." It was her sister-in-law, Pauline. Roisin knew her well enough to know that she was probably mortified.

She squeezed Tom's hand before turning to Pauline. "Sure, I've got plenty of everything. The drinks are outside the kitchen door. Help yourself." The cat's out of the bag now, she thought, and maybe it was for the better.

They went back inside. She looked around the room and felt a sense of satisfaction with how her life was going. Her body still felt the warmth of Tom's embrace, and she was sure her face reflected the happiness she felt. Why on earth did she wait so long to make this move?

Jimmy Tyrell had brought a selection of delicious snacks from the shop, dates filled with cream cheese, spicy wasabi nuts, stuffed vine leaves and a selection of cream cheeses. Someone suggested playing Charades. The reaction was mixed, but the reluctant players stood no chance against the enthusiasm of the majority. It turned out to be a great idea for breaking down any remaining barriers. Nobody stood a chance of evasion, and everyone got their fair share of teasing. Tom took the easy route and chose Dracula. When Roisin's turn came, she deliberately challenged herself, doing her best to mime War and Peace. She felt like a fool as she attempted to portray someone on a battlefield, shooting wildly about her. Then the contrast of the symbolic dove flying away. Wild guesses arose from the group, mixed with lots of laughter. Everything from Hitchcock's *The Birds* to *One Flew over the Cuckoo's Nest* was thrown open for suggestion. The more bizarre the theme, the more fun they had guessing, and the jokes were flying. Maggie and Helen seemed to have struck up a friendship. Jimmy Tyrell threw himself into the game, and himself and Blessing joined forces too. Any awkward moments were thus hidden in jovial activity. She tried to avoid direct eye contact with Tom but found herself constantly gravitating toward him. She had to remind herself to stay back.

When everything had quietened down after the game, Blessing produced a CD of African music from her basket. She inserted it in the player and proceeded to shake and sway her powerful body in time to the rhythmic music. She grabbed poor Tom's arm and threw her arms around his neck as she gyrated with unabashed rhythm. He looked mortified but quickly recovered as he began to get a feel for the music. Roisin winked over at Maggie who immediately took up the cue. Both of them shimmied over to shake their bodies beside the dancing pair. Even those reluctant to dance couldn't resist tapping their feet or swaying their shoulders to the lively music.

Tom came over to Roisin and raised his eyes to heaven in a good-natured fashion. Blessing was absolutely in her element. She was born to dance, Roisin thought, as she watched her. Her body responded to every drum beat as she threw back her head and closed her eyes, fully immersed in the rhythm. Roisin had always felt a connection to African and South American music and it was a delight to watch Blessing celebrate it.

Afterwards, when the music stopped, she clapped Blessing on the back. "That was brilliant. Why don't you start up an African dance class? I'd be the first one to join up?"

"Oh no, my friend. I don't have time for such frivolity." Blessing boomed out her powerful laugh again and it was as uninhibited as her dance style. "Have you any idea how many hours I work every week?"

"Yes, but you were born to dance. When else do you get the chance?"

In her inimitable deep African-English accent, she said, "Anyway, do you seriously think I could encourage a bunch of Irish people to throw themselves with abandon into my cultural arena?"

Roisin's face betrayed her hurt. "Yes, I do actually. Despite what you may think, Irish people have great rhythm ..."

"Oh, dear. I didn't mean you. You've got it, honey. Where did you learn to dance?"

"Too late, Blessing. Forget your flattery. Actually, I was a real disco queen back in the days. It's the only sport form I really enjoy, besides swimming. Hey, don't laugh. Dancing *is* a sport; at least it gets the heart beating and revs up the motor."

Blessing's laughter was infectious. She looked at Roisin with one raised eyebrow. "What if I did consider it? Would you be able to round up a group of interested people and find a venue? I don't have the time or inclination for any of that. And it will have to be on Saturdays. I really don't have any time during the week."

"I can probably think of at least five people who would be willing to join at the drop of a hat," she said, as she looked around the room. "Let's see what I can do."

After most of the others had left, Helen and Todd settled down with a cup of coffee in the living room as Roisin was clearing up in the kitchen. As she stacked the dishes in the dishwasher, Tom came in.

"I think I'll be heading off now, Roisin. It's been a long day, but great fun. Where did you find that wonderful African woman? She's something else."

"Just someone I met when I arrived here. I knew she'd be good fun. Besides, although she deals with lots of people every day, I think she's a bit isolated. You'd never think she was a doctor, would you?"

"A doctor of what? You've got to be kidding me."

She closed the door of the dishwasher and flicked on the switch. "No, I'm not. She's a medical doctor and has a very busy practice. By the way, why don't you come by for breakfast tomorrow? Helen and Todd are leaving early. We can spend the day together and if the weather is nice we can pack a picnic and head off somewhere."

He came over to her and put his arms around her shoulders, looking into her eyes. She felt his warm breath on her face. "Now that sounds like a plan. You must be a mind reader because I was thinking along those lines myself—well, not the picnic part. Haven't done that since I was a lad."

She reached up and kissed him gently on the lips. "Pity you have to go so early," she whispered.

"Don't tempt me, Roisin. There's nothing I'd like better, but you'd better get back to your guests."

She nibbled on her lower lip. "I know. I really should, shouldn't I?" She hesitated, not wanting to let him go and fully aware that she was sending mixed messages, but she suddenly wanted to throw caution to the wind. The wine and good company had loosened her reserve.

They kissed again and he pulled her closer, cupping her buttocks with his hands. She giggled and gently removed them. "Not so fast, Mr!" She didn't even mind the stubble of his chin brushing against her skin. His arms felt warm and protective, and she sank into his embrace. The sound of Helen's voice made her pull away abruptly.

"Come on, Roisin. What are you doing in there?" She could hear Todd chuckling.

"Yeh, yeh. I'm coming," she laughed. "See what I mean? It's too awkward with family," she whispered to Tom. "Bet I'll be bombarded with questions."

He came into the living room with her and said his goodbyes. Then she walked him to the door and stood on her tiptoes to kiss him once more.

"See you tomorrow then," he whispered in her ear before gently nibbling on her earlobe. Shivers of excitement ran up her spine. One last kiss on her forehead before he squeezed her hand and left. A smile played on her lips as she stood there for a few moments, rubbing her ear and watching his silhouette as he walked down the lane.

When she went back inside and saw Helen grinning from ear to ear. Roisin put her hand out, palm toward her sister. "No questions," she laughed.

"Ah, you're no fun, Roisin. He's staying on for a while, isn't he? What'll you do if Javier shows up tomorrow? He didn't say exactly when he was coming, did he?"

"Well, he knows he doesn't own me. He'll have to deal with it. Besides, that would be a bit too coincidental, don't you think? Fate couldn't be so cruel, could it?"

"You like him a lot, don't you?" Helen asked.

"Yep. I do, but you know what they say…if you want to know me, come and live with me. That's the real test. Anyway, you're asking too many questions."

"Okay, okay. You win. I must say though, Roisin, you're really blooming. I think this is doing you good; maybe it's the sea air." She winked at Todd. "Ah, come on, Helen," he chided her. "Don't give your sister such a hard time."

Roisin yawned. "Sorry, I'm exhausted. I've been so busy helping Maggie out in the shop. It's been great for taking my mind off things." She turned her attention to Helen. "Thanks for prompting me to finally make the move. I shouldn't have waited so long…" She sighed. "Still, I do feel guilty about Javier, I really do." Even as she said it, she knew it wasn't quite true. Why did she have to feel guilty? Was that a part of her Catholic upbringing? Did he deserve it? Roisin thought back to how she had felt, constantly trying to cheer him up, to pander to his moods and negativity. No, things would not change. Javier would always be part of her life, but she didn't feel emotionally connected to him anymore, nor did she feel responsible for him or his feelings. Yes, she was concerned about him, but she didn't like the idea of him following her there. "I can't write him out of my life with one swift stroke," she said. "Do you think I'm awful for flirting with Tom?"

No answer. Todd got up. "I'm going to have a smoke," he said.

Helen said to him. "Can't you answer her question?"

He shook his head. "I'm staying out of it." With that, he left the room.

Helen poured herself another glass of wine. "Since you asked, I'm going to tell you." She took a gulp of her wine and Roisin wanted to flee, fearing what was to come. She needn't have worried. Helen continued. "I know things haven't been easy between you and you weren't happy, but you're moving too fast. It doesn't look good."

Roisin took a deep breath. "Firstly, Tom is a friend and I'm getting to know him. Secondly, I've been loyal to Javier since I've known him." She felt her face flushing and waved dismissively in the air. "I didn't ask to meet Tom, but these things happen. He's a special man, Helen. Besides, I don't want to have to answer to anyone. No guilt, no excuses. I'm getting my life together and I have no idea how this will all end." She smiled and stifled a yawn. "Anyway, I'm too tired to discuss this right now. I'm off to bed."

Todd came back inside, rubbing his hands together. "There's a right nip in the air."
Helen yawned and stood up. "I think I'll hit the sack too. What about you, Todd?"
"If we want to be up early tomorrow, we'd better get some shut-eye."
Before Roisin went up to bed, she did what she'd been looking forward to doing all evening. She retrieved Tom's present, which she'd put on a shelf in the living room, and made herself comfortable. She took her time releasing the ribbons and removing the paper and folding it with care. It was a beautifully-crafted fountain pen and a blank hardcover notebook. The book cover was decorated with Celtic designs in embossed gold. He had written a few lines on the inside cover. *A pen, a tool with which to write cannot work magic. But let the words spring from the heart, for therein lies their beauty and their honesty. Roisin, I wish you all the very best. A new page, a fresh start! Tom xx*

She read over his words once more, tracing them with her finger. The pen in dark green enamel was inscribed with her initials and also decorated with a matching ornamental Celtic twirl. She would guard and treasure it.

# Chapter 22

The next morning, while they were sitting down to breakfast, Tom's car pulled up. Todd was sorting out his camera equipment for their excursion. He wanted to take a boat out to one of the islands and get some photos of the seals lazing on the slabs of rock. Roisin already had a picnic basket prepared for herself and one for Helen and Todd. When the doorbell rang, she met Helen's eyes. "Please, no smart comments. This is awkward for me, and maybe even more so for him."

Helen raised her hands, palms outstretched and laughed. "I promise. I'll do you proud. Anyway, we'll leave you to it. Just let me finish my coffee."

Roisin went to open the door and came in a few minutes later with Tom who looked like an urban gentleman in his smart jacket, blue jeans and tan leather boots. She admired the ease with which he dealt with people as he greeted the others. He had the right amount of respect, and his easy-going nature made people feel comfortable in his presence.

Roisin poured him a cup of coffee and excused herself while she went upstairs to get ready. Todd was showing him some of the photos he had taken, and she heard them discussing photo techniques as she went upstairs. Helen followed her up.

"He looks gorgeous, your mister handsome. I'm really happy for you, Roisin," she whispered as they approached the landing. "You should see the glint in your eyes."

"Cross your fingers that today goes well. He's staying here tonight."

"Have a couple glasses of wine and you'll be fine."

A blush crept up to Roisin's cheeks. "I'll call you tomorrow or the day after." You got me wondering though. What if Javier does show up? How am I going to deal with the situation? He sounded pretty desperate…and lonely."

"Just take it a day at a time. Try not to think too much," Helen said before going upstairs."

\*

Within an hour, they were driving through the countryside. Pink Floyd's *Wish You Were Here* was blasting out of the car speakers. She felt as if the world was the most perfect place. It was the kind of day that would lift anyone's spirits. The clearest blue sky hung like a blanket of finest voile over the landscape. It seemed to go on for infinity. A few solitary seagulls sailed the light breeze, as if they were enjoying their playground in the sky. It was easy to feel relaxed in his presence, and she chattered on about the upcoming exhibition and how Maggie had asked her to come to Dublin to accompany her to the show. "Sorry, I'm such a chatterbox this morning. It used to get on Javier's nerves at times."

"I enjoy listening to you. Can't imagine how anyone could find you irritating."

She turned to him. "Tell me, what have you been up to? Any new writing?"

"Yes. I've been messing around with some new song lyrics. Remember my friend the musician? He asked me to write some lyrics to a few new pieces he's written. I'm always my own worst critic, but if I may say so myself, they're not half bad."

"You don't happen to have a recorded sample, do you?"

"Well, as it so happens…." With one hand on the steering wheel, he retrieved a disc from the compartment under the dashboard. "Here it goes…"

She leaned back with her eyes closed and soaked in the sound of the classical string guitar intro which was followed by the husky voice of Tom's friend singing of lost love and yearning. She hummed along. The combination of lyrics and melody struck a chord in her heart and, before she could stop herself, her eyes had welled up with tears. Tom looked over at her. "That bad, is it?"

"Sorry," she sniffed. "I'm a sucker for sad songs. What is it about music that gets right under the skin? Need I say more? I love it."

He tried not to show his pleasure, but his eyes gave him away. "We never thought of joining forces before, but I have a good feeling about this. Talked him into booking a space at a local recording studio next month."

"That's fantastic. Look, if Elton and Bernie Taupin can do it, why can't you?" She listened carefully as Tom began talking about his life. Little by little, she was discovering more about him. He was definitely romantic; he had good friends, which spoke for him too. He was a poet; a deep thinker. So where were his faults? She could have kicked herself for looking for the proverbial hair in the soup. So what if he had some faults? It wasn't as if she herself was without any.

"Oh, my God! How rude of me," Roisin's alarmed voice cut through the momentary silence.

"What's wrong?" Tom kept his hands solidly on the steering wheel as he glanced over at her.

"I completely forgot to thank you for your gorgeous present. Honestly, I am so thrilled with it." She rummaged through her bag and took out the little book. "Thanks so very much. I absolutely love it. How did you know I love pens and writing? And your inscription is so inspiring."

The fine crow's feet around his eyes became more pronounced as his eyes twinkled with pleasure. They were heading toward the famous Cliffs of Moher, just about forty miles outside Lissadore. The road was narrow and, as Tom carefully took a corner, a car came speeding toward them. Roisin sat up with a jolt when she saw the driver's face. She didn't know if she was seeing ghosts. Was that really Javier who had sped by in a black Golf. No, it couldn't be, she thought, dismissing it as a figment of her imagination. Nevertheless, her heart was beating from the shock.

Tom slowed down. "Some people seem to think they're Formula 1 race drivers. I need to get used to these sharp curves."

Roisin chewed on her lower lip. Should she

tell him? No, if she did it would ruin the mood and would not serve any useful purpose. Her mind raced to and fro. Tom, oblivious, turned on the radio and drove on in silence. Javier hadn't specified when he was going to arrive. Of course it could just as easily be today? This would change everything. She pictured the scene if she arrived back tonight with Tom. It would cause all sorts of unnecessary aggravation for all three of them. What to do? There was no other way to deal with it than to tell him, but she decided to wait until they were on the way home.

They decided to avoid the cliffs. Majestic as they were, both of them had seen them umpteen times before. Besides, they suspected they would be teeming with tourists. Later, as they cruised along the coast road, they had a clear view of the full expanse of water and sky. It was one of those perfect days which threw a brilliant light onto the sea and made it look as if it was dotted with diamonds. Dapples of light danced on the water's ripples, and over on the horizon the lavender outline of misty peaks jutted towards the clear, blue sky. "Let's stop off here," Roisin said. She felt a headache coming on and rummaged around in her bag for her sunglasses. They served two purposes, blocking out the light and concealing the worry she knew was evident in her eyes.

He pulled in smoothly onto the next lay-by and turned off the ignition. They both got out. Roisin scanned the area, looking for a shaded picnic spot. "Let's move the old limbs a bit," Tom said. He stretched and she caught a flash of his trim waistline. They started to walk, and she removed her shoes and socks, enjoying the sensation as her feet sank into the slightly damp surface. She was aware that her silence was a total contrast to the loquaciousness she'd displayed earlier on, but she couldn't force herself to change that. About half a mile ahead they reached a secluded cove. She was locked in her tangled thoughts.

Desperate to distract herself from unwanted thoughts, she threw her bag down onto a flat rock. She looked out onto the water, linking her arm in Tom's. "Let's catch some sun," she said. The sandy cove was protected on three sides by walls of jagged rock. There was enough shade to guard them from the full blast of the sun. "I know it's probably madness,' she said, "but I'm going in for a dip. If I think about it too much I'll change my mind."

Tom's mouth fell open. "You're not serious! Nobody goes swimming in this weather."

"Well, I do." She was already removing her jumper. "Besides, what about all the Christmas swimmers…or the people who swim the channel? I'm going in, and you're not to peek."

"Spoil sport," he said, groaning, as he turned his back on her. Quick as a flash, she had stripped down to her underwear. She placed her clothing in a neat pile on a nearby stone. "Don't turn around until I give you the all clear," she shouted as she ran toward the water, yelping with glee as she hit the freezing Atlantic. The initial shock almost made her heart stop but she was soon up to her armpits in water and began swimming to get the blood flowing. She turned around to give him the okay and laughed when she saw him still obediently looking the other way. "You can turn around now," she shouted.

He turned around, shaking his head in disbelief. "Come on in," she shouted. "It's getting warmer already." He mustn't have heard her. She floated on her back and turned her head slightly to watch him saunter over to the nearest boulder. He propped himself upon it, chin in hand, looking very much like a Rodin sculpture. She wished she could sketch him but she would try to do it later from memory. Her body was becoming deliciously warm and tingling.

She hadn't thought about the practicalities of how she was going to get all the water off her body but it didn't matter. Should she tell Tom to turn his back again or would that be silly? The reality of her impetuousness struck her as funny. She flapped around to warm up, then glided through the water, flipping over on her back and lazily following the movements of the clouds.

She glanced over to see if he was still in his thinker pose. He was not there. Perfect. Trying to look as graceful as she could, she swam inward to the shallow water and half stumbled over the slippery stones as she headed for the cove. She saw him then in the distance sauntering back from the car, and admired his calm air and the way he held himself, as if he knew his place in the world. Shaking herself to get rid of most of the water, she plonked down in the warm sand as he approached her, carrying the basket of goodies. "I thought this might come in handy," he said as he handed her a roll of kitchen paper. She peered up lazily through the bright sunshine and grinned at him, taking the paper with outstretched hand.

"Practical as well," she said. "I forgot I'd packed that." She sat up, hugging her knees to her chest.

Tom discreetly busied himself with the picnic things while she removed her wet undergarments, soaking up as much of the water as she could and toweled herself dry. She pulled on her jeans and jumper and shook her hair dry, tying it with a scarf. "Oh, that felt so good!" She poured herself a cup of tea from the flask and began peeling a boiled egg. I'm ravenous. Swimming always does this to me."

"I was tempted to join you in there, but you looked like you were having such a good time all by yourself."

"You should have, Tom," she said, now munching on the apple so he wouldn't see her smiling.

After they'd cleared away the remnants of their little feast, Roisin sat on a flat-topped boulder. A crease formed on her forehead as she remembered the car swerving past on their way there. She had managed to convince herself that it was not Javier, but now she wasn't too sure. She almost jumped as Tom surprised her by coming up behind her and massaging her shoulders. She raised her arms up behind her to clasp them around his neck as she surrendered to his warm touch. He tickled the inside of her neck with light kisses, and they slipped down onto the damp sand. She didn't need the wine after all. She removed his shirt and snuggling into his chest, slowly running her hands up and down his torso. "Listen to that," she said, as she turned to look at the sky. "I think there's a storm coming." He took her face in his hands and pulled her toward him, kissing her with urgency. "Never mind the storm," he said. She tried to ignore the sound of the howling wind, although it added a sense of urgency to their love making. But it was no good. She disentangled herself from him. "I'm sorry, Tom. I can't do this."

He groaned. "Ah, Roisin. You're driving me mad. What's the problem now?"

"I just can't. Please don't ask me." She reached out to catch her jumper. The wind was that strong. She sneaked a sideways glance at Tom. His jaw was set firmly, and his eyes were like flint.

"I'm really sorry, Tom, but I think we'd better be going.

He reached for his shirt, grabbed his shoes and leaned against the boulder to put them on. The only sound of protest came from the howling wind. She shivered, not just because of the sudden drop in temperature.

She must tell him about Javier before they reached home, but how? She went over to him and tried to put her arms around him. He took her hands firmly, and pushed them away.

She hesitated a moment, aware that what she was about to say was probably neither wise nor was the timing right, but she had to tell him. "There's something I have to tell you, Tom."

He brushed the sand from his clothes. "Go ahead."

"I think my husband might be here. There's a possibility he might show up tonight."

He almost lost his balance. "What! You tell

me now."

"Well...I wasn't sure. He said he might be coming soon, but I never expected him to show up now. Remember the car that sped towards us on the curve as we drove here?"

Tom glared at her. "That was him?"

"I told you, I don't know. He drove by so fast...but it looked like him." She beat the flat of her palm against her forehead. "Stupid, stupid. Why did I have to tell you now?"

"Very, very bad timing. Fool that I am. Well, it looks as if you've got all the cards in your hands, Roisin. I can't pretend I'm happy about this."

"Neither am I." She sighed. "Do you understand now?"

"So, do you still love him?" His voice could have cut through steel.

She suddenly felt afraid and her voice sounded hysterical. "Love! That's a big word." She paused and took a deep breath. This time she spoke in a measured and slow voice. "It depends on how you define love. I suppose I do, in a way. Being away from him has taught me that. But I'm not in love with him. I think I'm in love with you." She laughed nervously. "I never thought I'd find myself in a love triangle before. Look, I have to make light of this otherwise it will do my head in."

"Hey, don't rush things here." His admonishing tone startled her.

She continued, almost in a whisper, as if she didn't hear him. "I did tell you I was married. You know I didn't deliberately orchestrate this, Tom. Come on. Don't make it harder than it is."

His jaw line moved in micro-contractions, and it was impossible not to notice the flicker of anger in his eyes. "Oh, no," he said, shaking his head. "I run a mile from situations like this. Too tricky." He clicked his tongue in exasperation. "I'm going back tonight. You really should have told me before, Roisin. I suppose I should have known there would be complications. That's the last thing I want, or need. You've got to make up your mind here. As I said, you've got the ace. Don't play around with me."

Now she was angry and frustrated with herself. Why did she seem incapable of getting things right? In her attempt to straighten things out, she had complicated them even more. "Play with you! Of course I would never do that. Tom, didn't you hear me? I said I'm in love with you. Have you any idea how precious those words are? These are not words I throw around lightly. How could you even think something like that of me?" In a rage, she packed the picnic things and stormed off toward the car. He followed. Almost at the car, she turned around to face him. "For all I know, you could have a bevy of women back in Knockadreen. We don't own each other, Tom." The sound of his laughter made her turn around. She challenged him. "What's so funny?"

"If a thunderbolt had a face, I know what it would look like," he shouted after her. "You should have seen yourself storming off, bottom wiggling. It just struck me as funny."

She turned on her heels again and kept on walking. He sprinted up behind her and caught up with her. She turned around to face him, fury still in her eyes. He put his arm around her. "Come on,

Roisin, let's not ruin the rest of the day. I want to show you something. It's not too far away and it might do us both good."

She was still pouting as she packed the stuff in the car and sat inside. She hated being misunderstood and wrongly accused. Her head tilted slightly, chin pointing upward. It had been a long time since she'd been so angry. She knew he didn't deserve it but she couldn't help herself. He was merely a catalyst for her pent up emotions and her inability to know what to do about the situation. She wanted to do the right thing and to be fair to both of them. Clearly, Javier could not see her with Tom. It would be far too painful for him. At least she was relieved she had pulled back from him earlier. She was not a loose woman, although she had been tempted. And after all that, the storm had blown over. Although it was still windy, a patch of blue sky showed up above.

Tom reached over with his free hand and rubbed her shoulder. "Are you ready for take-off?

Her anger, too, began to dissipate, but only slightly. It had been such a beautiful day and she didn't want it to end on a bad note. She turned her face away from him. "Sure. Let's go then." He started the car and switched on the radio. A catchy tune caught her involuntarily tapping to the music.

They continued in silence. She wondered where he was going to take her. Golden gorse bushes added a brilliant contrast to the rich green fields, but she couldn't really enjoy the scene. The landscape changed to hilly terrain, adding to the mystery factor. And everywhere the typical little stone walls flashed in front of her eyes.

Tom looked over at her. "All I ask is for honestly. You should have told me back in the car, Roisin."

"I know," she mumbled. "And what would we have done? Turned around again?"

"Probably," he said.

"Yes, but I still think you overreacted?" she said, continuing to stare out at the landscape. "I was honest. What I don't need is someone lording it over me and bossing me about. I've had enough of that."

More silence.

He took a gravel road off to the right and followed it for about a half a mile. Within minutes, they'd reached their destination. He pulled over to the side in front of a field that was partially hidden by hedgerows.

"This is your surprise?" she asked, still mulling over their argument. "I don't see anything but fields and more fields."

She followed him over a stile, pulling the brambles to clear the way for her. He marched ahead like a man on a mission. She trudged through, catching up with him, avoiding the cow dung and trying not to step on the primroses. A small forested area lay ahead. The mystery must be obviously concealed behind the trees. They walked in silence and she fell into step with him, keeping her eyes on the ground. If she had only worn more sensible shoes. The ground was uneven with pebbles and small clumps of earth interspersed. The scent of fresh grass, moss and other spring vegetation mixed with the ever-present tang of seaweed as they walked through an archway of trees onto a clearing.

He stopped and put his arm around her. "Remember before you left I told you I sometimes come out to this area?"

She nodded, avoiding his eyes.

There was a moss-covered headstone off to the right, almost concealed by a clump of trees. He took her hand and guided her over to the headstone. "This is where I come to tank up energy," he said. My grandfather came from these parts, and I spent many summer days here in my youth. He was the one who showed me this place. It's the burial place of one Ireland's greatest and least-known poets, Mol O'Riordan."

"Come off it, Tom. You're kidding me, right?" She caught his eye and saw a glint of laughter there. "You're such a tease. You must think I'm a complete idiot. Okay, so why are we here?"

"I really did used to come here as a boy, and this whole space—he made a sweeping movement to include the entire space—was left to me by my grandfather. I always dreamt of coming to live here someday. It's a grand piece of land, far away from everything, but with easy access to town." They continued on toward the house. "Whenever I'm out this way, I come and visit my old haunt. I like to believe that I get inspiration here." He took her hand. "Come." They trampled over the lush meadow and behind a row of trees she saw an old house, or what was left of it.

She drew in a breath. "It's beautiful Tom."

"I want to rebuild the house, keep these existing stone walls but add glass and wooden frames and beams." He pointed over to the sea view in the far distance. "Just imagine waking up to that view every morning." She watched him closely and saw his eyes light up as he told her. "The walls would enclose a courtyard with a glass roof. I'd have solar panels too. It would be a little oasis and provide light and shelter in these wetlands. The foundation has to be deep too in order to harness geothermal energy." He sighed. "Pipe dreams, I'm afraid, but it might just work. When the house market improves, I'm going to see if I can sell the house back home and go for it. It would be far too expensive at the moment, especially as this place is a bit too far off the beaten track."

"Would you grow your own food and have chickens and geese?"

He looked sharply at her. "Are you making fun of me?"

Her expression was serious. "No, not at all."

He bent down to pick up an old dried piece of bark and flung it into the distance. "So, this is what I wanted to show you. That's my dream. But I suppose we'd better be getting back before it gets dark."

They drove in comfortable silence, each locked in their own thoughts. Soft slow drizzle began to sprinkle, and low-lying clouds cast a shadow over everything. As twilight covered the land, the sun began to drop ever-so-slowly down low on the horizon, like a spider manoeuvring down from its web. The sky's palette changed to a swirling mix of soft purples, pinks and yellows.

Her mood began to sink too. How would she deal with Javier? And what about Tom? He'd be heading back to Knockadreen soon. Would they see each other again? She turned toward him and placed her hand on his leg. "Thank you, Tom. That was a lovely surprise and a lovely day…for the most part."

"For me too. Let's forget about the not so positive parts." He placed his free hand over hers and squeezed it.

She sank back in her seat. "I'll probably be coming back to Knockadreen in a few weeks. Can I call you?"

His voice held a tinge of sadness, or so she imagined. "Of course, you can always call me. Do you think you'll know what you want by then?"

"I think so, yes." It was hard to say this with conviction.

"Good." He cleared his throat. "There's something I should tell you, too."

"Okay." She closed her eyes as she waited for his revelation.

"Remember Sinead, the woman who was giving you a hard time back in the pub that evening?"

"How could I forget?" She remembered Sinead's probing questions and suspicious eyes.

"We had an on-off-relationship for a few years and it didn't end well. I thought you might have guessed that."

"Oh. So that explains her behaviour."

He continued. "I fell for her for all the wrong reasons. She didn't do my reputation any good either. Jealousy can do mean things to a person."

Roisin didn't want to probe further, thinking he would tell her as much as he felt necessary.

"Of course I swore I wouldn't get involved with a woman again. But even I didn't believe it. This time I want to do it right. Pity I had to fall for a married woman, eh?"

She sighed and shifted in her seat. "It's not as if I planned this. The last thing I was looking for was romance. But feelings cannot be turned on and off at will." She turned to face him. "Relationships are complicated. But you're right, Tom. I have to make a decision."

"Maybe I'm a romantic at heart, or my expectations are too high. All I know is that I've never been good at them."

She tried to smile but found herself biting her lip. "They say there's a lid for every pot. You just have to believe it."

He laughed bitterly. "Unfortunately, such clichés rarely apply to real life."

They were approaching Lissadore. Tom kept his eyes on the road. "I'll drop you off, Roisin, but I'm heading back straight away. When you've made up your mind, I'll be there. But I won't wait forever."

She turned toward him. His eyes were still fixed firmly on the road.

"God, I have a knack for tangling things up," she said.

"What do you mean?"

"Forget it, Tom. I'll just make it worse if I try to explain. It's just that I've spent so much of my life with Javier. I still care about what happens to him. It's not as easy as I thought it would be to walk away. Do you understand that?"

"Yeh, I suppose I do. Believe me. I've been there before. Unless you make a clear cut, you'll never move forward. No matter what happens between us, you should remember that. Finish one thing and move onto the next."

She sighed. "If only it was so easy. Why does life have to be so complicated sometimes?" Her question hung in the air.

When they finally reached her house, he turned off the ignition, reached over and kissed her cheek. He threaded his fingers through her long, wavy hair and moved to her lips, kissing her passionately. She didn't pull back. Finally, he said. "It's probably better if I head straight on home now."

"Yes, it probably is," she said, with great sadness.

"Let me help you get your things," he said. She didn't object. At the door, he took her in his arms once again and held her tight. She felt cocooned in his embrace, and when she finally wriggled free, she was reluctant to look into his eyes. She was overcome with a great weariness.

"Don't forget to call me when you come back to town," he said. "Whatever will be, will be?"

She gave him a weak smile and went inside without looking back. As soon as she closed the door, she leaned her back against it and let her tears flow. With a heavy heart and tired legs, she climbed the stairs.

# Chapter 23

The next morning she awoke from a dreamless sleep. Her heart was heavy in her chest. She pulled on her robe and trudged downstairs to make a cup of tea, switching on the TV as she passed it. The annoying chirpy chatter of the breakfast show hosts filled the room, and she listened half-heartedly as she sipped the hot drink. It was 9.30, late for her. The doorbell rang and she jerked back to reality. He certainly didn't lose any time.

She checked her reflection in the hallway mirror, smoothed her hair, and wiped the mascara smudge from her lower lids before opening the door. Javier stood there with a bunch of pink tulips. She was surprised he had even noticed tulips were her favourites.

She didn't know whether to laugh or cry. He looked awkward standing there with the flowers. They stared at each other, frozen, for what seemed like an age.

Her eyes welled with tears. He almost stumbled toward her, wrapping his arms around her. She blinked and pulled herself together. He handed her the flowers and she took them with a nod of acknowledgement, biting her tongue. Normally, he had only bought her flowers on birthdays or Valentine's Day. "Javier…why didn't you ring me first? She gave him a weak smile. "I suppose you'd better come on in."

He shrugged and followed her inside. Awkward moments passed as they sat opposite each other in the living room. "Oh, the flowers," she said, thankful to have something to do. She got up to fill a vase with water. When she returned, she sat on the edge of an armchair. They were acting like strangers, awkward and shy with each other. "How was your trip?" she said.

Javier rubbed his jaw. He looked at her and seemed unsure whether or not to say what he wanted to say. "Roisin, I've had a lot of time to think about us, about everything." He stood up and began pacing the room.

"Sit down please, Javier. You're making me nervous."

He continued as if he hadn't heard her. "You know this isn't easy for me. I was beside myself, Roisin." He stopped pacing and sat down again, wringing his hands and looking at the floor. "The one thing I feared most in life was to lose control. I'd seen my father go through this before and I swore I would never become like him." He looked up with such remorse in his dark brown eyes, it pained her to look at him. "I became him, Roisin. When I lost my footing, when we almost lost our house, I couldn't bear the mortification and the anger."

"But that part wasn't your fault, love." Had she said 'love?'

He continued. "I know that now, but it felt that way, and then the alcohol." He sighed. "That finished me off altogether." He sat upright and whipped in some air "That was some demon I had to fight, and I'm not out of the danger zone yet." He brushed a few stray hairs out of his eyes. We are all so fragile, Roisin."

She looked over his shoulder, at nothing in particular. Scenes came crashing back. She remembered the slap, the culmination of many unsaid things and pent up emotion. She rubbed her cheek and turned her eyes to him. "You know I did the right thing, don't you? I had no choice, Javier."

"I wasn't myself, Roisin. "You have to know that."

She sighed. "It's too late now anyway. What's done is done." She crossed her arms over her chest, still not sure how to react as she took in the pallor of his olive skin and tired eyes. He had lost some weight, but that suited him. But he had shaved and he wore a clean, blue shirt that set off his thick, dark hair.

"Let me make you a cup of tea. Have you had breakfast? There's a nice café in town. They do a great breakfast."

"A cup of tea is fine," he said. It's been a while since I had a bite, but don't worry about me."

She could see him from the kitchen and felt bad for not offering to make him breakfast, something she would have jumped to do in the past. But she didn't want to fall back into their old domestic arrangement. Making tea gave her a few moments to compose herself.

"I've been driving around taking a few snapshots of the area. So much has changed—all these new roads," he called to her.

She came into the living room with a tray of tea and biscuits. "Did you go down to the beach?" She almost said 'our beach.'

"No, no, I didn't, not yet." He sat perched on the edge of the couch, eyes glued to the television show that was still running. But he looked unsure of himself, sad even. Typical, she thought. He just cannot let himself go. Secretly, she cursed herself for being so unkind. It must be hard for him, she thought. He was a proud man and both of them knew what he was here for.

"When you've finished your tea, I'll show you the rest of the house," she said, chirpily. She busied herself folding laundry.

He nodded as he stirred his cup.

She carried the folded laundry to the door and turned to face him. She wanted to tell him to stop looking so morose and to lighten up because he was already dragging her down, but she couldn't bring herself to do it.

He sank back into the couch and grinned at her, almost as if he had read her mind.

"That's better," she said, while pleading with an invisible source to help her handle this right.

Javier arched his hands in a steeple. "Can you please sit down for a minute, Roisin."

She sat down opposite him. "What do you want to say to me?" She absentmindedly took one of the cushions and hugged it to her chest.

He was watching her intensely with his soulful eyes. "You're looking well, Roisin, reluctant as I am to admit it."

"Things have been going well for me." She bit

her tongue again, not wanting to hurt his feelings even more.

"Ah, come on, Roisin. This is ridiculous. We're acting here as if nothing happened. You're my wife, for goodness sake."

Her eyes blazed and she threw the cushion aside. "What do you expect me to say? You were the one who refused to talk whenever I tried to discuss things. You were also the one who told me not to come crawling back when things didn't work out. They were harsh words, Javier. As you can see, I'm doing fine. You think you can just show up and mess up my head again."

"Well, what did you expect? I never could figure you out. What was wrong with what we had? How do you think I felt? You just left me…"

"Whoa. Hold your horses. I didn't just leave you. I'd been trying to talk to you for years but you were always so emotionally detached. Have you any idea how lonely I felt? We were like spiritless robots with each other. Not exactly what I had in mind for the rest of my life."

He stood up and started pacing the room again. "Okay, okay. Don't you think I've had enough time to play this whole scenario out over the past few weeks? I've changed. That's what I'm trying to tell you." He sat back down again and cupped his jaw in his hands, running his forefinger back and forth under his lip. "I don't know…maybe it was all too much, this constant pressure. Work, mortgages, the whole shebang. It ruins people, Roisin. It's a trap, it gets under your skin, like a ball and chain around your ankles. Did you ever think how I might be feeling?

You were the one with the freedom. I had all the pressure, and then when I lost my job…."

"Here we go again. The same old story." She sighed with exasperation. "You had your role and I had mine. It's not all about who earns most money. What about all the years I juggled part-time low-paying jobs? The cooking, the cleaning, shopping, caring for your mother? You never appreciated that, did you? That was never worth much to you, was it?"

"Ah, come on, Roisin. This isn't what I came for." He sat back down again. "I've had a lot of time to think. I know I made a lot of mistakes but I'm willing to make amends. Don't you feel anything for me anymore?"

"Of course I do. Do you think it was easy for me to leave you, or my friends?" She didn't wait for a reply. "I knew I had to prove something to myself. If I had stayed, nothing would have changed. You know it, I know it."

He sat back, stretched out his legs and opened his hands as if he was going to show her a magic trick. "What would you say if I told you I've been looking for jobs here?"

She sighed. "I might say you've waited too long."

"You're the one who's always preaching about it never being too late. Give me another chance, Roisin. Please."

She knew how much it cost him to make such a plea. He was the most stubborn man she knew. He never apologised, ever. "Well, I'm not going back to where we were," she said. "If you get a job here, I'm not making any promises, can't you see that?"

"So, are you saying I should forget the whole idea?"

She smiled. "Don't put words in my mouth." It was awful to see him struggling. She hated to be the one to hurt him, especially now that he had been making such an effort. But she also felt a curtain of gloom close in on her as she realised her newly gained freedom was about to be thwarted. Why did he always make her feel so heavy?

"Can't we just spend a few days together and enjoy ourselves, without all this post-mortem analytical stuff?" he said.

She had been looking forward to a day of rest, just pottering in the garden and reading. Maybe even writing a few letters, but she couldn't turn him away. What was wrong with her? This was her husband. She didn't know how to deal with him or what to do with him.

She began fixing the cushions. "You have to be realistic, Javier. We can't just act as if nothing happened. We have to talk about it at some stage."

"I don't think you'll get them flatter than that. Would you sit down, for goodness sake? You're like a bloody jack-in-the-box." He poured himself another cup of tea and took a sip. "I passed through Knockadreen on the way here."

Oh, my God. She hadn't thought of that. Nobody had rung her, but of course she had been gone all the previous day and hadn't listened to her answering machine.

"You did?"

"Well, of course. How could I come and not see your family?"

"So, who did you stay with?"

"Brian and Pauline. The kids have grown so much."

"Yes, they have. Was it awkward?"

"Not any more than I thought. For the most part, they tried not to pry. I think they'd like to see us back together."

"Who would?" she asked.

"Well, Brian, for one. He said something about us falling into the trap of modern times, or something to that effect."

"Brian is a dreamer. If he had his way, women would all stay at home and have a houseful of children. He needs to wake up."

"I thought you were close to Brian."

"I am. I love Brian, but he has some quaint ideas." She hoped he hadn't mentioned her date with Tom.

"I also heard about your new friend."

She swallowed and felt the heat rush up her throat. "Oh, you mean Tom?"

"What Tom?" His expression changed in an instant to one of suspicion.

"Never mind." She felt a headache coming on and rubbed her temples.

He continued, as if he hadn't heard her. "I was referring to the friend you met here, the one with the shop."

"Oh! Yes, Maggie. She's been a godsend." Her mouth took off at a terrific speed, anything to distract him. She could have kicked herself, and hoped he wouldn't probe further. "I was so lucky to meet her, but you know my ideas about synchronicity and all that. It definitely was a stroke of luck." She began clearing away the cups and he helped her.

"It's as if it was meant to be, Javier. Everything has fallen into place. Why don't we drive downtown and I'll show you the shop. We can take a stroll down to the beach as well. I love it down there."

"Who's this Tom fellow?" *Ah, so his antennae were working fine, damn it.*

She had always been honest with him. Why change now. Besides, small lies can lead to larger lies and more complications, she thought. "He's someone from Knockadreen I met when I first arrived."

"Yes, and…."

"He's a very nice fellow, Javier."

"Gawd, Roisin, you don't waste time do you?

"Come on! He's only a friend."

The glint of fury in his eyes instantly made her regret having said anything.

"Will I show you the rest of the house and garden?" she said, as she began stacking dishes.

The suspicion had not left his eyes but he obviously thought better of pursuing the subject. "Why don't you show me when we come back? By the way, should I get a place tonight or can I stay here?"

"I think it would be better if you stayed in a B&B. How long are you here for anyway?"

He reached for his jacket. "All the B&B's were busy and I have to be back by the end of the week, but I have an interview lined up tomorrow in Galway—one of those new software companies. We'll see how it goes." She was surprised to hear about his interview but decided not to probe further.

Later, as they drove into town in relative silence, she thought about this new turn of events. What if he moved here, just for her? She presumed, even if he did get a job offer, he would have at least a few weeks to make up his mind whether to stay or not. That would give her time to think things through too. They parked the car and strolled along the main street toward the shop. She knew Maggie would be working, and debated whether or not she should go inside and introduce Javier. The problem resolved itself. As they came closer, she saw Maggie standing outside talking to a policeman. "What on earth is going on now?" she mumbled to no one in particular. Maggie was oblivious to their presence as a small crowd began to gather. Roisin didn't want to interrupt. The policeman, who was taking notes said to Maggie. "Are you sure that's the only thing missing?"

"Yes, I'm sure. I had just taken some shots and had uploaded them onto the laptop. I know I left the camera on the countertop. Everything else is in place. They didn't even go near the till."

Maggie turned toward the small crowd with an exasperated look. Then she spotted Roisin. "What are you doing here, Roisin? Don't tell me news travels that fast?"

Roisin rushed over to console her. "What happened? Are you all right? What about all our stuff?"

"I'm fine, thanks. The only thing that's missing is my camera."

"Are you sure?"

Maggie's eyes blazed with impatience. "I'm

sure." She pointed to the policeman who was checking the broken lock. Stress marks appeared on her throat. "It must have happened last night." Maggie's eyes rested on Javier. She raised an eyebrow at Roisin.

"Oh yes. This is Javier," Roisin said. "I think I mentioned he was coming for a visit."

Maggie extended her hand to him. "I'm sorry. It's not exactly the best day to meet. I'm beside myself. Believe me; I don't need this at the moment."

Roisin tried to console her. "At least they didn't take anything else."

Maggie's charm returned as she forced a smile on her face. "Nice to meet you, Javier. I suppose it'll all get sorted. Are you staying for long?"

While he told her of his plans, Roisin's mind was clicking things into place. She remembered the photos Maggie had taken of that fellow the day they had met in the pub. She had a niggling suspicion that the break-in had something to do with Bill Buckley and his cronies and she quickly told Maggie of her suspicions.

"I never even thought of that. I was too focused on the show and everything, trying to make sense of it all. Anyway, I've already uploaded those photos on my computer at home so they're out of luck."

"Keep your voice down, Maggie," Roisin said in a whisper. Although most of the crowd had left, it was possible that whoever was responsible was lurking around. The last thing Maggie needed was for someone to break in to her house.

Roisin gave her husband a quick run-down of

the events, looking to Maggie for confirmation. She also gave him a quick synopsis of Mrs. Walsh and her grandson.

"Are you serious?" he said. "I don't like this one bit. If you take my advice, keep out of it. You don't need this kind of stress."

"You're right, I'm sure," Maggie said. "But it's probably too late for that. Anyway, if we drop it we'll be playing right into their court. I'm bloody furious about the whole thing." She almost spat out the words. "And I'm not letting them terrorise us like this. I'd better get onto the insurance company and call the glass fellow to come and repair it as soon as possible."

"Is there anything I can do?" Roisin asked.

"No, you go off and enjoy yourselves. There's really nothing you can do at the moment. I suppose at least we're lucky that they didn't take anything else. If they had taken our collection, we could just forget the whole exhibition. When I think of all that hard work!"

The policeman had since left but Roisin told Maggie she planned on calling into the station when she was finished there, to tell them of her suspicions. "Maybe this will help the police to catch them."

"We still don't have any proof though. All we have is a couple of photos. I'm sure they weren't stupid enough to leave fingerprints in the shop. The hard thing will be proving a connection between the theft of the camera and the other events. But that's not my concern, I suppose."

Roisin turned to go. "Well, if you're sure I can't do anything, I'll see you tomorrow bright and early. If there's a change of plans, just call me. I'll check my messages tonight when I get back."

Javier and Roisin sauntered down to the beach, deep in conversation. In a strange sort of way, it was the best thing that could have happened to them, for it completely took their minds off their own situation. A soft warm breeze surrounded them and they stopped to sit up on the grass, watching the rhythmic waves crashing in on the shore. Several surfers were off in the distance. She admired their grace and stamina as they balanced on their surfboards, riding the waves. A little laugh escaped her. "Remember the time we camped by the beach and you lost all of your clothes?"

"How could I forget? I had to wrap your jacket around me and hide in that tiny tent until you returned with some spare clothes. We thought it was the worst thing that could happen to us, spending most of our spare money on a pair of jeans and a couple of tee-shirts."

Roisin smiled. "I can still see your face. Remember the time we were driving through France and you got violently ill from that seafood? You were happily munching away on your prawns and clams while the announcement was made on the radio not to eat the seafood. We didn't even know about it, and the restaurant owners mustn't have known either. After you emptied your stomach—I can still see your face, as white as alabaster—you got back on the moped and continued on. Now that was stoic." Roisin leaned her head onto his shoulder. "We do have many happy memories, don't we?"

"What was so bad, Roisin, that you felt the

need to leave?"

Roisin shifted her position and sat upright, facing Javier. She raised her voice a couple of octaves. "Bad? It just wasn't working. Have you forgotten already? You were in a negative space for so long. I couldn't get through to you, and the idea of a future like that was too overwhelming to even contemplate." She sighed in exasperation and rubbed her cheek in memory of the slap. "You raised your hand to me, Javier. My God, this is a waste of time. You still don't get it, do you?"

"Come on, Roisin. Let it go. They were extraordinary circumstances and you provoked me."

"Oh, spare me." She raised her hands in the air.

"Seriously. Is it so much better now?" He picked up a stone and threw it into the water. They watched it skip along the surface.

"Do you want an honest answer?" She turned her face to him and waited for his reaction.

"That doesn't do me any favours, does it? Not exactly good for my ego if you don't even miss me after all the years we've spent together."

"I never said that. It's just that I'm my own woman now. I'm proving something to myself, earning my own money. And, I'm living my life, making my own decisions.

He took a handful of sand and threw it. "That's the problem with women today. All that psychobabble filling their minds with rubbish."

"Come on, you're beginning to sound like Brian."

"Should I even bother with my interview

tomorrow?"

"It's up to you. You know the risks. I'm not promising anything. Only do it if you really want a change. I'm seeing this through, Javier, for better or for worse."

They continued sitting in silence. He put his arm around her shoulders, hugged her close to him and kissed the top of her head. "I've decided I'm going to go to that interview anyway and take it from there."

"I just wished you had tried years ago. It's not like I didn't try to tell you."

"What's the point in bringing up the past all the time?" He hit his forehead with the palm of his hand. "I may be a fool, but at least I'm making an effort."

Sitting so close to him, she felt that old attraction. His warm hand resting on her shoulder gave her a sense of belonging. He knew her inside out; she didn't have to invest an age in finding out his likes and dislikes. At the same time, she couldn't imagine ever returning to the life they had had together. She was touched, too, by the fact that he had made the effort to come after her. Or maybe he was escaping too. He pulled her closer and kissed her on the forehead. She didn't resist.

"Let's go and have lunch," he said. "Must be the sea air that's making me so hungry." His words, normally strong, sounded hoarse, but it broke the magic of the moment and dragged her back to the here and now. She let her thoughts fly off in the wind, out to the ocean. "Isn't it beautiful here?" she said. "I don't think I'll ever get tired of it."

He squeezed her hand but didn't say anything. In all their years of being together, she had yet to hear him making a simple statement like, "Yes, it's beautiful." It was one of the things that had irritated her about him, as if he was afraid of making a commitment.

"Tell me what you think? Is it beautiful or not? What's so hard about giving me a yes or no answer?"

He laughed. "Yes, okay, it's nice, but it could get a bit monotonous after a while. I know you; you'll soon get fed up with it and want to move again."

She sighed. "Just like I did in Spain, right? I only stayed there for twelve years. Just think about it, twelve years in that little village. Don't give me any of that. I won't fall for it anymore."

"Come on, Roisin, you didn't have a bad life. We had some nice times."

"Oh, Javier. Don't you realise we're doing it again? There's no point to this. We'll just go back to where we left off." They dusted themselves off and walked back down toward town.

The usual crowd of Sunday diners filled the room with lively chatter. Singles, couples, and families with their children gave the pub a cosy atmosphere.

They chose a table over toward the back in the dining area. It gave them a good view of the room and the bartenders who were pulling pints against a gleaming backdrop of sparkling glasses and bottles. "Would you mind driving?" Javier said. "I feel like having a pint of Guinness."

"Sure. You know me; alcohol in the daytime

makes me sleepy anyway."

After giving their orders to the efficient waiter, she scanned the room to see if she could recognize anybody. All she saw was a sea of strangers. She suspected most of them came from the outskirts. People enjoying a Sunday lunch together. The indirect lighting added to the intimate atmosphere.

A few minutes later, Javier lifted the dark brew with its rich creamy top to his lips and took a long sip. "Ah, that tastes good," he said. They both chose the Sunday roast special. While they waited for their meal, she filled him in on her early days in Lissadore. She chatted excitedly about the upcoming exhibition. "I'm really enjoying being creative again. It all sounds very promising too. I can see us having our own label." She slapped him playfully on the wrist. "What are you laughing for?"

"Just wondering how long till you get fed up with it. I thought your dream was to be the next J.K. Rowling."

"If it's meant to be, it won't pass you by. Besides, we don't have to plan every single step of our lives. That's boring. Maybe I can do both."

Their steaming dinner arrived, roast beef finely sliced, thin strips of green and red peppers and roasted rosemary potatoes with a spicy pepper sauce. They both ate, savouring the delicious food.

In between bites, she told him about how she'd met Maggie.

He did more listening than talking, but she could tell he was distracted. When he finished eating, he pushed the plate away, sat back and drained the remains of his drink. "Did I tell you you're looking great?"

She yawned. Nobody could accuse him of not trying. "Yes, you did. Thanks." Despite herself, she had to laugh at his pure obstinacy.

"Remember we always planned on buying a camper van and travelling? No, don't say anything. Just hear me out. I've been doing a lot of thinking. The job I'm applying for tomorrow would give me lots of free time. It's very well paid, Roisin, and I think I have a good chance of getting it…."

She nodded, letting him continue. And while the idea appealed to her, simply because she couldn't really see herself settling down just yet. It still didn't feel permanent, and she realised, upon seeing Javier again, how secure she felt with him, especially now that he was more like his old self, but he would need to do a lot more persuading to manage to convince her. Because her thoughts kept drifting to Tom. On the other hand, even if she could get away for a few weeks, a journey like that would certainly help her make up her mind.

He continued using his persuasive arguments. "Doesn't it sound great? We could go away for weeks at a time just like we always dreamed of doing."

"Why am I beginning to feel like a donkey? Come on, Javier. You can do better than that. Dangling a carrot in front of me won't change things!" Her words might have sounded convincing to him, but the more he spoke, the more she found herself being tempted by the idea of travelling from place to place, discovering new places, watching the sun rise in the desert, all of that. Javier may be many things, but he was, in his normal state, strong, uncompromising perhaps. He had that adventurous spirit too. He could turn his hand to anything and when he set his mind to something he pulled it through. The idea appealed to the gypsy side of her nature, and just for a moment she allowed herself to dream. But then she came to her senses as she remembered the other side of Javier. He knew her too well. He knew about her Wanderlust and that this vision would appeal to her adventurous spirit.

While he continued telling her about his plan, her eyes took on a faraway look. Perhaps he really had changed. She turned her attention back to him and saw the light in his eyes and the curve of his strong lips as he spoke. She could almost believe him if she allowed herself to. He was definitely more like the man she had first met, the one who was full of plans and who could be so convincing. Perhaps the change of place would suit them both. After all, was it really his fault that things didn't turn out as he had planned? The first few years, she had had complete and utter faith and trust in him. She had loved his youthful enthusiasm and his seeming ability to fix anything. He could always make her laugh too. She watched his hands as he gesticulated. She'd always liked his strong, warm hands and his long shapely fingers. She smiled.

His eyes lit up even more when he realised he was getting through to her. "Just think about it, Roisin. We could even travel down to Italy and Greece. Hey, we could even go to Morocco."

"Bickering all the way. No thanks. Anyway,

you were never interested in going down south. So, why the change of heart? Do you realise that we only ever went to places you wanted to go? You were never willing to compromise."

"Here you go again bringing up the past. See this as a new beginning. Come on, you can't be earning much in that job. What if it doesn't work out? Even if I don't get that job tomorrow, I'll do what I've been planning on doing for ages and set up a consultancy company. I can work whenever I want. It's a win-win situation. I've done my research, Roisin. There's definitely a market for my skills. Look at all the up-and-coming pharmaceutical companies out here in the west. They need people like me."

She thought of Tom and his parting words. Surely she couldn't be fickle enough to be swayed so easily. Out of the corner of her eye, she saw the silhouette of a familiar figure. She looked closer, gesturing for Javier to be still. Sure enough. Bill Buckley's cropped head stared back at her. He was leaning toward a slighter man, talking in what looked like urgent tones. Bill was in his Sunday best, but his jacket looked as if it was at least one size too small for him. She didn't want to draw attention to herself so she said to Javier, without obviously staring at Bill Buckley: "Don't look yet but the fellow at the bar is the one I was telling you about. The one who was harassing my old neighbour's nephew. Supposedly he has his fat fingers in dirty drug money."

Javier glanced over quickly. "Which one?

"Careful. Don't let him see you staring. The big fellow with the cropped hair."

She watched as big Bill Buckley handed something to his companion before abruptly heading out towards the back.

"So, what are you going to do now, Nancy Drew?"

"Very funny. Don't knock it. Maggie and I are a good team. I'm going to follow him. See where he's going. What do you think?"

He shook his head in exasperation. "You're impossible, do you know that?"

"I do. Now let's go."

There was no sign of Bill Buckley, but she had memorised a good description of the other fellow, just in case. Truly, she had no idea where this was all leading. But if she could at least make Mrs. Walsh's life easier, it would be worth it.

Unfortunately, it wasn't like the movies, and she didn't have the faintest idea where to look for him. He could have disappeared down any of the side streets or already be driving away. Reluctantly, she decided to head back home.

Back home, she showed Javier his room. It would have seemed absurd having him search for a place to stay now, and it was only for a few days. "I'm going to potter about in the garden a bit. What about you?" she said.

"I'll just upload the photos I took and play around with them."

The shrill sound of the telephone ringing caught her unawares as she was in the throes of ripping out a particularly resilient thistle. She rushed inside. It was Helen, curious as ever. She wanted to know how her night of love and passion went. "Well, you could say fate intervened," she whispered. "Guess who's here?" She gave her sister a quick rundown of the situation. Helen expressed her surprise and said something about bad timing.

"Maybe it was all for the best," Roisin said. "I'll ring you later. Yes, I'll tell him you were asking for him. Maybe he'll pop by on his way back to the airport." Roisin was surprised that Brian hadn't told her sister about Javier's visit yet.

In the evening, she had another unexpected visitor. It was Esther, the woman from the B&B. The change in her was obvious. Her former ruddy complexion was transformed, and she seemed much calmer. She handed Roisin a large bunch of flowers and a bottle of wine.

"Thank you so much, Esther. Come on in. I'll put the kettle on."

"Sorry, I couldn't make it to your party the other night," Esther said. "I wanted to thank you for that tip about the sage tea. I feel like a new woman." She stopped in her tracks when she saw Javier. "Oh, I'm sorry. I didn't know you had a visitor."

Roisin introduced them and left them to it as she went to make tea. Making tea was part of the ritual. You could spend all your life making tea, she thought, and that's what she loved.

"I hope you don't mind me coming unexpectedly," Esther said. "It's just that I can't believe how much better I feel." She smiled over at Javier and directed her attention back to Roisin. "I've just been telling your friend here that you shouldn't be surprised if you have a queue of people coming for tips soon. Word spreads like wildfire." Roisin had to admit that Esther looked much better. Her eyes had lost that frantic look. They now twinkled with good humour.

The woman continued. "I heard about Maggie's shop being broken into. It's terrible, isn't it?"

"Yes, we passed by there today. The police were on the scene, so I'm sure they're on to it."

"I wouldn't be sure about that," Esther said. "There are rumours, you know, about Maggie. She used to hang out with the wrong crowd. Something to do with drugs."

Roisin shook her head in exasperation. "What do you mean? Maggie has nothing to do with drugs. I could vouch for that; in fact I'd bet my life on it."

"Well, I'm just repeating what I heard."

Roisin remembered Fidelma's suspicious look whenever Maggie's name was mentioned.

"I don't know about the past, but I can assure you Maggie is a great woman. She's been very kind to me.'

Esther looked relieved. She settled back onto the chair. "I have nothing against her. I just thought you might need to know. I wouldn't want it to colour the way people look at you. It's so easy to be tarred with the same brush. You know how people are?"

Roisin laughed. "Indeed I do. Believe me. They're the same everywhere."

Javier continued to work on his photos and gave no indication that he was listening.

Esther put a spoonful of sugar into her tea and

stirred as if she was going to scrape the bottom off the cup. "They didn't take anything, I hear."

"No, they didn't. That was the weirdest thing." She decided not to mention the camera.

Finally, Esther must have got the message. She changed the subject. "So, how are you settling in here? It's lovely and quiet, isn't it?"

"It is, yes. I'm loving it. The whole area is gorgeous. I doubt if I could get tired of it." She glanced over to see Javier smirking.

"Have you met Mrs. Walsh? A lovely woman. Shame about her grandson. He's another one. They say he's a bit of a no-gooder."

Roisin shook her head and watched as Javier's grin grew wider. He pretended to be admiring the photos but she knew better. Funny, she hadn't thought of Esther as a gossipmonger. Was that why she came, to find out information?

"Yes, I've met Mrs. Walsh. I know she's very fond of her grandson. Thinks the world of him, in fact, so he can't be that bad."

They chatted for a bit longer. Esther stood up to go. "Well, I'd better get moving. Why don't you come to our Scrabble evening again sometime? The more, the merrier I say. Fidelma would love to see you there."

Roisin assured her she would. She stood at the door and watched her drive away. Javier's cheeky grin said a thousand words. "Well, I see you're getting to know your neighbours," he said.

"She's alright. Just trying to do her moral duty."

They both laughed and settled down to watch

a film. He sat on the couch and she sat on the armchair. The evenings were cool so she pulled the blanket over her lap.

"Come on over here," he said, patting the space beside the couch.

She hesitated for a few moments.

"Come on," he said. "I can warm your feet. It's getting chilly."

She was too tired to argue. "Okay then," she said. She took the blanket and snuggled beside him on the couch. As she lay there watching the actors on the screen, she thought back to all the times she would have wished he'd have watched a film with her. But Javier never compromised on such things, and so she had accepted it in the end. She had always thought a good marriage should give each partner freedom to follow their own passion. She had never expected, nor wanted him to do everything with her. But there had come a time when she had realized how alone she'd felt in the marriage. She suspected he was a loner at heart. It was enough for him. He did not need other people as much as she did. And she knew he loved her all along, but she needed more. She needed a true companion. Perhaps panic, too, had taken over as she had envisioned the type of future they would have had if she had stayed. They would have continued in that same routine, sharing meals that she had cooked and going for walks together; they would have had lively and heated discussions about politics and all sorts of things, and he would have become more and more stubborn as time went on. If she was honest, she was probably as much to blame because she, too, had settled into that type of lifestyle. She probably should have been more assertive and put her foot down more often, but experience had taught her that this often lead to more trouble than it was worth. Soon she was fast asleep. She awoke to a gentle nudging. For a moment she didn't know where she was. She groaned and looked around her, wild-eyed. "You might want to get to bed, Roisin," Javier said. "Don't you have to get up early tomorrow?"

She rubbed her eyes. "I hate when I do that. Now I've missed the film."

"You didn't miss much," he said, smirking.

He followed her upstairs, and he didn't hide his disappointment when she pointed him to the guest bedroom. "Come, on Roisin. For old time's sake."

"No, Javier. I'm far too tired and I need a good night's sleep." As she lay in bed, teary-eyed, she wondered if she was doing the right thing. It really was time to make a decision.

# Chapter 24

The shop window had been replaced when she arrived the next morning. Javier's interview wasn't until the afternoon, so she'd arranged to meet him back at the house after she finished work. Maggie was already in a flurry of activity, labelling, ironing and sorting her stuff for the exhibition. Roisin got to work, organising her side of things.

"So, that's the famous Javier."

"Yep!"

"I like him. It's obvious he still cares a lot for you, and I think he's sincere."

Roisin paused for a moment, folding the tissue paper over the hats in a box. "I've always said he's a good man. Pity he took me for granted, though. A little much, too late." She put the lid on the box and shoved it over to the side. "He's going for a job interview here today. Can you believe he wants to come and live here?" She continued with the next box, gently unfolding the tissue paper and placing a couple of scarves inside. "You know, I pleaded with him to do this years ago. He wouldn't budge. I suppose, in fairness, he was afraid. Never was a risk taker, at least when it came to uprooting himself and starting off afresh. Pity I had to take such radical steps." She stopped what she was doing and turned to Maggie. "Why are men like that?"

"Don't ask me. Do you see them flocking up here?"

"Oh come on, Maggie. I'm sure you have many admirers. A woman with your looks."

Maggie snorted in disbelief. "So, what are you going to do?"

"I have absolutely no idea. Tom is back in Knockadreen. Anyway, he doesn't want complications. Who does?" She stopped for a moment. "Where are the other empty boxes?"

"Out the back, under the cabinet with the sliding doors."

"Right, just a minute," Roisin said. She returned, carrying a stack of boxes. "We won't be able to see out of the car windows at this rate."

"It'll be okay," Maggie said. "I just hope they have plenty of parking near the exhibition halls." She continued asking about Tom. "You said he was back in Knockadreen."

"Yes. He made a quick exit when I told him Javier was coming. Who can blame him?

"For goodness sake, Roisin, why did you tell him?"

"Why should I lie? I hate deception. Do onto others and all that…it always comes back to bite you anyway."

Maggie slid the steaming iron across the garment and seemed lost in thought.

"Javier is leaving at the end of the week. I promised Tom I'd give him a call when we're in Dublin for the exhibition."

"Far be it for me to judge, Roisin, but don't you think that's a bit duplicitous?"

"Not really. I have to sort things out, and how else would I do it."

Maggie shrugged and changed the subject. "Did I tell you I've booked our hotel?"

"Yipee. Where?"

Maggie went to her laptop to search for the link. "Here, come and take a look.

Roisin clicked on the gallery of pictures. "I remember that place. It's in that alleyway near the Powerscourt Centre. It looks gorgeous and is really central."

Maggie's grin gave her impish look. "Maybe we can write it off in next year's taxes. I think we deserve it after all our hard work." She scanned the room, whooping with joy at all the boxes and piles of wares ready to go. "I've heard it's a great place for mystery scouts looking for undiscovered talent."

"Sorry?"

"The Trade Fair," Maggie said.

Roisin took one of the scarves from a pile and wrapped it around her neck. She reached in her bag for her sunglasses and put them on too. "What do you think?"

"I think we'd be our own best customers."

Roisin scanned the display in front of her. They could afford to be pleased with themselves. Their products looked great. She grabbed one of the hats and took long, exaggerated steps up and down the shop floor, flicking up her sunglasses with one hand and wiggling her hips. Maggie snorted with laughter.

Serious again, Roisin removed the hat. "Would you mind if I took an extra day off after the show is over. I'd like to go down to Knockadreen when I'm in the vicinity."

Although Maggie's tone was jovial, she looked disappointed. "You're planning on dumping me."

"No, don't be silly."

"Okay, but only if you promise to keep an eye out for me. I want a Tom too."

Roisin was about to make a retort when Darius came rushing through the door. He had been busy with exams the previous couple of weeks so Roisin had barely seen him. He took in the room and let out a low whistle. "You've been busy?" he said. "I tell you, gals. You're going to be great. Want to see what I've been up to?" He pulled a portfolio out of his bag and put in on the counter top, flicking through it and showing them some of his own designs. Roisin tried to make the appropriate sounds of enthusiasm when she saw tee-shirts in shrill colours. They looked as if they'd been put through a shredder and patched up again. Then there were Knickerbocker tartan trousers and what looked like cellophane raincoats for the modern urban man, as he put it. She couldn't imagine any Irish man wearing them but kept her thoughts to herself. Still, people never ceased to surprise her, and the fashion world was always looking for new, innovative ideas. Not that plastic raincoats were new, but Darius explained they were made of recycled, breathable, plastic which had been imbued with Nano-particles, making them ultra-light and allowing the skin to breathe. According to him, they were also wind-proof, rain-resistant and practically tear-proof. "If you look inside," he explained, "you'll find witticisms printed on the pocket labels, quotes and that sort of thing. The best part is that a percentage of the sales will be donated to a Rainforest project. See, it's not your run-of-the-mill polyethylene," he said with a wink.

Both Roisin and Maggie were impressed with what they saw. They loved the idea that he was working with such innovative fabric designers and doing something for the planet. Roisin was sure there was a market for those raincoats, perhaps even for his tee-shirts.

"Enough about me," Darius said as he closed the lid of his laptop. "Have you decided what you're wearing to the show?" He raised an eyebrow in good Spock fashion.

Maggie hesitated. "Not exactly."

"I took the liberty…," he said, "…of doing these sketches for you." He took out his sketch pad and showed them the drawings. Simple, but effective. Black fitted tee-shirts with their printed logo, high-waist Marlene-trousers and berets with flowers on the side, giving them a slightly vintage look. "I thought Maggie could wear the black beret," he said, "And Roisin, you could wear the red one. You've got to look the part, you know, darlings." He rummaged in his bag once more and took out a tee-shirt and a black beret and made a great show of handing it to the first taker. Maggie reached for it first. "Go, go, try it on," he said. Maggie obediently did as he said. She turned back and gave him a big kiss on the cheek. "You've thought of everything, Darius."

He feigned a bashful look. He always made them laugh with his exaggerated flamboyancy. He loved playing 'camp;' but it was all a show. He was thoughtful and interesting too. Once he had told Roisin that he had grown up in the country and had had a fascination for clothing. He had loved watching old films too and despised having had to wear the school uniform. Since his mother was an avid sewer, he used to bug her continuously with his sewing requests until one day she had said. "The machine is there, you can do your own sewing from now on." He had pimped up his school uniform by adding little touches that only he could see. He laughed when he told her how much fun he'd had knowing that the pocket linings of his trousers and jacket, and his boxers were made with striped silk or odd bits of velvet. "I felt as if I had conquered the system," he said. "All that grey—grey concrete walls, grey skies and dull classrooms—but I had colour in my heart and nobody could take that away." The down side of Darius's personality was his domineering manner. When he was on a roll, he tended to be insufferable, Roisin noticed. At such times he was outspoken and commandeering. Really, he was a born leader. He had what it took to go far one day.

It was decided. They applauded his idea and he agreed to take care of the details. They could make the berets themselves.

"I hope this goes well after all our effort," Maggie said.

Darius was in charge of dusting shelves once a week and decorating the window. He was dressing a mannequin and turned round in mock surprise after hearing what Maggie said.. "You'll be fabulous. Seriously, I think you'll be snatched up by one of those scouts. It's goodbye Lissadore, hello New York." He started singing the Lisa Minnelli song of the same name, waving his hands, fingers spread-eagled in time to the music.

"Careful or you'll break Miranda," Maggie said. That was the name she had given the mannequin. "She didn't come cheap, you know."

He stepped back out onto the floor and Maggie gave him a friendly punch. "You're incorrigible. Getting our hopes up like that."

"Believe me. I know these things."

Maggie grinned good-naturedly. "Who made you God?"

"This *IS* my *métier*, honey. Trust me."

"We'll see. But for now, let's get back to work. There's still a lot to do. We'll be relying on you to take care of the place when we're gone. Keep your eyes open, too, for any suspicious characters. I don't think the insurance will keep on paying if this happens too often." Darius had, of course, heard of the break-in but didn't seem to be too concerned about it. "I'll be fine," he said. "What could happen?"

# Chapter 25

The next few days passed by in a flurry of activity. Javier was up early and made her breakfast every morning. At the weekend, he had arranged for them to visit the Burren. The weather was perfect, and they walked for a couple of hours taking photos and enjoying he sights. Roisin was torn. She didn't want to give him false hopes. She also didn't want to appear to be ungrateful. The last thing she wanted was for him to bend over backwards, trying to satisfy her every whim, only to revert to his old ways as soon as she let him into her heart again. She was still wary of this newfound harmony. Sometimes she found herself slipping into a camaraderie they had enjoyed in their first few years together and she began seeing him with different eyes, even contemplating a future together. He was thoughtful and kind and much more relaxed. He even cooked her dinner a couple of times.

    At the end of the week she came home from work in a panic. She slammed the front door, threw her bag on the couch and let out a heavy sigh. Javier was listening to some music in the living room. The fire was lit, and the delicious smell of something roasting in the oven filled the room. He had even bought flowers.

    "What's up?" he said, turning to face her.

She wanted to be alone and he was an irritation. "Nothing."

"Dinner's almost ready."

"I'm not hungry."

"Well, thanks very much," he said. "Is my cooking that bad?"

Roisin sat on the couch and burst into tears. "I don't know what I'm even doing there. I'm out of my depth."

"You've always been like that, Roisin. "You take on too much, you get your hopes up and burn your energy and then you…"

She held her hand out. "Not now. I don't need your psychological analysis." She buried her head in her hands and shed tears of pure frustration. He came over and put his arms around her. She shook him off. His words stung. Was he right? And why was she feeling overwhelmed? She pulled herself together and looked at him through tear-filled eyes. "I wish I'd never agreed to go to this stupid exhibition,"

He raised his eyes to heaven. "I'll never understand you, Roisin. All that's wrong with you is you've been working too hard. Forget about the shop for a couple of days. You're stressing yourself out over nothing." She knew he was right. She had times like this, when she didn't want to meet people. She just wanted to go about her life without stress, become invisible even. Javier understood this. But another side of her was hugely extroverted and wanted to leave her mark in some way. She was independent and could never be satisfied with a boring, routine existence. Did she need him after all, someone who knew her better than she knew herself?

If only he wasn't so damn contrary. He let her away with nothing.

She sighed. "I've committed myself now. How do you suggest I turn off and forget about it?"

"That's easy," he said. "Do something completely different. It'll take your mind off things" Why could he never take her seriously? She got up and went over to check the oven. "What's for dinner anyway?"

"See, that's a start." He grinned. "Moussaka with aubergines. I made a salad too and got a bottle of wine." He sounded like a cheery telegram man, like someone who was trying too hard.

Her face lifted into a smile. "You cooked. Hold me while I swoon." Javier had never cooked, nor had he done much around the house. The cooking part was never a problem because she enjoyed it but the rest had often irritated her. She watched him uncork the wine. Were they going to fall back into old patterns, another location, same life? If so, would it be so bad? He was being too nice, too accommodating. How long could he keep it up? Maybe they were just not compatible. It was neither his nor her fault. Perhaps she had been swayed by a false ideal of how the perfect marriage should be. She had always had impossible expectations. One thing she knew for sure, staying married takes a lot of compromise, forgiveness and a huge dose of humour and tolerance

He shrugged, ignoring her remark. "We need to get out of the house for a while," he said.

"There's nothing to do around here," she said. Aware that she sounded like a spoilt teenager, and also realising that she was playing into his preconceived notions about her becoming fed up and bored with the place after a couple of months, she added. "Maybe we can go to that spa hotel I've been hearing about." Her eyes lit up as she began to think about it. "That would be perfect. We could spend the day in Galway, the night in the hotel and Sunday we can use the sport and spa facilities. I could even have a beauty treatment. "Gosh, I'm starving."

"I thought you said you weren't hungry."

"Well, I am now. What do you say? Would you be up for it?"

"Sure, why not?"

Roisin began setting the table. She poured out the wine and handed him a glass. "You know, I don't expect you to do everything I want. You hate shopping and you hate spending money on frivolous things."

"Once you don't expect it too often," he said, with a grin.

\*

The weekend away did them both good and it was just the thing Roisin needed to free her mind. The following few days saw her full of vigour and even looking forward to going to Dublin. She didn't even have time to think of the future or what it might hold. She was too busy preparing for the show. Javier kept himself occupied by visiting local spots and taking up his old hobby, photography. The fresh air and exercise were doing him good too. He already looked better. They spent most evenings walking along the beach, if she wasn't too tired, or just enjoying each other's company.

One evening as they were walking along the main street, they bumped into Blessing. Roisin's heart stopped for a moment. She was terrified Blessing might mention meeting Tom at the party, but.she should have known better. Blessing was far too smart and far too astute for such indiscretions. She asked Roisin, while taking a sideways glance at Javier, if she'd made any progress regarding the dance class. This was funny, especially because she was the one who'd initially talked Blessing into the whole thing. Now Blessing was pushing her to move it along. Javier, never the greatest at small-talk, excused himself while he went to a kiosk to buy the newspaper.

"I haven't had a minute," Roisin said, "But I have a few ideas, and as soon as our show is over I'll get onto it. There's no point in me putting in an ad when I'm hardly ever here at the moment," Roisin continued. "Besides, as you can see, I have a visitor."

"I noticed. Is that your husband?" Blessing said. "He's not very talkative, is he?"

Roisin found herself defending him. "He has his moments, but he was never one to push for the limelight."

Blessing's bellowing laughter filled the air. "I hope you're not referring to me."

Roisin winked. "Now what makes you think that? It never entered my head."

Blessing raised one eyebrow and shook her head in mock disbelief. She waved goodbye and sauntered off, wiggling her hips as she went.

Javier joined Roisin, who had picked up pace. "Who was that?" he asked.

"That's Blessing, the doctor. I'm sure I mentioned her. She's quite the dancer too."

"Well, she seems like a character. How did she end up living here?"

"Necessity, I think."

"In another hundred years we'll all be mixed together, all colours and creeds, maybe religion will be banned. It's the cause of all wars."

"That and inequality, if you ask me," Roisin said. "Why didn't you stop to chat; anyway? I think Blessing might have been a bit put out."

"You know me. I'm useless at small talk."

Roisin shrugged. "I tried to convince Blessing to teach a dance class. It took some convincing, but she finally agreed. Only if I organized it."

"You'll never learn! Don't you have enough on your plate?"

"I'm trying to do things differently here, get involved in the local community and do my bit. It's so easy to end up isolated, everyone doing their own thing." She turned to Javier. "I've had enough of that."

"What do you mean? You had me, you had your friends and your students. Wasn't that enough?"

"I suppose not."

"Don't forget the times you helped out in the kitchen for the homeless. Or the time you offered free classes in the local school. You ended up disappointed. People are ungrateful and selfish, Roisin. They don't appreciate altruism"

"Here we go again. I don't buy into that. There are many good people in the world. You just need to look for them."

"Yeh, and you need to take off your rose-coloured glasses. The good ones always lose out in the end."

She mimicked him. "Just look at history, blah, blah, blah." she said, deepening her voice to match his. She'd heard it many times before, too many. She was tempted to challenge him. Of course he was right about history, but she was sure there were as many cases of peoples' positive action in the world as there were of despots and bullies, conquerors and money-grabbers. The only problem was that despots usually used force to achieve their goals.

*

When it was time for him to leave again, she hugged him tight to her chest. "I'll miss you, Javier. I'm even getting used to your cooking. And who's going to light the fire for me and chop the wood?"

He grabbed her in a bear hug. "Suppose you'll have to do it yourself," he said. "But we got along great, didn't we? Just like old times."

She released herself and cupped his face with her hands. "It'll never be the same. We're both different now, but you'll always be my friend. Isn't that something?"

He opened his mouth to say something and began to cough. He turned to get his luggage, shoulders slightly drooping. She closed her eyes and took in a deep breath.

When he turned around again, his face gave nothing away. "Right, then. I'd better get going," he said.

She watched him walk through the departure gates, and she knew by the set of his shoulders and the tilt of his head that he didn't want to leave. He turned back when he reached the top of the stairs and gave her a crooked smile. His dark, wavy hair was thinning at the temples, somehow making him look vulnerable. But it was the unmistakable sadness in his eyes as he waved that tore her apart.

A gnawing sense of guilt overcame her as she thought of Tom.

Javier was in a much better space than he had been before she left. She knew she had done the right thing by leaving. Drink had never agreed with him. In fact he had never been one to drink much, but she knew it had been his only way of coping with their changing life circumstances. He had admitted as much a few days previously. Coming there and leaving Spain was a big decision for him to make too, especially knowing she wasn't prepared to give up her new-found freedom. He knew if he made the decision to come, he'd be taking a risk. She ran her fingers through her hair and sighed. It was impossible, the whole situation.

She decided to let fate take over. It didn't look as if Javier was going to be offered the job after all; there were too many unemployed younger Irish men with families to support. She recalled their conversation of the previous evening when he'd as much as told her that. "If I don't get it," he'd said, "I'm going to set myself up in business. I can do it from home."

"You'll need a big place, though, and that's not cheap."

"What do you mean? This is big enough."

"No, Javier. You'll need your own place."

"But that's ridiculous. It doesn't make sense," he had said.

Then she'd sighed. "Didn't you listen to anything I said?"

He'd clenched his jaw and stared at his empty hands, a habit he had to distract from his disappointment. He had then got up and cleared the table, whistling—another habit to convey false optimism. When he'd sat back down again, he'd taken both of her hands in his. "We'll discuss this when I come back, Roisin. I'm very close to having a buyer for the house. You'll see, everything will work out fine."

She'd squeezed his hands and given him a peck on the cheek. "I'd better get an early night," she'd said. "Tomorrow is another long day."

And now, she watched him walk through the departure gates. The set of his shoulders and the tilt of his head showed determination. When he reached the top of the stairs he turned back and gave her a crooked smile. Her eyes welled up with tears as she saw the look in his eyes. She forced a broad smile on her face and waved at him, miming that she would phone later.

As she walked back to the car, she was determined to set things straight on that score. But for the moment, she had other things on her mind. Tom was so different from Javier. But how genuine was Tom? She had lots of new things in her life now – everything, in fact. If she did accept Javier back into her life, she'd never know what it would have been like with Tom. On the other hand, although she was pretty certain that Tom genuinely liked her, they'd known each other for such a short time. What if he cheated on her? Maybe he was a heartbreaker? Perhaps she'd need to do a bit more investigation. She might ask her brother where he had heard those rumours. She'd learned enough to know that there usually was some truth in the old saying, *there's no smoke without fire*. Determined not to let this old familiar melancholy and churning of thoughts drag her down, she squared her shoulders and headed back to the shop.

# Chapter 26

When she got back, she called into Jimmy Tyrell's for a quick sandwich and a cup of coffee. He was his usual cheerful self, chatting away about the benefits of goji berries. He was so convincing that she left the shop with a 500g bag. If they did all he claimed they could do, she could expect to outlive Methuselah.

The town was practically empty at 8.30 in the morning. Apart from Jimmy's and a couple of other cafes, most shops and offices didn't open until 9 a.m. She expected to be in the shop before Maggie but she should have known better. Maggie was already there.

"Well, how did it go?" Maggie ran the duster over the shelves. "Did you see him off?"

Roisin looked at her watch. He should be taking off in about ten minutes. She sighed. "I did, but I feel so bad."

Maggie did her best to console her friend. "Think of all the worst things he ever did to you. That always helps." And it did. Her powers of recall were intense. She could see him back in their Spanish kitchen, face brick-red, about to hit her. She also recalled incidents where she had worked so hard to be cheerful, when he had walked out on her and stomped up the stairs, refusing to talk, refusing to go anywhere with her. There was no way she would ever accept that again.

"You should see your face," Maggie said.

The spell was broken. "I'm the one who's always talking about moving on and here I am dragging up old resentments. It does help though. I was beginning to forget why I left."

Maggie flipped the switch on the radio. Her favourite morning show host brightened the mood, and they busied themselves packing their wares into boxes and cases. "The shop is going to look so bare. I hope we do well," Maggie said.

"So do I." Roisin checked the price tags on the bags she'd made. The labels looked classy with their new logo. Everything had an organic feel about it, from the label fabric to the description, which was printed to look as if it was hand written. She folded the last bag and placed it neatly on top of the others. "Let's put them in the car so we don't have to do it tomorrow, shall we?"

"Sure," Maggie said, "but one of us had better stay here, not that there's much going on at the moment. By the way, I sold quite a bit yesterday. It was definitely a good day." She opened the till and retrieved an envelope, handing it to Roisin. "Here, this is yours."

Roisin took the envelope and opened it. There was a wad of notes, hundreds and fifties inside. She looked up at Maggie, eyes wide. "This is far too much," she said. "I can't take it. It's much more than we agreed upon."

"No discussion," Maggie said. "Remember we talked about extras if we did well? Well. We did. You're worth more than your weight in gold." It was clear that Maggie would not entertain any further discussion on the matter, and of course it was more than welcome. Next month's rent was due soon and Roisin's reserve was dwindling faster than she'd expected. She smiled at Maggie. "What would I have done if I hadn't met you? I could be working in a call centre or changing sheets?"

"You'll always survive, Roisin, and don't forget you're meeting Tom. You'll need extra cash when we go to Dublin."

Roisin nodded. Her fact lit up as she thanked the gods of fortuitous pathways and guiding steps for having arranged the meeting with Maggie. She hummed as she sorted through a stack of bags. Maggie tried hard to prevent her lips from twitching into a grin, but couldn't keep it in any longer. She chuckled and said. "Do you always do that when you're embarrassed?" Roisin looked up, blank-faced, and Maggie waved her hand in the air in front of her. "Never mind, I'm just teasing. By the way, Darius dropped in some outfits for us. Let me get them."

Her wooden clogs clacked rhythmically on the floorboards as she walked to the studio. She returned a few minutes later and handed Roisin a black dress and a canary yellow scarf. "Go try it on. It'll look great with that scarf. Here, don't forget this." Maggie handed her a sparkling black crocheted beret made with Sirdar's lovely cotton mix. "I'm going to try mine on too. Just a sec." Maggie held a tailored black two piece up against her body.

The two women went out the back and, in a mad scurry, threw off their clothes and put on the new outfits. "Just a dab of lipstick," Roisin said. "Black drains the colour from your cheeks." She dug in her handbag and pulled out a lipstick, handing it to Maggie. "Here, try this one." With a couple of deft strokes, Maggie applied the lipstick perfectly. "I'm not sure." Roisin squinted. "The style is great but I still think that black is a bit harsh for you."

"Well, you look great. Darius was right about the yellow. I know it's all in this year but I still can't get used to it."

Maggie adjusted the beret on her friend's head until it looked just right. She looked at herself in the mirror and frowned. "Yes, I think you're right. Black drains what little colour I do have in my cheeks. Hold on, I have an idea." She went over to a shelf, rummaged through a pile of garments and opened the middle drawer from under the large cutting table to retrieve a frilly wide collar. The cherry-colour complemented her pale complexion and jet-black hair perfectly. "Right," she said, as she posed in front of the mirror. "Now we've got that sorted."

Roisin stood beside her and linked her arm around Maggie's waist. "We make a good team, don't you think? Stylish without being weird. Talking about weird. I heard something strange this morning on the news. Do you think it could have anything to do with our little detective endeavours? It seems as if the police have foiled a huge drug smuggling operation off the West coast. They didn't give any details but I have a feeling in me bones," she said in an old crone's voice.

"As long as there's demand, the criminals will find a way to supply. I'm afraid I'm too cynical when it comes to human nature." Roisin sighed. "Still, that's definitely good news."

"Wouldn't it be great though? Imagine if we were instrumental in helping to stop this madness."

Roisin's eyes took on a wistful look. "I'd be happy if Mrs. Walsh could have some peace of mind. That would be enough for me."

# Chapter 27

They left Lissadore the next day when the dew was still sparkling on the leaves. It was Roisin's favourite part of the day. The watery sun cast its light upon the distant lilac mountains. There was still a nip in the air despite the fact that they were approaching the most carefree season, and the town was beginning to fill up with tourists. As they drove down the coast road past the camping ground, a group of colourful tents added to the carefree feeling. She saw surfers pulling on their waterproof suits. The tide was out and she witnessed a row of children, like exotic ants, carrying their colourful surfboards towards the water. A tanned, athletic young man led the group toward the frothy, teasing waves.

With one hand on the wheel, Roisin grabbed an apple from her bag and one for Maggie too. "Don't you just love spring? It seems to hold such promise. Doesn't everything seems possible when the sun shines? I'm so excited about this trip."

"Sure it does, but if we didn't have the other seasons we probably wouldn't appreciate it. Now I feel like Marilla talking to Anne of Green Gables. Sorry to run over your unicorn." She switched on the radio. The sounds of The Script's latest song blared through the speakers. Both of them sang in harmony, 'If one day you wake up and you're missing me....Those fellows are amazing. I love their sound."

"They've really hit the big time. I think their music appeals to all ages. I wonder if Tom's song will hit the charts. It's very good."

Maggie turned to look at Roisin. "You never told me he was a songwriter?"

"He's a man of many talents. I only found out the other day when he played it for me. Anyway, you're a bit of a dark horse yourself. How come you never married?"

Maggie sighed. "My love life has always been a disaster. I think I'm just not meant to have your typical picture-book scenario with husband, kids and all that lark."

"Nonsense," Roisin said. "It's all a matter of priorities. I bet so many people just fall into marriage without even thinking. They marry out of a sense of panic. You're probably a lot more discerning."

"Maybe. I've never thought of it like that before."

"Some people take a bit longer to find the right partner. Not everyone has to follow the same pattern. Maybe your dream man is just around the corner." She glanced over at Maggie and gave her a reassuring smile.

"I'm not holding my breath."

"They always come when you're not looking. I hate to sound preachy or anything, but it is my firm conviction that we've got to find happiness within ourselves first. Look at you, for instance. You've created your own niche in life; you're creative and you ooze self-confidence. I bet most men find you intimidating. Didn't you notice the way Jimmy Tyrell was flirting with you?"

"Go on out of that! He was not."

"Oh, yes he was. He really likes you."

"Well, I kinda like him too."

The thought crossed Roisin's mind that Javier could easily find someone else too. How would she feel about that? Not good. She felt her muscles tighten and consciously relaxed her lips when she realised she was pressing them together. Was that the true test of whether or not she loved him?" She stared out of the car window at the fields of green flashing by.

As if reading her mind, Maggie said. "Emotions can't always be rationalized. Do you realise that most people haven't got a clue about how to deal with their emotions?" Maggie peered at her face in a tiny hand mirror and brushed her cheeks with blusher.

"Where did you get that piece of wisdom from?" Roisin smirked. She inserted a new CD into the player and twiddled the knobs.

Maggie laughed. "Oh, I don't remember. One of my self-help books. Or maybe it was in a song."

Roisin felt a tickle of laughter rising up from her belly. "This is pathetic. I can't believe we're even discussing it."

"In all seriousness," Maggie continued. "We should stop over-thinking things. Just enjoy ourselves." With that, she reached into a box in the back, fumbling for something. She emerged with two large silver-coloured hair coils which she placed over her breasts. "How do you like my new look?"

Roisin laughed. "I think your blood sugar's

dipping. We'd better stop off for a bite to eat?"

"I'm so glad you enjoy eating too," Maggie said, throwing the coils back into the bag. "I couldn't stand it if you'd said, *Oh no. I just had an apple.* Let's check out the next place." She pointed to a road sign. "Ballysimon is only up the road."

Ten minutes later, they pulled in to a café restaurant at the top of the main street. A slate board advertised an all-day breakfast and the lunch offers. You could feel the warmth upon entering. The interior in shades of warm ochres, sand and browns was contemporary, bright and clean. They took a seat in a side room and immersed themselves in the buzzing conversations and cosiness of the place. Roisin looked around the room. There were photos and posters of Indian Chiefs. Other posters depicted battles between Native Americans and white settlers. Just above them, in a glass cabinet, she saw another array of faded blank-and-white photos of Native Americans, children and adults. There was something spectral about them. She imagined herself walking outside to a totally different landscape. As she stared into the eyes of a young girl in one of the photos, she became mesmerised for a moment. The young girl stood erect and unsmiling, with eyes full of sadness and depth. She was wearing a calico dress which looked as if she'd been forced into it and commanded to smile for the camera. Probably taken from the reservation and placed in a Catholic boarding school, Roisin thought.

"Kind of weird, isn't it?" Roisin made a great show of opening the menu.

"What, this place you mean?"

"Yeh, what's with the cowboys and Indians? You'd never think we were in Ireland, would you?"

The waitress, a tall brunette with a kind, open face came over to their table. Her every movement buzzed with efficiency as she took their order. A smart middle-aged couple who sat near the front of the room greeted her as she passed their table. They heard the woman address the waitress by the name Bridey. "Congratulations," the woman said. "Sorry we missed the opening. It's looking really nice."

"Ah, thanks," the woman called Bridey said. "Let's hope it goes well. We'll certainly do our best."

When the woman returned with their drinks, Roisin asked her about the Indian theme. Bridey told them she and her husband had just recently returned from living in the States where she had lived for over two decades. A friend from Arizona had done all the paintings, she said. In fact, her friend's great grandfather was depicted in one of the paintings. There was something authentic about Bridey, Roisin thought. She would have loved to know more about what had moved her to return after all those years, but Bridey was busy keeping everyone happy. She seemed to have just the right words for all her customers, most of whom she appeared to know on a first-name basis.

Roisin and Maggie ordered bagels and coffee.

"I forgot to check out some ideas for displaying our wares," Maggie said. "We'll have a pretty big stand. If we're lucky, we'll also have a wall in our booth for display purposes. But now I'm worried it won't be enough."

"It's hard to think of everything. We should

have organised a few mannequins, but, of course, that would have been out of the question. We'd probably trip over them."

"True, but we need to think of something…fast!"

"If we get there extra early, we can get a feel for the place and see what some of the others are doing. Just to be on the safe side, we could buy a few yards of black velvet to cover the table. I think the trick is not to put too many items out at one time. "

Bridey returned with their warm bagels and they began to eat with relish. Roisin took the top off hers and looked inside. "I must get myself a bagel recipe."

"Why bother when you can buy them in most of the supermarkets. Jimmy sells them in his Deli too. His are the best anyway," Maggie said.

"Ah, you do have a soft spot for Jimmy." Roisin's eyes teased her friend.

"Jimmy is Jimmy. I never thought of him like that. Besides, can you imagine listening to him going on and on? I'd never be able to enjoy a bite of non-organic, pesticide-riddled vegetables again. My system would probably go into shock."

"Well, you could do worse for yourself, Maggie. He's lovely fellow, not bad looking either."

"Are you trying to play matchmaker?"

"Just trying to get your mind off the exhibition."

"Well, it's not working."

As Roisin observed Bridey, she thought of all the Irish people who had been abroad, returning with little touches of the cultures they had experienced.

There was no harm in infusing the country with a mix of ideas and tastes from far-away lands. What she liked about Bridey's place, too, was that most of the menu was made up of traditional Irish fare. It wasn't microwaved frozen-food, or the type of Tex-Mex you could get anywhere. Not that bagels were traditional, but that was an exception. There was no harm in improving standards, as long as each country didn't become like a clone of the other. A tendency, she thought, which was invading the shopping malls and restaurants everywhere. She wondered if she would have even noticed such things if she had stayed in Ireland all those years. Maggie prodded her out of her reverie. "Come on, cowboy, time to saddle that old horse."

They paid up, giving Bridey a generous tip and promising to do some serious propaganda for her place.

# Chapter 28

Later, when they pulled up to the hotel, Roisin could hardly sit still. She looked up and caught Maggie watching her with a bemused expression. "Why don't I check in? I'll see you back here in about thirty minutes?" Maggie asked.

"Is it that obvious?"

"Go on. Call him," Maggie insisted.

Roisin smiled. "I'm pathetic, aren't I?"

"You've been bitten by the bug or smitten by the lug."

"He's no lug, but it is a dangerous bug. Like a silent invader, I never even saw it coming." She sighed. "And there's no antidote to this one."

Maggie tapped her heart area. "Oh yes there is. If you've been bitten once, you can encapsulate the site, close it off."

"Oh, don't be so melodramatic," Roisin said.

"You can talk. Now off with you."

"I'll check out the area and see you back here in a jiffy."

Soon, she was sitting outside a café in the pedestrian area down a side street from the hotel. While waiting for her drink, she took out her mobile and keyed in Tom's number. Her heart pounded with anticipation. What if he was still sulking? Maybe he wouldn't answer. She had to force herself to slow down. No answer. What now? She listened to his message and closed the flap on the phone. The waiter brought her drink. She took a sip and dialed the number again. This time she left a message, telling him she was in Dublin. She tried to sound nonchalant as she forced cheer in her voice and said she's love to hear from him.

*Put him out of your mind. He's not going to call back.* She finished her drink, paid and walked down to the main thoroughfare. She caught a glimpse of her reflection in a shop window. This is no good, she thought, putting a spring in her step as she walked briskly back to the hotel.

The exhibition was due to start in an hour, and Maggie was already busy arranging the wares.

"Sorry, Maggie. I hope I wasn't too long."

"He wasn't there, was he?

"No."

"Aw, come on, honey. Who needs men?" Maggie spoke in hushed tones. "By the way, check out yer man over there?"

Roisin followed her friend's glance. A lanky fellow with soft brown wavy shoulder length hair, and an infectious smile was unaware of their interest as he chatted animatedly to a couple of women. His nose was on the long side, his eyes a tad small, but the overall effect was pleasing. It was the smile and the way his eyes crinkled at the corners that gave him a particular charm. As was often the case, he appeared to sense their interest in him and turned to look over. He smiled and continued talking.

"He's got something all right."

"That's an understatement," Maggie said.

"Why don't you stroll around and talk to some of the other exhibitors." Roisin said. She sent a wish out to the ethers for Maggie. Maybe he was the one.

Maggie shrugged. "I don't know. Maybe he'll come over."

They busied themselves setting up their stall. "I wish I'd thought this out a bit better," Maggie said. She began fixing the velvet cloth and setting up the brochures and business cards in a wicker tray. "It doesn't look right, does it?"

"We still have enough time. Why don't you take a look at what some of the others have done? I'll be fine here. Besides," Roisin said, "I don't think it looks half bad. You just need some detachment, you know what I mean?"

"There's a lot at stake here, Roisin. All that hard work and everything. I suppose I just need to stop worrying."

"Exactly. Now off with you."

Roisin watched as her friend sauntered along the aisle, checking out stalls and chatting to the other exhibitors while all the while making a beeline for Mr. Leather Belts. A young woman from the neighbouring stall caught Roisin's attention.

"Mind if I try on one of those hats?" the girl said.

"Sure. Come on over."

The girl walked around to the front and began trying on a couple of hats. "Did you make them yourself?"

Roisin nodded, pointing to her friend. "It was a joint effort."

"Tell you what, if I earn enough today I'll buy this one," the girl said, admiring her profile in the mirror.

"Okay. Maybe I should put it aside for you. No two are identical, you see."

"Better not. What if I change my mind and you're stuck with it?"

Roisin shrugged and put it back in the box underneath the table, just in case the girl did want it later. The young woman's face was decorated with several piercings. It was almost impossible not to be distracted by the lip ring. It looked more like an injury than a decoration. The woman, who was no more than an overgrown girl, had lively dark brown eyes rimmed in dramatic dark eyeliner. Her heavily bejewelled index finger twiddled with her nose stud as she told Roisin she'd been sent by her boss to cover the stall for the weekend. "He'd never come himself," she said. "He would think that a form of prostitution. Considers himself an artisan, you know."

Roisin's laugh encouraged the girl, who then raised her eyes to heaven. "Beggars can't be choosers, I always say. Personally, I can't stand this gaudy stuff and he knows it, but I've been told I could sell oil to the Arabs so he'll never fire me." She emitted a low, throaty laugh. "Sorry, did I shock you? Anyway, here comes the throng. May the tills ring merrily."

They wished each other luck and the girl went back to her stall, chuckling to herself.

Where was Maggie? Roisin relaxed when she saw her deep in conversation with Mr. Bo Jangles. *The vixen, she didn't waste any time.* Actually, they looked good together. As if on cue, her friend came back towards her, wiggling her narrow hips in an exaggerated manner. As she approached, she said, under her breath: "Wipe that silly grin off your face."

"My silly grin! You should look in the mirror."

Maggie, pretending to examine one of the bags, said in a low voice. "He asked me to meet him later on."

"See, I told you. When you're least expecting it. What's his name?"

"Seamus."

Roisin winked. "You look really good together." Before Maggie had a chance to reply, they had their second potential customer. A young woman with wild ginger corkscrew curls approached the stall and asked if she could try on one of the hats. She was glad they had had the wherewithal to bring that large antique mirror and a hand mirror so the woman could admire herself from all angles.

Roisin got down to business.

"You've got a real hat face," she said to the woman, "it's gorgeous on you." She wasn't lying either.

The woman adjusted the hat this way and that before taking it off and checking the price label. "I really like it," she said. "Are you sure it suits me?" She beckoned to her friend who was admiring a pair of earrings at the next stall. The friend convinced her to buy the hat. Roisin took out one of their fabric bags with a Celtic logo on the front. "Actually, I want to wear it now, if that's okay," the customer said. "Can I have the bag anyway?"

"Sure. Wear it, by all means!"

And so it continued for the next couple of hours. All their hard work was not in vain. In fact, it seemed people were happy to part with their money because, when she finally had time to breathe, she noticed most of the other stall- holders were just as busy. Funny, she thought, all this talk of a recession—no sign of it here. She wondered now if the whole recession thing hadn't been overhyped.

Maggie kept glancing over at Seamus who had also had a constant stream of customers. "Seems as if he's doing well," she said to Roisin. "He told me he has a little place down in Tralee and does a good trade selling mainly to the tourists. He does all the leather-making and his friend designs the buckles. Oh, yeah. Did you know the press is coming tomorrow?"

Roisin stared at Maggie, her face flushing. "I'd almost forgotten," she said. The idea of being on television made her feel faint. She had a phobia about being photographed, never mind appearing on television. One day she wanted to embrace her inner scarecrow and find out what caused that fear. Her phone rang and she searched in her bag, trying to find it amongst all the lipsticks, pens, tissues, notebook and other paraphernalia. It was Tom; she had been so busy that he had completely slipped her mind.

He sounded rushed, breathless. "Hi Roisin. How's it going? Sorry I didn't get back to you earlier. I had some unexpected things to take care of here."

Roisin was silent for a moment, searching for the right tone of voice. "No problem," she said as she held her hand to her chest, as if that could still her racing heart. She raised her eyebrows at Maggie who was gesturing wildly at her, and walked away for privacy.

"Are you there?" he said.

"Sorry, Tom. Yes, I'm here. We've been up to our eyes."

"Well, what do you say?"

"Have you been running?" she asked him.

"No. Just a bit stressed. I'm coming up to Dublin tomorrow. Can we meet?"

"Suppose we could, yes."

"Great, look I have to rush now. Is Stephen's Green okay for you? Could you make it by eight?"

Roisin agreed and slipped the phone into her pocket.

Maggie was busy rearranging some bags on the hooks at the wall. She turned to Roisin. "Was it the man himself? Okay. I can tell by that sparkle in your eye."

"He's coming up tomorrow evening." Roisin's fingers trembled slightly as she flattened out some hats. There was no time to say more because Seamus came over to their stall and introduced himself to Roisin. "We're going down to the Old Barn for a few drinks. Come and join us if you want."

Roisin looked at Maggie who nodded enthusiastically.

"Thanks. I might just do that." In truth, she didn't feel like socializing, and she certainly didn't want to intrude on Maggie's date but it seemed, from the way he phrased it, as if they weren't going to be alone anyway.

After he had left, Maggie told her she was glad she was coming. "I'm a bit nervous, to be honest. It's been a while since I've done this."

"But he's so laid-back. Anyway, you didn't look too nervous a while back. You were flirting like an old pro." She punched her friend good-naturedly on the arm. "You'll be fine. Just be yourself. Are you sure you don't mind if I come along? I don't want to be like a spare wheel on the wagon."

"Don't be silly. You can at least come for a drink or two."

They stacked their boxes underneath the table and chatted with some of their stall neighbours as they walked toward the exit.

"See you later," Maggie called over to Seamus. He nodded and gave her a cheeky grin.

They had just enough time to unpack their personal belongings and freshen up, not that they were under any obligation to be somewhere at a particular time, but Maggie didn't want Seamus to think she wasn't coming. Their spacious room was on the third floor. It overlooked the inner courtyard and provided a good view onto the opened pedestrian area. While Maggie was getting ready, Roisin rested her elbows on the windowsill and leaned over, gazing outside at the people passing by. At least half of them were probably tourists, she thought. A young couple, who looked Spanish or Italian, although they were a tad on the tall side for that, were wrapped in a tight embrace. They couldn't keep their hands off each other. They stopped under a lamppost to kiss passionately, drawing stolen glances from passers-by. Both of them could have been models, she thought. A plan began to hatch as she pictured the woman wearing their designs. In a flash, she grabbed a brochure from the box on the table and ran out the door. Maybe she'd catch up with them before they moved on. Slightly out of breath, she reached the bottom of the stairs and was relieved to see them sauntering off in the distance with arms wrapped around each other. Half running, half walking, she caught up with them and lightly tapped the woman on the shoulder.

"Hi. Do you speak English?" Roisin said.

Both of them answered in unison. "Yes, a little."

Roisin took a deep breath. "Good. I'm staying in the hotel over there." She spoke slowly. Then it dawned on her that they might indeed be Spanish. She asked them and they confirmed but insisted on practicing their English. "I couldn't help but see you from the window," Roisin said. "Maybe you'd like to come to our exhibition tomorrow? In fact, I wondered if you'd like to model some of our fashion accessories." She handed them the brochure. Of course she could have found enough Irish models for the job, but this was a spontaneous idea.

The girl laughed, showing her perfect set of teeth. Her glossy dark hair framed her oval face as she looked at the pictures.

"How much?" The fellow's eyes held a touch of laughter.

"Well…I must admit I hadn't thought of that." Roisin chewed on her lip. *That's what happens when you're too impulsive, Roisin Delaney.* "I'll have to discuss it with my partner."

The girl grinned. "I think this is very good, nah?" She turned to her lover and he nodded.

"How long are you staying for?" Roisin asked them.

"We are staying for two more days in Dublin and then we are driving over towards the west coast, maybe down to Kerry."

"I have an idea," Roisin said. "Since I live on the west coast. You could use my place as a B&B. From there it's easy to make day trips. You'd save yourselves a lot of money. Does that sound fair? In addition, you can also choose one of our garments."

The couple exchanged glances and spoke in extremely fast Spanish, the words spattering out to form a waterfall of melodic sound. Finally the woman turned to Roisin. Her dark eyes held amusement. "My name is Maria and this is Rafael. How do you say, we seal the deal, yes?" Roisin was pleased with herself and silently patted herself on the back. She couldn't wait to tell Maggie.

Maybe it was a mad idea but it would help promote their products. Obviously Maria enjoyed prancing around and she would have no problem carrying it off. She could wear an old sack and still catch people's eyes. They could use her for their press photos too, should the couple grace them with their presence. She wasn't quite sure how she was going to organise it though. After all she could hardly expect Maria to walk around all day, could she? Maybe Maggie had a better idea.

When she returned, Maggie chided her.

"Where on earth did you disappear to? You've no idea what kind of scenarios were running through my head."

"I found us a model." Roisin was slightly out

of breath after taking the stairs two at a time.

"What?"

"While you were getting ready. I was looking out onto the pedestrian area and I saw this beautiful couple—I mean really beautiful. Did I tell you I'm sometimes a bit too impulsive?"

Maggie, good sport that she was, raised her eyes to heaven. "Go on!"

"I grabbed a brochure and ran downstairs as fast as I could. To cut a long story short, the woman is meeting us tomorrow at 10 a.m."

"But how on earth are we going to pay a model?"

"It's all taken care of. I told her we'd give her one of the hats or scarves in repayment…and that they could use my place as a B&B for a few days. They were planning on heading out west anyway."

"Well, what can I say? You seem to have everything covered, Roisin Delaney. I think I'll hire you as my new publicity manager." She looked at her watch. "Now let's go. I don't want to be late."

\*

Although it was early in the evening, the bar was crowded with locals and foreigners alike. This made it easier to blend in. Seamus was already there, sitting tall amongst a group and obviously enjoying the bit of fun. He was gentleman enough to stand up when they came in and to introduce them to the others.

"Come on, ladies, one each side of me. What are ye having?" His lilting Kerry accent added to his attraction; he was a natural raconteur. She could see Maggie relax in his presence. In the background, a fellow with a guitar and a fine voice sang some favourite folk songs and some of the customers joined in. There was nothing like a good old sing song to meld a group of strangers. Despite much protest, Roisin excused herself after an hour, insisting she wanted to get an early night.

## Chapter 29

Maggie was in fantastic form and buzzing with excitement the next morning as they ate breakfast in the hotel dining room.

"I can't believe it, Roisin. I feel as if I've been single forever and now this. I swear, there *is* such a thing as love at first sight. He's sweet and caring and so witty. Honestly, I thought my jaw would crack from the perpetual smile on my face. He invited me down to Kerry next weekend too."

"Whoa. Hold your horses, girl."

"You can talk. Cavorting with two men and I'm supposed to yank the reins."

Roisin sipped her orange juice. She looked at Maggie with a raised eyebrow. "Not exactly cavorting, dear. You make me sound as if I'm a Jezebel." Her lower lip quivered a little, and she twisted the corners of her serviette. "How shall I deal with Tom when I see him this evening?"

Maggie, oblivious to Roisin's emotions, said. "Just play it by ear. You'll be fine. Don't forget your lipstick—remember, press photos and all that."

Roisin gave her a weak smile, lowered her head and pretended to read the menu. She was truly happy for Maggie and tried to put her own concerns out of her mind as they focused on the day ahead.

Now that they'd become familiar with the place, the day was a breeze. As promised, the Spanish girl arrived on time. Maggie was thrilled with Roisin's idea. The girl cut a fine figure. Every hat she tried on looked good on her. She caught on fast and didn't need any particular direction as to how and when to model the accessories. Every hour she tried on a different hat or scarf or carried a different bag as she chatted with the other stall holders and handed out brochures. If they thought the previous day was busy, this day was buzzing with activity. They would be lucky if they had enough wares left to carry them through the day.

Early in the afternoon the Press arrived and took a few good shots of Maria modelling a quirky green hat which looked gorgeous with her dark glossy hair. She seemed to be having a wonderful time practicing her English as well and she regularly broke out into peals of laughter. The journalist, a young woman from the city, managed to interview both Maggie and Roisin about their business. Although Roisin still considered herself a blow-in with no real right to take any of the credit, Maggie was the one who directed the interviewer to her.

Another advantage of such a busy day was that Roisin hardly had time to think of her meeting that evening with Tom. When she did think of him, she convinced herself she had nothing to worry about. She was just meeting a friend, no more and no less. And she was living her dream. She didn't want to become the kind of person who looked back on her life regretting all the things she didn't do. We do not do ourselves or anyone else any favours by ignoring our own desires or playing the victim, she thought.

She withdrew from her reverie and focused on

the goings-on around her. Seamus came over a few times and started goofing around.

That's what worried Roisin a bit. Although it was all in good fun, he had a roving eye when it came to women. You didn't have to be a master detective to figure that out. He seemed to be particularly smitten by Maria, but then again who wouldn't be? She cringed for her friend but pretended not to notice his amorous ways in order to avoid upsetting her. It was Maggie who brought up the subject when they had a few moments alone.

"Did you notice my friend, Seamus, is a bit of a lady's man? I sure do pick `em, don't I?"

"I don't think you have to worry. He seems to really like you. And he's so charming, isn't he?"

"Oh, he is—no doubt about that. But I'm afraid of getting involved with a man who cannot keep his eyes and hands to himself."

Roisin smiled. "Ah, give him a chance, Maggie. He's just playing around. It's probably like the barking dog syndrome."

"I'm supposed to be meeting him again tonight, alone this time, so I'll see how he behaves. He's leaving tomorrow you know. By the way, what time are we heading off? We have to book out by midday. That'll give us plenty of time to make our way back leisurely. If we leave early in the afternoon we can be back by evening."

Roisin was more preoccupied with her date with Tom but she nodded in agreement. It was a wonderful feeling not to be responsible for anyone. There was nobody waiting for dinner, no shirts to iron, no boss to appease.

"Oh, I almost forgot," Maggie said. "Remember I told you I have to see Siobhan Hennessey from The Kilkenny Design Centre? How about if we swing by there tomorrow?"

"I think it's more than a swing. That's about two hours out of our way."

"We could combine the trip with a visit to some friends in Bansha, Tipperary. It's only an hour or so from Kilkenny, and I know they'll be delighted. Let me ring them now."

Roisin didn't even have time to protest as a woman stopped at the stall and started looking through the assortment of bags. Their stock was depleting by the hour.

Maria passed by and winked at Roisin. She was such a charismatic young woman and was in her element stopping and talking to people. Her boyfriend also stopped in for a while. He told them his mother's friend had a string of boutiques in Spain and asked permission to take some photos. Maggie later told her she had slight reservations; after all anyone could copy them, but as soon as you sold something you put yourself in that danger. "I'm going to seek legal advice on that," Maggie said. "It's exciting though, isn't it? Imagine our designs being sold abroad. This could be our breakthrough, Roisin." She ran her hand over her forehead. "I'm getting a headache just thinking about it. It's too big, you know what I mean? We'll definitely have to set up a website too. You're in with me, aren't you? I'm beginning to think you're my lucky mascot."

Roisin did think about it; in fact she didn't see why it shouldn't be possible. Still, it wasn't her dream, it was Maggie's, but she was truly happy for her friend. She just worried that it might all be too much for her. Maggie was already showing signs of being overwhelmed.

    The rest of the day passed in one crazy but exhilarating rush. Soon they were bidding farewell to new-found acquaintances and packing up their remaining stock. They were on a high from all that positive interaction. Maggie told the Spanish girl to choose a couple of items from the collection as a thank you for all her help. The girl rubbed her hands together. "I had such fun," she said. She chose a burgundy-coloured beret with gold embroidery in a Celtic knot design, and a plain black one with a tiny oak tree logo. She immediately wore the black beret. It looked great on her, but she could have worn an old burlap rag and still look stunning. Maria promised to call Roisin the following week. She watched as the Spanish lovers sauntered off arm in arm.

## CHAPTER 30

Stephen's Green was a popular meeting place and sanctuary in the heart of the city. The gates opened up onto an expanse of lawns, old trees, a lake and plenty of benches. It wasn't huge, but there was enough private space for lovers and friends who wanted to snatch some quiet time.

Her heart flipped about like a butterfly caught in a glass jar. Would she feel awkward with him again? What would she say if he started quizzing her about Javier?

She walked up to the gate with a heart full of misgivings. Maybe he wouldn't even show up. An insistent little voice kept badgering her. *He's not going to be there. He's back with his old flame. He thinks you're far too complicated, and so on and so forth....*

She spotted him amongst the crowd of people who were strolling in and out through the old wrought-iron gates. When she saw him, the butterfly went berserk, but she did her best to look cool as she began walking toward him. The temperature was perfect, not too hot and not too cold. There wasn't even a hint of a wisp of cloud in the sky, and the softest breeze filled the air.

Tom was leaning up against the rails reading a paper. Some inner sense must have alerted him to her approaching steps for he looked up and gave her a wide, cheeky grin, folded the paper and put it in his jacket pocket.

"Hello, Roisin." She stood there in front of him feeling awkward, but the moment was broken when he linked his arm in hers and brushed his lips against her cheek. It was more like a brotherly kiss than anything else, and she wondered if she had lost him already. The warmth of his body and his purposeful strength as he led her down the path quietened her misgivings.

"So how's it going? Have you sold everything yet?"

"Pretty much, yes. I need to pinch myself. I never would have thought I'd be designing and actually selling my creations. Really, I have you to thank for all of this, Tom."

"Me? How on earth do you come up with that?"

"Well—if you remember correctly, you were the one who gave me the tip to go into that pub." She stopped and turned to face him. "Why did you suggest that place anyway?"

"No particular reason. It just seemed to be a good stop-off point. Did you know that they have regular poetry slams there? I happened to be in the right place at the right time one evening and stopped off there for a drink."

Satisfied with his explanation, she continued filling him in on the weekend as they walked along, taking in the activity around them. "Looks as if Maggie's found herself a fellow. I'm so happy for her. Oh, by the way, I'll be having Spanish visitors soon." She continued chatting away like a babbling brook after a good downpour when she realised that he was as quiet as she was chatty. One glance told her he was miles away. Her antennae vibrated slightly as she tested the mood. Maybe she was talking too much? Or perhaps he was mulling over something that had nothing to do with her? She knew something was wrong before he even opened his mouth.

"Let's sit and watch the ducks a while," she said. They walked over to a bench overlooking the lake. "What's wrong, Tom?"

"Why do you ask?"

"Come on. I can tell there's something bothering you."

"Is it that obvious?"

"Yes."

He looked at the ground and cleared his throat. When he spoke, it was in a quiet voice. "I'm engaged, Roisin."

"What did you say?" She looked at him with wide eyes.

"I'm engaged to be married."

It was as if someone had prodded her with a long, sharp needle. She turned to face him. "Let me guess. It's Sinead, isn't it?"

He nodded.

"But I thought you told me…"

"She's pregnant. It's our last chance, Roisin."

"But….you said you didn't want children. I don't know, Tom. I'm not hearing love here."

His voice rose an octave or two. "Love. What is love? I can't leave her in the lurch. I'm very fond of Sinead, you know. We go back a long way, and we've grown close these past few weeks. Come on, Roisin. I don't want to spend the rest of my days alone."

"But…you could have anybody. Are you sure you're doing the right thing? You can still be a father without committing yourself to a lifetime of unhappiness. Support her financially, and emotionally. Be there for the child, but don't do something you'll regret."

He wrung his hands and his eyes held a pained look. She reached out for him and squeezed his hands.

"You don't know Sinead. When she wants something, she'll stop at nothing."

"Oh, yes. I got that distinct impression at the pub that night."

"But she's also the most loyal and generous person, if she's on your side."

"Hold on a moment. I remember vividly what you told me about how she treated you, how she did her utmost to ruin your reputation after you rejected her. Have you forgotten that?"

He released his hand and pulled his jacket closer to his chest. "You, more than anyone, should understand how difficult it is to cut emotional cords. Sometimes we just have to make priorities in life. I want this child. If I don't agree to the whole marriage thing, she's threatened to abort."

Anger welled up inside Roisin at the thought of how the woman was manipulating him. How desperate must Sinead be to resort to such devious methods? Although Roisin felt a strong attraction to Tom, she wasn't hooked so deeply that she couldn't disentangle herself. She was genuinely concerned about him and his happiness. But she knew there was nothing she could do about it. It was none of her business, and Tom was right, she had her own emotional issues to sort out.

They sat in silence looking out onto the lake.

He broke the silence with a sigh. "Anyway, that's the lay of the land. You know what's funny?" He ran his fingers through his hair. "That song I wrote. Remember the one I played in the car?"

She nodded.

"I'm meeting him tomorrow in the Arndale Studios. A big British record producer is going to take us on."

"That's fantastic, Tom! You've got two babies in the making." So he wasn't here just to meet her. She squeezed his hand again. "Everything will work out as it should. Just don't jump into anything."

Two swans sailed gracefully by and she followed their movement until they were out of sight.

"What about your husband? Have you made any decisions on that front?"

Now it was her turn to be in the hot seat. She answered a little too quickly. "I've been too busy. At least I won't be tempted by you and your handsome looks." She gave him a friendly punch on the arm. Maybe the hook was in deeper than she thought, for she felt sad. "Javier is still hell bent on coming here. I hope he knows what he's doing, Tom, because things have changed. I'm not the person I was a few months ago. But it's his risk, and I've made that clear to him."

He sighed. "We're a right pair, aren't we?"

"Yes, so what now? I'm getting a bit chilly. Let's go for a drink?"

"I could do with a tall, creamy glass of Guinness."

"Come, let's go up to that dance café in Dawson Street. You know the one I mean? There should be a good buzz there tonight." They walked in silence, meandering down past the Shelburne and down a couple of side streets, each locked in their own thoughts.

Tom broke the silence. "I'll have to think about your words, Roisin. Maybe Sinead is not the right woman for me. Maybe I am getting married for the wrong reasons."

"Call her bluff. You didn't need me to tell you that anyway. The worst thing you can do is to be coerced into marriage. It cannot work like that." She turned to face him. "She has no right to do that to you. Are you sure the child is even yours?"

"It could be. Hell, I want to believe it. Every man wants to see his image and likeness, to plant his seed. I'm a fool for denying that and for waiting so long. Sinead's like a changed woman, gone all soft and caring."

"That's only the hormones working. She'll be back to normal after the birth, and you'll be in it for life." She made an abrupt stop in the middle of the street. A woman who was walking behind her almost bumped into them and muttered something before continuing on her way. Roisin continued as if nothing had happened. She turned to him again. "Look, Tom, it really gets my goat when people manipulate each other. Sorry, it's nothing personal against Sinead. I don't really know her, but I think you're about to make a big mistake. I'd better shut up now before I say too much."

They entered the warm opulence of the café. It was still early enough in the evening so they found a cosy niche where they had a good view of the bar and dance floor. Tom ordered a Guinness and she ordered a glass of red wine. She should have known better, for alcohol made her way too amorous, but it also lightened her mood. They sat laughing and chatting as if they'd known each other for years. During a lull, while they both sat quietly, she found herself putting things in perspective. Surely she should be devastated by the bombshell he had just dropped on her. She had always lived by the credo that things develop as they should. If this was in the grand plan of the puppeteers, then so be it! Her philosophy was the result of many years of observing, not only the dramas in her own life, but also those of her friends and family. At least it would alleviate her from a difficult decision. Now she wouldn't have to make one at all as it had been made for her. Tom's voice awoke her from her reveries.

"Penny for your thoughts."

She snapped back into the present and smiled. The café was filling up and lively salsa music added to the din.

"Come on, let's dance." He took her hand and led her to the dance floor. It was easy to tune into the rhythm. A small group of salsa dancers, probably from a local dance club, were really into it, doing a much more professional job, but Tom and Roisin were oblivious to their surroundings. He pulled her close to him. "You smell lovely, Roisin."

She looked up at him with an incredulous stare. What's this all about? First he tells me he's going to get married and now he's paying me compliments again. No wonder she was confused. They moved their hips and feet in unison as the beat took up speed, abandoning themselves to the fluid flow of sound. Another plus for Tom. Javier had never been a dancer. He was embarrassed by any kind of public display.

Soon the dance floor was filling up, making it difficult to move freely. They returned to finish their drinks, exhausted. "Let me walk you back to your hotel," he said.

Outside the hotel room, they both hesitated, not sure how to say goodbye. Tom took her face in his hands and kissed her with passion. Her body and soul responded, and she floated in a wave of pleasure before removing herself from his embrace.

"Shall I come up?" he said.

She felt the tears welling up. "It's better if you don't. Remember what you said to me? I don't want either of us to have regrets. Let's keep this memory in our hearts and give each other time to sort things out. Whatever happens, we must trust it's for the best. It wouldn't be fair to Sinead, and it wouldn't be fair to Javier. I've never cheated on him before, you know."

He sighed. "We almost did, Roisin, don't forget that day at the beach."

She didn't respond. Instead, she brushed her lips against his cheek. They parted ways once more, but before he left he took her in his arms again. No words passed between them. What was there to say?

The light from the lobby reflected the moisture in his eyes. Before she closed the door, she watched his lonely figure illuminated by the street lights as he dug his hands deep into his pockets and walked down the cobblestone street.

# Chapter 31

The next morning she awoke from a dream that was still fuzzy in her mind. It left her feeling melancholic although she couldn't remember many of the details. Something about water crashing over a bridge and a bird flapping its wings in panic. Memories of the previous night lay heavy on her heart. It all felt so pointless. There was a soft knock on her door. "Yes, who is it?"

Maggie peeked her head around the door and asked if she wanted to go down to breakfast. After one look at her, Maggie said, "What's wrong with you?"

"Nothing I won't get over. Give me a bit. I'll just jump under the shower." She wasn't in the mood for Maggie's teasing; nor did she want sympathy.

In the restaurant, Maggie spread butter on her toast, gliding the knife in concentration as she made sure the edges were equally covered. She looked up. "I don't want to pry, but don't you think you'll feel better if you tell me what happened."

Roisin raised her hand in protest. "Not now," she said, as she sipped her orange juice and stared into the distance, not even trying to put on a brave face. "I'll be alright in a while. Maybe it's all for the best, anyway." Her weak smile did not reach her eyes.

Back in their room, both women were relieved

to have something else with which to occupy their time. Roisin smoothed the last item of clothing in her suitcase and turned to Maggie, who was brushing her hair vigorously.

"I'm sorry. This has nothing to do with you, but I think I'll take a while to lick my wounds. Would you mind terribly driving back alone? I wouldn't be much company anyway."

Maggie looked up at her with big brown eyes and nodded. "You do whatever you need to do. It would have been nice to have you with me when I go to the Design Centre, but I understand. We'll have other chances."

Maggie drove her to the train station. "Take all the time you need, Roisin." She rubbed her friend's back and kissed her on the cheek.

"I'll be right as rain soon. Don't worry. Anyway, I have to be back next week for our Spanish couple."

\*

Back in Knockadreen, Roisin took long walks by the lake and along country roads as she pondered the situation. There was not much she could do one way or the other. Silently she cursed herself for being so indecisive: it had always been her failing. Blame it on the stars, blame it on past conditioning. She felt incapable of making a decision without weighing all the pros and cons over and over again. She wanted to do the right thing.

Helen knew when to leave her alone, and they managed to tip-toe around each other without getting in each other's way. Brian and Pauline had asked her to mind the kids and she gladly accepted. Even Brian kept his opinions to himself this time.

Late that afternoon, she took Deirdre and Mark out for a walk. Mark was learning to ride his bike and still wobbling along, getting frustrated with himself for not yet being able to balance properly.

"You're almost there, Mark. I bet within an hour you'll be cycling like an old pro."

He threw his bike down on the curb, face flushed with frustration.

"If you carry on like that, you won't have a bike to ride." She urged him on. "You can do it. Don't be afraid." She worried about Mark. He was so down on himself whether it was on the football pitch, doing school work or now this. He was a bright boy, one of the best in his class, but it wasn't enough for him. She couldn't see why he was like this. It wasn't as if Brian or Pauline pushed either of the kids.

"Pick up the bike now, Mark, and try it again."

Something in her voice made him take heed, and he smiled, showing the dimples she loved so much. His was such a handsome boy with his dark brown hair and vibrant colouring.

He picked up his bike, hopped on and pedalled for all he was worth, wobbling at first but then managing to maintain balance. Deirdre and Roisin urged him on, and he turned his head to look at them, shouting. "I can ride." The bicycle began to wobble slightly and he turned his focus back to the task. He had succeeded.

Roisin called out to him. "You've got it, Mark. Now you will never forget. Keep going." Deirdre wanted to try next but Mark was not about to hand over his bike now that he was on a roll. Roisin was trying to play peacemaker when a car pulled up beside them. She took the bike and told the children to move onto the grassy edge as she gestured for the car to move on. The smile froze on her face when she saw Tom in the driving seat. He rolled down the window.

"Roisin, I thought it was you," he said. "What on earth are you doing here?"

Sinead was sitting beside him in the car with a smug look on her face. Roisin gave her a wan smile and tried to act nonchalantly but her voice gave her away. She avoided eye contact and concentrated on the children. Although she didn't want to show her humiliation, she knew her reply was too snappy. "I didn't expect to bump into you either, Tom." She nodded to Sinead and said. "I was sent on a mission. Isn't that right, Mark? Show them what you can do."

Deirdre looked at Roisin with a puzzled expression. She took in the situation in a glance and smirked. Mark hopped on his bike again and rode up the road. She was glad she had this distraction. It would have been much more awkward if she had been alone.

Tom looked as if he was going to say something but Sinead cut him short.

"We'd better get going, Tom. Remember we have to write the invitations." She flashed Roisin another of her smug smiles. "We'd love to have you come to the after party. Wouldn't we Tom?"

"Sure, sure," he mumbled. Roisin noticed his jaw clenching. He refused to meet Roisin's now challenging look but began instead tapping his fingers on the dashboard. The moment was broken as Mark called for her attention. Tom turned the key in the ignition. She saw his look of resignation and his shoulders drooping as he raised his hand to wave goodbye before driving away in a cloud of dust.

"I don't like that woman," Deirdre said, as she squeezed Roisin's hand. Roisin was about to admonish her niece, but since she felt the same way, it would have been hypocritical of her to do so. She remained silent.

*

Back in Lissadore, Roisin busied herself getting the room ready for her Spanish visitors. It helped to keep her mind off the humiliating meeting with Tom. Whenever she thought of it she felt furious with herself for her reaction, or lack of reaction. But her anger was really a mask for her disappointment, although she knew she had no right or no claims on Tom. Roisin was also angry with Sinead, but she knew that was not fair either and attempted to put herself in the other woman's shoes. Sinead probably did love Tom. She sighed and slumped on the chair and let the tears flow. They were quiet tears as she thought, too, of Javier. She truly did not know what she wanted and that was the most infuriating thing of all.

A pecking sound at the window brought her back to her senses and she wiped away the tears impatiently and rushed over to see who was making that insistent noise. It was a little bird, a tit or something similar, pulling bits of moss from beneath the windowsill for its nest. It was a sign, perhaps, for her to get moving too, and she threw herself into action.

And in that same vein, she remembered Blessing's dance class when she was in town in the afternoon. Now is as good a time as any, she thought, as she passed by the town hall. She went inside to make enquiries about renting a space. The woman in the main office seemed happy to accommodate her and gave her some information on prices etc. Roisin made a snap decision and rented the space for the coming Saturday week. That would force her to get the ball rolling.

When she got home, she spent ages online searching for images of dancers, and finally, happy with her choice, she downloaded a couple of pictures and created an attractive flyer. Not wasting any time, she took it in to a copy shop in town. An hour later she came out with a box of 500 flyers.

She sent Blessing a message telling her about the room and distributed the flyers all over town. Jimmy Tyrell gladly took a bunch and even agreed to come to the class himself.

If they managed to get ten people interested, it would be well worth the effort. They certainly weren't doing it for the money. It was a good form of exercise and there were worse ways to spend an evening. She could hardly believe her luck when, before the week was over, fifteen people had signed up. Even Blessing seemed to be excited, and Roisin was pleased that she, too, would perhaps begin to feel more part of the community. The town hall seemed to be empty most the time anyway, which was a terrible shame. In a sleepy place like this, which only came alive in the main summer months, it would add a spark to the normal routine. Now, if she could only find a way to draw in the younger crowd, keeping them out of mischief, she'd be a very happy woman. She could hardly imagine luring them with African dance but what if she hired someone versed in hip hop or breakdance or whatever the younger ones were into? It would have to be affordable too.

Amidst all that activity, she had had a phone call from Maggie one evening.

"You won't believe it, Roisin. Guess what has happened."

"Judging by the level of excitement in your voice, I'd say it must be big. Are you getting married?"

"Go away out of that," Maggie said. I'll give you a tip. Think Scottish bagpipers, high-class Department Store, London, glitz and luxury."

"Harrods comes to mind. Yes, and…"

"Roisin Delaney. You'd better sit down. They want to take some of our products on commission. I could faint with excitement."

Roisin gasped and blew a low whistle. "You're not serious! When did you hear that, and how come you're only telling me now?"

"I just found out an hour ago. I had to collapse on the bed for an hour like a Victorian lady, the excitement was so great. I didn't even believe, it. Thought I was being had, that someone was playing a joke on me. You know, it would be like something Darius would do. He's great at putting on accents. It was a phone call from one of the agents at the exhibition."

Roisin's mind was flitting all over the place, trying to take it in. "So what happens next?"

"They'll be contacting us soon, although he did say it could take a few weeks and probably our goods won't appear in the shop until autumn or winter. In the meantime we'll be in communication while he works behind the scenes to get things rolling."

"Well, isn't that just the way of the world," Roisin said. "All or nothing. You never know what's round the corner. I'm delighted for you, Maggie. Just imagine…" Her voice trailed off.

"It's ours, Roisin. It was your bags that sparked his interest in the first place. I take credit for having spotted your talent."

Now Roisin felt like falling into a Victorian swoon or at least having a glass of wine to celebrate. She was grinning from ear to ear as they arranged to set up a plan of action, concentrating more on the products that sold better and the ones that seemed consistently more popular. "But we mustn't get too many stars in our eyes," Roisin said. "We mustn't sell out either, remain true to ourselves."

When she had put down the phone, she opened a bottle of wine and settled in to watch a good romantic film, which only served to make her horribly melancholic.

*

Maria and Rafael showed up, as arranged, a few days later. Roisin had left the shop early to buy some food for them. She was a bit nervous at the idea of entertaining them and hoped they'd be able to occupy themselves most of the time. She needn't have worried, though. They were thrilled with their room and gushing with enthusiasm about the views. She set the little table out in the garden and they sat down to a meal of new potatoes, her special marinated steak and a fresh salad. Roisin told them about Blessing and the dance class and Rafael's eyes lit up, even more than Maria's. He turned to his girlfriend. "I think we should stay on for a while and check out this dance class?"

Maria didn't need much persuading. Roisin discovered that both of them were involved in dance back in their home town, and she got busy planning. But then she realized it made no sense to plan a future with the Spanish couple; they were only on holidays, and it was unlikely that they would be willing to come over regularly just to teach a dance class in a small Irish town. There were definitely enough talented dancers in Ireland, but she couldn't afford to pay too much, not until she was sure it would be a success.

Afterwards, as they sat together under the shade of the tree watching the sun set over in the far horizon, Maria looked with dreamy eyes at Rafael and sighed. "I think I want to come live here, darling. What do you say?"

"We'll talk about that later," he said.

Roisin left them to it and busied herself taking the washing off the line. Young love, she thought. Everything seems possible when you're young, not that she herself was old by any means, but she'd been around long enough to have many illusions shattered. She could hear them babbling away at a terrific speed. To an outsider, it would have sounded like an argument. When she returned, they were in each other's arms, kissing passionately. She remembered the first weeks and months after she'd met Javier. Really, they weren't much different back then, but time and responsibility can change everything.

With her arms full of washing, she walked over to them. "How about going down to the beach for a walk before bedtime?" she said. "There's nothing like the sea air to give you a good night's sleep, and if you want to explore the area tomorrow you'll need to get up early."

Later, as they walked barefoot along the damp sand, Roisin stared out to sea and watched the silver-tipped waves dancing their slow waltz in the soft moonlight. Maria skipped in delight, pointing to the deep blue skies. "Look. A shower of little stars. This is a good omen, no? Let's make a wish." Roisin closed her eyes tight and made her wish too.

## Chapter 32

The weekend before the dance class, Blessing and Roisin sat together one evening to plan the event. Together they flicked through a selection of CD's. Roisin had already introduced Blessing to the Spanish couple. Blessing thought it was a great idea to offer an additional contemporary dance class to attract some of the town's young people.

After placing an ad in the local paper, Roisin had spent at least an hour every evening replying to enquiries about the classes. Fiona from the B&B, Esther, Jimmy Tyrell and Maggie had also done their part, spreading the word, and so far they had six teenagers, ranging from thirteen to nineteen, due to come the next day. It was a good start, but a lot of work for a small showing.

"You really think this will go down well?" Blessing said, as she sipped her chilled wine. "Maybe I can dance, but I've never taught a group before. I don't even know if I want that."

"The way I see it, we'll all benefit, and you'll love it too. Isn't that the great thing about sharing cultural identities? I know you're busy and all that, but you have to have fun too."

Roisin knew what she was talking about, not that she could or should force her wishes on anyone else, but she had seen Miriam's eyes light up when she danced. There was a touch of an actress in that woman and a side to her that wasn't being lived.

Roisin clicked the remote and lowered the volume. "Just be yourself and shake those hips." Haven't you heard a buzz of excitement rolling through town lately?"

"I've been too busy for that, honey. The worst part is those endless reports and all the paper work that goes with running a practice."

"See, point proven," Roisin said. "You'll have to get someone else to take over that side of the business." She got up to close the curtains as it was getting dark outside. "I can't wait to see who shows up, especially since we haven't specified any age limit."

"Word is already spreading all right. Some of my patients mentioned it this week; they're having a hard time getting used to the idea of this other me." Blessing held her head back and laughed with abandon, the infectious sound of her laughter jumped over to Roisin. "God knows, I need something to laugh about. There's only so much you can take, and if one more person tells me about their haemorrhoids, I'm going on strike. Honestly, Roisin, you have no idea of the amount of people who come in and waste my time. It's the seriously ill ones who wait too long. If I didn't have a sense of humour, I'd have packed it in a long time ago."

Roisin was a bit taken aback. She had never discussed things like this before with Blessing. But it was understandable that Blessing had days of frustration too. She knew, from all accounts, that Blessing was a good, conscientious doctor. People liked her pragmatism and her non-judgmental and supportive manner.

"Anyway, I'd better be going," Blessing said. "I have a long day tomorrow."

"Not just you," Roisin said. "By the way, when are you going to come and look at the shop? Maggie is looking forward to seeing you again."

"One thing at a time, dear. I did happen to see that write-up in some women's magazine, though. Haven't you both done so well for yourselves? Is it true that you've been commissioned to design for Harrods?"

"What write-up?" Roisin's eyes grew wide.

"You didn't know about it?"

"No! It's the first I've heard."

"Sure. A photo of the two of you too, wearing hats."

The penny dropped. It must have been taken at the exhibition. She asked Blessing if she still had the magazine.

"I'll have to check. I subscribe to a handful of magazines for the practice. Keeps the patients from complaining when they have to wait. I sometimes browse through them before I put them in the waiting room. Let me see…" The woman put her long-lacquered index finger on her mouth as she thought for a moment. "No, I really can't remember, but I'll check through them later on."

"I'd almost forgotten about it," Roisin said. "Although it's huge news for us. I suppose I've been distracted between one thing and another. We can hardly believe it ourselves. That reminds me…I've got to do a few sketches for tomorrow. It's all go."

"Don't overdo it or you'll blow a fuse."

Roisin rolled her eyes to heaven. "Yes, doctor. I'll do my best."

*

Maria and Rafael used Roisin's house as a base while they toured the surrounding area. They had truly fallen in love with the countryside and were full of plans for moving there, buying a cottage and perhaps starting a family. She advised them to spend a winter there before making any definite decisions. In fact, it remained to be seen if she, too, could retain her enthusiasm when winter set in.

The next morning, she went to the shop to work for a few hours. Rather than slowing down in pace, there was lots to do as they now had a substantial order from the Kilkenny Design Centre and a few other exclusive shops throughout the country. They had had a crisis sitting as Maggie panicked about the increased stress. Her words still rang in Roisin's ears. "I never in a million years expected something like this to happen. And, to be quite honest…I don't know if I like it, Roisin. What do you think we should do? I'm going to have to take on a couple more people, and we might have to rent larger premises."

This all affected Roisin too. Neither of them wanted to end up selling out and becoming a mass-production company. The last thing they wanted was to end up like factory workers, producing their items under time pressure.

"Isn't life ironic," Maggie said. "I've waited so long for this, and then everything comes at once.

Careful what you wish for. Isn't that what they say?" She sighed. "To make matters worse, I hardly have time to see Seamus." She stared out the window. "I really like him a lot. Why does it have to be all or nothing?"

While Roisin offered her well-meaning platitudes, she thought about her own life and how things were working out. Talk about a fertile patch in her life. There was unstoppable growth from all sides; even her garden, which looked full and abundant, could easily turn into a wild jungle if she didn't begin to prune it soon.

*

The next day, when Roisin arrived at the shop, Maggie and Darius—the latter of whom was now off for summer and subsequently spending most of his days helping out—were busy stacking shelves.

Darius, normally so good-humoured, caught Roisin's attention, pulling her toward the back of the shop. "We were just about to have a break, weren't we, Maggie?" He rolled his eyes at Roisin so Maggie couldn't see him.

Roisin tried to hide her grin, but Maggie noticed it and turned to look at Darius. She was like a hawk when it came to things like that, never missing a beat. She was not amused either. "I'm not a fool, Darius. I know what you're up to."

He turned on his heels and went out the back. The sound of the kettle being filled broke the uncomfortable silence.

Maggie sighed as she placed a few scarves into one of their new gift boxes before wrapping them in tissue paper. "How are you today, Roisin? Any news from Javier?" Roisin was about to answer when the phone rang.

Maggie exhaled loudly. "That bloody phone never stops these days," she said. "Can you get it? I'm not here, and you don't know when I'll be back."

Roisin picked up the phone, listening intently and nodding. She scribbled something on a pad. Despite Maggie's instructions to do otherwise, she almost panicked and handed over the phone to her friend. One look at Maggie's thunderous face made her decide otherwise. "I'm sorry, Mr. Waters," she said. "Ms. Cassidy is not here at the moment." She should be back soon. Yes, yes. I've taken your number. We'll get back to you this afternoon."

She put the receiver down and let out a slow whistle. Her hand was shaking.

Maggie challenged her. "Who was it?"

"Wait for it," Roisin said. "It was none other than Jonathon Waters from Harrods."

"What! Why didn't you put him through? Are you out of your mind?"

Roisin's eyes blazed with anger. "What on earth's got into you? I'm not your Girl Friday, and I refuse to be at the butt end of your moods. You could cut the atmosphere here with a knife." Her voice softened then when she noticed Maggie's eyes filling with tears. "There's no harm done, really. Didn't you hear me telling him you'll call him back this afternoon?"

Darius came out with a sulky face and Roisin looked from one to the other of them, shaking her head in frustration. Maggie burst into tears. "I'm sorry. It's just that I don't know how to deal with all of this. It's over my head and I wish I'd never gone to that stupid exhibition."

"Come here," Roisin said, as she hugged Maggie to her. "You're doing fine. Hey, we're a great team. And this is what you wanted, right?"

Maggie's body shook as the tears streamed down her face. Poor Darius didn't know what to do with himself as he looked on. "So what!" he said. "In a situation like this you have to see the big picture. Now come on. Take a gulp of air and laugh at it. Harrods started small too, I'm sure, and they like your designs. That's a huge compliment." He handed Maggie a tissue and then, thinking better of it, dabbed her cheeks with it.

Roisin's patted her on the back. "Ah, dear, nobody's forcing you to do anything. You can always say no."

Maggie smiled through her tears. "I'm behaving like a bitch, and I don't like it." She sobbed again. "I never could handle stress."

"Why don't you take the day off and we'll carry on here?" Roisin said. "You need time to think about things. In fact, I have a better idea. How about going to visit Seamus for a few days? He'll do you good."

Maggie wiped her eyes and took a deep breath. A little smile began to play on the corners of her lips. She looked at her watch and stood up, bracing her shoulders. "Do you think so? Maybe I can make the 2 p.m. train if I leave within the next ten minutes. That'll give me time to throw a few things in a bag. Are you sure you can manage without me? You've got that dance coming up…and I don't want to miss it either."

"I'll be fine. Go!" Roisin shushed her away. "Darius will help me here."

Maggie rushed out the door, blowing kisses and almost tripping over the mat. A few seconds later she barged in again. "Just need to get that Harrods fellow's number. Mr. Water's, isn't it?"

Roisin ripped off the piece of paper on which she had written the name and number and handed it to her. "Now, hurry up." She remembered the magazine article Blessing had mentioned, but it could wait. Now was not the time.

"I'm going, don't worry," Maggie said, slamming the door in her rush. Peace reigned once more.

"Poor thing," Darius said. "It'll do her good."

They went over the sketches she'd made the previous evening, exchanging ideas on how best to combine materials for the new set of bags she had designed. It wasn't even what you could call an exchange of ideas, it was more like two worlds clashing and colliding. Their ideas of symmetry and design were at odds. That wasn't to say one was superior to the other. She had always considered herself creative, but she was untrained; it was something that came naturally to her. He was of a different ilk, visionary, even wacky at times. She remembered the portfolio he had shown her recently. This is what design school does to the creative mind, she thought.

"You've got to move on, Roisin," he said as he flipped through the fabrics she had chosen, tut-tutting in exasperation. "Hang on a minute. Let me show you something." She saw passion in his eyes as he opened his laptop and flicked on the switch. Within seconds, they were watching a fashion show, with running commentary, recently held in Edinburgh as part of the global awards for innovative young designers. While a selection of models strode down the runway with typically exaggerated posing, one young man, who looked like a mixture of a young Einstein paired with the singer Prince, was explaining the properties of the fabric he used for his bag designs. He had integrated mini LED lights which reacted to temperature. She watched, fascinated, as the colour of the bag changed from navy to various hues of blue. Darius stopped the video presentation and turned to Roisin. "This is just the beginning," he said. "I want to create something that's never been seen before. The whole face of fabric is changing. We must catch up with the times. It's all about recycling, mimicking plant structure and animal skin properties."

"Yes, but what's that got to do with anything? We are not catering to that sort of market. Anyway, this is all way above our means right now." She laughed at the absurdity of the situation. After all, through a set of bizarre circumstances, serendipity had landed her in a cosy and manageable world, a world of doing what she had always done and loved but had only ever seen as a hobby. She wanted to keep it that way, living for the day without planning the rest of her life.

"I'm not criticising you or Maggie, or any of this," he said, gesticulating wildly.

Roisin's eyes held a glint of humour. "Well,

that's big of you," she said.

He continued as if she hadn't said a word. "It's more about me. *I* need to move on." He resumed the video presentation. As it continued to run, he told her he would most probably be moving over to London in a few months to work with Imogene Wainwright and her design team.

She turned to look at him and saw that light in his eyes again. "I'm really happy for you, Darius, but sad for us. Have you told Maggie yet? Why leave now when things are going so well?"

"It's a chance for me. I won a scholarship. The applications were sent in from all over Europe. Only a handful of us were chosen. It's just timing. I didn't tell Maggie yet and won't until things are more definite, but I did tell her about my ambitions when I interviewed with her. Besides, she can easily find a line-up of students ready to take my place. I know a couple of really talented ones from my year, and I'll put in the word. You'll be needing a lot more manpower around here pretty soon." He stopped the video and put his laptop back into its case.

"I'll really miss you, you know," she said. "And I'll be waiting for an invitation to your big show. Don't forget us when you make the big time."

"Who knows...if the conditions are right, I just might come back here next year." He stood there in his purple V-necked sweater and fine plaid orange trousers, with one hand on his hip, as his eyes looked off into the bright future. Talk about stars in your eyes! This fellow was a comet about to take off.

"I hate to say this, but I'm glad Maggie's gone off for a few days. She was unbearable this morning.

Talk about a briar," he said.

Roisin shrugged. "That's the other side of the success sword."

"I don't know," Darius said. "I have the feeling there's something else behind all this. When I came in this morning, she was reading a slip of paper and almost in tears. She tried to hide it, but you should have seen the look on her face."

Roisin squinted as she made several attempts to thread the needle. "I'm going to have to bow down and get some damn glasses. This is ridiculous. Besides, why do they make these holes so tiny? Now that's something someone should invent, a decent-sized sewing needle hole." She turned to face him. "What do you suppose could have been on that slip of paper to make her react so strongly?"

"I have no idea but she had a frantic look on her face. It's probably nothing sinister. She'll come back like a new woman, I hope."

Roisin frowned. An uneasy feeling overcame her and she found it hard to shake it off.

Even later, she couldn't stop thinking of the note Darius had mentioned. There was no point in worrying over something she couldn't do anything about and so she tried to suppress the niggling feeling. She put on some music to keep her mind off it and began transferring the designs onto fabric. She cut, pinned and sewed the inside lining of three bags. Despite what Darius said about moving on and hinting about being more innovative, she stuck to her gut instinct. Her designs were proving to be most popular. People seemed to like the fabrics patterns she chose, and it looked as if she would have to train some new people to do this work in future. She was happy to design and oversee the process, but she knew she would soon tire of labouring over a sewing machine, especially under pressure. Apart from that, it wasn't economically viable to work like this. But they had made a pact not to outsource to cheap foreign labour shops. There were enough local housewives and young unemployed people who could do with the money.

Darius stayed out in the shop front dealing with customers. An hour before closing time, he asked if he could leave a bit earlier.

"I don't mind," she said. "It's not as if there's a whole lot going on here."

"Great. I'll open the shop in the morning and you can come in an hour later," he said.

## Chapter 33

She was awakened the next morning by the sound of someone hammering at her door. In her half-dream state, her first thoughts were of Mrs. Walsh. She fumbled for the alarm clock on the bedside table and squinted at the dials in the half light. It read 8.45 a.m. How could she have slept so long? The hammering persisted, and she stumbled out of bed and over to the window to see who was making such a racket. There was a police car in the drive. *This is all I need.* She pulled the curtains aside and opened the window, calling out that she'd be down in a jiffy. She pulling on some clothes and ran her fingers through her hair before rushing downstairs. All sorts of scenarios rushed through her mind. It was Garda Houlihan, the same one she had talked to that night outside Mrs. Walsh's door.

"I'm afraid I have some bad news, Ms. Delaney," he said.

She felt faint and nauseated. "What's wrong now? Has something happened to Mrs. Walsh?"

"No, no. She's fine. We have been trying to contact the proprietor of the shop in which you work, but I believe she's out of town. I'm afraid your colleague, Mr. Darius Dowd, was attacked early this morning."

Roisin sucked in a mouthful of cool air. "Not Darius! What happened? Did you say *attacked*?" She shivered. "Come in for a moment, Sergeant. I have to sit down. Can I get you a cup of coffee? I need one myself."

"Sure, sure. If it's no trouble." They sat across from each other with their cups of coffee, and she stared wide-eyed as the Sergeant told her that Darius had been beaten up as he was coming down the back alley toward the shop earlier that morning. "I'm afraid they did a nasty job on him, Ms. Delaney."

Her stomach churned. She held onto the edge of the couch as a thousand questions raced through her mind. This was a nightmare. Poor Darius. She tried to swallow. "Where is he now?" she asked in a thin voice.

"He is in the Mercy Hospital in Rush and is being well taken care of. It looked worse than it actually is, although he has some frightful bruising and lacerations."

She pulled her sweatshirt tighter to her body. "But…who did this?" Even before she spoke the words, she knew in her heart that it must be connected to the other episode, and to Bill Buckley and his buddies.

The Garda straightened his shoulders. "I am not at liberty to disclose any information, but it would greatly help our enquiries if you could answer a few questions."

She nodded. "I'll do my best, but I'm not sure I can be of much help." She remembered what Darius had said about the note Maggie had been reading the previous morning. Maybe that had something to do with it. He had said she seemed worried. Should she mention it?

The Garda had his pen at the ready. "Mr. Dowd was unconscious when a neighbour alerted us to the situation. When was the last time you saw him?"

Roisin thought for a moment. "Let me see. We were both in the shop yesterday and he left an hour before closing time, around 5.30, I think."

"Did he happen to mention anything unusual?"

Roisin cleared her throat. "No, not a thing."

The questions continued shooting out. "We have reason to believe Ms. Cassidy left yesterday in a hurry. Do you know her whereabouts?"

She wondered how they knew that. Roisin sat back into the couch and grabbed one of the cushions. "Maggie was a bit under stress. We encouraged her to take a few days off. As far as I'm aware, she's down in Dingle visiting her boyfriend."

"Do you happen to have an address?"

"No, but I do have her mobile number. Just a minute, I'll get it." She hoped she was doing the right thing. The last thing Maggie needed was more trouble.

She went into the kitchen to get her bag and returned with her address book. She always kept numbers and addresses in her address book, just in case. She'd lost data before on her phone and had an awful time trying to locate numbers again. The sergeant was standing at the window. "Grand view you've got here, but it's a lonely spot."

In light of the situation, his words seemed

ominous. She scribbled down the number and handed it to him. "Do you think there's a connection between Maggie's departure and the attack on Darius?"

"We are leaving all options open, ma'am. Did Ms. Cassidy ever mention anything about a Mr. Shane Daly?"

Roisin knew for a fact she had never heard Maggie mention that name before, and she told the officer as much.

"Were you aware of the fact that Ms. Cassidy's ex, Mr. Shane Daly, has been in trouble with the police before?"

She nodded. "Yes, although she never mentioned his name, she did tell me her ex had been in trouble with the police before."

"We have reason to believe she might be withholding information."

Roisin ran her fingers through her hair. "Is Maggie in trouble?"

The Garda gave a hint of a smile. "As I said, I am not in a position to disclose any further information at this time. The sooner we can contact her, the better. Are you absolutely sure you didn't notice anything strange about her behaviour lately?"

"No, as I said…she has a lot to deal with, with the shop and everything. It's understandable that she has been under stress. But she never indicated that there was something else bothering her." Roisin had decided not to mention the incident with the note Darius had seen Maggie reading, the one that seemed to spark off her bad mood. She wanted to try to contact Maggie first and hear what she had to say. It was all very confusing, and she didn't want to inadvertently get Maggie into trouble.

The Garda stood up to leave. "Thank you, Ms. Delaney. Without wanting to unduly frighten you, we advise you to take extra precautions. Do you live here alone?"

There it was again. She felt that familiar pressure on her shoulders. She rubbed the back of her neck. "Yes, I do, but I have visitors at the moment and am expecting more to arrive when they leave. I'm rarely alone for long." That wasn't exactly the truth, but she knew Javier would be coming back soon and Anastasia was planning on visiting from Spain sometime within the next month.

"Right," he said. He snapped his notebook closed and put it in his breast pocket. "Keep your doors locked at all times, and let us know if you notice any suspicious activity. We will do our best to keep the area under surveillance." He coughed in obvious embarrassment. They both knew the police didn't have the manpower to watch the house twenty-four-seven, but he was doing his best. She began shaking again as she watched him drive away.

*

As soon as he left, she keyed in Maggie's number. Just when she thought she was not going to answer, Maggie answered. Roisin cut to the chase immediately, telling her that Darius was in hospital and that she had just had a visit from the sergeant. She also told her to expect a call from him.

Maggie gasped but didn't say anything for a few moments

"Are you still there?" Roisin said.

"Yes. I'm here." Her voice sounded drained.

"Why Darius? It's me they're after. Look, I'll be back on the next train and we'll talk then."

Roisin showered and dressed. It would take her at least half an hour to cycle to the hospital. Although Fidelma had said she could borrow her car anytime, that it sat idle most of the time, she didn't want to take advantage of her generosity. The cycle would clear her head anyway.

First she cycled to the shop and posted a note on the door, stating that they would resume trading the next afternoon. Then she continued on to the hospital which was on the other side of town.

The door of his room was partly open. She took a sharp intake of breath when she saw him. His eyes were like slits in his swollen and bruised face. He turned his face to her and attempted to smile, and it took all her reserve not to cry. He was propped up in the bed with his leg in traction and his left arm bandaged, staring at the TV screen.

She rushed over to him, gave him a tender kiss on the cheek, and handed him two Calvin and Hobbs comic books and a box of chocolates she had picked up at the local bookshop.

"Darius. I'm so sorry. Who did this to you?"

"Cowards." He grimaced as he tried to adjust his position. "Doesn't look as if I'll be going anywhere soon, darling. And these hands won't be doing much sketching for a while either."

"Have you any idea why they did it? Did they try to steal your wallet?"

"No, but if they did, they wouldn't have had much luck. All I had was a student card and 20 Euro"

His voice was raspy and weak. "Maybe it was

an anti-gay thing. I have no idea, but as they kicked and beat me, they called me a faggot...." He exhaled a deep sigh and winced in pain when he tried to move. "I won't repeat some of the things they said." He shook his head. "What worries me most is what one of them said. I think it was the skinny fellow with the pale face who said it. He was one mean-looking individual. He said I was to tell that bitch to keep her mouth shut or she'll be next."

A ripple of fear ran down Roisin's spine. "Did you tell the police this? I'm assuming they've already been here?"

He winced as he shifted his position. "They were here earlier and I told them. What I could remember, that is. It all happened so fast, and then I was out for the count, or so they tell me. Maybe that was my saving grace."

"Darius, the police asked me about Maggie. I presume they asked you the same questions. Did you happen to mention the note?"

"I'm not sure. I think I did." He lifted his hand to reach for a glass of water on the bedside locker and sank back in frustration. She held the glass with one hand and supported his neck as he took a few sips. He leaned back. "What's going on? Is she in trouble?"

"I don't know," Roisin said. "But she's coming back later this afternoon and I'll find out more."

# Chapter 34

Maggie, true to her word, rang Roisin's doorbell later that evening. "Sorry I'm a bit late, but I had to check in with the Garda. I went to see how Darius was doing too."

"Come on in," Roisin said. Her friend's face was drained of colour. She looked as if she had been handed a life sentence.

"What I really need now is a good strong cup of sweet tea."

When Roisin returned with the tea, Maggie was prancing up and down the living room with a frantic look in her eyes. She plonked down on the couch and buried her face in her hands. The sound of her deep sobs cut through Roisin's heart.

Roisin went over to her. "What's going on, Maggie?"

Maggie took Roisin's hands and looked at her, pleadingly, with mascara-rimmed eyes. "I'm in deep trouble, Roisin, and I don't think I can get out of it this time."

"Tell me, for God's sake!"

Her friend sank back into the couch and propped the cushions up behind her. Her eye makeup was blotchy, giving her the appearance of a wild cat. She began to speak in a small voice, as she chipped away at her fingernails.

"Remember I told you about my ex, and how he was involved with some shady characters?" She paused for a moment.

Roisin nodded.

"I am due to testify against them next month in Dublin. I presume they are the same crowd who have been harassing young Johnnie Walsh. Anyway, I had to keep it top secret so as not to alert the wrong people. Remember I got some photos back there the day I met you in the pub? And you know there's a major crack-down now on these drug barons. Is that what you call them these days?" She snorted, laughing and crying at the same time. She took a deep breath and wiped her eyes, smudging the mascara even more. "It's about time, if you ask me. Anyway…" She stretched her skinny legs and fidgeted in her seat. "…the thing I'm not proud of is that Shane helped me set up the shop." She flashed Roisin a defiant look. "Please don't look at me like that," she said. "She who is without sin...and all that. I only found out that it was dirty money after the fact."

"Now you tell me." This was a lot of information to digest at once. Roisin's thoughts flitting to and fro. She remembered Maggie's strange behaviour that first day in the pub. She looked at her incredulously. "Are you trying to make yourself feel better…by implicating me?"

"Well, you've benefited too."

Roisin gasped in utter shock and disgust. "How can you say such a thing? That's ridiculous."

Maggie shot up from the couch and began pacing the room again. She spoke into the room without looking at Roisin. "I'm sorry. You're right. It's just that...I feel like such a fool, and I curse the day I ever met up with Shane."

Roisin turned pale. A flint of anger showed in her eyes. She crossed her arms, hugging them close to her chest. She let Maggie talk.

"This past week I've been getting threatening notes. Anonymous, of course. I didn't know who to turn to. I mean, who could I tell?"

Roisin released an exasperated sigh, raising her voice an octave or two. "You could have told me. Do you still have them? Maybe it's time you showed them to the police."

"That bunch of incompetents," Maggie almost spat out the words. "But yes...as it happens, I do have those notes." She grabbed her bag from the couch and opened a notebook, extracting three crumpled pieces of paper. She handed them to Roisin. "Here, what do you make of these?"

Roisin smoothed them out. Each of the notes held a different message, short but menacing. She was no graphologist, but, unless the blackmailer had deliberately tried to disguise his writing, it was obvious that he was not comfortable with a pen in his hand. Small, untidy and disjointed letters formed the words: "Open your mouth and you're history." Not exactly the most brilliantly formulated note she'd ever read. Not that she'd ever seen such a note before...except on crime shows. The second note, written in the same narrow handwriting said: "One word out of you, bitch, you're done for." The third note was written in a different script. This was certainly no private school felon. "If you don't want to have your name in the papers, keep your trap shut. Just so you know we mean business, you'll be getting a little warning. Shame about the pretty face."

Roisin repeated the last words, almost in a whisper. She turned then to her friend, took a deep breath and said in a deliberate voice. "Maggie. Listen to me. You must show these to the police. Tell them everything. You owe it to Darius, if nothing else."

Maggie plonked down again, her voice rising and breathless. "What if they don't believe me? I could end up in prison. All I've worked for." She sighed. "I suppose you're right though. I deplore these bastards. How could I have known they'd harm Darius? Believe me, if I had thought they meant you or Darius, I would never have left."

"So, that's why you were so quick to take us up on our offer to go away for a few days."

"Yes, that was one of the reasons. I wanted to have time to think things through." She took out a tissue and wiped the mascara from her eyes. "But I also wanted to see Seamus again."

"What about your ex? Where is he now?"

"The last time I saw him was three months ago. I have no idea where he is. I don't want to know either. I'll see him in court when he testifies against Bob the Boxer, the one he claims ruined his life."

Roisin's face relaxed. The anger left her eyes. It couldn't have been easy bearing that burden alone. "No matter what, Maggie, you'll have to tell the police. Besides, they probably already know about the court case. All they have to do is put two and two together. Don't let yourself be frightened off by these idiots' cowardly threats."

Maggie was near to tears again. "They've shown they mean business now. I feel so guilty about Darius. You could be next, Roisin. Have you thought of that?"

Roisin put her arms around her friend. "Don't worry about me. I'll be fine. If you give in to them, they win and everything will have been in vain. Why don't you talk to Darius again? Tell him everything and see what he says."

Maggie sighed, a deep, heavy sigh filled with regret. "I think you're right. I'm going to the police. This time I'll tell them everything. Even if I have to lose the shop, or pay back that 5,000 Euros Shane invested in the business. It'll be worth it."

"It's not as if you deliberately did anything illegal. Now, off with you. I don't think you should waste any more time."

Her friend put a brave smile on the situation and left with a new resolve. Roisin hoped she wouldn't change her mind on the way to the police station.

# Chapter 35

The dance was about to start in an hour, and she had arranged to meet Blessing down in the town hall. They had already checked the sound system and done a practice session the evening before. Rafael and Maria were busy packing for their departure back to Spain the next day. Their contemporary dance class would be their final gift to some of the youth of Lissadore. If it went well, Roisin intended keeping it up. It wouldn't be hard to find someone else to take it over, and if Rafael and Maria did return…well, they would play it from there.

"Before I forget," Maria said, as she handed Roisin a card. "Thank you so much for this wonderful holiday. I'm so glad Fortuna was smiling upon us that day in Dublin."

Roisin's face flushed with embarrassment and pleasure. "Luck was on our side when we met you." She opened the envelope. It was an invitation to come visit them in Barcelona.

"Don't wait too long. We are serious about coming back to live here. Aren't we, Rafael?"

He planted a kiss on the top of her head. "Wherever you go, I go," he said.

"I will definitely come," she said, "but we'd better be going now, or we'll be late. Have you got everything?"

Maria opened her satchel and took out a handful of CD's. "This should be big fun," she said, as she put her arms around her boyfriend and hugged him tightly.

\*

Blessing's dance session was up first. She wore a traditional African print dress in black and amber and had wrapped a matching scarf in her hair. Roisin watched her flounce down the hallway toward the ballroom. As soon as she had taken the proceeds and greeted the participants, Roisin planned on joining them.

Rafael and Maria had over an hour to spare before their class was due to start so they went up to the balcony to watch. Roisin unpacked her cash box and rapped her fingers to the lively sound of a reggae Afro mix resounding through the hall. The front doors were open, providing her with a good view onto the main street. Good ole Fidelma. She could see her and some of her friends heading her way.

Fidelma entered the city hall with a huge grin. "Look at you," she said, pointing to Roisin. She turned to the others women and said. "This is the famous Roisin."

Greeting and smiles all around. "Are we the first?" Fidelma said, as she opened her purse.

"You are, and it's lovely to see you."

Fidelma turned to her friends. "We're looking forward to this. Aren't we, girls?"

"Well, now that you've dragged us along," the short, bubbly brunette said, as she shimmied on the spot.

Fidelma rolled her eyes. "Ah, come on. Don't make a show of us all."

"Will you be joining us?" Fidelma asked.

"I'll take a look in when I've finished here," Roisin said, "but my Spanish guests will be giving a dance class for the younger folk when this is over, and I'll have to be back at my post."

"Great. It's about time this town had a bit of novelty," Fidelma's other friend, the tall, curvy one said, with a twinkle in her eye. "Always the same old, same old,"

Blessing heard the commotion and came toward them, all smiles and charm as she held out her arms in greeting like a great matriarch. Roisin watched the women follow her down to the ballroom, grinning.

She was barely able to catch her breath as one after the other came in. There were some unfamiliar faces, but most of them she had seen around town. It was hardly likely that Maggie would show up, but she might surprise Roisin after all. The last thing Roisin had heard was that Maggie had told Darius and the police everything. Darius had taken the news very well and was recovering nicely. Even better, he was beginning to have flashbacks of the event before he blacked out and was able to give some details about his attackers.

Just as she was about to close the doors, her mobile rang. She half expected it to be Maggie telling her she couldn't come, or her sister wishing her luck. To her surprise, it was Tom. Tom, whom she had successfully banished from her thoughts.

"Hi, Tom. Where are you?" A crease formed between her brows when she thought of their last meeting. "Look, I can't talk now, I'll call you back," she said, as another couple straggled in. Blessing was coming toward her, tapping her watch. Roisin nodded and ushered the new arrivals in before Blessing finally closed the heavy wooden doors.

She could hear the unmistakable sound of shuffling feet and muffled laughter coming from the ballroom as she counted the money before locking it in the cashbox. Not bad. They had made quite a bit of money, although she supposed the tax man would want his cut and they'd have to pay for the hall rental. At least she could reclaim some of the money she'd put into advertising. What pleased her most was the enormous interest in the dance. Blessing was in her element too, just as Roisin knew she would be.

Should she call Tom or wait until later? Why was he calling now anyway? There must be a new turn of events. Perhaps his bride to be was now expecting twins. At least Javier knew what he wanted, even if it had taken him too long to figure it out. There was no shillyshallying with Javier now. She decided to call later, when all the excitement was over. The last thing she wanted was to appear to be too eager. Tom had left her waiting long enough. Not that it was really his fault; she wanted to be fair about this.

No sign of Maggie, which was a shame, but she could understand her not showing up. Maggie just didn't feel comfortable with certain people like Fidelma, and that was unlikely to change. To make her already tricky situation worse, word had spread about Darius. She could just imagine all the awkward questions Maggie would have to endure, especially in light of the fact that several people seemed to be suspicious of her in the first place. Once rumours escape, they had a tendency to run wild. Maggie's future success depended on her unsullied reputation. She couldn't imagine those prominent retail outlets buying her designs if there was even a whiff of a scandal.

Rather than join the dancers in the ballroom, she went up the side staircase and sat with Maria and Rafael where they had a bird's-eye view onto the dance floor. She could hear Blessing's voice booming out instructions, and she went to peer over the balcony.

Blessing had made sure that everybody was on the dance floor. Fidelma and her friends were in hysterics as they tried their best to follow the complicated hip wiggles and feet shuffling while shaking their shoulders with arms extended like some exotic bird about to take off. "No honey. Loosen up the shoulders," Blessing said, as she swept over to Dolores and pressed down on her shoulders, circling them. "Not so stiff," she said. "Forget everything you've been taught in Irish dance class." Dolores, red-faced but obviously enjoying herself, seemed to get it finally.

Maria and Rafael, who had disappeared somewhere to sort out their music, joined her. Judging from their body language, they were having a great time. Esther and Paddy were doing something that resembled a waltz. Paddy looked most uncomfortable as Blessing zoomed in on them. Maria shrieked with glee at the fun of it all, and her boyfriend gestured for her to keep the volume down. Jimmy Tyrell had rhythm all right, Roisin noticed. He was dancing with a pretty, petite auburn-haired woman. If she was any judge of human nature, the chemistry was zinging between them. As the initial chaos and embarrassment of the class began to shape into something more fluid, the group began to meld with the music and forget their inhibitions. They proved to have pretty good rhythm too…well, most of them. There were, of course, a few exceptions. Harriet Walsh would never be a dancer, but at least she tried.

Roisin was delighted to see a few men there too and watched as Desmond Corrigan tapped Fidelma on the back and whispered something to her. Although Roisin had seen him a couple of times around town, she didn't know him personally. But he was also a topic of conversation because most of the women of a certain age had at least one eye on him, even the ones who feigned indifference. Not only was he handsome in a Brian Ferry sort of way, he was living out there in that big house all by himself. It was rumoured that he had inherited a substantial sum of money. His father had sold a lot of the land that had been in the family for generations. And, since his father had passed away a couple of years previously, Desmond was now, by all accounts, a very wealthy man. That fact made him even more attractive to certain women. But he wasn't one to flaunt it. She had heard that the interior of the house hadn't been done up in decades. Fidelma would be just the woman to add a bit of homeliness to his bachelor pad. There was speculation that he was gay but nobody was sure, and he seemed to have a spotless if somewhat boring reputation.

Her eyes rested on the swarm of moving bodies, and her thoughts moved to Tom. She wondered what she would say to him. What did she really want? Romance, certainly. Love, absolutely, but at what price? Did there always have to be a price?

Blessing looked up and waved for them to join in, which they did, although Roisin didn't have much time, as she had to man the desk before the next group arrived for Maria and her boyfriend's class.

She tried Tom's number before the next group arrived. He answered immediately, as if he had been waiting for her call. "Hi, Roisin. Thanks for calling."

"Sorry I had to cut you off then. I was surrounded by people." She was still recovering from her intensive dance session. She spoke in short, breathless gasps. "So, what's the story? How are the wedding plans going?" A little grin played on the corners of her lips, and she wasn't even ashamed of it. She listened.

"Well, you can't say I didn't warn you," she said.

"Roisin, I know I'm not your favourite person at the moment. Things aren't going well between me and Sinead."

She held her breath, waiting for him to continue. His raspy voice shook, ever so slightly. "It's not going to work, Roisin."

Roisin heard a woman's voice calling from the background. Sinead, no doubt. Tom's voice again.

"I have to go now. Can you meet me at the weekend? I'll be out your way, and we need to talk."

She tried to calm her breath while she considered her answer. "I have to stop now too, Tom. I see more people heading this way for our class." Her heart won over her pride, and she agreed to meet him the following week. This was interesting news indeed. But he need not think she would be his ping pong ball. A flush brushed her cheeks as she remembered meeting him and Sinead back in Knockadreen. She had been so angry at him. He had just sat there as if they were casual strangers when he could have said something to make her feel better. But, to be fair, what else could he have done?

The sound of voices jarred her back to the present. She went outside to check. There were two young fellows in black tee-shirts and baggy jeans hanging around near the front door, obviously reluctant to be the first. She called over to them.

"Hi lads, are you here for the class?"

The taller of the two, a fellow of about sixteen with short sandy-coloured hair, mumbled something to his friend and they both grinned. "Yeah. We thought we'd take a look in. Nothing better to do here tonight right, Gav?"

"Well, come on in," she said. "Have you danced before?"

The smaller one, who looked a lot like one of the singers in a popular boy band, answered. "A bit. But we're not great."

"You'll love it," she said, as she took their admission fee. "Just follow the sound of the music. It's the last door on the left." The hint of a smile formed on her face as she watched them ambling down the hallway. She wondered how they'd manage to dance with their jeans hanging loosely on their buttocks.

A popular sunshine song blasted down the hallway. She closed her eyes and swayed to the music. Soon other young people straggled in, mostly in small groups. Just before she was about to pull the door closed, she noticed a young fellow standing by himself over against the wall. His straight hair was brushed over to one side and hung down over his right eye; an obvious attempt to conceal his face. He was clicking keys on his mobile at a terrific speed.

"Hi there," she said. "I'm about to close the doors. Are you here for the dance class?"

He cast his eyes at her shyly and hesitated for a moment. "Yeah, how much is it?"

"Seven Euros."

He flipped his mobile phone shut and jangled a few coins from his jeans pocket, examining them in his hand. "I only have five fifty," he said.

"That's fine. Come on, hurry!"

He looked painfully shy but followed her inside. "I was waiting for me friend, but I can't get hold of her."

"What's your name?" she asked.

"Niall."

"I'll tell you what, Niall. You go on ahead and I'll leave the doors open for another ten minutes. Is that a deal?"

He seemed hesitant but gave her a shy smile which lit up his bright blue eyes. "Yeh, great. My friend's name is Julie." She had the feeling there was no Julie, but maybe she was wrong.

True to her word, she waited for another ten minutes before closing the doors. When there was no sign of Julie, she went up to the balcony for a bird's eye view.

While Rafael stood with his back to the group, demonstrating the moves, Maria wove her way through the teenagers, stopping every now and then to correct a move here, an arm there. She did this with fluidity and grace, her glossy pony tail swinging in rhythm to her hips. She never raised her voice or embarrassed the kids who were trying to keep one eye on Rafael, as they danced in deep concentration. They had chosen popular artists everybody knew, and the kids were obviously enjoying themselves. Sweatshirts and protective layers were ripped off and flung to the side, as the tempo increased. Maria spaced them out on the dance space to allow for more expressive arm movement. There was also a good mix of the sexes and that made for a more balanced group. Roisin noticed some of them definitely needed more appropriate shoes and made a note to tell them that on the way out. She didn't want them tripping over their shoelaces. And she certainly didn't want any law suits on her hands. She made a note to check out the appropriate insurance. Couldn't do anything these days without covering your back.

Roisin spotted Niall dancing unselfconsciously near the back of the hall. He didn't need Julie after all. The music was so enticing that she would have loved to go down and join them, but age barriers prevented her from following her instinct.

Her mobile rang. It was Maggie. She sounded

breathless. "Sorry I couldn't get there earlier," she said. "It took longer than I thought and I had to get some things sorted. Is it going well? I suppose it's hardly worth coming by now. It must be nearly over."

"I was waiting for you," Roisin said, not in an admonishing way. "It's going really well, but if you come now you can still catch the last quarter of an hour. I'll open the doors."

When Maggie arrived she looked a lot better than the last time Roisin had seen her. "So, did you sort everything out," Roisin asked.

"Yes. I think they were as relieved as I was. I'll tell you more later." She turned to open the door again. "There's a young fellow hanging around outside. He's one of Bill Buckley's fellows. Maybe he's going to turn a new leaf. What do you think, should I go talk to him?"

"No, it's probably better if I go," Roisin said. She went outside and pretended to check out a poster on the front door. The young man was sucking on a cigarette, looking out into space. She saw him glance her way briefly and she used the opportunity to catch his attention. "Hi there. Did you come for the class?"

He flicked a few strains of hair from his forehead and looked at her suspiciously.

*Looks kind of innocent, certainly not like an up-and-coming criminal.*

He turned towards her. "Yeh, I thought I'd take a look but the door was closed."

"If you want you can go up to the balcony and check it out. It's a bit late to join now, but if you like it, you can come next time," Roisin said.

He flicked the cigarette onto the ground and

stubbed it out with his foot. Then he shrugged his shoulders and followed her. He didn't look at Maggie when he passed her. She winked at Roisin. After showing him up to the balcony, Maggie said, "It might be a good idea if one of us followed him up there. You never know."

"Good point. Although I can't imagine he'll get up to any mischief. You go up, I'd better stay here. They'll be coming out soon, and I want to hear their feedback."

She opened the door to the dance floor and looked out onto the group of dancers. A couple caught her eye. They were oblivious to their surroundings and moved as one body, weaving in and out, and twirling, coming back to embrace, moving in sync with each other and yet each of them appeared to be locked in their own world. They had something special, something that was rare to find. The beauty of it made her heart catch in her throat as she felt her eyes flood with tears, because she didn't believe she would ever find that, not with Javier and not with Tom, and she felt infinitely tired and sad. The music slowed down and the man wrapped his arms around his dancing partner and kissed her. She leaned into his embrace. Then the magic was over and the music stopped. Rafael thanked them all for coming.

Roisin was in a daze as she watched the couple and how they were so in sync with each other. She remembered that psychic's card she had put in her purse. If she wasn't capable of making a decision, maybe the psychic could provide her with some answers. The woman lived in the next big town. Perhaps she'd do it next week before she met Tom.

The sound of movement and shuffling feet came up the hallway as the door of the dance floor was flung open and excited voices created a din. They came out, with flushed faces, in one long throng, happily chatting.

"Just a minute," she said, as she waved at them to listen. "I'd love to hear what you thought of the class. Are you interested in coming again?"

Niall answered first. "It was great crack, wasn't it guys?"

A resounding yes! "They're brilliant teachers, but I hear they're leaving," a bright-eyed girl dressed in tight hipsters said. Several voices fought for her attention and Roisin beckoned for them to be still. Feeling like a school mistress, she said, "If you're interested in continuing, please sign this sheet with your addresses and phone number. We will be hiring someone to take their place and I guarantee you, whoever it is will be just as good. The best news is, Maria and Rafael will be returning to teach the class on a regular basis." She smiled. "I'm sure you will all want to show them what great progress you will have made when they return." A resounding cheer filled the space, just as the Spanish couple came toward the group carrying their sound system. Some of the young people clapped them on the back and thanked them. Maggie came downstairs with the other young fellow. She addressed the group. "Hey, that was brilliant. If I wasn't so old, I'd have loved to join ye. Tommy here came a bit too late, but he is definitely going to come next time. Isn't that right Tommy?"

"If he's not too stoned," one of the girls said, and a few of the others heckled.

"You can talk, with the amount you drink," Tommy said, shifting his gaze.

"Now, come on, kids. There'll be no drugs or drink allowed on these premises. Anyone with even a hint of alcohol or drug use will be turned away." Now she was no longer a schoolmistress, she was a High Court judge.

Some of them had already begun to sign the list and wanted to know when the next class was to be held. She reminded them to wear the proper shoes next time, explaining that if someone had an accident it could be very costly. They understood this and took it in good spirits.

Maria plonked down on a chair when all the kids had left. "Phew. That was fun!" she said. A lot of those kids are naturals, although they tell me they've never taken a dance class in their lives, except for school stuff."

"Yes, but most of them grow up with music. Between all these X-Factor programs, I bet a lot of them have been practicing in front of the mirror. And you do have great music. It would entice anyone to get up and dance." Roisin said.

Maggie agreed. "Promise me if you come to live here, you'll also have a class for adults."

Rafael smiled and took his girlfriend's arms. "Let's go down to the pub one last time," he pleaded. "It won't be the same back home without all our Irish friends." The Spanish couple, Roisin and Maggie agreed to go down to McGee's on the corner.

# CHAPTER 36

As it happened, there was a 'bring your own' instrument sing-along this evening and the pub was already filling up as they arrived. The barman, a friend of Jimmy Tyrell's, gave Maria and Rafael a drink on the house. They were already becoming quite famous in that little town, where news spread fast.

The woman with the nut brown bob and impish face, who had been dancing with Jimmy earlier, was blasting out *A Woman's Heart* with all her soul. The barman whispered something to Maggie who then looked over to the niche on the left where Jimmy was raising his glass and beckoning for them to join him.

They all traipsed over and Jimmy sang Blessing's praise, saying how much he had enjoyed the dance. "I'm having a shindig over at my place afterwards. Why don't ye join me?"

"Where did you meet her, Jimmy?" Roisin asked, nodding toward the singer. "Certainly not at Scrabble."

He laughed. "No. She came into the shop and I gave her some of my Wasabi nuts. Well, the rest is history, as they say. They worked like a charm, and here we are."

"Good one, Jimmy. They must have been

some nuts. She's gorgeous." Maggie laughed.
*

Later at Jimmy's place, as it filled up, Maggie told Roisin she was thinking of moving down to Tralee to be with Seamus. "Don't look so crestfallen, Roisin. You can take over the shop here. I have so many orders." Her eyes lit up. "This is so exciting for me, Roisin. Come on." She poked Roisin playfully and raised her hands. "It's not like it's the other side of the world. I'll be back at least twice a month to check up on things."

Roisin chewed on her lower lip. She had half expected something like this. "But you know my situation. How will I do it?"

Maggie continued talking fast, gesticulating, with eyes wide and glowing. "I've thought of that, don't worry. I'll continue paying you an hourly rate at the beginning, and I'll pay the rent, of course. Darius said he'll come back next year when he's completed his apprenticeship. Where's the problem?"

"Yes, but….."

Maggie continued in a sing-song voice. "Time to commit, Roisin. Just think about it. You've got a good thing going here. You know so many people already and you've got the house and everything."

Conflicting thoughts swam around in Roisin's head. This would be a commitment of a different kind. But she owed it to Maggie…didn't she. Maggie's enthusiasm sparked something within Roisin. How could she say no? "Okay," she said, resting her chin in her hand as she stared out past Maggie, at nothing in particular. "Give me some time to think about it."

Someone tapped Maggie on the shoulder and she turned her attention toward them.

Roisin pondered the new situation. The problem was, she couldn't shake off the feeling that she might not even be here in a year's time. The future was still unknown, and this job had merely been a temporary solution, at least initially.

She watched Jimmy Tyrell and Jules, the woman with hair the colour of hazelnut, chatting and laughing. She was genuinely happy for them. Jimmy was such a good fellow. He deserved someone like Jules. Somebody had told her Jules lived in Cornwall but came here for the surfing. Her mother came from the area originally and she and Jules had spent many summers here.

Maggie's news didn't really surprise her. She knew as soon as she had seen Seamus and Maggie together that they were a good match, despite the fact that he was a bit of a flirt. Now that Maggie had got to know him better, she assured Roisin that it was all an act. Maggie and Seamus had similar interests and that was always a good basis for a happy relationship; both of them loved music and were creative. Roisin thought that luck had to be grasped when it appeared. So why did she hesitate to take Maggie up on her offer? It was that reluctance to commit again. Maybe it was time for a change in her attitude. Yes, she would take Maggie up on her offer but not commit for longer than a year. That would solve a problem for both of them.

Maria and Rafael were deep in conversation with a small group of people Roisin didn't recognise. She wondered if the Spanish couple would come to live here. It would certainly be a brave move, but they were young and she knew they would fit in and make a go of it.

A commotion off to the right caught her attention and she saw Maggie throwing a glass of wine in some fellow's face. The lively hum of voices stopped as all eyes turned to them. The fellow taunted Maggie "You and your drug buddies should get out of here. We don't need you." Maggie's eyes were blazing with anger and she stood there, hands on hips.

"You have no idea what you're talking about, Michael Dunphy. Besides, you're drunk. Don't you see the irony of the situation?" She turned around to the shocked party guests. "I'm so sorry about this," she said. Then, as he continued shouting abuse at her, she grabbed her bag, thanked Jimmy and left, slamming the door as she went. There was a stunned silence. Roisin asked Jimmy what the fellow had said to upset Maggie. He shrugged his shoulders. "One minute they were laughing and joking together and then he began groping her. When she pushed him off, he began to raise his voice and verbally abuse her." Roisin nodded, told the Spanish couple she'd meet them later at the house and rushed out after her friend. She heard someone trying to placate the drunken fool as she closed the door behind her.

Maggie was marching down the street with her head held high. The sound of her heels clacking on the pavement created an echo in the otherwise silent street. Roisin called out her name, running and skipping to catch up with her. "Come on, Maggie! Don't pay any attention to that idiot. He's not even capable of critical judgement."

Maggie came to an abrupt stop, swung around and looked at Roisin with eyes full of anger. "Sometimes I just want to get away from everyone. People can be so unbearably stupid."

Roisin pulled her friend close to her. "Don't let them get to you, Maggie. You're far too precious to let them drag you down. Besides, there are idiots everywhere. Don't judge everybody in the same light."

Maggie's tears spilled down her face and she wiped them away. "I feel so bad about Darius, about everything. How can I ever make it up to him?"

"What happened cannot be undone. It wasn't your fault, and Darius understands this, so don't beat yourself up over it."

"I just need a good night's sleep, Roisin, that's all. Wait and see, tomorrow I'll be right as rain." She sighed. "I bet you never thought you'd end up with so much excitement in this out-of-the-way place."

Roisin shrugged her shoulders. "I wanted a change, didn't I? But this isn't about me." She gave Maggie a hug. "Are you sure you're all right?"

Maggie assured her she was and walked off into the night.

*

The next morning, as the Spanish couple waited for the taxi to take them to the train station, they sat drinking tea with Roisin and discussing the previous night's events. "What was going on with Maggie?" Maria asked.

Roisin gave her a quick rundown of the situation. Maria nodded, pensively. "He was an idiot," she said. "I felt so sorry for her, but I think he made more of a fool of himself than of her."

They moved onto other subjects. "Maybe you can look out for a place for us to live. Something simple, not too far from the coast." Maria turned to her boyfriend. "Just think about it, Rafael, we'll be able to walk along the beach every evening. Maybe we can learn an instrument."

Roisin guessed that a lot of Irish people would give their right arm to move over to sunny Spain, but thus is the nature of humankind, she thought,—the yearning for the exotic. Whatever we have, we don't want. She had met so many people who would have liked nothing better than to live in Ireland. The locals, on the other hand, couldn't always see the beauty. They were sick and tired of the rain, depressed about the economy and disillusioned with so many things. It seemed to be getting worse lately. But one thing was for sure; there was no place nicer on a sunny day. Optimism and sunshine always seem to go hand in hand.

She was drawn back to the conversation as Maria spoke excitedly to her boyfriend. "… and we can teach Spanish and dance, maybe organise trips to Spain for the locals ..."

"I hate to interrupt, Maria," Roisin said, "but if we don't leave now, we'll be late."

As the train was about to take off, Maria gave Roisin a little package. It was beautifully wrapped in green tissue paper and tied with a sprig of ivy. "Don't open it yet," she said. "Wait until we've left."

Roisin blinked, trying desperately not to cry as

the train pulled away. Their two heads poked out the train window, blowing kisses to her against the backdrop of the steely sky. Although she was sad to see them go, she was more than pleased they had enjoyed themselves so much and were leaving with positive impressions of Ireland.

The town was abuzz with tourists now that the season was in full swing. She dropped off Fidelma's car, intending to go directly to the shop afterwards. As she entered the reception area to hand back the keys, Fidelma caught her eye and gestured for her to wait a moment. She was giving instructions to an athletic middle-aged couple in matching green polo shirts and baseball caps. A little smile played on Roisin's lips as she heard the hostess telling them of the Scrabble evening. "What about you, Roisin?" Fidelma called out. "Get that smirk off your face. You haven't been for a while. How about joining us tomorrow night?"

"Oh, Lord no, Fidelma. I'm up to my eyes at the moment." The couple grabbed some of the information leaflets from the counter and gave Roisin a friendly greeting on their way out.

"It's all go today," Fidelma said, as she ran her index finger over the bookings chart. She rang the bell for Esther, who promptly bustled through the door.

"Hi Roisin. "How are you?" Esther said. "Hear your dance went really well. Maybe I'll come along next time. Or is there an age limit?"

"Oh, no. Anyone's welcome. We'd love to see you there."

She wouldn't hold her breath. If people did all the things they promised to do, the world would look a lot different.

Fidelma asked Esther to watch reception for a while and beckoned for Roisin to follow her into the front room. "Come on in, Roisin. I have something to tell you." She giggled like a schoolgirl. As soon as she had closed the door, she whispered. "Forget the rumours; Desmond Corrigan is definitely not gay."

"You didn't, did you?"

Fidelma blushed and whispered. "I'm sure half the town knows it by now. That's what I hate about small towns. You can't pee in the garden but the trees will be whispering to each other. Before you know it, your deed is magnified beyond imagination." She sat down and gestured for Roisin to do the same. "Here's what I'd like you to do," she said. "If anyone mentions it, spin a yarn; lead them up the garden path. Do anything but just keep them guessing. Desmond is a fantastic man, he's just before his time, and he'll run a mile if he's cornered. Private doesn't begin to describe him." Her face flushed, and a secret smile spread from her vibrant blue eyes to her coral-painted lips.

Roisin laughed with delight. "Well, you are a minx! I swear you look at least ten years younger." She winked at Fidelma. "Don't worry, I'll see what I can do."

"It's all thanks to you. Desmond and I have known each other for years, but neither of us dared approach each other. I believed what I'd heard about him, and he thought I was stuck-up. Just goes to show you …" she said.

Roisin hesitated a moment as she contemplated saying what she was thinking. Would it be wise? "Well, em... There's something that's been playing on my mind. Now that we're talking about such matters and about false judgements, I couldn't help but notice your reaction to Maggie. It's been bothering me for a long time."

Fidelma made a brusque movement with her hand. "Oh, her!"

"See what I mean. I've come to know and respect Maggie. Whatever you may think about her, please give her a chance."

The woman took a deep breath and flicked away some imaginary fluff from her lavender cardigan. "I'm a very tolerant person, Roisin, but I draw the line at drugs. They have done and continue to do untold damage to our youth."

"I agree with you. But, Maggie was never involved in that scene. Just because she happened to fall for the wrong fellow. Don't tar her for life. That's not fair, Fidelma."

Fidelma's chin went up defensively. "Well, from what I've heard...."

Roisin tried to keep her voice calm although she was afraid of the direction this conversation could take. "Exactly, you've only ever heard rumours. Did you ever ask her?"

Fidelma swallowed. "How on earth could I ask her? Be realistic, Roisin."

"Well, listen to me. This is what really happened." As Fidelma poured them a glass of orange juice, Roisin gave her a rundown of everything she knew. Although the last thing she wanted was to break any confidence, she knew if she could get Fidelma on Maggie's side it would help restore her friend's reputation.

To give her her due, Fidelma listened to the whole story, nodding her head at regular intervals. She sat there with her arms crossed, not unlocking them until Roisin had nearly finished. Her features became softer the more Roisin talked. Finally, she relaxed her shoulders and sighed. "Poor thing. I can't believe how unfair I've been. Not that I ever spoke out openly against her, mind you."

Roisin stood up to leave. "Maggie could do with some good friends right now, that's all. We are all so fragile, Fidelma, but we forget so easily."

Fidelma nodded as she accompanied Roisin to the door. "I see I have my work cut out. Let's hope it's not too late."

Roisin noticed Fidelma's eyes watering. She smiled at her, reassuringly. "I didn't tell you this to make you feel guilty, Fidelma. But you're a woman of clout in this town, and you can help set the sails in a different direction."

Fidelma nodded. "It's the least I can do." She thanked Roisin for pointing it out to her too and told her she'd keep her informed of any new developments.

## CHAPTER 37

The sky emptied its burden in great buckets of rain. It was the kind of day you either embraced with heavy-duty rain gear or sat out in the comfort of your home. She zig-zagged her way to the car, finding shelter where she could and trying to avoid the puddles which were quickly filling up. The welcoming light of Maggie's shop sign, *Eye Catcher,* was a comforting refuge, and she looked forward to getting her creative juices flowing again and just sitting down to her sketch pad and sewing machine. Maggie was rearranging the display in the shop window. Roisin tapped on the glass and waved. The sound of upbeat music filled the warm and bright shop, adding another layer to the cosiness of what had become her second home.

Maggie, who was on a step ladder re-arranging some stuff, called. "Morning, Roisin. I'll be right with you."

"I'll put the kettle on, okay?"

Maggie turned to face her. "Would you be a darling and run down to Jimmy's and get us a couple of those delicious nutty croissants? I could do with some comfort food."

"Sure, but watch yourself on that ladder. You're pretty close to the edge." That's all they'd need is for one of them to have an accident. Roisin filled the kettle and grabbed an umbrella.

Jimmy was his usual optimistic self, whistling Bolero and doing a pretty good job of it too. "Morning, Jimmy. Sorry I had to leave in a hurry last night."

He looked a little worse for wear. "No problem. How is Maggie doing?"

"She seems fine today. Nothing like a good night's sleep, I always say."

"That fellow is an idiot. He won't be stepping over my threshold again, I'll tell you that." He handed over the croissants. "Here, try some of this new wild garlic cheese. It's delicious." He gave her a slice to try and put some in a little tub for her to take back for lunch. They'd need sustenance to get them through the day. It was going to be a long one.

Roisin popped the cheese in her mouth as she looked at the new spice sets. She almost choked as she read the label on one of the tins. Spicy Dicey, she repeated. She looked at another couple, Chili Billy and Giddy Biddy. "Who makes these anyway?" She peered at the label.

"All home mixed. Some new company down in Ennis. The fellow is about sixty, used to be in property development and lost it all. Says cooking saved him." She loved hearing inspiring stories like this. Instead of giving up, he had tried his hand at something new. She took all three, wondering which of the spices made Biddy giddy and handed them to Jimmy to add to her bill. "How long is Jules staying for? Will we get to hear her singing again?"

"She'll be around for a few more days. She might even play again in McGee's on Friday if you want to pop in." He showed no signs of sadness at her departure so she assumed they'd be seeing each other again soon.

"Well, let me know if she does, won't you."

"Sure, why don't you come along anyway?" He handed over the bag and her change.

She said she would and turned toward the door, almost bumping into Michael Dunphy of all people, the fellow who had annoyed and insulted Maggie the previous evening. He averted his eyes, and she debated for a moment whether or not to say anything to him. Rather not. There would be enough others to rub salt in the wound, and she hoped it would sting. So much for Jimmy saying Michael Dunphy would never cross his threshold again. She wondered if Jimmy would throw him out and turned around to wink at Jimmy before she left. Pity she couldn't hang around to hear the ensuing conversation, but she doubted Jimmy would confront him.

Maggie was clattering away at the sink and set one of the smaller tables for their lunch. She took a couple of side plates from the little cupboard and they sat down to eat.

Maggie unravelled the corner of her croissant. "Lovely, buttery, calorie-laden delicious. Tell me, Roisin. Have you thought about my proposition yet?"

Roisin took a sip of coffee. "I have and I will. On one condition."

Maggie's face broke into a wide grin and she wiped away the crumbs. "What's that?"

The tinkling of the doorbell interrupted her. "Hold that thought. I'll go."

While Maggie was dealing with the customer, Roisin started an online search for some new fabrics. She wanted to introduce some simple but classy tops, pants and dresses to their range and this is what she told Maggie when she came back in.

"So, is that your condition?" Maggie wiped the crumbs from her shirt and crumpled the paper bag, throwing it into the wastepaper basket and hitting the target like a pro.

"Yes," Roisin said. "There's no harm in testing the waters, but I need some variety." She was silent for a moment.

"Come on, spit it out. There's more, isn't there?"

Roisin took a deep breath. Would what she had to say sound totally egocentric? Her friend had been so generous to her already. "Well, em …" She cleared her throat. "Do you think I could have this project in my name?"

Maggie blew a low whistle. "Right," she said, toying with the idea for a few minutes. "You're pretty savvy yourself, Roisin. I don't see that being a problem as long as we get our orders filled. How about Cassidy and Delaney? That has a nice ring to it. Unmistakably Irish too." She repeated the name. "Yes, I like it."

Roisin exhaled and released the tension in her shoulders. "Are you sure you don't mind? It's just that I'd hate for us to become stressed out. My wish is that we continue to do what we love, at our own pace. If it gets too much, I'll run a mile, and it's only fair I let you know this about me." The doorbell tinkled again. "I'll get it," Roisin said. "You finish your coffee before it gets cold."

*Well, look who's here!* Roisin was just on time to catch a grand view of Blessing's well-rounded backside as the woman leaned over and shook her umbrella out onto the pavement.

"Holy Geronimo," Blessing said as she turned around and stepped into the shop, depositing her umbrella in the stand by the door. "I'll never get used to all this rain."

She wore a shapeless beige rain coat and flat black lace-up shoes, not exactly complimentary, and a far cry from the exotic-looking turbaned-woman who had been at the party. Blessing, like a person with no time to waste, took in the shop's interior in one cool glance. She swooped in on an earring display, picked up a pair of amber dangling earrings and held them up against her creamy mocha skin. "What do you think?" she said.

"Very lovely. Here, try this." Roisin gave her a red boxy hat, decorated with a thin shiny brocade rim. It was too small to fit over Blessing's big hair. They laughed as she tried on a few more. "I think my head is too big for Irish hats," she said in mock despair.

"Be happy you're not in China, then," Roisin said. "We can make one to fit. Just choose the style and colour and we'll have it for you by next week." Roisin already had her measuring tape out. "Here, let me take your vitals."

Blessing, who was a head taller than Roisin, stooped down obediently and let her take her measurements. As they deliberated over the colour, Maggie, upon hearing the commotion, came out to join them. "Ah, Blessing, it's you. I thought I recognised that voice. Sorry I was too late for your dance class. I heard it was a real hit."

"Yes, I enjoyed it a lot, and it's awakening all sorts of longings in these old bones. I feel Africa calling." She laughed loudly at her own joke. "So many people have stopped me on the street. I've even noticed my patients are more open to me now that they know I'm human like the rest of them."

"Which reminds me," Roisin said. "Have you thought about how often you want to offer that class? I need to book the hall on a long-term basis."

Blessing was busy draping a wide scarf over her shoulders and admiring herself in the mirror. "Definitely not every week. How about every two weeks?"

Roisin closed her order book. "Sounds okay to me, but I'll have to check with the county hall and see what bookings they have first. I'll give you a ring as soon as I know."

Blessing handed her the earrings. "I'll take these, but I'd better be getting back to work now." She called out to Maggie who was busy fixing a shelf. "Will you come next time, Maggie? I think you'll really enjoy it." Blessing was one astute woman, and Roisin knew she was concerned about Maggie but didn't want to interfere. This was her way of including Maggie and letting her know she was on her side. Blessing was also a survivor and one strong woman to have come so far.

Maggie came back into the shop. "I just might do that. Thanks for stopping by."

"It was my pleasure," Blessing said as she

retrieved her umbrella. "You have a lovely place here."

It was a successful and a busy day, and between sewing, serving in the shop and working on her new designs, Roisin felt a sense of accomplishment. This had the added benefit of taking her mind off recent events. Tactfully, she avoided the subject of Maggie's upcoming court case. Roisin knew Maggie would talk about it if and when she was ready. Meanwhile, Roisin wanted to pop in to see Darius after work but it was awkward getting there, and the walk would take her far too long. She took a taxi instead and had the most exhilarating ride with a woman called Josie. Josie was a character. She told Roisin she was the first female taxi driver in town and had been successfully driving people up the wall for years. "I'm replacing the local priest and have taken the oath of allegiance and secrecy" she said. "You've no idea what people get up to when they've had a few." She proceeded to tell rude jokes all the way to the hospital and said she liked to have people in stitches before they entered those sterile wards. Soon, Roisin was in great spirits. It was a rare gift that Josie had. She liked to shock, but her intentions were pure gold. Meeting Josie had a domino effect, too, because Roisin then transferred the good spirits onto Darius. Although his voice still sounded a little wobbly, he was doing much better and was expected to be released the next day. He was determined to restart work the following week. "If I stay away, they'll think they've won," he said, and she had to agree with him. So, although she had put the events of the past few weeks pretty much behind her, Garda Houlihan's words of warning still left her feeling uneasy.

*

Later in the evening she went out to do some much-needed weeding and cutting of grass before it got too dark. Mrs. Walsh's house stood empty as she was on holidays somewhere in the south. Roisin suddenly felt lonely. The sun had come out late in the afternoon and, miraculously, had dried up all those puddles and taken the drenched look off the countryside. She ripped out a stubborn old thistle and threw it over onto the other pile. Weeds—she contemplated the nature of life and the purpose of weeds such as thistles and others that were greedily trying to take over her garden. It was a never-ending battle. She thought about the day's news and the riots in London and other English cities. It did nothing to uplift her spirits but rather added to the feeling of foreboding that had slowly and silently crept up on her ever since she had left work. Although she loved living alone, she didn't like when the dark hours set in. Maybe it was a throwback to all those ghost stories she had heard in her youth, but there was something about the darkness that caused that primordial angst to shift something within her. Before turning in for the evening, she put all the weeds into the wheelbarrow and covered it with an old plastic bag in case it rained later. The sound of a car engine driving slowly past her house saw her turn her head to see if she recognised the owner. She caught the tail end of it as it turned the corner and slowed down even more near Mrs. Walsh's house. Probably nothing to worry about, she thought, as the car drove off, but she was glad to be inside again.

She forced herself to think of more pleasant things and suddenly remembered the card she had received from her good friend Anastasia the previous day. Anastasia was coming to visit at the end of the week for a few days. Roisin could hardly wait to see her again. Would Anastasia change her tune now when she saw how everything had worked out? Then of course she was going to meet Tom in a few days. She wasn't sure how she really felt about that. Javier had been sending her emails and keeping her up-to-date about his plans too. She missed the familiarity of having him around, but she knew things would never be the same between them again.

Tom had arranged to collect her after work on Wednesday after visiting his grandfather's place. Despite her attempts to overplay the niggling negative mood, it was still there. Before she turned in for the night, she double checked to make sure all the doors and windows were closed, just in case. As she rummaged in her bag to find her mobile in order to recharge it, she came upon the present Maria had given her. It was almost too nicely wrapped to open. She undid the sprig of ivy gently and unfolded the wrapping paper. It was an exquisite little silver angel pendant. She immediately put in on and admired it in the hallway mirror. It rested nicely in the hollow of her throat. She opened the gift card.

*Thank you so much, Roisin. We had a wonderful time. Wear this angel of protection and joy at all times. You will always be our Irish angel. See you soon. Much love from Maria and Rafael.*

How thoughtful of them. Although it was probably pure superstition, she did feel a bit safer now that she was wearing it, and yet…she still couldn't shake off that sense of foreboding. She thought she heard a car engine again and all the tiny hairs on her arms stood to alert. Creeping over to the window, she peered outside. It was too dark to see anything, so she went to the kitchen, poured herself a glass of wine and settled in to watch some light-television to settle her nerves.

## Chapter 38

It was no good. Her feeling of unease was growing in intensity. She debated what to do, and although it seemed a bit radical in light of the fact that it was merely a hunch, she called the garda station. All she got was an answering machine. How foolish she felt leaving a message about her fears and feeling of foreboding. She then called her sister and told her of some of the latest developments. She also told her about her rising panic. Helen managed to set her mind at ease. "That's not like you to be so nervous. What are you reading at the moment? I always get like that when I've been watching crime shows or reading thrillers." Roisin told her she had been watching Crime Watch the previous evening and realized it probably had had an effect on her after all. There were several instances of break-ins and one old man had been beaten to death with a hammer. She had sat there, mesmerized and horrified at the violence and lack of empathy these criminals displayed, but she couldn't turn off the tv. She had to watch it till the end. It was better to be informed, or was it? After talking to Helen, she checked the windows and doors once again. I really should get a dog, she thought. But she quickly dismissed the idea; dogs require a lot of care and she was gone most of the day.

She left the landing light on with her bedroom door open and finally fell asleep. It seemed like mere minutes before she awoke with a start and sat bolt upright in bed. The clock radio showed 2.35 a.m. There was an unmistakable hammering coming from downstairs. That must have been what woke her up. She covered herself, terrified and unable to move. Every muscle in her body tensed up. Her breath caught in her throat as the banging persisted. She broke out in a clammy sweat. It sounded as if they were breaking down the door. Her gaze darted to the wardrobe, but she realised that was no option. She was trapped, but hiding wasn't going to do her any good. Whom to ring? Her mobile was beside the bed and she tried the police again, sighing with relief when garda Houlihan answered. She kept her voice low, but her heart thumped in her chest, making it hard to get the words out. "Hello, Garda Houlihan. This is Roisin Delaney. There's an intruder trying to get into my house." She held the phone out so he could hear the loud hammering noise for himself.

"Stay where you are…and lock your door. Under no circumstances are you to open it. I'll be there as soon as possible."

A surge of adrenalin, fired by anger, propelled her to follow the garda's instructions. In her haste, she forgot she couldn't lock the door because the keys were in one of the drawers downstairs. The hammering sounds intensified. She looked around her frantically for something, anything she could use with which to defend herself. Nothing, she felt like a bird with a broken wing being chased by a cat. She crept onto the landing. Her eyes moved to the small window overlooking the back yard. If she could make it out the window before whomever it was broke through, she could run under cover of the trees until the gardaí arrived. Breathing fast, she yanked the window open and looked down. The sight made her dizzy, but it was a choice of taking a risk and jumping down onto the dormer window mantel, or waiting for a fate unknown. The memory of the state of Darius's face fuelled her into action. She climbed out and balanced herself on the ledge as she held the wall for dear life. Then she almost toppled but managed to propel herself forward, landing on the ground with a thump. A piercing pain shot up her leg, but by some super-human effort, she half-ran and half-dragged herself over to the next clump of trees where she was able to take cover, concealing herself for the moment. Still no sign of the police. What was keeping them? The landing light was still on and she watched with terror as two hooded fellows rushed past and on into her bedroom. Although she had had the wherewithal to half push the window closed before she jumped, it wouldn't take them long to realise how she had made her escape.

She made a dash toward the road and was stopped in her tracks as she heard loud shouting coming from the open window from which she had made her escape. Silently, she prayed the gardaí would show up before it was too late. Her heart was beating at a terrific rate and her legs felt as heavy as two blocks of cement. She weighed her odds. No, she couldn't run. Maybe they even had a gun. The front door opened…they were making a beeline in her direction, shouting. The moon moved in behind the clouds and darkness enveloped the scene. She dragged herself over to a nearby hedge. They were getting closer. They must surely hear her heart thumping. Just as she thought she was going to pass out in terror, the urgent sound of police sirens screamed into the night.

She heard one of them call out. "The bitch called the police. Run out the back, Podge." Well, if that was all she had to go on, at least she now had a name and a not-too-common one either. They took off toward Mrs. Walsh's place and the moon illuminated them for a few seconds. Judging by the speed at which they were running, she guessed them to be in their early to late twenties. One was short and stocky; the other was long and lithe. Both were dressed in dark colours and wore hoodies. She shouted out to the garda who had just darted out of his car.

"They've gone that way," she shouted. A second garda followed and both men ran in pursuit. One of them shouted to her. "Get back into the house, quickly!"

She half dragged herself into the house, wincing at the pain. What if they sneaked back inside? There was nothing for it but to wait. She went into the kitchen. At least she could lock that door. She fumbled about in the dark, not wanting to put the light on in case of the worst…and waited.

Finally, she heard swift footsteps coming down the hallway.

"Ms. Delaney. Are you there?" Relief. It was Garda O'Houlihan's voice. Roisin switched on the light and opened the door.

"You're safe now," he said. "We caught one of them."

She breathed a sigh of relief.

"But it might be a good idea if you stay somewhere else tonight," he said.

She looked at her watch. "Yes, maybe you're right." In truth, she had no intention of disturbing anyone at such a late hour. Besides, who would she ask? The thought of staying in the house now with the broken door giving free access to any marauding burglar didn't exactly appeal to her, and she weighed up the pros and cons of staying or waking up Maggie or even Fidelma.

The garda must have guessed her reluctance, because he refused to leave until she had worked something out. She had no choice but to dial Maggie's number while he looked on. It took a while for her friend to answer and when she did, Maggie's voice was groggy with sleep. Roisin gave her a quick rundown of the situation, and Maggie said she would come right away. Driving in the garda car with that thug in the back seat beside her was certainly not an option. Remarkably, Roisin felt calm, apart from the painful throbbing in her ankle. She rubbed it gently. It felt hot and swollen. She'd better have it checked the next day if the swelling didn't go down. While the garda waited, she packed an overnight case and included some phials of homeopathic remedies. Maybe all she needed was to rest and cool her ankle.

She thanked the garda and he waited outside in the car until Maggie arrived. True to her word, Maggie arrived within what seemed to be mere minutes. Time had lost its significance anyway, and she felt as if she was in a dream. She heard her friend exchange a few words with the gardai. Now that the adrenalin rush was over, a feeling of exhaustion overcame her. All she wanted to do was sleep. How on earth had she got herself into such a nightmare situation? Hearing Maggie's voice brought a cascade of questions to her mind as she pondered on the significance of her meeting with Maggie that day in the pub. It was a two-edged sword, bringing her luck on the one hand, and danger on the other. For better or for worse, they were now inextricably connected, at least until this was all sorted out. Roisin hoped the court case would resolve a lot of the problems and allow Maggie to get on with her life.

Maggie was in a worse state than she was. She apologised over and over again. "I'm so sorry, Roisin. This is a nightmare. When I think of what could have happened…." She broke down, sobbing, and Roisin ended up consoling her friend instead of the other way around.

Roisin sighed and gave her a weak smile. "You couldn't have known, and there's no point in rehashing what's past. Now all I want to do is fall into bed." She rubbed her ankle again and winced. "I was lucky, that's all that matters."

It was strange leaving the house with that broken door. Even though breaking into someone's house seemed to be effortless for such criminals, a closed door gave one a sense of security.

The swelling had indeed reduced the next day, but walking was still painful. She was lucky to get an appointment with Blessing straight away. Blessing, in her motherly and competent fashion, put her mind to rest, assuring her there was no real damage done apart from a strained ligament. Roisin mentioned having taken some homeopathic remedies and Blessing made no bones about the fact that she didn't put much faith in them. Roisin didn't even bother to argue with her. She knew what she knew.

\*

Tom was coming the next day and Maggie taxied Roisin around as she organised a replacement door. That would set Roisin back a pretty penny but it had to be done. She was lucky to find a local handyman with good connections. But then Maggie surprised her once more by insisting on paying for the door. "This is the least I can do," she said. "If you don't take it, I'll find another way of giving it to you."

"But why should you pay for it?"

"Maybe it will appease my conscience," Maggie said. "You'll be doing me a favour."

When Roisin arrived home that evening, the new door was already in place. Miraculous by Irish standards. It was a gorgeous solid red door, even nicer than the old one. She hoped Betty, the owner, wouldn't be too upset.

Work was a great occupier and Roisin threw herself into it the next day. Surprisingly, she didn't feel any fear, and it was as if the events of the previous night had happened in a dream. She had other things on her mind—Tom, for instance. She could see his face and his kind eyes clearly in her mind's eye, but he had shown himself to be so human and flawed by his handling of the situation with Sinead. He had sat there in the car as if he hardly knew her. She fumed with shame at the memory of it. But she'd get over it and, in truth, what could he have done in light of the fact that he had been planning on marrying Sinead.

She had bought a bottle of wine and some snacks and made up the spare bed just in case he wanted to spend the night. It was unlikely that he would be returning to Knockadreen after such a long day. Every time she met him, she was nervous. It was like meeting a stranger or having a first date all over again. Who was she kidding? First date! Perhaps he had changed his mind again and was still planning on marrying Sinead, and it wasn't as if Roisin even had her own feelings sorted out.

So, how should she react? What should she wear? Something seductive, or jeans and a tee-shirt? She decided on the latter. She popped some homeopathic pilules under her tongue and hobbled upstairs to get ready. Every step hurt. She was careful to put the weight on her good foot. After showering, she stood in front of the wardrobe searching for her favourite jeans. She hadn't worn them in weeks. She sat on the bed and gently pulled them on, still careful of her injured ankle. It was beginning to swell up again. Really, she should be lying on the couch with her legs up. As soon as she had manoeuvred the jeans up over her hips she knew she had dropped a size or two. They were roomy at the hips and decidedly loose at the waist. Funny, she hadn't noticed she was losing weight. In fact, she hadn't even thought about weight at all lately. Maybe because she had stopped waiting for something to happen. She had heard that somewhere, that play on words and now it seemed appropriate. Ever since she had turned thirty she had been trying half-heartedly to lose those excess pounds but despaired of ever getting back to her youthful shape. Now, although she still had a few little rolls of fat around her hips and belly, she felt surprisingly cheerful as she pulled on her t-shirt. She added a floral scarf in earthy tones to her hair, flicking out some tendrils from the back, before checking her watch. He should be here any moment.

# CHAPTER 39

Back in the kitchen, the bottle of wine caught her attention. She was tempted to take a glass. But no, it would make her too sleepy and she didn't need false courage. Or did she? She put the finishing touches to the nachos, adding some olives to the tray and popping it in the oven. She scanned the room and, satisfied that everything was as good as she could make it, she hobbled over to slip some CDs in the player. The only thing left to do was to make the salad. She flicked through her music collection and hesitated at Leonard Cohen. No, most men found it to be a turn-off. Del Amitri could work but he did tend to sing a lot about broken relationships. She listened to a couple of tracks but decided it was far too sentimental. Finally, she chose Jamiroquai's *Funky Odyssey* and flipped it in the player. Immediately, as the sounds filled the kitchen, she felt upbeat.

  While the nachos were sizzling in the oven she heard his car pulling up. She hobbled out to the front door and opened it. He stood there looking as handsome as the first day they'd met but with a sheepish grin on his face and a sorry bunch of wild flowers tied together with ribbons of grass. He handed her the flowers. "I'm afraid they didn't like the heat."

She smiled. "I love wild flowers. Let me rescue them before it's too late." Stepping into the role of platonic friend, she reached up and gave him a kiss on the cheek. "Come on in. I hope you're hungry. "The honey scent of the blossoms filled the air. "They're beautiful, Tom. Thanks so much."

"I wasn't being cheap, but I knew all the shops would be closed."

She hobbled on into the kitchen. "Don't be silly. Anybody can buy flowers, but you took the time to pick them."

He followed her into the kitchen. "What happened, why are you limping?

She brushed it off. "Oh, I just tripped in the garden." He mustn't have noticed the new door, and she'd never had time to tell him all about Mrs. Walsh and that whole saga. It didn't seem appropriate now either. He had enough on his mind.

"Here, let me get these," he said, as he helped with the wine glasses.

While she filled a vase with water and began arranging the flowers, he took some plates down from the cupboard and set the table.

Happy with her flower arrangement, she placed the vase on the middle of the table.

"How are you managing, you know, getting in and out of town? You can hardly ride your bike in that state."

"People have been very supportive. Jimmy Tyrell's been firing everyone up about the importance of car sharing, how we can all save on insurance and road tax, and about the necessity of releasing the whole concept of ownership. The world is changing,

Tom."

He grunted something and laughed. "Were you down in Kerry lately?" he said, popping an olive into his mouth.

"Kerry, why?"

"I thought you might have kissed the Blarney stone."

"Very funny!" Was she talking too much?

He pushed a chair under her and gently helped her into it. "I have an older mini sitting out the back that I rarely use. Next time you come down, you can take it with you. I'll sort out the insurance."

"Are you serious?" She jerked her head around, mouth open in disbelief. Tom was over at the cabinet getting another spoon from the cutlery drawer.

"It's seen better days, but has sentimental value to me. I don't want to sell it, but it needs to be used." He took a gulp of wine. "You'll be doing me a favour."

Why was everyone being so generous? The last thing she wanted was to appear to be helpless. She neither wanted nor needed charity. And she was doing fine without a car. She told him as much. But it was a waste of time. He refused to listen to her arguments.

"What colour is it?" The cheek of her! They both laughed.

"Pink."

"Go on, Tom, you're pulling my leg."

"It's bottle green. Really classy with wood paneling. A few rust spots though."

She already saw herself driving round the

countryside in it. Could she accept such a generous gift?

"Think of it as a loan" he said. "Could you live with that?"

She reached over and squeezed his hand. "I do miss my car." Which was true. Just because she could manage without one didn't mean she wouldn't like to have one. The buses and trains were expensive and limited her ability to be spontaneous. Everything had to be planned, and the weather wasn't exactly conducive to bike riding.

The crease over his eyebrow was replaced by an endearing dimple smack in the centre of his strong chin. His voice was hoarse as he filled their glasses with wine. "Did I tell you how lovely you look this evening?"

She blushed. "You don't look too bad yourself." His crisp blue shirt complemented his dark hair and healthy-looking complexion. Today he smelled particularly nice, a mixture of fresh air and good old soap.

"How did your day go?" she said. "Did you sort out what you came to do?" She didn't want to ask him directly about his wedding plans.

He cleared his throat. "I've been doing a lot of thinking these past weeks." His eyes shone with enthusiasm. "I'm going to start rebuilding my grandfather's place this summer." She pictured him living there with that woman and a few little ones. Concealing her disappointment, she turned to remove the tray of nachos from the oven.

"Let me get that," he said.

After planting the hot tray on the table, he

stood in front of her and placed both hands on her shoulders. His warm hands felt good. "I'm not going to marry her, Roisin."

She tried to mask her feelings, but her lips twitched into a smile. No matter what happened, she didn't want him to make a grave mistake. "Does she know it yet?"

"Yes, I told her a few days ago."

"No wonder you needed to get away."

"You were right. It never would have worked out."

She put some food onto his plate. "Well, I have to digest that piece of news. Here, help yourself to some salad." She raised her glass. "I can't pretend to be disappointed…although I do feel a bit sorry for Sinead." Strangely enough, she meant it.

He leaned over toward her and cupped her face in his hands. "I couldn't stop thinking about you, Roisin."

She swallowed and turned her eyes to the bunch of flowers. And then, almost in a whisper, she said. "I never had to be jealous with Javier. He was always there for me, in his way…" Tom's face was so close to hers. She continued. "…but I felt so jealous when you told me about marrying Sinead. At the same time I knew I had no right to be." She sighed. "And then I thought about it, and I realised that I would feel the same way if Javier found someone else." She tried to avert her eyes from his. "So you see. We are all flawed. I know I can't have both of you but now I know I don't want to lose either of you. Everything I said was true, though. It would have been a disaster if you had married Sinead. I was truly concerned for you."

"Roisin, one thing you need to know about me. When I commit, I commit."

She shrugged. "None of us know what will happen in the future. But apart from that, I think you did the right thing, Tom."

He took a gulp of wine. "She's not going to make it easy for me. It was a good time to busy myself with another project." He told her of his plans to reconstruct the house, maintaining most of the original brickwork. "I'm going to sell up and move out here, Roisin."

"Really?" Her heart skipped a beat. She tried to hide her excitement. "That's great news. When?"

"If I start soon, I should be finished by next spring."

She raised her glass and hoped he didn't see her nervous swallow. "Let's drink to that."

"How about you? Any news from your side?"

She sighed. "Javier still wants to come live here."

That crease was forming again on his forehead. Ever on the alert to people's moods, she change the subject. "Could you put the kettle on, please? My foot is beginning to swell up again?" She began chatting about the shop, anything to steer away from difficult topics. When she told him about Maggie's offer, he made some half-hearted comments, but she could tell he was displeased about something.

He let the water run for a few seconds. "How do you feel about that?"

"It's not a bad idea. I knew Maggie wouldn't

be hanging around here for long, especially in light of what's happened."

"I was referring to your husband?"

She shrugged her shoulders. "Not sure. I wanted that for so long…when we lived in Spain. Javier said I was a hopeless romantic and that I'd soon get fed up with it. He has always loved Ireland. He said it was a great place to visit…but he didn't want to live here. And now…I don't know. Too many things have happened." Her eyes met his, willing him to let it go. "I've learned to get out of my own way and not try to steer the boat too much. It took enormous courage…and energy to make this move. Now I'm going to let things happen, as they will. See which way the die falls."

He rubbed his chin, looking pensive.

Steering the conversation to even safer grounds, she told him her Spanish friend was coming the follow week. "There's a lull in the shop at the moment so I'll take a few days off and show her some sights. I think she was worried when she heard about my house break in."

"What break in?"

She tried to sidetrack, but it was too late.

"You're hiding something from me, aren't you?"

She released the tension in her shoulders and stretch her stiff and swollen foot. "You had other things on your mind."

"Tell me, what happened?" he said.

And she did. She told him about hearing the banging noise and how she had no choice but to jump out of the window.

"Heck, Roisin. You could have been killed! No wonder you're hobbling." He frowned and rubbed the back of his neck. "Do you think it was a random act?"

"No, I know it wasn't." It was a relief to tell him the whole truth. For the next ten minutes he listened intently, finally taking a long, deep breath. "Why didn't you tell me any of this before?"

She sipped her coffee as she contemplated how to answer. "As I said, you had other things on your mind. I didn't think it would touch so close to home. As far as I was concerned it was Maggie's problem, and Mrs. Walsh's problem—something I had no control over. Besides, we didn't find out about the threats until Darius was attacked, and you were busy with your wedding plans. If I had called you, you might have thought I was vying for your attention."

He crossed his arms and rubbed his chin. "I'm still not happy with you staying here by yourself. What if there's a next time?"

"I don't think there will be. It was more of a scare tactic." Even as she said it she wasn't entirely convinced. Not with the way they'd been hammering down the door. And when she recalled how they'd stormed upstairs, she was even less sure. She told him the police had captured one of the fellows. "Maybe they even have the other fellow already. Maggie's ex's court case is coming up soon, and I think they now have enough to go on. She thinks it will all be sorted soon."

"Well, I still don't like the sound of it. Seems to me as if these people are not to be messed around with, Roisin. If I were you, I'd keep way out of it."

She stuck a fork into a black olive and dipped it in the melted cheese. "You're right, of course, but I never asked for any of this. And if everyone ignores the problem it will never go away."

"Just remember Veronica Guerin?"

Yes, she remembered, although she had not been in the country at the time. "Veronica Guerin was one brave woman, but maybe she took too many risks or underestimated the danger. I'm not an investigative reporter. I'm just a peripheral witness who happens to have stumbled upon a hornet's nest."

"True, but promise me you'll be more careful in the future. And, no matter what time it is, you can always call me."

She agreed and promptly changed the subject. "Any progress on your new song?"

"Well, as you happen to mention it…just give me a minute, it's in the car."

When he returned, he popped the CD into the player.

As soon as she heard the first refrain, she knew it would be a success. The music was catchy, and the lyrics would be sure to appeal to anyone who had ever been in a tricky romantic situation. *Tangled up in You* was a real tear-jerker and hit too close to her heart. She fought hard not to make an idiot of herself and turned to clear the table so that he wouldn't see the tears welling in her eyes.

But nothing escaped Tom. "You're not crying, are you?"

She sniffed and wiped her eyes. "Don't make fun of me. It's just that…well…" She was lost for words. He came up behind her and put his arms around her. She released herself gently from his hold and turned to face him.

"You must know I like you a lot, Tom, but you were right. I have to clear things up between Javier and myself before I can move forward."

His jaw clenched, but his voice, when he spoke, was deep and husky. "Are you ever going to know?"

"I hope so."

Why was she such a fool? She had agreed to meet him, even cooked him a nice dinner. Was she kidding herself? But now the mood had changed and both of them were trying to gain footing in unknown terrain. They spoke a bit about Finn and the band's plans to go on tour in autumn, but it was obvious they were filling an uncomfortable gap.

It was too early to go to bed so she suggested they watch a film. She had a couple new DVDs and they chose to watch *Children of Men* starring Clive Owen, a heavy, dark film, not for the faint hearted. The wine was probably a mistake, though because despite her attempts at self-control, she was too aware of the electricity between her and Tom. But then she became so involved in what was going on in the film, she gripped a pillow and hugged it, hoping the characters would be able to make it to their destination. Tom patted the couch beside him. "Come closer, Roisin."

She didn't hesitate and snuggled up to him. The wine had made her drowsy and she had a hard time concentrating on the film. Because the couch wasn't wide enough for both of them, she was lying in his arms, with her back to him. She hoped he couldn't hear her heart beat. He kissed her on the inside of her neck and continued running his lips down toward the hollow of her throat. Shivers of delight coursed through her. He slipped his hand gently inside her tee-shirt while turning off the remote control with his other hand, like a pro. He accidentally pressed his leg against her injured foot, and she winced with pain. She gently drew him down onto the carpeted floor and their love-making took on a more urgent note. Even if she'd wanted to, she would have been unable to resist his expert touch. She responded with passion as he pulled off her tee-shirt and unhooked her bra in one seamless movement. She fiddled with the buttons of his shirt, giggling at her own impatience while writhing out of her jeans. Sparks flew up the chimney, making both of them chuckle for a moment. He pulled her up closer, locking his mouth on hers. The flickering flames threw shadows into the room, reflected the rising and falling of their own rhythm as their bodies joined together. Any resolve she had had faded away. Desire won.

   Later, still drowsy but warm and satisfied, she examined his face. He propped himself up on his elbow and played with a tendril of her hair, questioning her with his eyes. She placed her finger on his lips. She closed her eyes and fell asleep in his arms.

\*

She awoke with the first rays of sunlight shining in through the window. Through slanted eyes, she perused the room, the empty bottle of wine and the burned down candle. She was alone. Delicious memories of their lovemaking flooded her thoughts. For a moment, the horrible thought entered her mind that he might have done a disappearing act.

But no, not Tom. He came in bare-footed with two mugs of steaming coffee and pulled the curtains back, letting in some more light. She pulled the blanket close to her body and pulled herself up to lean against the couch, groaning after the hard floor. Her foot was particularly stiff and she stretched it this way and that. He knelt beside her and massaged it in slow, gentle movements.

"Hand me the coffee, will you, Tom?"

She cupped the warm brew and sipped it. "Just what I needed. What time is it?" she said, rubbing her eyes. Reality began to sink in. "I have to go to work." She placed her cup on the coffee table and struggled up, kissing him, before heading upstairs to shower.

\*

He was closing the dishwasher door when she came down. He looked at her sheepishly.

"You're a strange one, Roisin."

"Why?" She was genuinely surprised.

"All that passion under the surface? Mixed messages, and now you act as if nothing happened."

"Maybe I'm afraid to say the wrong thing."

"You're not feeling guilty again, are you?"

Was she? For once, she had put Javier out of her mind. "No, I don't feel guilty." She blushed thinking of her abandon the previous evening.

"Well, that's good to hear. I'd better get an early start."

She gave Maggie a quick call and told her she didn't need to pick her up.

\*

As he drove, she sneaked a glance at him. Strong, muscular arms held onto the steering wheel with an intense resoluteness. Her gaze moved up to his face but his eyes were set firmly on the road in front of him.

He looked over at her with a weak grin. "So, what's the diagnosis?"

"You look tired."

His grinned. "It was a long night and a hard floor…but it was…." He winked over at her. "…I don't want it to be our last."

They continued in silence as the sun's rays shone down over the distant hills. It was a rare cloudless sky, and the earth appeared to shimmer with the promise of a hot, dry spell. Occasionally, they passed small groups of tourists walking in the hills.

They were approaching the main street. She knew she had to do this right, but she struggled for the right words. She didn't want to lose him but neither did she want to give him false hopes. "So, what will we do, Tom?" She buried her head in her hands. "Will someone tell me what I want?"

"Maybe if you know what you don't want that'll be the first step to knowing what you want."

"Process of elimination, or what?"

"It helps."

He pulled up at the curb near Maggie's shop, switched off the ignition and turned to face her. "I don't want to lose you. The more I thought about marrying Sinead, the more I thought of you. Then when I saw you out there on the road with the kids, I felt so miserable."

"I'm complicated, Tom, and I've never been good at staying in one place. Feelings can change, you know, and love is such a delicate thing. I don't know if I can commit to loving someone for evermore."

"I never said I was easy either." He took her hand. "All my life I've tried to avoid commitment, but now it's time for me to change that pattern. We should give it a try."

She thought of Javier and his ensuing visit. It would break his heart to see her with another man.

They parted with a warm kiss, but his words echoed in her mind throughout the rest of the day, tormenting her.

# Chapter 40

Darius came in for about an hour to help out before lunch. It was lovely seeing him again. Apart from some swelling, his face was almost back to normal, but his spirit was still subdued. He had heard of her lucky escape and, as in a black comedy, they laughed as she told him of her escape out the window. "I still don't know how I got out that window. Honestly, Darius, if anyone had told me I'd attempt an escape like that, I would never have believed them."

"Did you ever have the feeling we're in some sort of a theatre piece?" You know, sometimes life can be so surreal. I'd like to know who is orchestrating all this. Is it my subconscious, 'cause if it is, my subconscious is one sick creature."

She slid the garment she was sewing out from under the needle tracker and turned her head toward him. "I've had that same thought many times, Darius, and I've come to the conclusion it's a waste of time trying to figure it all out. We'll never find the answer to that one, I'm afraid. You know, when I was living my ordinary but peaceful life, I dreamt of a new adventure. I suppose you could say I attracted adventure into my life, but I forgot to specify what kind of adventure. How about you? Was any part of you looking for this? I mean, did you somehow attract it to yourself?"

He had been swirling around on a swivel chair, and he stopped to face her. "I don't know, Roisin. What stuck in my mind most from being beaten up was the horrible verbal abuse. Did a part of me have those feelings about myself? Was it some sort of mirror?"

"You mean the anti-gay comments? Come on, Darius. That's ludicrous. You seem so comfortable in your own skin."

He rubbed his chin absentmindedly. "We all learn to wear our masks, Roisin."

She snipped off a loose thread. "Well, you had me fooled."

"So, you think there could be something to this whole cosmic-orchestrated theory?"

"Maybe," she said. "That would make me a figment of your imagination? Which is all getting too complicated. If I'm thinking that I might be a figment of your imagination. That would imply …" She laughed. "This is all getting too confusing, and I'm getting hungry. Shall we hobble on down to Jimmy's?"

\*

They linked arms, supporting each other down the street. The light was unusually bright and she wished she had worn sunglasses. Several tourists sauntered by in their colourful paraphernalia. Many of them were in town for the surfing event due to be held that coming weekend. Helen and Todd were coming to visit too, and she was looking forward to seeing them.

Jimmy's deli was abuzz with customers, and

Jimmy winked at her, indicating that he'd be with them in a few minutes. They browsed through the shelves, picking up this and that, and finally going over to the crystal section. "Maybe we need to get some protective stones—just to be on the safe side," she said. She picked up a rose quartz that fit nicely into her palm.

He showed her a smooth black stone on a leather thong. "I like this one," he said. He read the descriptions of the semi-precious gems and their supposed attributes. "According to this, obsidian protects against negative energies."

"Let me buy it for you. I have my angel." She took out the silver pendant concealed under her tee-shirt. "Maybe this is what saved me from harm. Maria and Rafael gave it to me."

The last customer was being served and they went to the counter. To the left of the counter one wall was used for signs, advertisements and business cards. She was alerted to one in particular. *Rabea de Silva, Astrologer and Love Psychic.* It had been a long time since she'd consulted any psychic or fortune teller, as they used to be called. While Jimmy served Darius, she popped a card into her purse.

"You're up to your eyes today, Jimmy," Roisin said.

"Aye. Sure, it's great, and it'll be over soon enough when all the tourists leave. Here, try some of this." He always had a plate of crackers and some samples of his home-mixed cream cheeses, olive paste, filled pepperonis or some other delicacy for his customers to sample. He handed each of them a cracker spread with a spicy tomato paste.

She pointed to Rabea de Silva's card. "Do you know this woman, Jimmy?"

He peered at the writing on the card. "Not really. Jules went to her when she was here; she was impressed, I think. Why, are you thinking of going?"

"Maybe. I need to make a few decisions myself."

A new customer came in and greeted Darius, nodding to the others. He was a handsome young man with sandy-coloured hair. Dressed in a bright yellow tee-shirt, khakis and brown flip flops, he looked perfectly casual in a continental sort of way.

"Brendan, is that you?" Darius said. "How are you doing? It's been a long time."

"Joe. How's it going, buddy? I thought it looked like you coming in here."

Darius laughed. "This is where it gets difficult," he said. He directed his words to Brendan. "It's Darius to my friends."

If she wasn't mistaken, there were sparks flying between them. Darius turned to her. "Brendan and I went to school together. His family moved away and we haven't seen each other since."

"Pleased to meet you, Brendan," she said. While she gave her order, the two fellows were deep in conversation. Wouldn't it be great, she thought, if Darius found a romantic partner, especially in light of what he had gone through? She gestured to him that she was going back to work. Far be it for her to disrupt something so important. She could feel it in her bones, as her grandmother used to say.

Back in the shop, ten minutes before opening time, she took out Rabea De Silva's card and examined it again. Part of her wanted to call right away, but another part told her to forget it. What did she expect to hear? Would it influence her if she was told she should go back to her husband, or if the psychic told her Tom was the one for her? She didn't want to be dependent on someone else's opinion, but she was curious at the same time to hear what the psychic would tell her. Then the whole inner dialogue began again with questions to which she had no answers. Is our fate written in the stars or is everything that happens to us just random? Of course she could make up her own mind in the end, but she was afraid of making the wrong decision. She seemed to have temporarily lost her ability to make decisions. Rabea De Silva's name had a nice ring to it. It must be a stage name. Maybe her real name was Mary Riordan or something like that. The name ran off her tongue like liquid silver. She picked up the phone, keyed in the numbers and heard a recorded message. She then left her details, requesting an appointment.

Darius came into the shop about an hour later. He didn't mention his meeting with Brendan but, judging by the light in his eyes and the look on his face, life had taken on a new sparkle.

She was busy fixing the last details on Blessing's hat. "What you do think?" she said.

The cinnamon-coloured hat would look lovely on Blessing. Roisin tried it on, adjusting it slightly to the right to give it a cheeky look. It could be folded, peaked or adjusted to give a different look each time, making it versatile and interesting.

"Not bad," he said, "but it's missing something. "How about adding extra detail? He took a wooden box of ribbons and brocade bands from the shelf and rummaged through it until he found a piece of thin black embroidered band with tiny yellow and nut-coloured flowers. He wound it around the rim of the hat. "Don't you think that adds to it?"

"I'm not sure if Blessing will like it though. How about if I add some detachable decorative touches? She'll have the option of either keeping it plain or attaching one of these doodads if she feels like it."

They settled on that and joined heads to come up with a slick and quick way to add the details, using tiny strips of Velcro. She ran up a little pouch from the same material as the hat and embroidered Blessing's name on the front with her fancy sewing machine. Darius helped out with customers while she continued sketching some new designs.

Maggie showed up for a few hours. When she saw Darius, she ran over and hugged him. He ended up consoling her, assuring her it wasn't her fault. Darius was a great believer in Astrology and Eastern Philosophy. He did not see himself as a victim of circumstance. Neither did he think he had attracted that violent event. Maggie wasn't particularly communicative, but Roisin knew the court case was pending and she didn't want to put pressure on her to be sociable. They worked side by side for the rest of the afternoon in easy companionship. She decided not to tell her about Tom's visit, although it would have been nice to share some light-hearted chit-chat with her. Sometimes it was better to keep silent, and she listened to her instinct.

The first thing she did when she arrived home

was to check to see if Rabea had left a message. She hadn't, but her friend Anastasia had. The enthusiasm in her friend's voice was infectious, and she began to get excited about the visit. Anastasia was particularly interested in historical sites and old houses. There was no shortage of those around.

*

A couple of days later, she was on her way to Rabea de Silva's house. The woman lived in a nearby town. Roisin's ankle was almost back to normal, and she walked slowly up the side street to a row to cottages where the woman lived. Full of anticipation, she rang the doorbell. A petite, dark haired woman with sallow skin opened the door with remarkable vigour. This was no Mary Riordan.

The woman held out her bejewelled hand. Roisin warmed to her immediately. "Pleased to meet you. Do come in. I hope you're not afraid of dogs." She laughed as a beautiful, almost white golden retriever came bounding towards her, tail wagging and shiny eyes full of trust looking up at her. The dog's wagging tail sent a whish of air around her.

"Can I get you anything to drink?"

Roisin followed the woman into a room off the hallway. "Just water please."

While Ms. De Silva went to get the glasses, Roisin scanned the room. It was bright and uncluttered and looked out onto a small but well-tended garden. Apart from a painting of swirling vibrant colours that took the shape of angel wings, the only other decoration in the room was a large porcelain angel on the windowsill. The figure was holding a lighted tea-light in her opened palms and wore a peaceful expression on her face. Roisin sat down on one of the comfortable wicker chairs on either side of the round table.

Rabea came in with a tray holding two sparkling glasses. She poured two glasses of water from a crystal jug over on the sideboard and handed one to Roisin. "Have you ever had a reading before," she asked.

Roisin shifted in her chair and cleared her throat. "Yes, but it was many years ago."

"Right. Just relax. Remember, I am not reading you but get messages from my spirit guides. If you can, try not to interrupt me as that slows down the information." She smiled and turned her intense eyes on Roisin. "If you have any questions, you can ask me after the reading. My guides never say anything to frighten, although they do try to nudge you on the right path."

Roisin nodded. Did the woman say *guides*? She didn't like the idea that incarnate beings were looking on. She sat straighter and tried to clear her thoughts. What she liked was that the woman did not try to extract information from her. She seemed sincere, and Roisin decided to go with it.

Ms. De Silva took a few deep breaths. "There's something new coming on the horizon that will end all of your confusion." Her face furrowed and she mumbled "Oh dear. It's something you least expect. It has to do with a man."

Roisin fought to dispel her cynicism. *Hello, Einstein. Isn't it always either love or money?*

"There's a lot of confusion around you." She

looked at Roisin for confirmation, but Roisin was determined to keep her poker face. Ms. De Silva continued. "They're telling me this will soon pass. I'm seeing the number three. Now this could be three weeks or three months." *Great, it could even be three years.* As if reading her mind, the woman chuckled. "Don't be too quick to dismiss. We are looking at developments that are likely to occur within the next year. The hardest thing to predict is timing because we are merely under the illusion of living in linear time." She turned her attention back to the cards. "All will become clear to you, and you'll know what you have to do. In fact, you don't even have to do anything big; it will all happen as it should. They're telling me you should be more flexible and look for cosmic winks or signs from the universe. Be more trusting."

Roisin's mind was working overtime. It was a relief knowing she didn't have to do anything, or make any decisions. So, she would continue as normal and see what transpired. "I don't want to hurt my husband though." She hadn't meant to reveal any information and now she'd done the exact opposite.

Ms. De Silva sighed. "Remember what I said, all will work out as it should. Do not feel sad at what it about to transpire... ." She paused for a moment as if looking for the right words. "You have fulfilled your contract with your husband. Do not feel guilt. All is as it should be. Your place is here; this is where you belong, and you will see that everything has been divinely planned." She focused her eyes on Roisin. "Did you live abroad? No, don't say anything yet. I'm seeing a lot of sadness in the past. You were not very happy? Your guides are saying you shouldn't berate yourself. You did exactly the right thing."

Roisin nodded and smiled. "I just don't want to hurt anyone," she repeated in a small voice.

Ms. De Silva looked at her with compassion in her big brown eyes. "Sadness and hurt are part of life. Our time here on earth is pre-ordained. Remember that." She took a sip of water and continued. "There will be a period of sadness, great sadness, but after this you will move into a new place. All confusion will be gone. Remember, no guilt. It is not your fault." *Why was she repeating that?* A chill ran up Roisin's spine. What was about to happen? She began to regret her visit because despite the overall positive message, she had a sense that there was something important Rabea was not telling her. The woman, in turn, enclosed her hand in hers and squeezed it slightly. "It does not always serve us to know everything. Sometimes there are valuable lessons to be learned when we make our own decisions. You must remember that this is the way things appear to be developing now, based on your intention. Should you have a change of heart, situations will rearrange themselves." Roisin nodded. It made sense. Maybe she had been imagining something, and although she still didn't know how things were going to go with Tom, she would follow the psychic's good advice and let things unfold as they should. Now that she had the confirmation that everything would work out, a warm sense of comfort spread over her.

The woman gathered the cards in one swift movement. "Do you have any further questions?" she said.

Roisin hesitated. "I'd love to know about one particular man."

Rabea closed her eyes for a moment. "There will be some tears, but tears like laughter are part of life, like the cycle of birth and the transition of the spirit. Remember to leave the past behind and live for now. I'm being told to make sure you know that the decision is yours. It could go either way. He has made up his mind." She smiled. "I like him. Do you have any more pressing questions?"

Roisin hesitated and the woman continued. "Spirit usually responds best to specific questions. I'm not getting anything else. The book is closed. But if you have a definite question, they usually answer."

She couldn't think of anything else to ask. Rabea poured each of them another glass of water and they chatted a bit about nothing in particular. She had so many questions, about Rabea, where she came from, if she had always had this gift etc. but she decided not to ask. Time would tell as to whether things would transpire as she had predicted.

As she drove home, a great sense of relief flooded through her, especially knowing she didn't have to make any major decisions. She had suppressed the mild warning about tears and sadness and would have to wait and see what that was all about. Her friend was coming the next day too, and that would take her mind off things. They'd have a few days to themselves before the crowds hit town. Her sister and brother-in-law had met Anastasia several years beforehand so she knew they'd get along well.

## Chapter 41

The next day was miserable and wet and it put a damper on things. Roisin wanted Anastasia to see her new surroundings in a positive light, but there was nothing she could do about that. Equipped with hat and umbrella, she drove to the train station in Galway to collect her. The station was busy with commuters, and she peered into the crowd looking for her friend's face.

A familiar voice called out. "Over here." She turned to see Anastasia waving and pulling a huge suitcase as she struggled toward her.

"Anastasia, you made it," she said as she hugged her. "How was your trip?"

"Next time, I'm hiring a car," her friend laughed. "Honestly, I had to change trains twice to make it here, and I've been travelling since 4.30 this morning."

"Never mind. You're here now."

"You look fantastic," Anastasia said. "Let me look at you. Hey, the weight is falling off you."

"Ah, come on. Flattery will get you everywhere."

"Seriously, whatever it is, I want some of it too."

They chatted all the way to the car, taking

turns to drag the luggage. Roisin turned to her friend and laughed. "What have you got in here anyway? Are you planning on emigrating?"

"Many a word of truth is spoken in jest," Anastasia answered. "I think you've opened Cassandra's box for me."

"Pandora's is more like it. Or maybe a can of maggots."

"What…you've lost me."

"Never mind."

They had always enjoyed silly bantering and it was nice to see nothing had changed.

They spent the afternoon catching up on the latest news. Later at home, after Anastasia had explored the house and garden, Roisin suggested they could either cook something or open a bottle or two…" She let out a little laugh remembering their many shared evenings drinking wine and singing, or dancing. "Or we could walk down to town this evening and I'll show you around."

Anastasia pointed to the rain splattering on the windowpane. "Do I look like a fish?"

"Okay. Then that's settled. I've got a great film we can watch. Maybe the weather will have cleared up by tomorrow. I certainly hope so, especially as there's the annual surfing event taking place this weekend."

"Don't worry about that. You are not responsible for the weather."

"Yes, I suppose you're right. I thought we could take a drive down to Kilkenny. There's so much to do there, lovely walks too. We can hop from the Design Centre to the local gallery and then have lunch at a riverside restaurant. You'll love it. If it's too wet, we'll stick to inside activities."

"Everything sounds great to me. Do you miss Spain at all? It's not the same without you."

"Of course. I miss many things about Spain, but I've been having a ball here. Honestly, Anastasia, I've been so busy, I've hardly had time to think about what I left behind."

Anastasia looked around the living room. "You've certainly made this place your own. It's lovely and cosy, if a bit secluded. Aren't you afraid living out here by yourself?"

She hadn't told her friend much about the spot of trouble, or about Mrs. Walsh and her nephew. She had merely alluded to it on the phone once. "Not really. In fact, I love living on my own. Sometimes I go down to the beach for a walk and never meet a soul. Only the crashing waves and the ever-changing skies. Mind you, I believe it gets even quieter in winter. Ask me then."

\*

The next morning they headed down to town. They had hired a car for a few days. Roisin drove to the purple guesthouse where she introduced her to Fidelma and Esther. They welcomed her with warmth, and Fidelma asked her if she'd be around the following Friday for the next dance evening.

"I'd almost forgotten about that," Roisin said. "But it's a great idea." She turned to Anastasia. "You'd love it. Maybe you'll even snatch a local man." She winked at Fidelma who was twiddling with her pearl necklace.

Their next port of call was to the Eye Catcher. Both Maggie and Darius were there and they, too, made Anastasia feel welcome. She finally had to drag Anastasia out of the shop. "Come on before you spend all your money in one place." Maggie placed the items into a bag. "This is a gift from us," she said, as she popped a glass necklace into a little pouch and gave it Anastasia."

Her friend proudly wore the long dangly earrings and the hand-painted silk scarf she had bought. Anastasia had taught textile design in one of the colleges and they had met through a mutual friend many years before and hit it off immediately. So the woman knew quality when she saw it. She talked about the possibility of importing some of Roisin and Maggie's wares. "I think they'd love this stuff back in Spain," she said.

Roisin told her friend about the order they'd been working on for Harrods and that Rafael's aunt was interested in selling some of it in her chain of boutiques in Spain. "We might even see some of our stuff at the Kilkenny Design Centre when we're there."

"I always said your true path was in the creative arena. So, you had to come back here to find that out. This place is doing you good."

"You know what they say. If you keep doing what you've been doing, you'll always get the same results. I made a move. That got things rolling." Roisin looked pensive. "It's almost as if the universe responds when we make the first move. How does that saying go? *God helps those who help themselves."*

"Are you trying to tell me something?"

"Maybe."

Roisin couldn't help but feel a sense of pride when she saw her mobile phone pouches and some of her bags on display in the visitor's shop of the Kilkenny Design Centre later on. Anastasia agreed they looked classy there amongst the sparkling silver jewellery, crystal vases and hand-made writing paper.

As Anastasia filled her basket, Roisin teased her. "You'll have no money left if you spend everything on your first day."

Anastasia grinned and flashed her credit card.

"Those things are dangerous," Roisin said.

"Yes, but fun. I've worked hard all year, and I'm going to live for today."

The shop assistant looked smart in her moss-coloured sweater and tie. All of the shop assistants wore items from the shop and, since they had obviously all been chosen for their good looks and charm, they were a great advertisement for the products. The assistant's deft fingers wrapped the vase Anastasia had bought in bubble foil and put it in a box. "Would you like it gift wrapped?"

"Yes, please," Anastasia said. She winked at Roisin, who knew her friend loved to have the presents she bought for herself wrapped. She remembered Anastasia buying herself presents for Christmas, having them exquisitely wrapped and putting them under the tree. Roisin always thought there was something both infinitely sad and yet humorous about that. There was a lot to be said for old friends. No lengthy explanations necessary. They could tune into one another with ease.

*

Later, when they sat at the window of The Thimble, a charming traditional restaurant looking out onto the river, she told Anastasia about Tom.

"So that's your secret. I can't believe you didn't tell me this before." She had a twinkle in her eye. "I knew there was something up. Will I get to meet him?"

"I doubt it."

"I can't help but feel sorry for Javier though," Anastasia said. "He must be lost without you."

"Well, he should have realised that earlier."

Anastasia took a sip of wine. "Don't you think you're being a bit harsh?"

"Hey, whose side are you on?"

"Did you at least tell him about Tom?"

Roisin felt a flush creep up her face. Her voice raised an octave. "Let's change the subject." She took a deep breath and said. "On second thoughts. Why are you suddenly so interested in Javier's needs? You above all people know what things were like between us. Don't you remember what sparked it all off, why I left? Do you think it was easy?"

"No need to be so defensive. Of course I don't forget, but his heart is in the right place. I think it all got to him and he was under extreme stress. Maybe he was just going through a negative phase."

Roisin frowned and rubbed the back of her neck. "Yes, but when the negative phase takes over your life, it's time to make choices."

"I've seen him several times," Anastasia said. "He asked me about you last time we met at the supermarket; said he'd been here. He's missing you, Roisin. I can't believe you won't give him a second chance."

Roisin concentrated on her meal, squeezing lemon juice onto her salmon. They continued eating and avoided any further discussion on that particular subject. Her thoughts turned to her visit with Ms. De Silva.

"I never told you, but I went to see a psychic the other day."

Anastasia perked up. "Really. I didn't think you'd fall for that nonsense."

"She was pretty impressive."

Anastasia leaned in closer toward Roisin. "What did she tell you?"

Roisin gave her a rundown of what the woman had said. She laughed at the expression on her friend's face. "For someone who was mocking it a few minutes ago, you look pretty captivated. Shall we give her a ring?"

"I must admit, I'm tempted," her friend said.

"I knew you would be. She lives in the next town. Maybe if I ring her now we can get you an appointment for tomorrow."

"What if she tells me something awful? I don't know whether we're supposed to know the future, assuming that anyone is even capable of predicting it." She thought for a few moments. "Go on then, I suppose it could be fun."

Roisin found the card and called. As it happened, Rabea had had a cancellation for three the next afternoon. She put down her fork, folded her serviette and stared out onto the slate-grey river, remembering Ms. DeSilva's words. *You don't need to do anything. It will all work out as it should.* "It looks as if the sun is coming out. How about if we go for a walk along the river afterwards? Or, we could do something more strenuous and climb that mountain we passed outside town."

"That wasn't a mountain, it was a hill," Anastaia said. "Besides, it wouldn't be good for your ankle. You're still hobbling a bit."

Roisin laughed, "Come on then. I was hoping you'd say that, but a bit of exercise will burn off some calories, at least."

# Chapter 42

Roisin drove Anastasia to her appointment with Ms. DeSilva. She'd walked through the town, window shopping, while she waited for Anastasia. There was a lovely restaurant on the main street and they'd arranged to meet there for an early dinner afterwards. While Roisin was browsing through the menu, Anastasia came in, beaming.

She sat down, pulling off her scarf and smoothing her hair. "That was amazing. If all she said comes true, I'm in for a magic carpet ride."

Roisin grinned. "Go on, tell me. Don't keep me in suspense?"

"Wait for it."

Roisin handed her the menu and while she glanced at it, Anastasia told her she was in for a new romance. "She said I'm so close to meeting the man of my dreams. Can you believe it?"

"Really? Did she describe him?"

"She gave me the initials P and R."

"That's pretty vague. Is that all?"

"No, she said I'd meet him at a large social gathering. My life will be totally turned upside down." She spread her arms expressively." She said I'll change everything: my job, my home, the whole lot."

Roisin's eyes widened. "That sounds exciting. Did she ask you any questions beforehand? I had to bite my tongue several times. It's so easy to unwittingly reveal information, although I really don't think she is a fraud."

"No, she didn't probe, didn't even seem to want to know anything. But I can't help thinking we shouldn't meddle in these things."

"Ah, come on. It's too late now. Besides, that's just your Catholic upbringing speaking. Why would people be given such gifts if not to use them?"

Anastasia thought about this for a moment. "It has nothing to do with the church. I couldn't care less about that. It's just that hearing something like that might influence me. Now I'll be looking for Mister Right at every gathering. What if she's wrong? I had given up hoping for a burst of excitement, let alone a complete life change."

"You have a point. But you should see the light in your eyes. And you know, the fact that you now have new hope makes you look so much more vibrant. So, that's not a bad thing." When she saw Anastasia's reaction, she laughed. "No, don't get me wrong. You looked great before, but you look even better now. Just wait and see what happens."

"Let's drink to that," Anastasia said as she called the waiter over.

The weekend crept up on them. Roisin allowed herself to play tourist in her own country. Her friend was uncomplicated and delighted with everything. Even the moody weather didn't put a damper on their fun. She hadn't seen her sister for a while and was looking forward to Helen coming. Todd had come down with a dose of a cold so her sister was coming by herself. They arranged to meet in town because Anastasia wanted to take one last walk along the beach and buy a few presents. Although there was a stiff breeze, which Roisin presumed was good for surfing conditions, the sun shone down upon the water creating silvery ripples on the surface. It resembled a star-spangled mirror. Her friend sighed. "Pity I have to return on Sunday."

"Well, you could stay."

"I don't know. It all sounds so good in theory, but I don't know if I could really do it." Anastasia stood still for a moment, peering into the distance. She pointed over toward the rocks. "Look over there. If I'm not mistaken, isn't that Javier sitting over on that rock?"

Roisin's heart did a skip and a jump. "What, where?"

Anastasia pointed to a large boulder in the distance. A lone man sat watching the surfers riding the waves, which were much wilder over that side of the bay. He appeared to be lost in concentration.

Roisin picked up speed. Anastasia followed close behind her. "I don't believe it," she said. "How can that be? He would have told me he was coming."

Anastasia tried to keep up with her. She fought against the wind. "Maybe he wanted to surprise you." Anastasia said.

Roisin bent down to take a pebble out of her shoe and turned to her friend. "That's not his style." Anastasia didn't reply. Roisin was too busy to notice as she continued marching off in his direction. When they had almost reached the rock, Roisin called out his name. He turned around abruptly and smiled. His dark hair shone in the sun. For a moment her breath caught in her throat. She was beginning to see him in a different light. After Anastasia's description, she had expected him to look haggard and pale-faced. Instead he looked rejuvenated, tanned and totally relaxed. She called out to him. "Javier. How come you never told me you were coming?"

He walked toward her and took her in his arms, almost suffocating her in his warm embrace. "Aren't you pleased to see me?"

"Sure. I just wasn't expecting you so soon." He turned to Anastasia and winked at her. "Hi Anastasia, fancy meeting you here." Of course he must have known she was coming. He turned his attention once again to Roisin. "It was a rash decision. I finally sold the house and decided to celebrate. I wanted to tell you in person and check out some properties while I'm here. Planned on surprising you later on today."

Roisin looked from Javier to Anastasia. She could have sworn there was a brief exchange between them. Maybe she was imagining it. She fought for the right words, but even to herself she sounded like a robot. "So, you managed to sell the house?" She released herself from Javier's embrace and sat on the rock. "That's fantastic news. You look as if a weight has been lifted from your shoulders."

"Oh, it has Roisin. If only you had waited. I haven't felt as free for more years than I care to remember."

While Anastasia and Javier chatted, Roisin

had a few minutes to let this surprise sink in. Her eyes were on Javier. She took in his broad shoulders and strong physique. The sunlight framed his strong, handsome head with the waves of dark hair curling to the edge of his shirt collar. It was as if something clicked in place for her. When she had first met him, she had found his looks, but particularly his charm, to be irresistible. His deep, brown eyes were capable of showing such passion and warmth, but also could turn almost black and sharp as flint when he was angry. Sometimes, when he had been asleep or lost in concentration, she used to watch him. She had only ever wanted to love him, and now she realised, with a start, that her love for him was not completely lost. She wanted to believe it, but was not completely convinced he had made a turnaround. She needed time to think things over. "So, you're here to look at some houses? Where?" Roisin said, warily.

"A fully furnished place in town, just down the road from your shop. And a house about a mile outside town."

Roisin gave him a small smile. "You're really serious about this?"

Anastasia walked over to the shore to take photos, leaving them to it.

"I can't believe you're doing this, Javier. You know….I told you I can't make any promises. I have my own life here now." He looked crestfallen, and she immediately altered her tone. She placed her hand on his arm. "Sorry, love. It's just that you've taken me by surprise."

Anastasia was walking toward them.

Roisin turned toward her. "Did you know

about this, Anastasia?"

Her friend looked from Roisin to Javier.

Javier cut in. "Come, I want to show you something."

He took her hand and led her over the dunes and onto the main road. He stopped abruptly in front of a colourful Volkswagen Camper that was parked along the curb. The name *Voyager* was printed in Celtic script along the side. It was decorated with hand-painted flowers and squiggles. She didn't know whether to laugh or cry.

Javier looked at her sheepishly. "What do you think?"

She felt light-headed and tried to fight back the tears. "Ah, Javier. You're doing my heart in." Why had he waited so long to hear her? And why couldn't she just forgive and forget, erase the past and look to the future without remorse? A definite transformation had taken place—in both of them. How could she disappoint him now? They had travelled this path too long together for that. What did she really have to lose by giving him another chance? Tom had said she should make up her mind. He was right. Lost in her thoughts, she traced her fingers over the colourful flowers. "You're not making this any easier for me, Javier."

Anastasia stood to the side, looking on.

"Hold on a moment," he said. He rolled the sliding door aside to reveal the interior. "Step inside," he said, taking her hand. He had written a poem on one of the panels:

*We trip and tumble over unseen stones*

*Losing our path in the twilight zone*
*I may not be perfect but neither are you*
*I've been telling you that till I'm black and blue*
*But no matter the sorrow, the pain or the strife*
*I'd rather have you as my number one wife*

### *The Clumsy Poet*

She looked from Javier to Anastasia and burst into tears.

"I know I was a fool," he said. "Will you give me another chance? Don't look at me like that, Roisin. I'm not asking you to commit yourself. Just give me this one break and come with me in my magic bus."

To hear him even use the word 'magic' was so out of character. That and the painted flowers and squigglydoops seemed absurd. People can change after all, she thought. At the same time, she felt irritated at being pushed into something she didn't want. Not that she didn't want to go on that trip with him, but it felt like manipulation. And the look of expectation in Anastasia's eyes made it even more difficult for Roisin to know what to say.

"Go on, Roisin," Javier said. "Give it a go. I took the liberty of arranging things with Maggie. She has agreed to delay her trip to Kerry or wherever she plans on going."

"You have it all figured out, haven't you?" She turned away for a moment, shaking her head. He had gone to such trouble. She sighed. "It's not a good time. I can't do this to Maggie. She needs me now. Let me think about it, okay? She kissed him. "I hope you understand; it's not that I don't appreciate it. Where were you planning on going anyway?"

"Italy, Morocco, Greece."

"But you never wanted to go there before."

"Sometimes it takes a half a lifetime to learn what's important." He put his arm around her. "We still have time. I'll wait for your answer."

They drove back to the house while Anastasia dropped the car back at the B&B.

Although she knew she had disappointed both Anastasia and Javier, she knew she had done the right thing. To break the ice, she teased him about the poem. "How long did it take you to write that?" she asked.

"Well, now that you mention it; it took me a whole day."

"It was sweet of you." She leaned over and squeezed his hand.

"It wasn't easy getting the tone right. You know I'm no poet," he said.

She glanced over at him and could see from the set of his jaw that he was trying to put on a brave face. Would it work out between them? Time would tell. He looked as if he had been exercising. Although he had always kept his body trim and healthy, the light had begun to fade from his eyes these past years, and he had been letting himself go. She realised that by moving out, she had done both of them a favour. The spark was back in his eyes and he had broken free of his self-induced inertia.

# Chapter 43

Helen arrived the next day. They were about to attend the surfing championships.

"I think we'd better walk down; parking will be a nightmare," Roisin said.

"Are you up to it? Javier said. "You're still limping a bit."

"I'll manage. Don't worry about me." But he insisted on dropping her off and joining them later. She knew he hated crowds and would make any excuse to get out of it. But there was no point in trying to change him. She tried a different tactic. "I bet you could get some fantastic photos. Maybe you could send some into the local paper. They're always happy to have something new." He mumbled something about there being enough photographers around, but she knew she had caught his attention.

The beach and the surrounding hills were filled with groups of spectators. Ice cream and fish and chip vendors were cashing in on the occasion. Despite the windy weather, there was a cheerful buzz in the air. Most of the locals were out and about. Roisin was delighted to see Mrs. Walsh, who sat wrapped in a tartan wool blanket in a camping chair. She greeted the old lady and introduced her to her husband, Anastasia and her sister. Later, when the others were distracted, Mrs. Walsh called her over. "I never did get to thank you properly, Roisin. My grandson is doing so well now. He and his girlfriend have moved to England and are starting a new life. They have invited me to come over for a visit in autumn. You have no idea how happy that makes me feel."

"I'm so thrilled," Roisin said. "But, I cannot take any of the credit. It's all your grandson's doing. He alone has extricated himself from this scene. Most never manage to. If he didn't have such a loving grandmother, he might never have made it." The old lady, with teary eyes, patted Roisin's arm.

If only Maggie's situation could be alleviated as easily as that. Although Roisin knew there was no such thing as happily ever after—not for everyone—she dared to hope it would all work out well. Who was she kidding? Mankind has always sought a way out. There would always be dealers and tokers, and if it wasn't one thing it would be another. We all have our drugs, she thought. But she also knew that people turn to drugs for a reason. So it stood to reason that that void must be filled. Young people needed a goal, a reason for living, another way to get their highs. There were many sporting activities and youth clubs around, but not all kids were into sports, and they had to be catered for too. Never one to be blind to her own failings, she realised she was no better. She was addicted to change, to excitement and perhaps even to Javier. And as the moment of her great revelation hit home, she was determined to change that and remember the reason why she had left in the first place.

*

Watching the surfing championships on that windy beach was more exciting than she had expected. It was becoming an international event with competitors from all over the world. She'd had no idea how popular this Irish surfing scene was. One young man from New Zealand told them he had sold his car to attend this year's event. She was torn between rooting for him or for the local surfing hero, Richard Murphy.

Later on, after they had freshened up, she, Javier and Anastasia went to the dance class. Helen didn't want to go. There was an even greater showing, mainly because they had handed out flyers at the beach earlier. She told them to go ahead onto the dance floor while she manned the desk, greeting old and new faces. Blessing showed up armed with a handful of CD's. Roisin watched her floating down the hallway in her billowing African print gown, looking flamboyant and obviously in her element. As if she knew she was being watched, Blessing turned around and blew her a kiss. "This time I want to see you on the parquet, Ms. Delaney. No excuses.

"Yes, Mam," she called back. In truth, she was looking forward to it. Maybe she could even drag Javier out onto the dance floor. See if he was really willing to change his spots. If he was willing to dance, there might be a chance he'd make an effort in other ways too. Although it was never wise to expect anyone to change, they would both have to make serious efforts to avoid falling into the same old rut again.

After the last group had straggled in, she closed the doors, locked the money away and joined the happy crowd. The dancers abandoned themselves to the rhythm of the salsa, reggae mix. She shimmied over to Javier who was doing his best to hide behind a small group. Reluctantly, he joined her on the dance floor. She knew he was uncomfortable, and as soon as the music stopped for a moment he made his escape.

Blessing was doing her best to get the dancers coordinated into small groups. "Shake those hips," she said. "Look. Watch me. Imagine your belly button is a tiny coin in a big bowl. Try to shake your hips without the coin hitting the sides of the bowl. That's right. Keep the centre steady but shake that bowl." It was hilarious watching everybody having a go at it.

"Come on, everyone can dance," she said. "You just need to lose yourself in the music. Forget what you look like. Lose those inhibitions." She continued to boom out instructions. She was a natural born motivator, and she glided through the dancers, adjusting a shoulder here, placing her hands on the small of someone's back, and always with encouraging words. Some of them were doing their own thing. Blessing wagged a finger at two young fellows who were wobbling their heads at a terrific rate and doing some sort of a fast moon-dance movement.

Later, as she was chatting to Javier, Fidelma came over, obviously curious to know who he was. "Are you going to introduce me?" she asked, eyelashes fluttering in Javier's direction. *What a tease*, and where was Fidelma's new man?

Roisin turned to Javier. "This is Fidelma. She is the owner of the most charming little purple guest house near the main street."

Anastasia interrupted her and coaxed Javier onto the dance floor. His protests fell on empty ears and he finally gave up the fight.

"So, are you two back together again?" Fidelma asked.

"Maybe, but on different terms. He's been my friend for so many years and that won't change."

"Okay. He must be the owner of that colourful van outside your house. I saw it the other day as I drove by. Anyway, I won't probe, but I had heard there was a mystery man on the horizon too."

If Roisin didn't know Fidelma better she would have told her to mind her own business. But she was curious to know who was spreading rumours.

"Really. Where did you hear that?"

"You know how small this country is. Marjorie's friend knows someone from Knockadreen."

And to think she had come here to get away from this sort of thing. "Tom is a good friend. We both helped each other out in difficult times, that's all."

"Well, I like your husband. You look so good together."

Roisin smiled. "Yes, isn't life strange? Sometimes we need to distance ourselves from a situation to realise what's really important."

Fidelma straightened a few strands of hair that had come undone. "It doesn't always work out like that though. At least not for me."

The ensuing silence spoke volumes. Not wanting to touch any tender wounds, Roisin didn't ask about Fidelma's new friend. But Fidelma was no fool. "You're wondering where he is, aren't you?"

"Well, I was hoping to see you together."

"He had to do some business up in Galway."

Fidelma's blue eyes held a shadow of doubt, and Roisin decided not to probe.

The tempo was notched up a bit and Blessing encouraged everyone to dance. Roisin and Fidelma had no choice but to join Anastasia and Javier on the dance floor, mimicking Blessing's moves and letting themselves sway to the music.

"Use your whole body," Blessing boomed out. "Now lift your feet as if you're stamping out ants. That's right, faster. Now pretend there's an annoying bee bother you. Swish your arms, left and right. And don't forget to smile." She flashed a big smile at them.

Roisin couldn't believe Javier was actually joining in. In fact, he was really letting himself go. How hungry people were for something new? And how easily they had embraced it too. This was the *new* Ireland. Although it was only the beginning, she hoped there would be a blending of cultures, without compromising the uniqueness of the country. She hoped Blessing would stick around for a long time.

In the frenzy of the dance, she had lost sight of Anastasia. She remembered seeing her talking to a tall, grey-haired man during the break. He was dressed in a suit. While trying to follow Blessing's instructions, she scanned the room. Finally, her eyes rested on her friend. There she was, hips wiggling to the music as she shimmied forward with outspread arms. Good old Anastasia. She had rhythm. But where was the fellow? No sign of him.

The younger kids would be coming for the next session. Roisin had organized a young dance teacher, who specialised in hip hop and Latin, to teach that class. If nothing else, Roisin was proud of herself for her, albeit small, contribution to her new community. Things like this had a domino effect. Blessing had found an outlet for her creative talents, and the young people had an outlet for their energy. But lord, Roisin was no Pollyanna. She was just following her whims and having a good time.

The next day, Anastasia was beaming from ear to ear. Although they were very good friends and Roisin was curious to know about the fellow Anastasia had been with, she would let her talk if and when she wanted to.

Anastasia wanted to say goodbye to Fidelma before she left; she'd hardly had time the previous evening at the dance. She and Roisin called in to see her. Fidelma was busy rushing around clearing up after breakfast. By the looks of things, she had a full house too. The lobby was busy with people checking in and out, and they'd almost tripped over suitcases on their way in. Still, she took a few minutes to chat to them. "What fun we had last night" she said. "I'm feeling it today though. And young Pat McEverly said his friends really enjoyed their class."

Fidelma extended her arm to Anastasia. "It was lovely meeting you. You know there'll always be a welcome here for you."

"Oh, how nice of you. I love it here, and if you ever feel like it you can come over to my part of the world. I'd love to have you," Anastasia said. Fidelma turned to Roisin. "What about you? I suppose you'll be leaving us soon."

"What? Me! Oh no. What makes you think that?"

"Well, since your husband has followed you here, I suppose he's trying to convince you to go back with him."

"I'm here for good, Fidelma. This is my place." *At least for now.* "Didn't I tell you that Javier is moving here? He's looking at a place here on the main street."

Fidelma raised an eyebrow and was about to say something but obviously thought better of it. Instead she said, "Well, if you'll allow me to interfere and give you some advice: live in different quarters and you'll be fine. If I'm any judge of character, he's a good match for you. You two looked so comfortable together."

"Yes, like a pair of old shoes. Time will tell, Fidelma."

Without her having to ask, Fidelma began talking about her new man. "He's set in his ways, Roisin. You know what they say about changing an old leopard's spots?"

"Oh, well, give him time. Don't push him."

Fidelma sighed. "No expectations here."

Somebody rang the bell and Fidelma bustled off toward reception. "I'll give you a call later in the week, Roisin."

\*

Roisin waited at the airport lounge with her friend. "Tell me to mind my business, Anastasia, but did your man's name begin with P or R?"

Her friend looked as if she was going to burst with excitement. "It's just a coincidence, but yes, as it happens, his name is Robert."

"You're not serious!"

"I'll probably never see him again," her friend said quietly.

"Well, what did he say? Did he take your number?"

"He did, but I'm not going to hold my breath. It was a fun night and I'll accept it for what it was." She turned to hug Roisin. "Thanks for a wonderful holiday. I'll definitely be coming back soon."

Roisin's head had begun to spin with all the endings and beginnings. "Don't forget to call me when you arrive home," Roisin said, before waving her friend off. It was time to get back to work.

# Chapter 44

Maggie was in the shop as she had hoped.

"What a nice surprise," Maggie said as Roisin came in. "I'm up to my eyes trying to get these orders sent out on time, especially if you'll be leaving me soon."

"Well, that's what I wanted to talk to you about," Roisin said. "I'm not going. It's not the right time."

"Of course you're going? I have no problem with that. Once we get these orders out we'll be pretty well caught up. I'll be well able to manage for a few weeks, and I have the students too. I can always go to Kerry at the weekends until you return."

Roisin shook her head. "I know. It's really kind of you, but it's too early yet for me to go on such a long trip with Javier."

Maggie looked deep in thought. "Javier was very sweet and very convincing. He really loves you, Roisin. I wouldn't let this chance pass you by."

"I know. But it's not passing me by. I have time to think it over. Javier is okay with it."

Maggie shrugged. "Well, we'd better get to work then."

The shop buzzed with customers. Roisin finally got to see the two new girls Maggie had hired. One of them, who looked as if she was about seventeen, was serving customers. It was soon apparent that she knew exactly what she was doing; her manner was relaxed but confident. The other girl was busy doing accounts on the computer. Roisin gave them a little wave on her way through to the workshop where Maggie was sorting through a new delivery of materials.

'Take a look at these gorgeous new materials."

Roisin went through the fabrics, imagining what she could make with them. Most of them were more suitable for bags and purses than for hats. There were floral tapestries in swirling greens with vibrant reds, like village gardens, embroidered canvases, cottons and other fabric mixes in beautiful shades of teal, indigo, purples, greens and creams. She could have kissed the gods in the design world who had finally declared colour to be *en vogue* again. They had begun to import finer Indian silks with the intention of adding some more elegant designs to their collection. "We could add some beading work. It's really in at the moment," Roisin said.

Maggie considered this. "I don't know. Beading takes a lot of time. It would really push the price up. But I suppose it's worth a try. We could make a few samplers and see how they sell."

Maggie walked over and closed the door between the shop and the studio. She turned to Roisin and spoke with a lowered voice. "The court case is on Friday. I hope that will be the end of it. My lawyer says I shouldn't have a problem, but I'm a nervous wreck."

"It'll be fine. Wait and see. Whenever I have

to go through something awful, I always tell myself that in a year it will all be forgotten. That really helps. Now you've come so far, there's no turning back. It sounds as if you have a good legal team behind you. What about your ex? Will it be hard facing him?"

Maggie sighed. "I'll have to deal with that too. He's like a stranger. I could say I curse the day….but what's done is done. He just made bad choices; I made bad choices."

"Do you want me to come, you know—for moral support?"

Maggie finished sorting the fabric. "You're a good friend, but I'd rather go it alone. The sooner it's over the better."

"If you change your mind, you'll know where to find me."

"Thanks. I've been so wrapped up in this whole drama—but what about you? Are you all right?"

"I'm fine, just still a bit confused. It'll be strange having Javier here, and I'm not over Tom. He's still waiting for me to make a decision." She didn't tell Maggie that Tom was also planning on moving there. "It doesn't mean we'll go back to where we were. I've decided to keep my own place and that won't change. I'm enjoying living by myself with no-one to answer to."

"What's Javier doing with himself today?"

"He's just hanging around the house waiting for a call from one of the estate agents."

"So he hasn't signed a contract on a flat yet?"

"No, unless he did it this morning. I think our chances of remaining good friends are much better if we live in separate houses."

*

She arrived home in a great mood. They'd had a productive and busy day. She dropped her bag on the couch and went down to the kitchen to put on the kettle. Javier was sitting at the kitchen table reading the paper. She caught a quick glimpse of his face and immediately felt uneasy.

"Hi," she said. "Did they call?"

His eyes squinted as he turned to her "What's going on between you and this Tom fellow?"

She busied herself putting the kettle on and taking out cups, thus avoiding his interrogating expression. "What do you mean?"

"You know what I mean. Don't mess around with me, Roisin."

She took a deep breath and sat down opposite him, holding eye contact. "I told you already. He is a friend who helped me out when I first arrived."

"Well, it didn't sound like that. The phone rang when I was taking a shower. I thought it was the estate agent so I listened back to the call. He sounds like a lot more than a friend."

She took a deep breath as she tried to collect her thoughts. His face had taken on that pinched expression, and she felt sick to her stomach as she thought of going back to the verbal battlefield. It was always the same; just as she thought things were going well between them, he'd turn angry for no apparent reason. Okay, maybe he did have a reason now, but if it wasn't one thing it would be another.

He was still looking at her in a menacing way.

"Don't look at me like that, love," she said. "There's no ownership here."

Once, he would have been even more furious, but now she could see that he was trying hard to control himself. Something had definitely changed between them and he knew she meant business.

She looked him squarely in the eyes. "You know I've never lied to you, and I'm not about to begin now. I already told you about Tom."

"You don't even know him properly."

"I know him well enough. If he's that great, how come he's not married? Or has he ever been?"

"So, you're saying being married is a measure of one's decency or normality?"

"Don't put words in my mouth. Just think about it, Roisin. Why isn't he with someone already?"

"Maybe he was wise. He didn't jump into marriage like most of us did." At his attempt to interrupt her, she raised her hand. "No, I'm serious. Most people follow the crowd. Call it peer pressure or whatever. Maybe it's instinct, the longing to reproduce, I don't know. Some people are just not cut out for marriage. And now look, just look around. All those big wedding celebrations, all the promises—for what? How many couples are still together?"

"What's that got to do with anything?"

"Tom never wanted to commit. That's all there is to it. He watched his parents go through misery in their marriage."

"Most of us did."

She shook her head in exasperation "Why am I even telling you this? Tom is a good person, and…I don't know why I'm even defending him. This is ridiculous. Besides, it's you who is sitting at my kitchen table. Just think about that." He didn't have a leg to stand on and he knew it. After an ensuing silence, he went outside to do some minor repairs on the van. When she was sure he'd be gone for a while, she called Tom's number and explained things to him. He had arranged to drive up with one of the builders at the weekend and wanted to see her. "I don't think it's a good idea if you show up here," she said. "Javier heard your message and demanded to know what was going on between us."

"And, did you tell him?"

"I told him we were good friends."

"Well, that's not a lie. Can you come out here on Saturday? Say you're working extra hours or something. I have to see you, Roisin."

She could hear Javier coming back and so she hastily agreed to meet Tom at his grandfather's place on Saturday before noon. She hoped her husband didn't notice the flush that was creeping up her cheeks. If he did, he didn't show it.

\*

On Friday, her thoughts were mainly with Maggie. She hoped everything would turn out well for her. Things appeared to have gone quiet on the drug front; at least she hadn't heard much about it on the news, although that might indicate that there was a lot going on behind the scenes. The last she had heard was of two large drug hauls in the capital. It seemed as if many hauls had been intercepted on the mainland too. Finally, international police forces were working together and cracking down on these criminals.

She wasn't proud of herself for telling Javier

that little white lie about having to work the next day. But the alternative would have been to worry him even more. He asked no questions when she told him she would have to drive to a nearby town to deliver an order. His face was hidden behind a newspaper and, when she asked him what his plans were, he mumbled something about driving up the coast to take photos. Although he seemed preoccupied, he gave no indication that he was upset in any way. They had never been the type of couple who did everything together, but she felt that, in view of what had happened in recent months, he had changed.

    Maggie rang on Friday evening after the court case. Roisin had been thinking of her all day but didn't want to call in case the news wasn't good and Maggie wanted time alone. Her friend sounded exuberant. "Now I can finally breathe a sigh of relief. That era of my life is over. I've nothing to fear now, and I hope it will put an end to rumours about me. It remains to be seen how the press deals with the story. If I'm lucky, they won't even mention my name."

    "That's fantastic, Maggie. So what happened? Were they able to convict Big Bill?"

    "That's still ongoing, but it seems unlikely they'll need me to testify any more. I've made my statements and my ex has been ordered to pay seven and a half thousand Euro. If you ask me, it's a petty fine. And it beats me why the big criminals have been walking free for years. Everybody knows what's going on. Surely they must have ample evidence to convict them." She sighed. "The whole thing is a farce. Anyway, I met him for a coffee afterwards and told him I'd pay back the five thousand Euro toward his fine. Now we're quits. He's happy, I'm happy. But he's a mere sardine in a lake of piranhas; I think he's finally coming to his senses."

"That's really good news. Did Bill Buckley have to take the stand?"

"No. He sat there as if he was the most upstanding citizen. He wore a suit and tie, the whole shebang. His bald head shone like a nicely boiled egg, shaved and polished for the occasion. All *Yes Sir, no Sir, I promise, Sir*. I tell you, these fellows know no scruples. He even nearly had me convinced. And that fellow, Podge, was sitting up in the back row with some of his pals. Did the gardai ever get back to you on that?"

"No, but I expect they will soon enough. You know how long it takes them to get things sorted. They're probably up to their eyes."

"True," Maggie said. "Guess who I bumped into on the way out of the courthouse?" She sounded so relieved and the words tumbled out of her mouth. Without waiting for Roisin to guess, she said, "Fidelma. She's alright, you know."

"Why, did you actually talk civilly to each other?"

"Aye, we did. She told me she's been meaning to come into the shop because she heard such glowing reports about it or something to that effect. She said if I have any business cards she'll display them in her B&B. Get some more tourists in. I could have done with that support a couple of years ago, but I suppose I should be grateful. Wonder what caused her change of heart?"

"Sometimes we just have to get to know

people properly, Maggie. In any case, that's good news all around."

Roisin hoped it would really be the last of the troubles, for all of them.

## Chapter 45

Javier left early the next day. He took his camera and his wetsuit with him, saying that he might go for a dip. She knew he'd never go in the water without a wetsuit. He couldn't get used to the coldness of the Atlantic. On his way out, they kissed. She rubbed her finger against his smooth cheek. "You smell nice," she said.

He smiled at that. "What time will you be back?"

"Probably before six," she said. "Should I make dinner this evening?"

"No, don't bother. I'll probably have a pub lunch."

It was hard to read him; he seemed to have forgotten their earlier spat, but she couldn't be certain.

\*

She could see Tom's car as soon as she pulled up to the site. He came out to greet her and sauntered towards her, strong and fit. The shirt with rolled up sleeves revealed his nicely tanned skin. Her heart did a little somersault when she thought of what she had to tell him. Their greeting was awkward at first. He took her good naturedly by the arm and showed her around, pointing out the deep foundation, explaining what all the pipes and pumps were for and how he was going to harness the geothermal energy for the house. She tried to concentrate on what he was telling her, how the heating and hot water costs would be a fraction of normal costs, making the initial investment well worthwhile. Her mind was elsewhere though, and she knew his was too. Would this be their last meeting? Was it over before it even began?

She was jerked out of reality as he pulled her to face him.

"I think you're doing the wrong thing, Roisin."

In light of her latest encounter with Javier, she suspected he was right. She could feel his strength and the warmth of his hand on her arm. He lifted her chin toward him with one finger—commanding, self-assured. "Remember what you said to me?"

She nodded.

"I knew it deep down, but you stopped me from making a big mistake."

"There's a difference," she said. "You've never met Javier."

She thought back to her conversation with her husband and how she had tried to defend Tom. Now she found herself doing the same thing in reverse. She told him how sweet Javier had been, how he had bought and even decorated the camper van. That he was willing to come and join her here. "I have to give him another chance. Don't you see that, Tom?" She sighed. "And now, I'm not going to second-guess myself again. We love each other, partners for life. I know that neither of us can change overnight, but it's worth giving it a go."

"Is that your final answer?"

She looked up at him with tears in her eyes. "Yes. I wanted to come and tell you in person." He took her in his arms and gently kissed the top of her head, holding her for what seemed like an age.

"I have to go now, Tom," she said, as she pulled away from him gently and tried to hide her face. If he only knew how hard this was for her. She turned toward the car, ready to leave, but he caught her arm.

"Please, Roisin. Not like this. Let us at least have lunch together. I promise I won't bring up the subject again."

She lifted her eyes to his. "Don't you think it will make everything worse?" Even as she said it, she knew she couldn't leave him like this. "Oh, come on then."

They agreed to drive in separate cars and to split up after lunch. "Unless you get the urge to go for a swim afterwards," he teased. She blushed and slapped him playfully on the arm.

"I'd rather go somewhere quiet," she said. "Off the beaten track." She told him that Javier was out and about and she wanted to avoid them bumping into each other, even if it was highly unlikely.

"I know just the place," he said.

She followed his car until he stopped at a little pub about fifteen minutes from his grandfather's place. It was in a tiny hamlet hidden behind a forested area, overlooking a river. She stopped the engine and got out of the car. "What a lovely spot," she said. "I'm surprised they can even sustain a pub out here. It really is off the beaten track."

"You'd be surprised how busy it gets though,"

he said. 'Let's go in."

There was no-one else inside except for a couple of staff but, judging from the clatter of pots and pans, it sounded as if they were expecting an army. Somewhere in the background, the sounds of piano music filled the air. It was like finding a glass chapel in the middle of a desert. Nothing seemed to fit.

He led her toward a table at the back, overlooking the river. As they browsed through the menu, a waitress came to take their orders. They both ordered fresh crab cakes with mixed leaf salad, peppery cheese dressing and homemade baguettes.

"I'd love a big glass of the black stuff now," he said.

She sympathised with him but argued it would be better if they stayed focused. They both had to drive, so they settled on a jug of iced water.

She was painfully aware of the fragility between them and guessed he felt the same. Determined not to sit in morose silence, she made some banal comments about the view. Her words rang hollow, even to herself.

He made no such pretence. She asked him about his music. He told her he hadn't been in the mood for writing recently. "Writing is like playing an instrument," he said. "If you don't feel it, all you get is something that sounds like cats crying in an alleyway." He took her hand in his. "What are you going to do if things don't turn out as you wish?"

"I'll cross that bridge if I come to it. I have my life here now, and Javier knows things between us will never be the same as they were."

"This life is a funny old game, isn't it?"

"It sure is. We have no choice but to celebrate the moments of bliss and take the rest in our stride."

He sighed. "Will you keep in touch, Roisin?"

"Of course I will."

"I'll tell you what. I'll get Frankie to drop off the car tomorrow."

She placed her hand on his and squeezed it gently. "No, please don't, Tom. It would only rub salt in the wound for Javier." She reached over and caressed his cheek. "I appreciate it more than you know, but it's not a good idea."

He nodded. "We'll wait and see then"

The tables began to fill up as their meals arrived.

"Where are all these people coming from?" Roisin said.

"I told you it's a well-known address. I think it was featured in The Best of Irish Culinary Venues. That magazine is distributed internationally. At least twice a week a bus load of tourists arrive. Just our luck that today is one of them."

"I can see why it was mentioned," she said, as she tasted some of the crab cake.

They were distracted by a lively group who made a point of choosing seats in close proximity to theirs. Tom and Roisin exchanged glances. Tom raised his eyes skywards and grimaced. "Will you let me know how things work out, at least?" he said. She nodded and blinked away her tears.

"This is very hard, Roisin. I wish things had gone differently."

She put down her knife and fork. "Remember

your promise, Tom. They say everything falls into place as it should, maybe they are right, the wise ones, whoever they are."

It was a relief to have the noisy neighbours there to distract them. Neither of them were doing a good job acting as if everything was all right. It was almost time to part ways. Tom signalled to the waiter to bring the bill, and Roisin excused herself while she went to freshen up. She knew what she was about to do was wrong but she couldn't bear the idea of saying goodbye to him. On the way downstairs, she grabbed a postcard advertising the local sites and scribbled a note to him, telling him it was better this way, then she asked the waiter to give it to him. She drove away with tears streaming down her face, and hoped he would forgive her.

Once she was home, she tried to pull herself together again, but it was easier said than done. There was no point in feeling regret. She had made up her mind, but that didn't stop her from attempting to purge herself of any last remnants of doubt. She took out the pen and notebook Tom had given her and tried to sort out her thoughts by writing them in her journal, but ended up throwing it down in disgust. It was no good. She changed her clothes, putting on some old jeans and a tee-shirt, and went out to the shed to get some gardening tools. A bit of manual work might get her mind off things. Where on earth was Javier? He should definitely be back by now. A growing sense of unease gnawed at her as she went over to the far end of the garden and began hacking at the thistles and other weeds, or what looked like weeds.

The hours went by and there was no still no sign of him. Because he absolutely refused to have a mobile phone, there was no way she could contact him. She had no choice but to sit it out and wait.

Her sleep that night was patchy, as she tossed and turned, worrying about Javier. She just didn't feel right about him not returning back. No matter how angry he had ever been with her, he had always come home. She cried into her pillow thinking about the sacrifice she had had to make with Tom too. What a muddle.

The next morning, there was still no sign of Javier. He must have stopped off somewhere and spent the night. Still, it was highly unusual for him not to let her know; he could have at least pulled in somewhere and called her from a mainline phone. She began to get seriously worried and paced up and down the room, wondering what to do. Just as she was preparing to go out and look for him, the telephone rang. It was Fidelma's voice on the other end, raspy and breathing fast. "Turn on the news. Quickly!"

Roisin pressed the remote button in time to hear an urgent male voice reporting that a man had been found dead after falling from the Cliffs of Moher. A thousand chills ran up and down her spine like icy ants. While she watched the reporter's mouth moving, she felt as if she was falling down a dark tunnel. Words blurred as she heard the reporter interviewing a Garda, who said the accident probably occurred sometime in the early evening. *It is presumed that the man was taking photographs and ignored the warning signs, stepping too far near the edge of the highest cliff.* Pictures of the scene flashed on the screen, and she looked on in horror as she saw the unmistakable van with the name Voyager clearly visible. Her body felt as if it had no substance, as if she could melt or fly away. The loud beating of her heart reverberated in her ears.

She sat there, staring at the television as if in a trance. Her body began to shake uncontrollably and her knees turned to jelly. She sat back on the couch, barely registering the sound of Fidelma's voice coming from the receiver. With a heavy hand, she held the receiver closer to her ear. "Sit tight, I'll be over right away," her friend said. She mumbled something into the phone but Fidelma had already disconnected.

*

Fidelma gave her a shot of whisky to calm her nerves. Poor Garda Houlihan was once again called to her house. After he had spoken to Roisin for a short while, Anastasia took over. She made him a hot beverage while Roisin kept a low profile in the background. She felt like something pliable, like rubber. People could do with her as they pleased.

Over the next few days she followed orders as her friends rallied around her, offering support and nourishment, both spiritual and physical. Maggie and Fidelma proved stalwart in the face of tragedy, and Jimmy and Fidelma provided everyone with enough to eat as people came by to offer their condolences. Blessing gave her some sort of herbal concoction so her already detached state was cushioned by a sense of floating in serenity. And yet, beneath the surface, her sadness threatened to engulf her. She feared she wouldn't be strong enough to face it.

Occasionally she'd see Javier's face come into her consciousness, as if he was trying to make contact with her. Several times, as she almost drifted into sleep, she would see his face zooming up close to hers, like a virtual photograph, half real and half imaginary. Even in this detached state, a terrible feeling of regret, even guilt scratched her insides, making her heart feel like a raw place of infinite pain. But then, another emotion would take over as she felt angry with him for trying to make her feel guilty. She had never wished him any harm and he should have known better than to step so close to the edge. Helen, who had come at once, instinctively knew this and kept telling her it was not her fault. "He didn't feel any pain," Helen had assured Roisin. But what about the pain Roisin had caused him by abandoning him in the first place? Then she would enter that cocoon where memories fade, where feelings are numbed, and it seemed to her as if she was composed of a million shards of glass that refused to come together in any coherent form.

# Chapter 46

Roisin had to identify the body, of course. The only way to get through the whole ordeal was to force herself to function and try to block her feelings. It was as if she was on automation, hardly noticing the man who accompanied her to that cold room. She shivered, wrapping her arms across her belly in an attempt to get warm. She wasn't even aware she had been holding her breath, a habit she had acquired whenever she didn't want something to touch her emotionally. One look at Javier's serene face caused her to expel that captured breath. At first, she barely recognised her own loud and uncontrolled tears of raw grief. *Breathe*, she said to herself, over and over. It finally worked. When she had gained control of her emotions, she sent Javier a silent blessing, leaned over and placed a kiss on his cold forehead.

Somebody had contacted his only remaining relative, a brother with whom he had not spoken in years, and she had spoken to him, but only briefly.

Funeral details were set up, and she knew it would have been his wish to be close to her. They had spoken of this a few times and Javier had often said he wanted to be buried wherever she was. She recalled that graveyard she had visited when she'd first arrived, and she wondered whether that was why she'd had a feeling of unease back then. It was one of those things that could not be explained by logic. She had read somewhere that all timelines merge, that life is not linear, and it gave her solace to think that she would one day meet up with him again in a different realm.

Legal affairs had to be dealt with, too, and her brother Brian proved invaluable here. One of his school friends had studied International Law, specialising in matters of estate and property. Since the existing property was in both of their names, dealing with it proved to be less complicated than she might have originally thought. At least he had managed to sell their holiday house. She could not have faced going back there, not yet anyway. Brian's friend had also arranged for their house in the village of Bacca to be put on the market. She had signed reams of paper work, not even caring to examine the fine print. It all seemed so futile now, and she knew she could trust this man whom she vaguely remembered from a distant past. After listening to her wishes, he had explained to her that if the house could not be sold, it could be rented out. She agreed, although she would have to figure out the financial ramifications of all of that later.

The funeral was due to be held the next day, and friends and family had begun to arrive. She dreaded the event more than anything else, being forced to mingle with friends and acquaintances at a time when all she wanted to do was retreat into her own world. She was not one of those people who could control her emotions, and she felt overwhelmed at the idea of having to face people. Anastasia was coming later on in the evening, and she had had a touching note and a wreath from Maria and Rafael who had been contacted by Jimmy.

When Anastasia arrived, Roisin fell into her arms, crying deep sobs of despair. Later, Anastasia, though tear-filled eyes, told her something that gave her great solace. "His passion was always photography. Just think about it, Roisin. He probably got the best shot of his life. At least he died a happy man. Have they given you back the camera yet?"

She nodded and pointed to a drawer in the cabinet where she had put his few personal belongings. She remembered Fidelma had quickly put them in the drawer, out of her sight. Remarkably, the camera had remained almost intact. The lens was broken into smithereens but the body was merely scratched, a small miracle when she thought of how it had apparently been ejected during the fall. She had assumed the police would have checked through the photos, but what did she know about these things?

Her friend inserted the chip and downloaded the images onto the laptop. "Are you sure you're up to this, Roisin?"

She nodded.

They looked through the pictures in silence. There was a series of spring flowers, so delicate as they forced their way up through the rock crevice. He had also taken a couple of shots of seals that blended so seamlessly into the rocks as they soaked up the afternoon sunshine. The next picture showed an old man sitting on a rock, smoking a pipe and staring out onto the Atlantic. There was something so strong in his demeanour, in the silhouette of his profile, and something so tender about the image. She could imagine how he had been staring out at the sea and contemplating his life. But there was also a fragility there in the unspoken moments of solitude. A fresh wave of sorrow overcame her once again as she thought about Javier. If only she could have turned back the clock, but no, it was useless to even contemplate the impossible. How much life is taken for granted. Anastasia handed her a tissue and she wiped her eyes and continued clicking through the remaining pictures. Tears turned to smiles as she looked at the photos Anastasia had taken of her and Javier in front of the van. They both looked happy together, happier than they had been in a long time. More landscape photos followed. He must have taken them on the days when he had been away by himself. Clicking on to the next photos, she gasped in shock when she saw a series of shots of herself and Tom together. How on earth did they get there?

"Oh, my God," Anastasia said.

Roisin felt dizzy with confusion and shock. Thoughts flitted through her mind as she tried to recapture the events before the terrible accident. It all looked so wrong. She buried her face in her hands. Had he jumped?

Her friend placed her hand on her arm. "You never told me," she said.

"No, it's not what you think. She explained to her friend how she had wanted to make things right, and how Tom had insisted on meeting her to try to dissuade her from going back to her husband. "I owed him that much, at least," she said. "It was never meant to turn out like this." She stood up and began pacing the room. "Javier must have been following me. He had confronted me about Tom after listening to the answering machine one day when I was at work. He was waiting for a call from a real estate agent. I told him everything, and I thought that was the end of it?"

Guilt gnawed at her insides once again, and she thought she was going to lose her mind. What a fool! Why hadn't he confronted her right there and then? She looked at Anastasia, who tried to console her.

"It's not your fault."

How many times had she heard this? No amount of consolation could make her feel better. Poor, stupid, Javier. Her friend poured her a glass of whisky but she pushed it away. Roisin sank into the armchair. "What'll we do now?"

"Here's the deal," Anastasia said. "What we have just seen is between you and me. What has been done cannot be undone. Nobody needs to know. It will serve no purpose." Anastasia stood in front of Roisin and placed her hands on her shoulders. "Do you understand me? Now, pull yourself together." Surprisingly, it helped. Roisin was relieved that her friend was taking over. That was just what she needed now. A strong hand and a decisive mind.

Roisin flipped back through the photos, looking for answers. Some of the landscape shots Javier had taken were particularly stunning, especially the last ones of the cliffs and the moody sky with crashing waves. There was a photo of him sitting outside a pub, biting into a thick sandwich and lifting a small glass of Guinness outside a sign that read O'Shaughnessy's Cliff View.

Anastasia jabbed at the screen. "See how happy he was there? That's what you have to remember."

Roisin broke into sobs again. "It's so unfair. What kind of cosmic joke caused him to appear at exactly that time? And how come we didn't even notice him? Surely we would have heard the van pull up?"

"I suppose he must have parked some distance away and followed you up there," Anastasia said. Roisin shook her head and spoke, almost in a whisper. "It doesn't make sense. How would he have known where I was going? I didn't see a soul."

"Maybe he followed you another day. That's the only explanation. Anyway, enough of this surmising. Remember what I told you? Banish those thoughts."

Anastasia made some phone calls and organised for the scenic photos of the cliffs and the ones of him and Roisin to be used as a backdrop at the funeral service. The priest was cooperative and told her friend they could hook the laptop up with the church's projector, which they sometimes used for weddings and other events. Although the priest found the request a bit odd, he saw no reason why they couldn't do it.

Before she went to sleep, she made herself a cup of tea, sat at the kitchen table and wrote a heartfelt tribute to the man who had been the love of her life. She didn't try to make him out to be a super hero, but mentioned the hills and valleys of their time together. Tears streamed down her face as she remembered all the little incidents, the trips, and the joys and disappointment of not being able to have children of their own. All the emotions came rushing through her, leaving her exhausted but cleansed. She kissed his image and knew he had forgiven her, as she forgave him.

Upon Blessing's advice, she had begun to wean herself off the medicine, and although it hurt so much to once more go through all these emotions, she knew it was necessary to hold herself together. Gradually, she began to feel stronger, but she didn't know if her strength would be sufficient to get her through the funeral and that final, heart-breaking shovelling of the earth onto the coffin. How would she stand up and talk about him to all her friends? Would they judge her, as she judged herself?

\*

The moment came when she was sitting in the little church with all the mourners behind her and her friends giving her support as they sat in the pew beside her. Some force imbued her with a strength she didn't know she possessed, and she carried herself with grace and poise, going through the motions and rituals. This is just a play; it's not real, she thought as the priest nodded to her. With a backdrop of the photo taken of them both in front of the van, she walked up to the pulpit and recited the words she had chosen with care, meaning every word, and yet feeling as if she was detached from herself, as if she was observing the scene from above.

> I see you gathered here with tears
> In eyes that cannot see me now

I am not far from you, my dears
A thought away, I take a bow

Rejoice and let me go ... for now
I'm summoned to a greater light

The boat is ready, I must row
To old seashore that's shining bright

Be assured that I'll be there
Whenever you may think of me

To hold you tight with love and care
But wish me well, for I am free.

She could hear people sniffling, but it was not her intention to make anyone sad, and so she continued sharing intimate, funny and sad moments, as if there was nobody else in the church. Just her and Javier. Once, when she thought she would lose control, she focused on the beam of light coming in through the stained glass window, showering the room in a golden glow. This gave her focus and enabled her to channel her words directly from the heart for all ears to hear.

Later, at the graveside, the part she dreaded most, after the priest had given his last blessing, she gently dropped three white roses onto the coffin. A quiet peace swept over her, along with the gentle breeze that came in from the Atlantic.
She could have sworn she heard Javier's

voice whispering in the wind as she absentmindedly watched a robin pecking at some insects in the upturned soil. The bird looked up at her with his beady eyes and hopped off toward the back near the row of trees. She followed his movements with her eyes. The last time she had been there, she remembered seeing the robin and now he appeared to be communicating with her, and although it was unlikely to be the same one, it could well have been. Of course she knew that was delusional, but she followed its movements.

  He appeared to swoop and stop, turning around every so often. The priest's voice droned on and she continued following the bird with her eyes. The shadow of a man was standing over behind one of the trees. She knew he hadn't been there before; at least she hadn't seen him. It was Tom. She was pretty certain. He appeared to be staring directly at her but she couldn't be sure because the brilliant sun was half blocking her light. As she looked around her at all the friends and family who had come to support her and to pay their respects to Javier, she knew everything would be all right and that this was where she belonged.

# Acknowledgements

Many thanks to everybody, especially Moya, Cathy and Tina for cheering me along, and to Frances, Debbie and Billy for your support and feedback. Special thanks to Jennifer Doran for being a great mother, for your incredible generosity and kindness, and for instilling a love of reading in me and my siblings.

And to Georgie Doran R.I.P. for all the stories.

Much thanks to Sharon Brownlie for helping with technical issues. You've been fantastic.

And of course to you, the reader. I know how much pleasure we can get from books, and how we can be transported to a fictional world for a while. I hope I have been able to give you some pleasure. You can keep up with me through my Amazon Author Page.
I'd love to hear from you.
Liz Doran

# ABOUT THE AUTHOR

Liz Doran is an Irish writer who lives in Germany with her husband. She has also lived and travelled extensively in the U.S.A, and has spent several months living in London and Tuscany. Liz loves colour, art, reading, film, design and travel. Her lifelong interest in metaphysical and spiritual matters has taken her on many interesting journeys. She trained as a Naturopath in Germany, specializing in classical homeopathy and colour puncture. She has two grown sons.

Printed in Great Britain
by Amazon